THE COURT OF COMMON PLEAS

Books by Alexandra Marshall

Fiction

GUS IN BRONZE

TENDER OFFER

THE BRASS BED

SOMETHING BORROWED

THE COURT OF COMMON PLEAS

Nonfiction

STILL WATERS

The Court of Common Pleas

Alexandra Marshall

A MARINER BOOK
HOUGHTON MIFFLIN COMPANY
Boston • New York

First Mariner Books edition 2003

Visit our Web site: www.houghtonmifflinbooks.com
Visit the author's Web site: www.alexandramarshallbooks.com

Library of Congress Cataloging-in-Publication Data
Marshall, Alexandra.
The court of common pleas / Alexandra Marshall.
p. cm.
ISBN 0-395-96794-5
ISBN 0-618-25753-5 (pbk.)
1. Judges' spouses—Fiction. 2. Women medical students—Fiction. 3. Married people—Fiction. 4. Midlife crisis—Fiction. 5. Retirees—Fiction. 6. Judges—Fiction. I. Title.
PS3563.A719 C6 2001
813'54—dc21 00-053887

Book design by Melissa Lotfy
Type is Monotype Fournier

Printed in the United States of America
QUM 10 9 8 7 6 5 4 3 2 1

For Jim

Acknowledgments

At the Case Western Reserve University School of Medicine, I'm grateful to Gaylee McCracken, M.D., who gave me her precious time and insight, and to Dr. Albert C. Kirby, Thomas Jacobs, M.D., Marlene English, and Ellen Rosenblum. Also in Cleveland, Dian and John Haynes provided helpful references and encouragement, and Augustus and Nina McDaniel were generous guides. I've learned about the independent pharmacy from Herman Greenfield, about nursing from Patricia Pingree, Vicki Carroll, and Susan Babcock, and by the examples of my own doctors, Richard Pingree and J. Gregory Kane. I'm particularly glad for my dear aunt Margaret McDowell Walker, my traveling companion during the writing of this novel.

Interior monologue of the poet:
the notes for the poem are the only poem

the mind collecting, devouring
all these destructibles

the unmade studio couch the air
shifting the abalone shells

the mind of the poet is the only poem
the poet is at the movies

dreaming the film-maker's dream but differently
free in the dark as if asleep

free in the dusty beam of the projector
the mind of the poet is changing

the moment of change is the only poem

—Adrienne Rich
From "Images for Godard"

PART ONE

I

THE SKY BRIGHTENED into shades of gray and, from Overlook Road in Cleveland Heights, silver-plated Lake Erie. The steel skin of a small airplane caught the daylight and turned to chrome, pressing like a fender against the air above that horizon. Nearer, in the middle distance of the back yard, the branches of a forsythia looked like feathers rubbed the wrong way. Straight as a tent pole the buckeye tree stood its ground, prompted by an early spring to veil its poisonous young shoots in gauzy spires of colorless bloom.

In the foreground, Audrey was reflected in the kitchen window. She had wakened as usual without the aid of an alarm, slipping from the mystery of a dream that was enthralling if only because, custom made, the dream meant what it meant to her alone. Already the dream had given over to dread, vanishing from consciousness like some amazingly intricate insect whose whole life cycle takes no longer than a headache and leaves even less of a trace. She hadn't known dread could come in three equivalent dimensions, nor that the deepest could have been the most easily prevented. It wasn't within her control to be accepted to medical school, and neither was it possible to know whether, if she was admitted, it would eventually turn out to be the right decision to have made. But she'd chosen not to tell

Gregory of her application, and, standing at the kitchen counter they'd shared for the twenty years of their marriage, as she watched the first light infuse itself into their view, she was afraid that her good reasons for not telling him weren't good enough.

In their bed he was still asleep, embracing his king-size pillows, laboring through dreams that, like his work in the court system, always had elaborate plot lines. Travel-brochure dreams was what he called these journeys beyond the wonders of the world. In them, every now and then he traveled solo, but the more elaborate they were, the more essential to them was Audrey, who couldn't speak any of the languages—whereas he could speak them all—but whose first-aid kit kept them safe from every disaster. He'd never tell Audrey this because, as he'd be the first to admit, it was all plagiarized material.

Sleeping, he escaped the nightmare of being awake to contemplate the senseless death of Rob Wallace, a younger judge with more promise than one person was ever given to contain, of a heart attack at forty-one. Every time he thought about Rob, Gregory felt a sharp heat behind his eyes. Rob's reputation for genuine wisdom went not just beyond his years but beyond even the legal code. Oh sure, every lawyer was expected to exercise judgment informed by the mind and the heart, but in Rob it was like watching instinct and learning in a fusion made stunning by its seeming effortlessness. Gregory wasn't often persuaded by hyperbole, but he'd believed Rob was a genius. The violation of his sudden early death—might over right—offended Gregory's entire belief system, but more, it pained him horribly, personally. Not even Audrey fully understood it made him want to quit altogether. At sixty-three he'd already seen everything, some of it twice.

The trouble was, her own future was coming toward Audrey like too good a pitch not to take a swing at. She had always wondered why it was considered better to believe in a "half-full" glass when a "half-empty" glass creates a greater urgency to make it full. By this logic her life felt invitingly half empty. She was more ready for this upcoming birthday than for any previous milestone, because this time she'd given herself the gift of believing in fifty—fifty-fifty—as half of adulthood. What better opportunity could there be than the convergence of plain ambition and the mythic empty nest? The intervention of Rob's death was a tragedy, certainly, but it was also an instance of ordinary bad timing, because it coincided with Audrey's application deadline, which, although perhaps mistakenly, she'd decided not to miss. Louise Schneider, the physician in charge of the MetroHealth Clinic, where Audrey worked, had convinced Audrey that the best thing she had going for her was that few veteran nurses ever voluntarily jumped overboard into shark-infested waters. Who could resist sending a rescue boat to bring her in alive?

The sky was taking on color, a comfortingly pale pink like the inside of an infant's mouth, and Lake Erie had become, all the way to the border with Canada beyond the horizon, the shiny, smooth metallic rose of those American sedans driven by elderly women. In the middle of this continuum Audrey felt a combined gratitude and hope that made her feel both lucky and unfulfilled. Now she could see in the back yard that the grass needed to be cut, and with equal light outside and in, she could no longer see her reflection in the kitchen window. Anyway, she'd switched from the nuisance of eyeglasses to the ease of her contact lenses, transparent slices of perfect vision unrestricted by frames. And since Overlook Road rode the hip of the hill above Case Western Reserve University, the medical school was practically already within her view, even if only literally. Her question was, what else was she overlooking?

This nicely sited Colonial had been their starter house because, by the time Gregory married, he was already a judge elected to the same Common Pleas Court as, by now, he'd spent his entirely contented career. But since the court isn't officially in session without the judge present in the courtroom, she'd been the one to accommodate her work schedule to the needs of their daughters, so that, for example, she'd never missed a weekday lacrosse game. Today's was conveniently at Magnificat and, for a change, she wouldn't have to rush all the way across the city to get from Metro to the game. Her note to Gregory told him she and Sally would stop after the game for the makings of a special dinner. It went without saying that she'd choose a favorite of his in order to try to cheer him up a little, no matter that, ever since Rob, nothing much could.

It was just as well, then, that they'd postponed their anniversary trip to Paris, settling instead for one overnight at the Ritz-Carlton above the Cuyahoga River with a dinner of Dover sole slid away from the bone by their white-gloved waiter. Twenty years before, they'd spent that same March night there too, but the next evening, that time, they'd used their tickets to Paris. Gregory had known from the start that, unlike himself, his new wife loved surprises, so they'd flown into their marriage on Air France, Première Classe, and, because he'd retrieved his good French with a fresh round of lessons, all the flight attendants complimented his accent while offering them endless amounts of the best champagne onboard. For their tenth anniversary they'd returned to Paris for those intimate interiors of restaurants and museums, and a deep hotel bed that was half the size of their own at home.

Audrey shivered as she shut the door behind her, trading the kitchen's relative heat for the chilly, damp garage. Even in March she had twice experienced Paris as both the City of Light and of Warmth, and for this revisit she'd imagined their extended conversations in compassionate detail. The one about medical school would have gone well because it could be continued from morning to night to morning, until Gregory agreed with Louise Schneider that, unless Audrey gave herself the option of applying, the possibility of her ever becoming a physician would remain an opportunity missed by the feeble excuse of an unasked question. Any actual encounter here at home, in the context of Rob's death and their own lives, could only by definition go far less well. This anticipation alone almost made Audrey wish she would be rejected.

When the walk-in clinic opened up every day, patients who'd been able to wait through the night arrived promptly, lining up for diagnosis. It was her job to be ready for anything, and Audrey found she liked this methodical problem-solving aspect of the work, verifying her powers of observation, expanding her caring skills.

"Any day now, I hear," Louise confided obliquely, not wanting to divulge the contents of a letter that was already in the mail. She couldn't imagine herself beginning medical school again, but no doubt this was because she knew all it entailed. Similarly, Audrey had said she couldn't think of having another baby at this point in her life, notwithstanding that she was perhaps still biologically capable. And yet, if Louise were to ask Audrey's advice about whether or not to have a baby at her age, no doubt Audrey would be encouraging. Just as nobody could argue against a prospective mother who was both eager and mature, in Louise's opinion the medical profession should require all doctors to be nurses first. Audrey was going to be a far better physician than most, because she knew how to handle, hands on, someone who wasn't feeling very well.

Audrey asked, "And?" But she didn't let Louise say anything more. "No, never mind, don't say anything. You can't be sure until—"

Louise laughed and said, "Until you open the envelope?"

"Some call this the scientific method, but its other name is—"

"Superstition?"

"Pessimism." Audrey handed Louise a folder and said, now gravely, "Just as in the examining room right now we have either a terrible fall or a serious case of child abuse." All too often the women were also abused, but they rarely brought themselves in.

This was the worst part of the job, so Louise displayed an appropriate reluctance, hesitating at the door. "How will we ever get our women to come in preventively? Can you answer me that?"

"Not yet." But in fact this was the very question motivating Audrey's medical school application.

Out in the waiting room there was a chronically asthmatic family of six, none of whom had slept through the previous night. A third-grader had a sprained foot and was glad for the borrowed crutches but very disappointed not to have a bone fracture requiring a cast. A regular customer read the paper in her usual seat, needing the company of this room in addition to the proven benefits of medication and psychiatric social work. Audrey was acutely aware of the burden it was to provide solutions to real problems, but never more than now, when Louise had practically just told her, by a sly wink, what she seemed to know for a fact: all of this would one day be hers.

They were more or less the same age, so Louise represented not only the current goal but the alternative opportunity Audrey might have had in the first place. That is, if she hadn't had two older brothers setting the vocational tone, maybe the decision-making would have ended up differently in her own case. But as it was, Johnny and Neil went directly into the family business—Morrow's Pharmacy, the last independent not to sell out to the Rite-Aid chain—so it didn't occur to their parents to reinvent the wheel. It was only after their father's death nine years ago that Neil moved to New York, asserting his own wish to teach grade school and live with a partner of the same sex.

Audrey was at Kent State that deadly spring of 1970 when Ohio college students were fired upon, ending the era when it was still possible to expect a daughter to want a life not unlike her mother's. "You'll want to choose something you can go back to once your kids are in school" had been her father's kind-intentioned advice. This was in their one and only conversation about what Audrey wanted to be when she grew up, when they'd sat at the kitchen table one Sunday afternoon.

In those days it was a diner-style booth built into a corner, and Audrey remembered leaning against the wall. Her father had been working his crossword puzzle, his glasses resting low in a bifocal effect.

She'd responded, "You mean, like a teacher?" and he'd said, "Yes, sure, or maybe a nurse. Your good grades in math and science qualify you, I bet."

And that was all there was, and all there ever was, to it. Audrey's mother, Celia, had entered the Flora Stone Mather College for Women on Euclid Avenue, but she had never finished. No woman on either side of the family had ever gone to graduate school, so when Audrey continued on for her M.S.N., she'd had no reason to think this degree wouldn't be enough. And in one sense her father was correct, even prescient, in knowing that once her kids were in school—although of course he'd meant elementary school, not college—she'd return to the fulfillment of her own ambitions. Where he was wrong was in not knowing that all her life, Audrey, his youngest child and only daughter, wanted just one thing she'd never had: to be the one in charge.

But on the wards, ironically, the nurses were the ones "in charge." Although the doctors gave the orders, they took advice from the nurses, who were there on the scene and could observe either progress or decline. It was more of a partnership, before two things happened to change the relationship between doctors and nurses, malpractice suits and managed care, each of which forced doctors and nurses into opposite corners. And if it was less rewarding to be a nurse these days, it had also become more challenging to be a physician required to become more collaborative while being the bottom-line decision-maker.

"Doctor, can you please tell me how much longer it will be before I can be seen?" The woman never made eye contact with Audrey, so there was no point in Audrey's correcting her to say she was still just a nurse. "Sure, Helena" was Audrey's ever-tolerant reply, every day, "just let me check." She picked up the phone to dial the extension for the office a few doors down the corridor. "They can take you right away," she said, knowing as did her counterpart in counseling that Helena would need another few hours.

But this is just what Audrey meant. Instead of being the one, or one of the ones, who shuffled Helena from place to place while supplying comfort along the way, she would rather provide the cure. She wanted Helena healed once and for all, so the poor woman could spend her life somewhere other than in this windowless room, hour after hour, day after day. There had to be some discovery out there, but not yet made, that in Helena's situation would make all the difference. Yes, Audrey was admittedly foolishly overambitious, given that the psychiatric social worker in charge was doing the best he could. And yet Audrey needed to try, just as Helena obviously needed the help.

"Don't let him get away!" was her father's only other direct advice to her, to marry Gregory Brennan. Gregory was nine years older than her brother Johnny, but because he'd poured his heart into the justice system he'd become forty-three and unmarried. Audrey was already twenty-nine at the time, so from her father's point of view it was practically too late. Needless to say, Audrey and Gregory had had their kids immediately, which turned out to be a good thing, because Jack Morrow had only ten more years to get to know his grandchildren.

Audrey watched Helena settle down again with the newspaper, and she found herself wishing that her father were alive so she could tell him he'd been right, twice.

Gregory sometimes allowed himself a "snooze" bonus, knowing that only one, at most, was his limit. Taking best advantage of these nine extra minutes, he would take inventory, performing a checklist worthy of bench science. These days his inquiry concerned mortality, and the question he asked himself was whether or not any progress had been made on why senseless death still occurred.

There was Rob's in particular, although of course this didn't mean he was incapable of caring about natural disasters wiping out whole populations, not to mention countless innocents in war zones. For the greater good there was one who should have been spared, because Rob Wallace's rare intelligence was organic, manifested with the giant ease of a tree making oxygen from daylight. Rob's imagination was so large with promise, the size of his absence was increasing every day instead of diminishing. Missing Rob was like discovering, item by item, how much more than you reported at the time the thief actually made off with.

The alarm sounded again, to signal the end of this nine-minute opportunity to feel worse about the morning than when it had first interrupted sleep's unconscious balancing of plus and minus. This time there was no proof of the possibility of self-improvement, just the destructive power of a cheap plastic box the size of a hardball. Now he was required to rouse his daughter Sally, who'd roll into another school day of this senior year rendered utterly untroubled four months ago by Early Decision. Sally's immediate future at Virginia was by now so thoroughly imagined, the prolonged anticlimax seemed to make her restless all over again, as she admitted to envying those classmates who were just learning what options they had, or not.

Still, Gregory got out of bed and went down the short hall to his daughter's closed door. "Sally? Honey?" He always announced himself, no matter that while he was sleeping his younger child had turned eighteen's corner into adulthood. He opened her bedroom door and, because there was nothing subtle about Sally, shook her. "Sally? Honey?" The expression on her face was so unpleasant it was almost ugly.

He hated this, the one part of the job he wouldn't miss when Sally went off to college. "Get up!" he said like a tyrant, which he also hated, although nothing less had ever proved effective. Good luck to her roommate, he told himself as he returned to the sanctuary of his bedroom, and that went for everybody including, one day, he hoped, her future husband. Gregory caught himself hoping he'd still be alive for that day.

But if you did the math, it wasn't altogether self-pity that caused Gregory not to take another decade for granted. Even without the shadow of Rob's depressing death, it was a fact that he was born during the Great Depression. If you asked him, the impact was obvious.

And yet, more like a man with everything going his way, he showered and dressed in one of the European tailored suits he always wore even though only ten inches of trouser showed beneath his robes. He matched his tie to the thin blue of the sky, pretending to optimism. Downstairs, he could see that the *Plain Dealer* was in its plastic bag at their door ahead of the *New York Times,* and he took this as a good sign, validating his decision, at the time unheard-of, to leave a major Wall Street firm for a hometown practice. Wait. This choice had been corroborated so thoroughly, so long ago, why did it even come to mind?

"Hey, Dad," Sally allowed in her morning monotone, slumping into the kitchen so gracelessly it seemed impossible to believe she was the star of her own lacrosse video, prized by college recruiters with outsized budgets, who'd flattered her with such overblown promises she thought they could only be false.

"Hi, champ."

She never said anything more, nor did he, usually. But he said, "Good luck."

"Huh?"

"Today's game."

She squinted at the refrigerator door. "Magnificat," she read from the athletic schedule posted there.

In this undefeated season he knew better than to ask which was the better team, so Gregory merely repeated, "Good luck." His own West Side alma mater, St. Ignatius, currently had the best high school football team in the nation, but he was more invested in Sally's games.

"Okay," she said, but with an expression that could be the ancestor of a smile. At least something gave her pleasure, even if winning was always, by definition, at someone else's expense.

This generation of kids had everything going for it. Above the garage, to attract their first daughter in off the road once Val got her driver's license, a storage area had been outfitted with soft furniture, a mini-kitchen, and music, including a fairly decent drum set. Now that Val's friends in her band, String of Pearls, were off in their first year of college—including Val, whose precise destination had been unresolved until late summer—Sally and her own friends used the soundproof room for the sports channel or MTV, taking utterly for granted the privilege it represented. Yes, he knew how old he sounded. Well? He felt old.

He knew too much, so for instance he couldn't simply drive down Euclid Avenue on an early April Wednesday morning without noting like a guidebook that it started out an Indian trail, which then became a stagecoach route. Streetcar tracks ran down the center of the street as once, before World War II, a hundred kinds of cars were manufactured here in Cleveland, where the steering wheel and the attached horn and windshield wipers were invented. The corner of Euclid and the street named for the city's distinguished former mayor Carl Stokes—Euclid and Stokes—was the site of the country's first hand-operated traffic signal, a device invented by another African-American Clevelander named Garrett Morgan. One block over, stretching along Carnegie for sixteen blocks, was the fourth-best hospital in the world, the Cleveland Clinic, which was the city's largest single private employer, of more than eight thousand. "Thank you, Moses Cleaveland, our fine city's esteemed founder," his girls teased him when in their opinion he sounded like the Chamber of Commerce.

"Seriously, look around you," he'd refute them, without having to mention the Rock and Roll Hall of Fame. Every now and then he wished he had some out-of-town relatives to show around and show the place off to: "First there was the Indian trail, and now there's the World Series champion baseball team of the same name."

So by the time he got downtown, Judge Gregory Brennan had cheered himself up considerably with the honest history of this city where he'd been born and had outlived a lot, not the least his own stubborn fears. Now his chambers were located in the modern Justice Center, across the street from the original Cuyahoga County Court House he would always prefer. There was no thrill equal to the experience of climbing those front steps each morning between the paired seated statues of Thomas Jefferson and Alexander Hamilton and then, inside, gaining reinforcement from no less than Aristotle, whose words were carved into the marble—"AND THE RULE OF THE LAW IS PREFERABLE TO ANY INDIVIDUAL"—for none to avoid. Here in the Justice Center, uplift took the mundane form of elevators.

"Good morning, Judge," Marjorie McCarthy greeted him from her secure place behind her massive oak desk. When he responded, as always, "Good morning, Marge," she corrected him, "Call me Esquire from now on," to which Gregory could only ask, "Pardon me?"

"I've decided I'm going to become a lawyer too." But she had to look away from him so she wouldn't ruin her own joke.

Gregory stared at the brass nameplate on her desk, as if to attempt to conjure the adjustment. The old courthouse was being restored so faithfully it was difficult to believe anything beautiful had the power to change. The dense terracotta paint was being mixed according to the original formula, and the brown leather on the padded swinging doors, though new, was identical to what it replaced. By the door to his chambers, and by each judge's, had stood the ribcage-high nameplate that looked like a miniature gas pump dressed up with brass flourishes, including back-to-back C's signifying Cuyahoga County, or as Audrey teased him—though never Marjorie—Coco Chanel. He'd had to leave all that behind, moving into the twenty-four-story granite cube of the new Justice Center. No, he couldn't begin to imagine losing Marjorie too, on top of Rob.

He was unable to meet her eyes because—now she would be as shocked as he was—his eyes were filling with tears. If she ever quit, so would he. And now he saw he was serious. Still, he had to come up with something to answer, so he told her the truth: "I'm sorry to have to tell you how very sorry I am to hear that," which caused Marjorie to chime, "April Fool!" Her own day had begun with a series of fake disaster calls from her nephews, so this seemed tame.

Gregory sat in the armchair beside her desk and broke the rules for a second by taking her hand in his own. "As you know," he told her, "I've always thought you would have made an excellent lawyer. But don't ever leave me, please," he begged her. "Promise?"

Marjorie said, "Only on a stretcher." This she regretted as well, since it was the awful way Judge Wallace left, when he left.

Before Gregory could respond, she said, "But Judge Wallace's wife—widow—called already this morning to thank you for inviting her boys to do something with you on Saturday morning. She said to say that they'd love to, and you only need to tell her what time." Her approval was evident in her sweet smile. "What time shall I tell her for you?"

"Nine? Ten?"

"Nine. My nephews would already have been up for hours."

"Okay. Thanks." Gregory pushed against the arms of the oak chair and stood over Marjorie. "You see how much I need you, Marge, don't you?"

At his own desk Gregory turned his back on the present and, like the restoration project, returned to the past to take guidance. Maybe it *was* time to retire. His own mentor, Judge Osborne, had taken cases on assignment from the Ohio Supreme Court until his death at eighty, but Gregory's own expectation had been that he'd run for one more six-year term and call it quits. Now he wondered about forgoing that last term. Swiveling in his leather chair, he looked out his window and over the roof of the old courthouse to the Burke Lakefront Airport and a little plane climbing into the air like a squirrel up a tree. The future provided inspiration far better than the past: why not make that postponed trip to Paris to celebrate Audrey's fiftieth birthday? Or why not take her off in a new direction—to Martinique, say—or, like Gauguin, who stopped in Martinique for five months, keep on going all the way to Tahiti? Maybe he could take up painting too and, like Gauguin, suppress the third dimension. For this recent canceled trip to Paris, he'd once again renovated his French. Why *not* retire?

Gregory and Audrey often compared their work, law and medicine both being self-contained worlds—with hierarchies, yes, but this wasn't the point—that existed for only one purpose. People passed through the systems of medicine and law to get help, and it was a privilege, as he and Audrey would agree even on their worst days, to provide it. They were like Noah and his wife, transporting the survivors.

But his hands were shaking, so he held each with the other as his pulse jumped. That he might retire early was an idea he'd never had, except in relation to other people. There was Judge Osborne's powerful example, never to quit entirely, but then there was his own father, who'd hit a tree at such a high speed it wasn't termed an accident. The night of the crash, the police spared the widow and her two boys the most telling detail—no skid marks on the road—when delivering the news. Gregory then became the obsessively studious son of a father who had been a failure at everything but his own death, who died too young to set him any example but the wrong one.

"Please approach the bench," Gregory instructed both attorneys as, off the record, he accused the defense of stalling. "Am I clear?"

"Yes, Your Honor." They sounded like identical twins.

Jury selection was moving so slowly even Gregory had trouble staying with it. To the young lawyers he counseled, he often compared being a judge with his having been a catcher as a boy: if you lost your concentration behind the plate, you were to blame for any subsequent error. It could happen in the courtroom as out on the baseball diamond, and now he wished he could tell the jurors that, if they were bored, it wasn't their fault.

"Ladies and gentlemen," he said, rotating in his chair to address them, "I've asked counsel to refrain from needless and bothersome interruptions, so we will proceed with the jury selection process and begin the trial after the recess. You have been exceedingly patient with our sometimes tedious justice system." He turned back and ordered, "Proceed," which obliged counsel to reply, "Thank you, Your Honor."

But when court resumed, the first witness to be called by the state seemed to be missing from those gathered in the hall outside the courtroom. Gregory extended his arm and pointed it at the defense as if holding a zigzag bolt of lightning. Both lawyers stepped forward again, the one insisting it was a simple misunderstanding, whereas the prosecutor argued that while there were indeed other witnesses to be called, the girlfriend was crucial. The vehicular homicide case against her boyfriend was based on her grand jury testimony, where she'd described driving the defendant's car when he grabbed the steering wheel during an argument, causing her to lose control. There was no point in the judge's saying "Find her. Get her in here," but it seemed to Gregory that he had no other real option. In a baseball game there could be a rain delay, when both players and spectators would have to wait, often hours, while it was decided whether or not to call the game. To the jurors he made this analogy as a way to let them know the case would continue. The large modern windows with their panoramic lake views were sealed against any and all weather, but you could see freighters make their way from one destination to the next, the way he himself always had.

During the lunch break, this being Wednesday, Gregory went as usual to get his shoes polished. Joe Ricci was a guy who'd also worked the marble courthouse halls his whole career. A dedicated Indians fan—"But who isn't these days," he'd say, "when it's easy"—he made shoes shine like new cars in a showroom. Some of the younger ones out there relied on paper shields to protect the socks—"Would you believe what people will pay for socks these days?"—but Joe was old school, a real pro. His brother Frank ran the barber shop—"From top to bottom, right, Judge?"—because they knew that the justice system remained the kind of workplace—"One of the few left, am I right?"—where people would still attempt to look as good as they could. Where they had to. Where their lives depended on it.

"You're looking good, Judge."

"You too, Joe." Or, "You too, Frank."

"How's everything?"

"Good. And you?"

"Good too."

Their talk never got more personal than that, except the week Joe and Frank's mother passed away and each of them mentioned the fact, as then Gregory did around the time his mother died. And when they talked about—while avoiding—the death of Judge Wallace.

Today was a little different, because Gregory was more tired than usual. As he sat impassively and watched Joe Ricci labor over his shoes, he felt like the professional loser he'd already been, in personal terms, when he arrived at work this morning and missed Marjorie's April Fools' Day joke on him. At least he'd had the idea of bringing Rob's boys in on Saturday morning for haircuts. But this was an exception to the day's lapses. It was almost as if, in the absence of testimony by the key witness, the jury could find against him instead. For insufficient everything.

But he'd never liked being taken by surprise, so he was frustrated that the prosecutor appeared to have been manipulated by a witness who had suddenly become reluctant. She'd told the grand jury that the defendant, her boyfriend, had been screaming at her when he grabbed the wheel, causing her to swerve into the oncoming car, in which the driver had been killed. Clearly, her version of the events was crucial in order for a charge of vehicular homicide to be brought against the defendant. Gregory shifted in his seat, knowing how hard it was to ascribe state of mind. This much he knew from his personal experience, having spent fifty years trying to imagine what his father's thoughts might have been as he flew off the rainy road at a high speed.

At least he and Audrey spoke up when something was bothering them. He'd had to learn how to do this, but she'd made it easy for him because, for his fiftieth birthday, she'd organized a surprise party, telling him one lie after another in order to fool him into thinking she would never, ever do that. Then of course he'd walked into a room and nearly had a heart attack from the shock of encountering a parade of faces he'd hoped to have left far behind.

He had a small cramp in one calf, which he ignored. And anyway, that was more than a dozen years ago, and nobody at the party could have known from his behavior that this wasn't the thrill of a lifetime. The next morning he'd found a way to break it to Audrey, then too blaming his father for ruining surprises for him.

"You're not looking too good, Judge," Joe told him for the first time ever.

Gregory was about to reply, "You too, Joe," but caught himself.

"Me too," said Joe. It turned out to be his pancreas. He never knew he had one.

Gregory vigorously protested the news, as if Joe must be mistaken. "Pancreatic!" he said, tipping his face to the ceiling as if it were the great dome of the Pantheon and a circle of light could pour down upon Joe from the heavens and deliver the instant cure.

"So whatever it is with you, you get better quick, you hear me?" Joe pressed the two brushes together and set them down, bristles coupled, and draped the flannel finishing cloth across the footrest of his second chair, where he placed himself in its lap, leaning into a detailed description of the diagnosis. "So I had to tell them, 'Sorry. I don't believe in the death penalty.'"

Gregory heard Joe ask, "You don't either, do you?" All speech caught in his throat, but Gregory made an effort to offer Joe the appreciative chuckle Joe expected from him no matter what.

"Do you?" repeated Joe.

"No, me neither." Gregory knew about pancreatic cancer even though, by the end, it was perhaps the only kind his mother didn't have. She'd wished for it, in fact, because she'd heard how quick it was, how little time it took to be over.

During Audrey's lunch break she'd gone home to check the day's mail and, in her front hall, had become her own fight-or-flight case study. Her breathing was so rapid and so shallow it felt to her as if she'd just had sex. Her dilated pupils blurred the bulk of the text, but she could read at least one word: "Congratulations." Audrey's agitation made it impossible to read whole paragraphs, but she'd memorized the first three phrases, welcoming her into distinguished company.

When was the last time she'd had such a secret as this? When she'd had sex for the first time and only she and one other person knew? That part of the experience hadn't felt right that time either, but the rite of passage, then as now, was nevertheless pure exhilaration, reinforced back at Metro when she was greeted by a bouquet of long-stemmed white tulips. Louise was so practiced at patient confidentiality there wasn't a card to be misinterpreted. It was as if Louise were the teenage boy she'd just had sex with, promising her he'd never be the first to tell.

At the end of that afternoon, Audrey stood behind the Hathaway Brown bench at Magnificat, watching Sally dominate play. Although both teams wore the crisply pleated miniskirted uniforms of their private schools, with their menacing mouth guards they all had split personalities. Sally wore a rolled-up bandana, warrior style, and was flicking her stick, charging, dodging, faking, flinging the ball at eye level. She played attack and ran like a racehorse far ahead of the pack, galloping down the field, reaching with her thin muscular legs as if she had two pairs of them.

Audrey had learned to keep boots in the back of her station wagon, so she could always be covered from the ground up. Spring sports were frequently enough played in the freezing rain as to have warned these practiced bystanders, who huddled gamely, hunched under their turned-up collars. It was still the first half, but, on its own terms as always, the sky was providing insufficient daylight, guaranteeing minor injuries and disputed calls by the referees. There was no question as to which team was winning.

Sally had been promised longer seasons at Virginia. To have gotten this good in this climate under these conditions—or so the recruiters had lined up to tell her—proved genuine greatness. Sally's ambivalent but essentially good-humored older sister began addressing her as "Your Greatness" with a familiar mock reverence. "May I approach the bench, Your Greatness," Val would joke during halftime as Sally rested her legs for fewer minutes than it takes to soft-boil an egg.

Audrey always made sure Sally knew she was there, but because the coach and backup players supplied adequate noise, the sidelines fans were free to chat or, as the cell-phone dads did, link up the office and the lacrosse field by satellite, keeping a simultaneous eye on the game and the Asian markets. Since Audrey was preoccupied, she was relieved not to have to make petty conversation today. How could she honestly answer "Not much" to the casual question "What's new?"

And in the car on their way home Audrey knew to count on Sally not to inquire about her day. For someone so active, Sally wasn't at all interactive, and because there was the lacrosse game to debrief, she was in no danger of confiding in Sally before she had a chance to tell Gregory. Even before she had a chance to tell Sally what a good game she'd played, Sally said, "I'm freezing!" and turned the heater's fan so high it filled the car with icy air. Displaying added impatience, Sally complained that the refs were all such fools it wasn't right that the coaches should be required to call them "sir." It wasn't enough that Audrey quickly and completely agreed. Sally was prepared to inventory each call, all the way home.

Because this wasn't a conversation, Audrey didn't feel obliged to listen too carefully, so instead she wondered who would dare to be the first boy to have sex with Sally. Of course it was possible that Sally had already been initiated—this was the point of having a doctor you could talk to once your mother laid the groundwork—but Audrey suspected that, even as a virgin, Sally would be the one to initiate. In an all-girls school like Hathaway Brown, there were no lessons in passivity because there was no reason to be compliant.

And yet Audrey hadn't been so confident about her older daughter Val's ability to be led by her own desires rather than those headlined in the teen magazines. Val had followed each adolescent trend with a true-believer fervor and, needless to say, the statistics also presumed sexual activity. Every conversation with her mother on the subject ended prematurely because Val had always rushed off, as if speed were the same thing as accuracy.

"Val's not coming home this weekend, right?" Sally had quieted down, moving on from the immediate past into the near future.

"Not that I know of," said Audrey. Val had told them very little about her life at the University of Cincinnati, but this didn't mean they'd suspended their worrying about her, since, if she were to succeed, she'd doubtless find some way to fail. The real cause for concern wasn't the fender-bender the day she got her driver's license, nor her losing track of the time her first night without a curfew, but that Val could always be counted on to sabotage her own success, along with her own best interests. Audrey looked forward to calling Val with her good news, and hoped that she might inspire Val, who was another late bloomer.

"So can I use your car?" Sally said, picking a scab on her shin.

Every time Audrey was asked this question by either of her daughters, she answered, as now, "Maybe." She never gave permission to any plan involving a car without consulting Gregory, who was irrational on this issue alone.

"We'll talk about it at dinner," said Sally, supplying her mother's all-purpose reply. Then she changed the subject to, "What're we having?"

Audrey said, "We'll get whatever we want." They were near the famous West Side Market—"designed by the architect of the Museum of Art," as Gregory never failed to mention whenever they were on this side of the Hope Bridge, "named for Bob Hope's father, who was a stonecutter on the project," he always said—and Audrey pulled into an empty parking space near the entrance. With a hundred or more merchants under that great vaulted roof, every ethnic identity was represented. Audrey answered Sally's question by suggesting, "Let's celebrate."

"Winning?" Sally was always at the exact center of her world. She knew it was her job in life to be.

Audrey sounded more like Sally—like a winner—when she said, "Yes!" The other medical students would be closer to her daughters' ages than to her own, but today she'd felt younger and younger.

With their bags of food in the back of the wagon, they headed home. Food fragrances escaped their various wrappings to fill the car with the sure promise of feasting. Audrey regretted withholding her news all the more, now that they'd picked a meal worthy of the good champagne she'd put in the fridge on her way back to the clinic. Tempted, unable to resist, she chanced, "How do you think you'd feel if I ever went back to school?" She knew how manipulative this was, but she risked the offense.

"You? You mean, like Dad with his French?" Sally's own interest in the French language consisted of her discovery that *le jeu de la crosse* came from the Old French for "the game of the hooked stick."

"Sort of."

"Frankly, I'd think you were both having a nervous breakdown. He's bad enough as it is." Twisting in the passenger seat as if making one of her aggressive moves on the field, she told Audrey, "It was so embarrassing, Mom. Him talking to Madame Jacob in French class on visiting day, pretending like he's French. As if Madame Jacob, who *is,* couldn't tell the difference."

"Dad was only being polite."

"If you ask me," Sally said, "parents shouldn't be beginners. It looks foolish."

Even Audrey had to admit she had a point.

Scrupulous about measuring, Gregory always added an equal amount of tap water to his ounce and a half of scotch. Usually he waited for Audrey to get home, but the news was already on.

All these years, out of loyalty to Walter Cronkite, he'd stayed with CBS. It was obvious that Uncle Walter had retired way too early, and Gregory wanted the network bosses to know that this fact hadn't ever escaped his notice. For local news he as faithfully watched Fox 8 for the weather—for the weather*man*—because Dick Goddard never quit, not even at sixty-five. Gregory had startled himself that morning with his concrete consideration of retirement, because his assumption had been that he'd follow Judge Osborne's "senior status" example and take occasional cases into old age so as to keep himself alert while helping to prevent a judicial backlog. Few other professions were so well suited to gradual change, once past the age of seventy when it was no longer possible to run for reelection. As Gregory relaxed in his favorite chair, he was content. In his profession the goal with each election was to ensure reelection six years later, but suddenly he had options. Audrey's was a good example of the opposite, having required perpetual education to keep up with technological advances. Actually, because of computers it might have become easier—for their generation, that is—to be a doctor than the nurse who had to know how to use the new equipment. Not that his and Audrey's fourteen-year age difference made them, technically, of the same generation. Gregory took a long sip of his scotch and turned his attention back to the news.

He could remember the moment of Dan Rather's on-the-scene transition from local reporter to national, on that day's broadcast from Dallas when Cronkite had to put on his glasses to read into the TV camera President Kennedy's precise time of death. Throughout all the intervening decades Dick Goddard's tinted hair gave him a perennial advantage, so that, like the Jerry Lewis Telethon hosted locally by Goddard for three dozen years, with him it had long ago become impossible to tell one year from the last.

"April first weather trivia," announced Goddard. "Are you ready? Where does the expression 'raining cats and dogs' come from?" All Cleveland knew he ought to know the answer, since he had five cats of his own. "I'll have the answer before the end of the half hour," he promised, "and a *snow* forecast. No fooling!" Gregory had no need to know—who did?—but he nevertheless caught himself in momentary speculation. Such was the idiotic power of the news that the next immediate question posed by the anchor team was prompted by the city's lead story of the evening: what is the real meaning of these drive-by shootings? Gregory didn't fail to note that the answer to this question was more obvious, which didn't make it the easier to answer.

There was a time in his career when he'd wondered what it said about him that he was less interested in criminal than civil cases, and when he'd come to understand he was a logician. So, naturally, the problems he preferred solving were those created by the mind more than the heart. Crimes of passion, ironically, seemed to him to be a lot less complicated than those where the motivation had to be investigated. Temperamentally, he was perfectly suited to finding cause when the law itself allowed interpretation.

But then, when his wife's headlights flashed against the window, announcing her arrival as she turned into the driveway, Gregory became aware of his acute relief, which was how he could recognize his overpowering concern for the safety of his family. In these past few weeks he'd experienced Rob Wallace, belatedly, as the son he might have had if he'd had his kids—as so many of his classmates did, on account of Korea—while still in college or law school. By this measure, he was able to acknowledge that if anything ever happened to Audrey or either of their kids, he too could prove himself capable of committing a crime of passion.

Sally dropped her cleats onto the linoleum, and rounds of earth rolled like coins from a spilled purse. She always waited to be asked, especially when her team was undefeated.

Before he had a chance, Audrey said, "Six to zip," as she set the shopping bags on the counter, freeing her hands in order to reach out to him with a greeting, as if she had any idea how much he needed to matter to her right now.

"Mom's in a good mood," said Sally, "so she insisted on lobsters flown from Maine."

They were both so noisy he almost felt overwhelmed, though he nevertheless said, "Congratulations."

"Yeah." If Sally weren't an adolescent, she'd have wanted to shower before dinner and given her mother the chance to tell Gregory her news, but she never did. She didn't even wash her hands before plunging them into the silverware drawer.

Less to criticize than from mere professional habit, Audrey washed her own hands. She didn't wish to give orders, and yet, if Sally were still a child it would be possible to send her off on some small manufactured errand for just the right amount of time.

At least she grasped the glasses by their stems as she announced, "Mom said she chilled champagne."

"Careful," cautioned Audrey as she evaded Gregory's questioning look by watching their daughter place three glasses on the table with the flair of a professional bartender. These had been a wedding present, so they were official antiques.

"Sorry. What else?" After a game, Sally always brought equivalent energy to the next thing, leaving her fingerprints everywhere, the way in lacrosse season her signature effort was stamped on every goal. "I'm not in the mood for dog food ads," she said as she clicked off the television with the remote. "My theory is, they think anyone who watches Dick Goddard has to be an animal lover, so they're targeting that consumer audience."

Gregory must have decided to abandon all hope, because he heard himself asking in vain, "Where does the expression 'raining cats and dogs' come from? Anyone have an idea?"

Audrey washed the lettuce, then spun it dry. All winter the lettuce had been hydroponic, but this small head had been grown in the earth and had actual flavor. Soon the ground would be dry enough to plant lettuce seed in the downtown allotment gardens Audrey had helped to organize by calling on Cleveland's memory of Charles Lathrop Pack, the wealthy local lumberman who in 1918 began his national campaign for home food production. As a result, five million victory gardeners had grown more than five hundred million dollars' worth of food. By comparison, her own community gardening program, started on a few abandoned lots, seemed meager. But today, after two dozen years, well-established gardens flourished as, side by side, cultures also cross-fertilized. Until a year ago Audrey kept up a plot Val worked with her, but with Val in Cincinnati, Audrey contented herself with daffodils in the back yard, because they self-propagated.

Sally was checking the phone messages, but she'd heard her father ask Dick Goddard's trivia question. Her answer to him was "Who cares?"

They ate quickly, and Sally cleared the plates before going upstairs to make phone calls in the absence of real homework this late in the school year. Audrey and Gregory sat with mugs of decaf and the biscotti she was unable to resist at the West Side Market, despite the fact that once she had broken a tooth on one of those petrified nuts embedded in these seemingly kiln-dried cookies. The champagne had turned out to be a bad idea, even though she'd nursed it and, she could joke, it made for a logical sequence to move on from that to doctored coffee.

Gregory could see that she had something to say, so he waited for her to speak.

But she began by asking, "You know that phone call?" Now she sounded like a kid making excuses. "That I took in the other room?"

Was it really necessary for him to answer "Yes?" They were strict about not taking phone calls during dinner, but Sally refused to keep herself in suspense, so—this was the extent of her defiance of parental authority—she always answered it in the nanosecond before the machine took over.

"Well, it was this doctor from Case Western Reserve, congratulating me." Audrey took in enough oxygen to light a fire, but it produced only a spark. "On having been accepted to medical school." She couldn't seem to bring herself to insert a personal pronoun.

Ambiguously, he responded in silence, shifting in his chair as the earth moved beneath him.

"That is, on *my* acceptance letter. Here it is." Now she placed the large envelope on his placemat, like a next course.

In the courtroom Gregory was famous for deliberately not betraying any emotion, a trick—an exercise, really—he'd perfected over the years. Now he called on this skill, but instead of projecting neutrality, he couldn't relax the muscles of his face.

He couldn't begin to make his voice work either, not that he would know what to say. He refused to open the envelope without some form of acknowledgment—an apology wouldn't be inappropriate—that she'd violated a trust. He could see it in her face, the way she looked both proud and ashamed.

She was examining her teaspoon, like a silver appraiser looking for the stamps that signify its value. More actively, she was setting aside the first several things she'd thought of to say. It was untrue that she'd thought she wouldn't get in: she knew she might. It was unfair to assume that Sally could resent her for impinging: nothing interfered with Sally's self-directed focus, and besides, Sally's future had been firmly established three months before her own final deadline. It was unkind to blame the effect of Rob's death on Gregory. The only thing left was the available truth. "You knew I'd thought about it seriously enough to take the test. And you knew I'd done well enough."

This shocked him more. "That was *last year!* Has it been that long since you told me anything? And what else don't I know? What *else?*"

She said nothing more than "Nothing" at first, but then added, "And it wasn't last year, it was last fall. I told you that Louise Schneider encouraged me to consider the idea. The deadline forced me to go ahead, since the deadline coincided—"

"Who?" Of course the name was familiar, since Audrey began most sentences with "Louise" whenever he inquired about the clinic. Not unlike the way he'd so often mentioned Rob, he'd have to admit, if he weren't feeling betrayed.

"The way Rob, for you—"

"Don't you *dare* blame him!"

"I'm not," she protested.

"It's unforgivable for you to mention him in this context. It's not *his* fault he died. Or mine either." Gregory was so tense he was trembling.

"I know. I only meant that the timing—"

"Was unfortunate, yes." Gregory glared at her.

"—prevented me."

He stood opposite her, gripping the back of his chair with both hands. In his courtroom, or anywhere, nothing bothered him more than making excuses, except the thought that he wouldn't recognize it when he saw it. Did she think he'd let her get away with making her dishonesty his own fault?

He asked, but she couldn't answer him. No matter how wrong, it wasn't dishonest. It was a fact: horrible, as the saying goes, but no less true. She couldn't risk making things worse by saying this.

"You should be ashamed of yourself," he said.

Here was her chance. "I am." Audrey raised her face to meet his gaze. "But how could it not have been worse if I'd ignored your suffering? Disregarded you?"

"But you did."

"No," explained Audrey patiently, "no, I didn't. That would be if I'd decided it was sad about Rob, but not quite sad enough to prevent me from needing you to take on the burden of my own concerns."

"Well, it *was* 'sad enough' for me," he said in a sarcastic tone she'd rarely heard. "So don't use Rob as an excuse ever again. It offends me. It offends him."

The table was in the new part of the kitchen, once the side porch, incorporated into the house by replacing the brittle screens with seven large state-of-the-art sheets of thermal glass that knew to keep the seasons straight by holding heat in and cold out, or the reverse. All Audrey needed from them right then was the evening air, but they were sealed shut.

Now her silence had the effect of pushing him deeper. "You seem to have forgotten who I am," he continued, "or else you would never for a single minute think I wouldn't feel as I do. Completely undermined." And though he couldn't have put into words why "undermined" was accurate, Gregory knew it was.

Audrey couldn't extract herself either, so she said, "If you think I've neglected who you are, then what about me? Why can't you be happy for me? Or at least proud?"

"Oh, please," he said dismissively. "Of your having been devious? The better question is, *why* would you do this?"

There was no way a last sip of decaf could compensate for the champagne she wished she'd never chilled in the first place, but she finished it anyway, like an actor giving herself a meaningless task to perform, a small gesture to indicate her character's inability to defend herself. The decaf had grown cool and had no taste.

"Sometimes, Audrey, I think you have no idea who I am." He managed to avoid acting like some schoolyard bully, but he couldn't come up with anything more creative, despite the fact that her question was a good one: why hadn't it been possible for him to feel happy for her?

So she repeated his "Oh, please," as if she'd caught him, like a cop, in a speed trap.

"Don't condescend, Audrey."

"Then don't you speak to me in that smug tone."

"Not smug, hurt. Hurt." Exhibit A.

She quit, but like a kite when the wind dies.

"I feel betrayed by you." His voice was just as theatrical, though quiet. "The way I'd expect to feel if you fell in love with someone else. I see I'd be the last to know."

"No, it's not the same thing."

"Speak for yourself—"

"I am." She stared at him. "At least I'm trying to."

"—because this is my point. You and I are different. You and I have an essential—an enormous—difference." Now he let go of the back of his chair, in order to produce Exhibit B.

The muscles in her neck knotted.

He opened his hands so she could see how they trembled. "What you forgot about me is the thing you know very well about me. I come damaged. Damaged goods means broken,

-hearted and -spirited, which in turn means I'm incapable of being surprised like this. I can't take it. You've always known this about me, and in case you'd forgotten, Rob Wallace's death was a sufficient reminder."

In a voice made sharp by the chaos of feeling, he said, "I don't like surprises and, as you know, I don't do well with them." Now he returned his hands to his pockets, and he jingled the coins to make this last point. "You could call it my only inheritance."

Next came the dispiriting experience of wishing it had gone otherwise. As it was, her success had become a failure.

If only Gregory hadn't seized the moment, when their champagne glasses were raised, to salute Sally for her win. Sally had already announced that this was a celebration—"Mom's in a good mood" were her words—so all Audrey would have had to add was that she also had good news. One or the other of them was bound to ask, "What?"

The water bubbled in the glass as she rinsed it, and she carefully placed it in the dish rack, making a point not to snap the stem like a twig. Audrey had inherited her mother's delicate hands but short fingers, making it hard to wash these flutes, which were too fine to be put in the dishwasher. Drying her hands and returning the red-and-white-checked linen towel to its place under the sink—her mother's were the same, in blue, from a special shop in Pittsburgh—Audrey remembered a morning from her senior year in college when she was home from Columbus for a weekend and had slept late, notwithstanding the commotion.

That day her mother was also drying her hands, but only as a way to keep them occupied. Her father had spoken in an agitated voice familiar to Audrey, but only in relation to his children, or occasionally an employee, never his wife. "Celia, you've deeply disappointed me," he'd said. Audrey had been on her way into the kitchen, and she'd stopped still as a statue, even balancing on one foot.

Her mother had explained, "The delivery truck was late, Jack." Audrey hadn't been able to see Celia's face, but this soft voice didn't sound like someone who had done something wrong.

"That's no excuse, Celia. It's worse than an excuse."

"I'm sorry, dear." She'd apologized right away, but her husband wasn't finished.

"Only a sneak would act like this. Only a—"

"It wasn't a crime to want new furniture without obtaining your approval. All our marriage I've been in charge of our home, the way you are at the pharmacy." Celia's tone was so flat it was still hard for Audrey to guess what the problem was. "And anyway, you surely got your way in the end, didn't you?" But now her voice caught, like a thread in a zipper.

And Jack took advantage of her by saying, "Don't make it seem like I'm some cheapskate!"

"I'm not."

"Yes, you are. It isn't about money!" But now he'd sounded defensive.

"No, it was about something else." And now it was as if she'd seen it was over, but in the way a lost opportunity is. "I just wanted some privacy," Celia added in a small voice.

"Distance, you mean," he'd replied. "A distance between us, you mean."

"No, Jack. A little privacy, is all." A subsequent generation would call it "personal space."

"But why?" And now, finally, he'd softened his voice too, as if it weren't too late for that.

"Not even you could understand, you whom countless women confide in every day."

"Yes, exactly. That's my point exactly."

"I said, '*Not* even you,'" she'd repeated with the same emphasis, "because you clearly don't." Then she'd added, "This too shall pass." Audrey couldn't tell whether her mother was quoting him or the Bible, or being ironic or sarcastic. She couldn't yet tell what the "this" referred to.

And so her father spelled it out. "You yourself said I know all about the change of life, as I do, but believe me, this is different. What just happened here, my dear, was a radical act on your part."

"Don't make it into a protest, Jack, like I'm some college kid. I'm a mature woman who only wished not to share a double bed at this time."

"A matrimonial bed, it's called." Then he'd been the one who'd sounded like a schoolboy.

"Well, I measured for a king-size mattress, but I found it wouldn't go up the stairs. Twin beds seemed like the solution. And a common headboard might have provided—"

"Admit it, Celia, there was no way I'd have agreed." There was a chance Jack had possibly heard his own words, because he added, "As was just made quite clear."

But by now Celia was weeping. That is, now it was possible for her to tell him he'd humiliated her, by ordering the delivery men to take the new mattresses back to Halle Brothers, and by the sad looks on their faces, pitying her for having married this brute. She'd already washed the pretty new sheets and aired the new lightweight wool blankets, and was planning to make up the beds, covering them with the single king-size bedspread designed to make the point that this change was really about night sweats and nothing more. She'd only wished—now, in her exhaustion, she sobbed—to wake up every two hours and not wake him, and not have to see in his face every morning what a tough night she'd given him. It was hard enough to get through them on her own. Why was that so hard for him to see? Why was it necessary for him to humiliate her?

Audrey had retreated like a cat burglar. To her knowledge, neither of her parents was aware that she'd been there in the next room, nor, as far as she knew, was the issue ever again discussed. Audrey's guess was that her mother might have borrowed her empty bedroom down the hall from time to time, but she never knew this for sure, and to this day Celia slept—alone now, for these past nine years since Jack's death—in that same double bed.

Audrey crossed the kitchen to make sure her own daughter wasn't in the living room, caught, like a spy in the old days by border guards in the compartment of a train, with no exit. What could be worse than if Sally had listened in, the way she herself had, on a conversation she'd wanted nothing to do with? Now, though, seeing the empty room, Audrey felt even stupider, since of course Sally would have barged right into the kitchen tonight, to referee.

She also saw this might not have been a bad thing. Just as her mother might have wished she'd found a way to discuss the matter in advance of the delivery truck, she too would rather have had Gregory know she was thinking of applying to medical school. Why hadn't she told him? Wasn't it for the very same reason? What could be worse than to be prevented from having an idea?

2

AUDREY MOVED ABOUT the first floor of the house with authority, switching off the ceiling lights in the kitchen, the shaded standing lamp next to Gregory's favorite chair in what he called the den, the pair of wall sconces on either side of the front-hall mirror, and the cut-glass miniature chandelier at the top of the stairs. Nevertheless, she didn't have the nerve to open the closed door to Val's bedroom.

From that end of the hall she could verify that Gregory wasn't in their bed, which was just as he'd have made it in the morning, the king-size spread as wide as a river. From their bathroom an acute triangle of light fell across their mattress, dividing it on a diagonal. Having learned her mother's painful lesson the easy way, she and Gregory had started off their marriage with a king-size bed even though, except for the maple rocking chair in which she'd nursed their babies, there was little room for anything else. On a normal night he could be sitting in the rocker with his blue-veined ankles exposed between his white oxford-cloth pajamas and cordovan slippers. On a cool night like this he'd be wearing his English flannel bathrobe, and across his lap would be an accordion file fastened tight by winding a string into a figure eight, the way a boat is secured to a dock.

Audrey knew that filling her body with air wouldn't help, except in getting a little oxygen to the brain.

She stepped from her square-toed heels but put them by the bedroom door for the next morning. The forgiving carpet yielded to each footstep as she left meandering tracks like a rabbit in the back yard. Making her way to the sink to remove the contact lenses she'd worn since the day's first light, Audrey was aware that her eyes were more exhausted than the rest of her body, which was as alert, and as alarmed, as any rabbit.

Val's room hadn't become the official guest room because she'd gone only a few hours away to Cincinnati, but during the fall and winter, if Gregory woke in the night he would often bring his overnight reading there, where he'd made a place for himself. Never, so far, had he slept there. Audrey could tell from the way the air didn't penetrate far enough into her lungs to steady her that, evidently, this was what his plan was. It didn't take a detective to note that his bathrobe was missing from its hook on the back of the bathroom door, nor to discover that the alarm clock wasn't on the night table. There was no moon, so their bedroom windows appeared to be wide open to the void.

She sat on his side of the bed, not to claim it as her own but to attempt to inhabit it fully enough to imagine why Gregory might be entitled to such an eloquent hurt. What might he have done to her to equal her disregard? If, say, like their neighbors Herb and Sheila Golden or Lou and Betty Brown he'd invested in a retirement community in Florida or Arizona without asking Audrey if she had a preference as to climate? She could feel the premise kick up energy, but before she could get defensive, she prevented herself from having the need to: it wasn't a bad example, since she'd only given herself a viable option, which wasn't the same thing as moving out, whether to the Sun Belt or down the hall. Applying wasn't the same thing as enrolling! Why, then, did it now feel as though their bedroom windows were open, as though the wind from Canada were racing across the vastness of the lake into her face?

He had argued that it was as if she had a lover, a comparison she'd dismissed as irrelevant in addition to inaccurate. This had never before come up in their marriage, not that they were indefinitely protected against marital betrayal, but because they made the effort to stay in touch. Did they? When, exactly, had his touch last brought her so fully out of herself as to be beyond the confines of her own body? Well? But Audrey interrupted herself, since the advantage of a twenty-year marriage was that, not unlike life, it had a cyclical nature. Not even a single-celled organism was absolutely accountable.

In the hall outside Sally's room, Audrey saw that the white ceramic doorknob was like one of the perfect tulips Louise Schneider had given her that afternoon, and the comparison made her both nearly laugh and almost cry. How would she ever answer Louise's question about how she'd celebrated? The only advance over the day before was that now she could know for a fact whether or not anyone in the world believed Audrey Morrow Brennan was qualified to become a doctor.

"What's *his* problem?" Sally asked her mother. But the point wasn't to know the answer, only to register that nothing ever got by her, neither out on the field nor here at home.

For that reason Audrey always tried to tell her the truth. "We're in the middle of something, but don't worry." The available truth often sufficed. This time it would have to, because Audrey could tell by the lurch in her stomach that there was no easy, honest, complete answer.

"Okay, I won't." Sally yawned like a lioness. "At least not until tomorrow, when you can explain to me why Dad's in Val's room with the door closed, like he's being punished. Okay?"

"I love you, Sal," Audrey said as she leaned down to kiss her daughter, who reached up to encircle her mother's neck. She'd been named Sarah after Gregory's mother, but Val had picked “Sally” so it could rhyme with her own name. Audrey chose to say nothing about Sally’s wet hair.

“I know, I was in a hurry, as usual,” said Sally, who’d let the towel drop into a heap as if this were a locker room. “I love you too.” She closed her eyes, allowing herself be kissed.

As Audrey turned off Sally’s bedside lamp, the phone rang sharply, once. When Audrey answered it, a voice requested, as an operator would, “Can you hold on a moment, please?” Light was restored to Sally’s room, but a full minute seemed to elapse before there was another word. And then the feeble word was “Mom?”

Since it was Val, Audrey could feel herself relax, even to the point of experiencing a thrill. The solution would be to persuade Val to come home this weekend for a family meeting, where for once Val could take pleasure in knowing that the agenda hadn’t been set by a dilemma of her creation. In other words, Audrey had immunized herself against yet more bad news.

“They’re making me call you.” Val’s speech was slurred. “Because they wired my jaw.”

“You had *surgery?* And nobody informed us?” Sure, Val was, technically at least, an adult—it wasn’t about permission—but she’d undergone surgery? Alone? Who would ever let that happen to a nineteen-year-old away from home for the first time?

Sally sat up straight with her hand over her mouth. Surgery meant a knee injury, which could mean the end of a career. In such a case, a college like U.Va. immediately withdrew its offer, or so she’d heard.

Whenever she was on duty in the emergency room, Audrey imagined finding her own father, whose life had come abruptly to an end in a similar lighted corridor on one of those narrow stretchers. Since then, she’d tried to represent the wishes of the parent or child who would give anything to be there right then, knowing that for every patient there was always someone who cared. Even at the clinic she never minded it when patients brought extras along. Better too many than too few.

Now it seemed the other voice was back on the line and capable of providing the rest of the information. This was the floor nurse, who said Valerie had just come up from the recovery room and was understandably still a little bit groggy. "But she's doing real well" was all she volunteered to say.

So Audrey introduced herself, and her voice changed as she claimed the authority not only to ask questions but grasp the answers. First, though, she thanked the nurse for initiating the call. Otherwise she'd never have been aware that a person she so loved could be in so much trouble.

Val was ten and Sally nine—and Audrey forty—when her father died. Of all possible causes, for the girls it seemed adequate for her to say his heart had stopped, avoiding "attack" and "failure" (thus fault or blame) and emphasizing that he'd lived seven whole decades, almost to the minute. Batteries run out too, Val told Sally with a shrug, without knowing there was no comparison.

But here there was both fault and blame, because what had stopped short, abruptly, wasn't Val's life but her fallible judgment. Audrey heard the nurse say Val had a concussion, but what this proved was that her consumerist daughter was immune, in this one and only instance, to the science and art of advertising. "She was in a car accident," the nurse reported, "without wearing her seat belt."

Audrey wanted to shout loud enough for Val to hear, "Don't you know never to give away your only advantage?" But then, instead of blaming Val, she got mad at herself for not encouraging Val to go to Cleveland State, where she could live down the hill on Euclid Avenue and work first on getting her act together. Instead, she'd gone off to the University of Cincinnati as if, along the way, this might turn into a better idea. Now Audrey saw she could blame Gregory, because he'd been convinced that Val could take care of herself. And now she did.

Gregory was under the covers in Val's bed, curled like that lobster tail she'd have enjoyed if he hadn't ruined that too. She said, sharp as a pencil point on a scorecard, "Val will need her own bed. She's just been put to sleep so her face could be rearranged." Audrey turned on the overhead light. Her real point was "How *dare* you accuse me of being unconcerned about anyone but myself!"

And now Sally stood behind her mother at the bedroom door, looking like a police officer ready to arrest him for being in his daughter's bed. There he was, at sixty-three, in a bedroom decorated with matching Laura Ashley wallpaper and curtains, sheets and bedspread, in a color Val chose at twelve because she said it matched both roses and violets, no matter that roses are red, violets are blue. There was neither a reason to explain himself nor a simple enough way to.

It was irrelevant that in court he was protected against outbursts and insults like this—not that he was known for finding in contempt without adequate cause—because he could see she seemed to have a case: she held a small duffel by the handle as though she were running away from home. Now from Val's drawers she grabbed a few things, but she used no more time than it took to tell Gregory that Val could have died, tonight, the exact same stupid way—driving off the road, hitting a tree, alone—as his father did.

And if right then he were to have a heart attack, would that be his own fault as well? As it was, his heart was absent from his body, trying to get to Val, to supply the help he obviously hadn't provided. He collapsed into the news, which surrounded him.

Audrey claimed the power of her own momentum. She'd just had the true-life experience of seeing how little there was to separate life and death—a mere membrane—and how little cause was required—practically none—for a car crash to turn fatal. She'd always known people could die for no reason, but now she *knew* it differently. Standing in that bedroom doorway, she was already rushing to Val's real bedside, her mind racing along Route 71 the two hours to Columbus and the two more on to Cincinnati. She was speeding through the spring night like a human ambulance, sounding her sirens unapologetically like every single medical cliché in the world. It was as if in a public space someone at death's door had called out frantically, "Is there a doctor in the house?"

At Val's bedside Audrey was given the recliner, having presented herself at the hospital in the middle of the night. Unlike Sally, whose body rested during sleep, this daughter had always been a restless sleeper, and in this altered state, without knowing she wasn't free, Val had rattled the bars of her cage with her every move. Audrey had tried to soothe her in a calm but ineffectual voice, as if it were a coma, not just a ditch, she'd fallen into.

Now it was Val who was in a reclining chair—the front seat of her mother's car—on her way home to Cleveland. She'd been discharged by midmorning and told to come back in a week, no matter that she couldn't see out of one eye or open her mouth except to insert a straw.

The return trip took longer with other people out on the road. Another difference from the trip down was that daylight made unavoidable the signs reminding drivers that in the state of Ohio, seat belt use is mandatory.

"I know," Val admitted to the crime. "I must have thought I was still at the movies." In fact, she and her roommate had gone from the movies to an off-campus party where, several rum punches later, Val left alone, her roommate apparently having met someone she couldn't keep her hands off of.

On the first day of nursery school Val's teacher told Audrey at the noon pickup, "Valerie learns from experience." Already she'd raced up the steps and flown off the end of the slide intended for the bigger kids, who knew first to watch the others to see how fast a slide it was. All Audrey could answer was yes, this was why she'd told the teacher the story of Valerie's first staircase. In her little life she'd learned everything by doing it.

But now Val told Audrey in a shaky voice, "I feel so lucky

you're a nurse, because I didn't—it's not that I didn't trust them—*like* them. Every single one who came into my room had to ask how it happened, and then, like they were doing a survey, if I was wearing my seat belt. I finally said, 'Look in my chart!' Like it's not bad enough to see everything red out of one eye, like the world's on fire or something. Or soaked in blood." She stopped to consider the possibility, then she asked her mother, "Is it?"

"Is your eye soaked in blood? In a way, yes. So you're very lucky it's not worse, and I'm really not saying that to make you feel guiltier for not wearing your seat belt, but because it's true." Audrey gripped the wheel with both hands, the way a young child holds on to everything for dear life. All she wanted was to lay her forehead down on those hands as a way of expressing how grateful she felt. "We're all very lucky."

"I know," Val agreed. Then, because it hurt too much to talk, she slept all the way from Jeffersonville to the exit for the Motorcycle Heritage Museum, when she began to cry, but silently, and wept all the way to Bellville. There she resumed, "What I meant about the movies was to ask if you ever have the impulse at the movies to fasten your seat belt like you were on an airplane." Val was trying to account for an honest lapse without admitting to the rum. Was that lying or not? "So do you believe me when I say I'll never do it again?"

"Yes, I do." A kid at the movies who reflexively reaches for a seat belt is a kid who is in the habit of wearing one. So there was another explanation, which Audrey knew they'd get to later on. Unlike Sally, Val was never any good at keeping secrets.

"But does Dad believe me?" Now Val sounded worried.

"I couldn't honestly tell you," Audrey responded as honestly as she was able.

"I mean, what if I can't drive anymore?" They were past Medina, evidently close enough to Cleveland for Val to feel she was entering her father's jurisdiction. Obviously enough, she meant what if he refused to let her drive?

"Your eye will heal," Audrey chose to say, "so one day you'll be okay to drive again. But you'll be a passenger for quite a while yet." With Val in profile, she couldn't see the bandage covering that eye, but the metal particles had been removed with an electromagnet, and proper compresses applied. Audrey knew little more than that about how to fix eyes. Of course this could change soon, by starting medical school in four months, not that this news would mean anything to Val except to exaggerate her confusion.

Val chose to pretend that her entire question had been answered. "That's a relief," she said. Then she slipped into the utter security of what amounted to clinical sleep, and stayed there the rest of the way to Cleveland Heights.

Heading straight for Lake Erie like the lead goose on the last leg of a migratory journey, Audrey was as tired as she ever remembered. Was she up for those notorious all-nighters no medical student did without? As she suddenly felt her muscles go as slack as power lines during a freak April storm, this had become a very good question. What if, as this daughter of hers was wondering about herself, she can't do it? Permission aside—so yes, she'd understood this was Val's point about her father—was she physically capable of it?

When Audrey and Gregory first met, her schedule was so irregular it required him to become spontaneous. Since this was a new experience for him, at first he was awkward with the hunger she'd come home with, waking him up with the cozy fragrance of scrambled eggs and toast, or else the other hunger, after some horrible outcome, of her need for the bodily reassurance of sex. He'd been a slow learner, feeling ambushed by her assaults on his dead-to-the-world body, but after a while he'd come to feel a disappointment when he'd wake up at the regular time and find her merely asleep beside him. "Wake me up," he'd request. "Ravish me!" he'd beg her, no matter that some nights she was in no mood for a pitch-dark encounter with him or anyone. Nothing personal.

Along Overlook Road on either side of the uniform slate

front walks, each square of earth had been raked of winter debris and appeared poised to deliver bouquets, depending on what bulbs were planted in the fall. In her own yard, in addition to the Dutch Master daffodils about to come, there were at the moment saffron-colored crocuses pushing their way up to the surface, waving their fingery foliage like hands wanting to be called on. Audrey's classroom image caused her to doubt her own ability to know the correct responses to questions as invisible as bulbs planted so many seasons ago it wasn't possible to know if they were underground until they reappeared. Who said she would still be able to get by on fewer hours of sleep than a newborn's nursing mother? Sure, she'd managed, but so had she once been able to read Latin.

In the voice of herself as a child Val asked her mother, "Are we almost there yet?" but Audrey couldn't tell if the intent was ironic or, its opposite, involuntary. She'd stayed asleep during the quick stop at Morrow's Pharmacy to fill the hospital prescriptions, but now she was awake enough to add, "Weren't we so lucky to have Gram there for when we got sick?"

Audrey said, "Yes," and "I'll call her," but she was struck by Val's sense of her equality with Sally, when in fact Sally prided herself on her perfect attendance. If she ever got sick it was during school vacations, whereas Val was always having to make up for lost time. Still, it was true that it was good to have Celia available to sit with Val, who could no more be left alone as an experimenting teenager than as a little girl. "Gram will be delighted with the task of puréeing your daily requirements of vitamins and protein, won't she?"

For these past nine years since Jack's death, Celia had kept busy with her volunteer work, delivering prescriptions for the pharmacy one day a week to those who weren't able to get around anymore. "Give me something to do" was Celia's standard request, which now caused Audrey to wonder why she hadn't applied to medical school years earlier. This wasn't a serious question—because she'd have missed time with her daughters, that's why—but it was a good one. As her mother often observed, nobody Audrey's age was ever available these days to drive from one elderly shut-in to the next, since like Audrey they were all too busy devoting their energies to what Celia termed their nonvolunteer jobs.

Audrey brought Val home to their empty house and made her comfortable in the purple bedroom that, as Val herself observed, matched her face. Then she went down the hall to her own bedroom. She called Celia, who answered the phone before the end of the first ring.

"Why hello, Audrey," Celia said, her concern paramount no matter that she'd expected this call a while ago. "How's Valerie doing?"

"I'm sorry I didn't call earlier," Audrey began.

"Gregory called, first thing. You just stopped at Morrow's, Johnny tells me, to fill her prescriptions." The difference between Celia's son and her late husband was that Johnny knew everything too, but told it. Jack had been discreet. To a fault, if you asked her.

"Right." Audrey's brother Johnny was like a surveillance camera, as opposed to Neil, the younger one, who'd left town primarily, he claimed, so he wouldn't always be the last to hear about his own life.

It had also been in Audrey's own nature to conceal. As a child she'd had more secret hiding places than most other kids, and like a series of bomb shelters she'd kept them all stocked with what provisions (such as a dime or a stick of gum) fit in a Band-Aid tin. Audrey's personality no doubt derived from having that pharmacist father, whose job it was to keep everybody's secrets. Jack Morrow would know, for instance, who was being treated for depression or infertility. He'd been among the first to dispense AIDS-related drugs—not that he or anyone knew in those early years what the disease would come to be called—to unfamiliar men from the suburbs who wished to be fully anonymous. Secrets were safe with Jack Morrow, and as a result, two of his three children, Audrey and Neil, were quite capable of blank faces.

Celia added, "Johnny didn't see Valerie, though, because she stayed in the car."

Audrey felt like saying, "Yes, I know, *I* was there, unlike yourself," but she just answered the question. "Val's doing okay, but it's not a pretty sight."

"What happened?" Celia's theories were these: either some drunk who shouldn't be out on the road, or an older person like herself who shouldn't drive after dark. Were there any other causes of accidents?

"Inexperience," Audrey explained. The most frequent cause, according to statistics. "Youth."

"How would she like company? This morning I made some soup and Jell-O for her, also tapioca for the eggs. And cinnamon applesauce. I could stay the day tomorrow, since I already switched my library volunteer day with Florence, who just joined a rheumatoid arthritis study group. It's amazing she still gets around." Celia paused. "So I'm free, is all."

"And I'm glad you are. Val's already asked for you."

"You're so busy," Celia said. "I'm sure that you'll have to go to work."

"Right now I'm only going to sleep. But tomorrow, yes." There was no point in saying she'd missed today.

In the silence it wasn't clear, even to Celia, what she thought. Then she said, "But it isn't inessential work, at least, is it?" She meant, given that her daughter chose to work, if she had to choose a job other than at the pharmacy, she could have done much worse. On the other hand, if she'd picked a different field, the way Neil did, teaching grade school, then it wouldn't have seemed so like a rejection, would it? Jack always felt it was, as if Audrey seemed to consider the work he did beneath her.

Now the silence was Audrey's own, as she deliberated whether in her mother's opinion medical school was or wasn't inessential. At least, since her own daughters hadn't yet been informed, Audrey couldn't be faulted for not letting her mother in on her good news. At this rate, Audrey barely knew if the news could still be called good.

"I'll just drop the food off today and see if she needs me. And tomorrow morning, I'll be there long before she wakes up." But Celia reconsidered. "Unless she'll have trouble sleeping, in which case you ought to say I'll check in on her when I get there. What's your guess? I suppose I should say your *advice*, since you no doubt have a better sense how she's doing."

"I think the pills Johnny gave Val will help her sleep." Audrey was aware that she made her brother sound like the doctor.

Along the arc of their marriage was displayed, like laundry on a line, the challenges of being a working couple whose evenings weren't free either. At the end of the day, when they found that they'd already spent all their energy, they would still make it a point to voice their confidence that there'd always be the next day, and in this way they had managed their marital renovations without resorting to the services of demolition experts for whom there's no tomorrow. Gregory considered himself lucky that all he'd wanted for the next phase of his life was the one woman he already had. His fantasies—don't laugh, he'd say—lay in the pages of glossy travel brochures he perused like pornography. His sexual ideal—he'd call himself a poster boy for the industry—was side-by-side seats on an airplane during takeoff.

Gregory had discovered this within twenty-four hours of their having been introduced. That day was as clear as the memory had remained, of their circling their lives from the sky directly above. Gregory's choice to return to Cleveland reversed the decision others had made on his behalf, to fulfill their own dreams for him. That day he'd shown Audrey how small a world his was, by telling her that she'd filled it. He'd had to shout over the engine noise in order to be heard.

Here was his point: diligently, he'd married at age forty-three after providing stability for his dependent mother and kid brother; conscientiously, he'd fathered for these subsequent twenty years two exacting children he dearly loved and who were sources of pride and worry; finally, now that he'd almost reached retirement age, he'd learned how to lavish attention on himself too, although in little increments of time. It just took a minute to picture himself in a puffin colony in Iceland or among the sultans' ghosts in Byzantium. His permanently younger wife was of course always younger by the same amount, and yet it had always been correct to assume they were equally at the center of each other's lives. Since she would likely be left behind when he at last adventured to the afterlife, it hadn't seemed presumptuous to count on her to want to be in that adjoining seat on the airplane while they still had the chance. Couldn't she see herself on the other side of the world, touching down like a seed?

If once Audrey could, at the moment she seemed content to invest her wanderlust in her children, prompting them toward independence, concentrating her own narrower needs at Case Western Reserve, down the hill from their house. Everything she could want was contained in that hospital complex, as if she were his age and preparing for her final decline. After their two decades as contemporaries, only now was their age difference an obstacle. And only now was he second-guessing his giving up the enormous world of the New York firm, in case it meant that right from the start he'd given up on himself. This was his last thought as he pulled into the double-width driveway, the only asphalt he owned.

Val sat at the kitchen table with her back to the door opening from the garage, and as she turned in her chair, in slow motion she watched her father see Before and After in each half of her face. In his courtroom he'd seen countless bandaged faces like that, but only as photographic evidence in lawsuits.

"Hi, Dad." The swelling and discoloration had spread from

under the bandages like a spill leaking from behind a refrigerator door. "That bad, huh?" she said, not attempting to stand up because the medication affected her balance.

Gregory closed the door behind him and moved to Val, but like a magnet, repelled as well as drawn. "Valley, Valley," it came to him to say, an echo from the days she called him "Daddy! Daddy!" as she ran into his wide-open arms.

Now she only smiled and said, "Thanks, Daddy," taking the paper cone of purple tulips he offered her. "Still my favorite color, too." The flowers looked like plums.

"I'm glad you're home, home safe." He placed the palm of his hand against the better side of her face and pulled it down her neck, across her shoulder, not really daring to touch but needing to. Then he squeezed her arm, the gesture of a mourner trying to convey a feeling there isn't a proper word for because it combines the opposites of misery and hope, hope and misery.

"Me too." She was also glad for the distraction of the pale stems that needed a fresh cut. "Can you get me a vase, and the scissors?"

Gregory was just as glad for the chance to watch her hands at work, imitating her mother's, but he could see that the vase he'd picked was too deep, and its mouth too wide.

"Mom's upstairs asleep," Val said like a mind reader taking credit for stating the obvious, "but aren't you early?" Because she also knew what her father would say next, she wished for a way to avoid having to tell him what happened.

"I was worried about you, so I left as soon as I could. I wanted to know what happened."

"I know," she said, stalling.

That he could wait, and wait, was Gregory's one professional advantage.

And of course in theory Val could lie to him, but in practice it hadn't ever been altogether possible, as if she believed he could send her to jail like anyone else.

He'd outwaited the best of them.

Val drew in a breath she expelled, rejecting it, and tried again. "I went to a party and it's true what they say: your reflexes are slowed down by alcohol. Which happened to me at a curve I didn't see soon enough. I guess I hit the rear-view mirror along with the windshield. I also guess it could have been much worse. That's what Mom said about my eye."

Where should he start? For one thing, he was still wearing his overcoat and could start by taking it off, taking his time hanging it up, returning to his chair at the kitchen table. He could take in a breath and slowly release it. To begin to learn how to relax a little, he could take up yoga, and should.

Now Val was the one who waited.

The skin around Gregory's eyes settled into folds, like a blind gathered on hidden cords, and it was a darker color than the rest of his face. Here, his disappointment concentrated like that pigment, so that from a distance his eyes appeared sunken, like coins in a wishing well. In the courtroom, when he examined people, what they wished was that they weren't guilty.

"I'm not blaming the alcohol, though. It's my fault." For his sake, if not yet her own, she'd better put it into words. "For two reasons. I'm underage and I should never drink and drive. Nobody should."

"That's right, that's good," Gregory acknowledged. But he couldn't continue, because it had never occurred to him until just now that he didn't know whether his father had had alcohol in his blood at the time of his accident. And if he had, would his death have been any less a suicide?

"I didn't tell Mom yet about the drinking part. We only talked about the seat belt part. But I will. And yes, I know that's a state law too."

"Yes, it is." Gregory took Val's hands into his own and patted them like snow into a ball, holding them tight enough to melt them. "Thank you for not lying to me, dear," he told her, sounding like one of those timid signs from the days before city ordinances prohibited smoking in any public space.

Val thought about saying that she rarely drank anything but beer, then changed her mind. She doubted that in this context he'd be reassured to find out that, as her generation had learned to make these distinctions, alcohol was never her drug of choice.

Gregory distracted himself—from the problem of not knowing how seriously to worry—with wondering about his father. Those were the days before routine blood-alcohol testing after traffic fatalities, and maybe his mother hadn't ordered an autopsy in order to avoid discovering more secrets about her husband than she could handle. But if she did know, did she lie to her sons about their father? And here was the bigger question: was this why he'd become a judge? To pass judgment?

Val didn't want to have to ask him explicitly how he planned to punish her. "Dad?" Now she wished she'd included the drinking part in the version she'd told her mother, so that the disclosure phase—her father's terminology—would be over.

Gregory had let go of her hands to cover his own face, and he showed her his pale throat, like an animal surrendering. But Val didn't want that much power, after all. She was about to propose that she shouldn't be allowed to drive for the rest of the semester. She would require this of herself in order to earn back their trust.

Against the dark screen of his closed eyes, Gregory was picturing Val in what was the next-to-worst-case scenario. She wasn't dead, so he refused to witness that, and fortunately, unlike the current case in his courtroom, there wasn't an innocent victim. Nevertheless, he pictured this vulnerable daughter of his reciting the alphabet while walking in a straight line in the headlights of a cop car, and said, "I think you've been punished enough."

What time was it? Audrey was peripherally aware of Gregory, who moved around the edge of her consciousness the same way he moved silently about the room. It was only because he said

"It's six-thirty" that Audrey knew she had spoken. Night or morning?

She was still wearing the sweater and slacks she'd chosen a day and a half ago, before she knew how appropriate was her choice of the dull, practical green of army fatigues. The bright-spirited quilt covering her could have come from a Doyle Yoder photograph of Holmes County's Amish country, and the early evening light blended other incongruities: the colors of grainy mustard, grapefruit pulp, ash. The pigment in the paint on the wall by the window had vanished.

Gregory sat with his back to all this, on the narrow bench at the foot of their bed. It pained him to wear these highly polished shoes, but because he didn't want to further burden this encounter by mentioning Joe Ricci's pancreatic cancer, he simply, though carefully, removed them. In his stockinged feet the rug was densely soft, like a putting green.

Along with the insufficient light, their silence grew thin enough to disappear. He moved to the rocking chair and spoke. And she heard herself answer him this time. She said, "Okay. You?"

"I saw Val. We talked." But he stopped. "No, first I want to say I'm sorry for last night. For my reaction to what could have been good news."

She didn't say it still could be good news because, in a day, this had become harder to believe. She rolled from her back onto her side, to face him as she said, "Thanks for saying that."

"And I'm also sorry for your inability to have discussed it with me."

Wait. Was he making that *her* fault?

"Or no, I mean the inability was mine, I guess you felt."

Guess?

"With reason." Now Gregory admitted to a new worry, which surprised him since it was so enormous. "Do I make you censor yourself? Have there been other important things you haven't dared to tell me because, as I demonstrated last night, I—"

"No," she said aloud, failing to see the correct answer would be yes, certainly. Continually. Look at just now.

"That would be wrong." He even tipped forward, toward her, to say, "That would be very wrong."

Hold it. So it was her own fault again?

But he meant he wouldn't want that, as was clear in his sincere expression and by the authentic way his voice was fragmented but held together, barely, like safety glass.

She said, "I can't seem to talk about this right now. There's too much going on, and you and I have such a long way to go. But I appreciate your apology."

He leaned away from her, rocking back and holding that position with his foot on the edge of the bed frame, as if making a turn at one end of a swimming pool and pushing off in a backstroke. "We *do* need to talk about Val's drinking problem, though, so as soon as you're ready, just let me know." And when he got up from his chair it kept on rocking without him.

"Wait." Audrey almost thought he could mean the problem it was for Val to drink water without a straw, with her jaw wired; Val could hardly get her pills down. "Wait." Audrey reached for Gregory. "Tell me."

He did.

Hathaway Brown had a Drunk Driving Awareness Day, when a flatbed truck would pull up to the school and display the wreck of a car in which five drunk teenagers had been killed instantly. Audrey had to wonder what more it would take to impress Val. "Instead, she gave me some theory about seat belts at the movies. I should have guessed."

"I'm sure she wanted to tell you on the ride home," he said, because Val had said so, "but just couldn't."

"Still, she told you." Without ambivalence she said, "That's the main thing." Nevertheless, it was a first. Audrey marked the transition with the ambiguous grief peculiar to parents of teenagers.

"Val said there was a lot of blood." Gregory didn't want to omit anything.

"There always is with a head wound." But she didn't want to sound like a clinician.

"No, I mean they focused on that, not the drinking." Then with an odd smile he added, "As you know, I'm not in the habit of believing it's better not to get caught. But in this case—"

"You'll make an exception?" She laughed. In his courtroom he was so unfailingly fair, it was strange to find he seemed to have a sense of humor about equal application.

He smiled, showing his even teeth, which, like everything else, had been fixed by Judge and Mrs. Osborne, whose own Charles, Gregory's best friend as a boy, drowned the summer before he would have gotten braces.

"Or," Audrey suggested, "maybe it wasn't noticed because it wasn't obvious. Maybe she'd had less to drink than she thought she did."

"Let's hope," he said. One more thing they could agree on.

Audrey pulled herself to her feet. "I'll be down soon. Just so you know, I'm not going to mention medical school tonight." It would have been better timing not to have heard for another few days, but she'd already delayed the process until the last minute, forcing her to present herself at the Admission Office in person, as if she didn't trust the postal system. As it was, the first day of school was in four months.

In a precise imitation of their daughters he replied, "Whatever," camouflaging, the way they did, his passionate concern.

Audrey took such a long shower the tips of her fingers wrinkled. Fastening her wet hair into a ponytail, she dressed in Val's brown and gold Hathaway Brown fleece pants and a school sweatshirt she'd inherited from Sally. If she looked a lot younger than her age, as she was often told she did, wasn't it relevant that she wore the clothes of adolescents? She also wore moisturizer, and lots of it.

Audrey had an underdeveloped sense of style, which she said was due to the fact that she wore uniforms at work. But the real reason her daughters never borrowed her clothes was that practically everything in her closet was handed down from them. The way frequent travelers never had to buy bath soap, it had been years since she'd bought a good sweater just for herself. Even Val, whose generic wardrobe was all black, liked the unique feel of cashmere.

From the kitchen came the fragrances of foods Celia had prepared and, like Meals on Wheels, delivered. All that was necessary to do was to slice her oatmeal bread and ladle the stewed chicken over the rice. In Celia's girlish handwriting were instructions to serve Val the chicken and rice soup that was the inspiration for this menu. That chicken was shredded, and that rice had absorbed enough liquid to be spongy. There was page after page of notes, as if Celia were documenting every thought she'd had while preparing the food. There was enough chocolate pudding for everyone, Celia wrote, since she'd be making more tonight, which she would bring over tomorrow. If there were any special requests, let her know.

Sally got a ride home and burst through the kitchen door, calling, "Val?" After today's rigorous lacrosse practice the coach made the team shower, Sally told everyone, so their parents wouldn't see how muddy they were. Now she looked like a shampoo ad, because the car heater in her face had fluffed her hair absurdly. She turned her attention to Val, exclaiming over her bandages, demanding every detail. Neither of them had been in serious trouble—except Val, academically—so this was a breakthrough story. None of Sally's athletic injuries compared, not that she was in a position to complain.

Gregory sat with his ounce-and-a-half, having missed Dick Goddard's Fox 8 weather. Audrey would have enjoyed the extravagance of vodka, oily and metallic at once, but she played it safe with a small glass of white wine. They both ought to set an example by not drinking anything at all, but this hadn't occurred to either one of them in time. Sally grabbed a bottle of peach nectar and, as they all drank to Val's health, Val turned toward her mother to say how much more important nurses are than doctors, then how essential it is to be as excellent a nurse as Audrey, because some can be very mean.

"Rushed, overburdened," Audrey excused.

"That too, sure," allowed Val, "but the doctor barely showed up, so, if you ask me, nurses need to be nicer."

"Nurses are always expected to be nicer, no matter what. We like to say that the definition of 'rounds' is the doctor walking around the bed and, without looking under the covers, asking the nurse, 'How's the patient?' So don't be too hard. We always get the blame, never the credit." On this subject she could go on and on, but, "Never mind. There are pluses and minuses either way you slice it. Sorry." This was no time to treat lightly the way Val looked: like a textbook illustration in the chapter on suturing.

Gregory was afraid Audrey might have changed her mind about not bringing it up, so he tried to change the subject. "Celia's chicken is delicious, isn't it?" By telling him she wouldn't mention medical school tonight, she had let him relax, but now he'd become tense again. Under the table, one of his legs jittered like a wind-up toy.

But the last thing she'd want to create was greater complexity. "The secret Morrow recipe," she said, thinking that her sole ambition ought to be to learn how to cook such basic comfort food.

"So how come you never cook it?" asked Sally. "Because Gram's still around to?" To Sally, to be in your mid-seventies was to be ancient history.

The purple tulips looked as if they were trying to climb out of their unnecessarily deep vase, which was the feeling Audrey had. She had chosen for their renovated kitchen a distressed pine table and cushioned chairs that were comfortable enough to sit in, if necessary, for hours. "Because she's the pro," Audrey answered. "It's her job." This was the dish Celia always made for her friends and neighbors when anyone got sick or whenever somebody died.

Val asked, "What about when *she* dies?"

When Audrey was growing up her family always ate in the dining room, in straight-back chairs, at six-thirty sharp, and they were each expected to tell something about their day. Something charming, if possible.

The first time Audrey arranged to bring Gregory to meet Jack and Celia, she suggested lunch instead of dinner, and a restaurant instead of the club. "Not the club? Why not?" asked Jack, enough times to force her to answer with another question: "What if, as a judge, he's uncomfortable in places that discriminate?" Insulted, Jack argued that, thanks partly to his own work on the membership committee, all kinds of people could belong there now. Besides, he didn't personally know any restaurants with a Sunday buffet equal to the Canterbury Country Club's. "Perfect for the after-church crowd," he'd said, so she'd responded, "See?"

Every Sunday throughout childhood they'd gone downtown to the church on Public Square—with Tiffany windows and a dress code to match—and then back out to Shaker Heights for the club's buffet, where the parents had their martinis or manhattans, made by a bartender who knew what brands and how much to pour, while the boys and girls impatiently waited until the dessert gimmick of make-your-own sundaes.

Back then, the pharmacy could afford to be closed one day a week, when Jack gave himself permission to relax with his pair of straight-ups, with two pearl onions on a plastic sword-handled toothpick in the club's colors. Jack's point was that, though she'd already disappointed them a few times with men she deselected, he wanted to show off his club to his prospective son-in-law.

The round tables were too big to permit confidences, and because of the buffet there was frequent coming and going. The route by their table was the most popular, so Gregory was at the center of things, and he came up with something charming to answer each of Celia's proper-hostess questions.

They'd already covered the difference between "beyond a reasonable doubt" and "a preponderance of the evidence," so Celia asked, "How would you describe the difference between the *letter* and the *spirit* of the law?" Touching her napkin to each corner of her mouth, she was proud of herself and very glad that Nancy Drew had hooked her, at age eight, on detective novels.

Gregory had the ability to focus his attention with the precision of a lens and to make a person believe that he hadn't already thought everything out. "A very important question, so let me see. Well, for example," he began, letting his gaze drift up as if to snatch an idea from the air, "just this morning I came out of my apartment and, on the sidewalk, there was a woman walking her dogs without a leash. Welsh corgi, I think they're called, the kind Queen Elizabeth has, those short-legged ones that could have been collies in another life? These were a pair, waddling side by side. Now, we all know there's an enforceable leash law, and it's not like they're feral dogs or anything. Still, there are people who are afraid of dogs no matter what the breed is. I would never say anything in a situation like that, but I did want to make eye contact, so I did. In response the woman said, 'Look again, buster.' The leash was about a foot long, leashing the dogs to each other." Gregory paused to see if Celia needed him to spell it out any more specifically. Apparently not.

"*Buster?* She called a *judge* buster?" Celia lost her bearings momentarily when she asked, "Couldn't you *arrest* her?"

This threw him off, so he answered, "Well, no, that's not within my powers. I'm not a police officer."

"No, for *contempt*."

This made Gregory laugh out loud, picturing himself as a

meter maid with a book of tickets he could issue as he pleased.

His laugh alone charmed them sufficiently for them to hand Audrey over to him from then on. Celia let him know this with her most sincere smile. And Jack knew enough, from television, to throw in that he was seconding the motion.

So it was a good introduction all around, which was why, tonight, Audrey longed for the man he'd been when they met. She missed that man who was resiliently undepressed, cheerful practically to a fault. She wanted back the man who had told her that the simple answer to her mother's question about the difference between the letter and the spirit of the law was that there was no difference.

But, though it was uncharacteristic of him to have canceled their Paris trip without consulting her, Audrey's larger disappointment was in missing the opportunity to console him after the loss of Rob. This regret worked like blood, insinuating itself between the layers of her skin to make Audrey feel the way Val looked. She felt swollen with it, her fingers too thick for her rings and her leather shoes too tight for her feet. Regret clumped in her stomach like indigestion, souring her. Ambition had no value for its own sake, Gregory believed, as Rob's early death confirmed.

Last night at this table he'd asked, "But *why* would you do this?" He didn't add, "to me," but his anguished eyes supplied it. What she should have said, and wished now she had said, was "This isn't about you, Gregory. It's about *my* being accepted to medical school. It's not about punishing you. It isn't *about* you!"

Over time he'd tried to educate her to argue more like a lawyer—not like that, the sort of thing a teenager shouts—in order to be more persuasive. "I can't do anything to make you feel less hurt," he'd instruct her, "unless your argument is strong. Don't raise your voice at me because, in my line of work, that signals to me that the facts aren't with you. Plus, if you don't know the answer to a question, always say so."

It was possible she didn't know the answer to his question because, if in a few words she could have told him why, she would have. She regretted not having been able to reconcile security and insecurity. Wasn't it permissible to have some of each?

If she'd felt more confident of being admitted, she'd have confided at least in her brother Neil, who knew what it was to dare to change his life, by leaving it behind like an expired passport. Neil had kept his own fundamental secret half his life, until a few years after their father's death, when their mother finally came to recognize that, as handsome as Neil was, he wasn't "eligible." Of the three of them, only their brother Johnny appeared not to strain against their parents' definition of him. Instead, in fact, most mornings to this day, Johnny still borrowed their father's neckties.

But Audrey believed he wore them voluntarily, was the point. The benefit of a steady childhood was that there were choices, one of which was to stay the same. Audrey wondered whether she'd be the pharmacist in the family if she'd been an only child or if, for whatever good reason, both her brothers had moved away. And if she *were* the pharmacist? In that case she doubted she'd have thought to go to medical school, even though these days everyone was compromised in the same way—by the insurance companies—and for the same reason. Their father was always independent, and he would have hated being regulated. The irony was that the fight wasn't against his sworn enemy, the goddamn Big Brother government, but against his dear old friend, Big Business. The paperwork was just as bad.

Audrey went upstairs, where there were no surprises. Sally was on the phone, passing along a melodramatic rendition of Val's accident. Down the hall Gregory sat in the rocking chair, holding the accordion file across his lap. And from the room over the garage came the muffled thumping of Val on drums.

The drum pulse sounded like the human heart through a

stethoscope, an amplified staccato anatomy-class exhibit. Clearly Val was feeling the sticks with stiff fingers, but the regulated rhythm was so steady it steadied her. It always had.

As a young child Val's imagination preferred the vocabulary of sound. Neither words nor pictures pleased her nearly as much, and she'd had a dexterity that allowed for free expression. Her first band was called One Girl Band, and she'd played kazoo, harmonica, and bongo backup to her own rhymed vocals. Never had she been self-conscious in performance, which Audrey determined had been Gregory's gift to Val, since, although without flamboyance, this was what he did at work all day long. In middle school she'd submitted to lessons and sung in the glee club, where her wide stance and tight upper body made her look like a young bird in flying lessons.

Audrey sat at the top of the stairs to listen to Val, a riff that had the fluidity of a saxophone, the individuation of a piano. Val was able to reconcile these opposites, while her own strengths and weaknesses were in conflict. Her sense of success and failure was that they were the heads or tails of a coin toss. Risk didn't have to be explicitly chosen because it was always present. This was what had Audrey worried.

Now Val took off, leaving behind all decorum, sounding like the car wreck she'd experienced, which was the point, and the beauty. Beginning in sixth grade Val presided over drum kits that were top of the line, like all the equipment at Hathaway Brown. And because the school was known as fashionable, Val had named her band String of Pearls. The band played at every open house—Val at center stage, making huge sound—to encourage parents of daughters to ask themselves if, in any coed school, in Cleveland or anyplace else, the drummer in a rock band would be allowed to be a girl.

The essay topic on her application was to write about a "nonmedical" interest, so Audrey had written about the civic needs met by the Community Gardens Initiative. In plots no larger than fifteen by twenty-five feet it was possible to construct particular botanical worlds. There, in immigrants' gardens, okra and yams flourished next to bitter melons known as foo gwa, garlic and red grapes grew beside chili peppers, green peas and carrots alongside the basics—corn, beans, squashes—first grown in this earth by Native Americans. There was cultural overlap in this produce exchanged without language over fences serving as two-sided trellises, not barriers. She'd never pretended to be anything but an idealist.

In their own plot she encouraged Val to grow watermelons and pumpkins for size, sunflowers and asparagus for their drama, and raspberries and cherry tomatoes for their manifold yield. She was looking to compensate for Val's lack of self-confidence by giving her this means of self-satisfaction. The first season the weather cooperated, so that by the next spring, Val remembered the pleasures of such success as she'd never been able to experience. Even the essential lesson of the purpose of thinning out made sense when first applied to a row of radishes and, secondarily, to a page of multiple-choice answers. In that conversation Val was amazed to learn that, as a nurse, ruling out diagnoses—R/O—was what Audrey did all day. Call her earnest, but who could argue with convincing a little girl whose teachers decided she "had some problems" that she was capable of growing more fruits and vegetables than she could carry.

Audrey also taught Val that Cleveland jokes were no doubt still told on the East and West Coasts, but out there at either extreme nobody had what was called a hometown. Here at the center of the country, kids could learn to place themselves by looking at a map: Cleveland was, not surprisingly, right where the heart would be. Not the eyes or ears, not the gut or the reproductive organs—and, okay, not the brain either—but what body ever functioned without a heart?

In 1952, the school of medicine at Case Western Reserve transformed the education of American doctors in two ways. It reoriented medical learning, away from the study of separate subject areas and toward an understanding of the human body as a linked series of organ systems, and it did away with grades and ranking in the first two years by introducing a new concept — teamwork — to those whose college years were a hard-fought scramble for extra points. The incoming medical student was assigned, rather than the traditional cadaver, a pregnant woman to follow, beyond delivery into her baby's first few months of life. The emphasis on clinical, patient-centered care was what made the program compatible with Audrey's skills and interests.

"You're good at this," Louise Schneider began telling Audrey one day when Audrey caught something she'd missed. "Have you ever thought about it?"

"Reinventing the wheel, you mean?" And then Audrey laughed.

"You know, there are wheels in need of reinvention," Louise said, "so don't laugh. You ought to think about it."

"Wheels within wheels, no doubt," Audrey quipped, refusing to enter this conversation.

As a surgical nurse she'd hardly ever been asked to offer her opinion, so it had made her uncomfortable at Metro, at first, to be asked what she thought about the doctor's own thinking. Gradually, Louise had conditioned her responses until they were the literal opposite of what they'd been. "Don't say 'No thank you,' say 'Yes please,'" Louise coaxed her, until one day Audrey proved to be as coachable as her own athletic daughter.

At Metro there were six core clerkships offered in Primary Care, so Audrey could imagine herself not having to leave the building. Louise wrote the letter of recommendation before Audrey asked if she would, and like a mom Louise kept track of the deadlines. It was also Louise who suggested getting help in preparing for the required MCAT Audrey then scored surprisingly well on, given that she was no doubt the only one in the testing room with so little at stake. Like a disease, the decision was internal, incremental, until the day it was full blown.

Audrey came from the bathroom and Gregory closed his file, so together they pulled the bedspread back and folded it onto the bench at the foot of the bed neither one had slept in the night before. She didn't find it a good sign that their bed looked as wide as a river.

They faced each other like brackets around a blank space into which a footnote would be inserted, once the source had been determined.

"I'm exhausted," she admitted.

"Me too," he said, but his tone was competitive.

She pretended not to notice. "Dinner was fun. Wasn't Sally funny? Wasn't she great with Val? Sometimes it takes bad news to get siblings to be nicer to each other, don't you think?" She sounded like her mother.

"Bad news improves situations, does it?" His face folded vertically into pleats unless he smiled. He didn't smile.

She said nothing.

"You're not the only one," he said.

"I know."

"You're not the *only* one, you know."

"I *know.*"

"If we had one of those marriages where you asked, 'And how was your day, dear?' you'd know."

"So then tell me," she said, but didn't sound entirely sincere.

This could be why Gregory said something as stupid as, "For your information, I'm somebody," when all he meant was that he wasn't nobody.

"You can pull rank in your courtroom, but don't bother—"

"And you think you're qualified to be a *doctor?* You have so little empathy, common decency. Talk about bedside manner!" But now, since he was only on the other side of this same bed, Gregory had missed his own joke.

"Oh! You should talk!" And so had she.

Gregory took a few steps back, pulling his tie from its slip-knot, unbuttoning his shirt collar. "I'm not going to let you disregard me this time," he insisted. At last he'd found the correct word. "Dis-re-gard me."

She dropped her hands from her hips, clasped them behind her.

"In my court this morning a witness claimed spousal privilege and became exempt from testimony, no matter that she'd married the defendant only yesterday. Can you imagine what this is like for a judge? Do you *care* to know what it's like?" He unbuttoned his shirt so quickly he gave the impression of unzipping it. "It's called an abuse of power to marry the accused to avoid testifying against him. Spousal privilege—based in the belief that the state mustn't undermine the family—is a loophole." He slid his belt out of its loops and flung it out like a lasso. "Does it *matter* to you that I had no choice but to dismiss the charges? An act of recklessness resulted in a *death*, and criminal charges won't be brought because the driver can't be forced to testify against a man who, according to what she'd told to a grand jury, grabbed the wheel from her and shouted, 'I'm going to fucking crash this car!'"

There were no words, was her feeling, so Audrey didn't even try. But her expression conveyed sufficient understanding for Gregory to see it, if he could.

It seemed he could, because next he crossed the few steps to the window and, before lowering the blind, searched the dark sky for blinking lights. His deep-set brown eyes—devil's food, she'd characterized the color the night they met—seemed to take her into himself, to both feed her and devour her. He was needy of a wife so devoted, she'd marry him all over again. "You and I are different. Perhaps I see too much." Now his dark eyes grew still darker. "I worry more than you ever will, Audrey. About everything."

She nodded agreement. Look at all she took for granted. Look how much she ignored. Look what she'd missed.

"Do you know *how* different you and I are? All yesterday, I imagined buying airplane tickets with, for once, an open return. I pictured going to Paris, or flying to Martinique and on to Tahiti. Or anywhere, or *any*where!" Gregory paused to formulate his next words carefully, attempting not to seem to be blaming her while also acknowledging their dilemma. His hurt was hard. "The distinction, however, is that I'd want two tickets. And you only want one."

3

THEIR MARCH WEDDING had been such a cause for celebration that it didn't matter, not even to Celia, that the arrangements weren't those she'd have made if Audrey had delegated the job to her. Jack was helpful in this regard by reminding his wife that their daughter wasn't ever likely to want a typical wedding. "Isn't it enough," he asked, "that she finally wants to get married? Don't make me ask her to let me walk her down the aisle just to please you." But in the end, there was no aisle in the courtroom Gregory chose for their ceremony, which was Judge Osborne's own, with him presiding in a robe that looked sufficiently ecclesiastical that to Jack it seemed a small price to pay. "What would you prefer, Celia, that she pick someone *un*distinguished?"

Still, Celia was disappointed. When she asked Audrey, "How could you go to church week after week without imagining your wedding?" Audrey might have reminded her that she hadn't gone to church week after week for more than ten years. That would have been a way to distinguish *her*self, if only from her mother.

But unfortunately, Audrey was neither wholly dependent on her parents nor completely independent of them, so these sorts of decisions fell to Gregory by default. Maybe what became established that day—"from this moment forward"—was this pattern of decision-making that, for the first time in their marriage, she'd violated. Because, as for actors, for a nurse it was a professional advantage to be able to take direction, nowhere better than in her training had she learned the value in telling people only what they wanted to hear.

In Audrey's one-day absence from Metro, the white tulips Louise had given her had come into their own. Their petals had opened wide, and some choreographed pairs leaned in identical arcs like dancers suspended in defiance of gravity. In the middle of the bouquet a trio stood vertical, as if on pointe, possessing their own austere grace. Even the pale green leaves appeared to be costumed, some as curls and others cascading like streamers. They took up more room now than when they first arrived.

Louise Schneider said, "Welcome back." The first patients were already in formation too, poised to overwhelm the clinic by the end of the afternoon. But first Louise asked Audrey how Val was doing.

"She'll be okay. It was the floor of the eye, a blowout fracture and some double vision, inflammation, no big damage. Dislocated jaw, wired. She looks battered but vows not to let it happen ever again." Audrey realized as she said this that this was an accurate comparison with victims of domestic abuse, which was frightening. In order to remember this was a car accident, Audrey pointed to her own face, where the top of the jawbone joined the nine bones supporting the eye. "She hit the rear-view mirror, here."

Louise nodded, concerned. "And you?" Because Audrey opened a file and seemed prepared to get on with—to rush into—the day's business, Louise asked her again, "And you?"

Now, since she'd been caught evading, Audrey couldn't look at Louise as she said, "A case of unfortunate timing, because my husband doesn't seem to share your encouragement. I'm carrying around the notification like a letter from a lover, consulting it to make sure it says what it says, feeling elated and at the same time almost wishing I hadn't gotten it. If this were still the day before yesterday, Val would be intact, too." Audrey laughed as she said, "So does that answer your question, Doctor?"

When Louise smiled, her teeth looked set back because her chin protruded, but her gold fillings flashed like new wealth. "I'm going to take you to lunch," she said, "and you're going to say more."

"Yes, sir." As Audrey presented the first patient's file to Louise, she added, "And will that be all, sir?"

The morning was undramatic but too busy with the ridiculous paperwork required for referrals. Finally a child came in with an acute problem that could be resolved without blood work or ultrasound: a double ear infection. At one point it became clear that it was raining out in the world, and those arrivals caught in the downpour were like pans of water on radiators or wood stoves, their saturated clothes humidifying the whole waiting room. Then it was lunch time.

The cafeteria contained a cross-section of the hospital's population. Residents draped their stethoscopes around their necks like Olympic medals, whereas veteran doctors tended to try to pass themselves off as civilians. Louise and Audrey each filled a plastic bowl from the salad bar and paper cups with Diet Coke. The cookies were notoriously good, so they deliberated then selected one oatmeal-raisin to split between them. Without their white coats they looked like any visitor, who wouldn't be there if not for having a loved one upstairs.

"Start with Gregory," said Louise. "What's his problem?" The vernacular tone made her sound less than half her age.

Audrey swept cookie crumbs into the palm of her hand as she said, "Not good timing. Awful timing. He had other plans."

"So?"

"So he had other plans. He wants to take trips." Audrey knew this was an unfair way to characterize his wish to travel, but for now she didn't correct the impression.

"Fine. The only thing certain about medical school is that it's finite. Four years, that's it." Louise forked a chickpea and a green olive and demolished them. "The whole world will still be there in four years, tell him."

"But it seems he wants to retire sooner." It was embarrassing to be making such excuses for him, as if his entire life he'd been spoiled extravagantly.

"So? Then retire! Don't tell me he expects you to make him his lunch! Not *that* cliché." She herself represented the other cliché, the wife her physician husband left for a nurse in order to avoid having to be equal.

"It's not rational," Audrey started to explain.

"No kidding. What is?" Then Louise said, "Eat your lunch."

So Audrey tried. "But I can't be cynical about him, because I can't blame him for what he wants. I'd want it too."

"If you didn't want something else?" Louise was trying to recall their other conversation, when Audrey concluded that she ought to go ahead and apply, and worry later on about finding the right time to tell Gregory. There was no debating the deadline for submitting her application. Already, hers was almost late.

"No, I mean I *do* want to travel too." After a little pause Audrey said, "But not right now. Or in the immediate future."

Louise, who was so good at diagnosing, asked, "Then how about when you're sixty-three?" It was unnecessary to add that this was their real problem.

With her shoulders hunched as if to protect her heart from such scrutiny, Audrey said, "Last night's dinner was as if nothing new had happened, neither bad nor good. We sat around the kitchen table and offered up family stories and laughed." She laughed now too, thinking about Sally's perfect imitations of the others on water skis. "The reminiscing was about recovery, and it worked. It was about being glad that we were all together, all safe."

Louise wasn't unmoved, but she still said, "Let me guess. So now you're feeling guilty."

"It's that obvious?"

"It's that basic." Louise's voice softened. "I don't mean to sound like a know-it-all, but who wouldn't be glad? And then, who wouldn't wish there weren't still the problem between you and Gregory, and feel bad for having created it, so to speak, by—"

Audrey straightened up and raised her face so that she could look Louise in the eye. "By daring to want something for myself?"

Louise just smiled her smile.

All afternoon Audrey used available pockets of time like jacket pockets stuffed with used Kleenex and loose change. Whenever she could think two things at once, she did, so that by five o'clock she was doubting the importance of her being at the clinic while at home her daughter was on steroids to reduce the inflammation behind her injured eye. Then again, how about altering the dynamic in order to acknowledge Celia for simply being there?

When as a child Audrey was sick, Celia had been her personal nurse, not that she'd given her mother any of the credit for her choosing to join the profession. Right this minute Celia was tending to Val's needs, making her feel properly safe, helping her heal. Sure, she would complain to Val about her own ailments, also about the horrible muzzle-like whiskers now in fashion—don't those men know they look like terriers?—and of course about the loudness of the music, even though she liked the spirit of it, and so on and so on, nothing too unfamiliar. But Celia wasn't ignorant. For a long time, she had persisted in referring to her younger son, Neil, as "still unmarried"—wishful thinking—until one day she became the one to invite Neil's partner to the Thanksgiving dinner at Audrey's house that year. Always claiming some good reason, Neil had been absent at holiday tables for the past few years. Celia had noticed.

Audrey had to wonder about her father, though, and whether,

if he were still alive, Neil would have accepted the invitation. No, that's not it. What she wondered was, if Jack were alive, if her mother would have had the courage, since it was all too easy to picture her father saying, "Absolutely not." He was an Ohio Republican, he'd say, and proud of it. "The issue isn't Neil, the issue is traditional values," he'd say, "without which you wouldn't have had more U.S. presidents from Ohio than from any other state in the Union except Virginia. So someone still has to be old-fashioned." Then he'd ask one of the grandchildren to list the Buckeye presidents and to select one to hear more about. Almost always they would ask for President McKinley, to get their grandfather to describe the second presidential assassination, the point-blank shooting rarely mentioned in history books.

What would her mother say, that it had been "a small price to pay" to outlast the transition to her own menopause? For all Audrey knew, her mother had come to interpret her "act of rebellion," as Jack called it, as a symptom of the same condition afflicting her. In any event, it seemed to have been turned into an advantage, according to Jack, who tenderly called his wife his "very own rebel." The added advantage was in sending the message to their kids that, if what he meant by "rebel" was their mother, they could pretty well forget about trying it themselves.

The hours used themselves up in the intersection of these thoughts with the normal heavy traffic of all Friday afternoons at the clinic. Nobody wanted to need help on Saturday morning and have to go to Emergency, so they came instead with problems that could often wait until the clinic opened up again on Monday. "Better safe than sorry," was Audrey's Friday afternoon refrain when a patient apologized for coming in. She would rather have it be too busy than too quiet, especially today, when her being here meant she wasn't home with Val.

And then a young woman brought two toddlers and an infant into the examining room with her and made up for everything else by needing help. She apologized for bothering the doctor—

and Audrey didn't correct her right away by saying she was only a nurse—but it wasn't like this before, with the other two, she explained.

Audrey asked how so, and Tasha Howard explained as Audrey noted her slight fever and the pallor of her fingernail beds and mucus membranes. Was her tongue sore? Was she feeling dizzy? Iron-deficiency anemia was the most obvious possibility, but was there a history in the family of sickle cell anemia? No? When Audrey described the condition better, it turned out the answer was yes. But not so fast.

In the delivery of her baby, was there anything unusual? The baby was beautiful, Audrey said, and the two older kids were so well behaved—she kept picture books in a drawer for this kind of visit, to entertain during the boring, talking parts of the exam—and, well, yes, there was, Tasha Howard answered, because the baby came early, also real fast this time, and she wasn't here in town because her boyfriend got a job at the Lordstown plant, where they were visiting, so the hospital was small. While they were real nice and everything, by the time she got registered, the doctor was in the middle of someone else's delivery. It worked out okay, though. And the tired young woman smiled wearily.

Audrey asked the older children to move into the corner closer to their mother's head, and she helped place Tasha Howard's heavy legs into the stirrups. While she arranged the drape, Audrey asked if she'd had time yet to go in for a follow-up visit, if she'd been seen since the baby was born. The baby had been seen, but no, she hadn't had the time for her own self yet.

"You know," Audrey told her, "most women don't bring themselves in to be seen. They bring their kids, like you do, but they figure they'll be fine. I'm glad you came in, and I do wish more women did. Just lie back now, so I can take a look, okay?" She adjusted the drape and sat at the foot of the table on a low stool. If Audrey hadn't known better, she'd have thought the woman was dilated—that is, she *was*—which was how she knew to suggest, calmly, that these two bigger kids seemed capable of waiting out front, okay? Sure, they could bring all the books, and the sleeping baby could stay right here in the carrying chair. She'd just get the doctor real quick, to confirm things, but first she asked what had been the exact delivery date. Well, she asked instead, when was the baby's birthday? And sure, Audrey said, she could understand completely: nobody could be expected to think straight in this situation. So it had been three weeks.

While Audrey watched, Louise removed the purple clots like spoonfuls of stuffing from the wide-open cavity of a turkey, one after the other until the shallow pan was full, and while she did this, Audrey held Tasha Howard's hand and explained that, after the birth, the placenta hadn't been entirely removed. Her body didn't know she'd already had her baby, so it continued to provide all this blood, because that's its job. The reason she couldn't know this was happening was that blood is supposed to clot, and her cervix kept it all inside her, like a valve, until the pressure from within her caused it to open up, more like a door. The reason she's been so tired is that, unknowingly, she's been losing all this blood. That's what happens sometimes, so that's why it's important to get the placenta out. "Are you feeling okay so far?" Well, at least the patient didn't have to worry about sickle cell anemia.

Louise left the examining room to make the phone calls to see who was still around for Ob-Gyn in Day Surgery, no matter that it was now the end of the day. The best doc available was on his way out the door, but he was snagged back like a yoyo. That's the other thing that happens sometimes.

Audrey called for a volunteer to watch the kids until a relative got there, someone who could take everybody home after the procedure. It was a D and C she'd need to have, Audrey explained, although in fact only the C, since by dilating, her body had already done the D on its own. "Never," Audrey answered when she was asked how many times she had seen something like this before. But then, nor had she ever wheeled anyone into an operating room—down a corridor and into an elevator and down another corridor—who was all the while holding her busily and contentedly nursing baby.

Audrey had asked the receptionist to call home to say she'd be late. When she finally arrived at the house, none of the others seemed to need to hear her excuses, and they surely didn't want the situation described at the dinner table. But Audrey insisted, because, she said, this story was the proof.

Celia said, "I didn't realize today had been an experiment." She and Valerie had played gin rummy and hearts the whole day long. "What was it you were trying to prove?"

The dining room wallpaper wasn't very old, but even though the pattern included songbirds on flowering branches, to Audrey it seemed dreary and formal. The moiré drapes looked vulgar when the intended effect was elegance, and the silver on the sideboard was a tarnished yellow, unless this effect was the result of the candlelight. It had been so long since they'd used the dining room other than on a holiday, the whole experience was unreal. Whose idea was it? Her mother's? Gregory's? As a way to put them all on their best behavior?

"I'm not arguing, just asking," Celia argued.

Val's place at the table looked like the tray of a highchair: only soft-food choices. Sally's plate, as now, was always the first one empty, so she helped herself to more meat and potatoes and yet more milk. Gregory was relying on his tried-and-true avoidance skills. He didn't meet Audrey's gaze, whether or not he could, or would.

"I only proved something to myself," said Audrey, as if that weren't enough to count. "I love my job, that's all. I'm good at it."

"That's true. I'm the expert," Val said, and made a lopsided effort to smile. "I wouldn't have made it in the hospital without you."

"Thank you, Valley." When Val used to tell her she was the

best mom in the whole wide world, it felt as good as this did. So, with either nothing or everything to lose, and because sooner or later she would have to, Audrey said it: "I have something else to tell you. I applied to medical school. I applied to medical school and I got in. I got into medical school." Audrey looked around the table. The exaggerated expressions on their faces made them look drawn by a caricaturist.

Only Val spoke. "I could use one."

Sally slumped in her chair as if she'd collided with her own teammate.

Celia looked to Gregory to stop this nonsense right this instant.

"I mean it. At the moment I need one," said Val.

"Be quiet, Val," Sally ordered. "Say something, Dad."

Gregory didn't say how he'd wished Val's accident could have invalidated the option of medical school. He'd apologized to Audrey for his initial reaction, and although that exchange hadn't been perfect, it could have been worse. At dinner, everything had seemed fine, like old times. But he was wrong, again. This was his fault, for not having been capable of censoring the final thing he'd said, when he'd accused her of wanting a ticket to medical school in order to leave him behind. He hadn't meant to give her any ideas.

"Don't tell me she didn't tell *you* either!" Sally's profound shock sounded more like blame.

What was the accurate answer? She both did and didn't tell him.

Sally took advantage, scoring. "Why can't I have a normal life?"

"You do, Sally, dear," said Celia, "thanks in part to Cleveland." If her Jack were alive he would agree, so she said it again. "Your life has always been very normal." Conservative, she meant.

"Normal *parents*. People who don't *change* all the time!"

"There's nothing wrong with change," Gregory said. "And we're all believers in change, so let's not be blaming change." For having said the word three times, he wasn't very convincing.

So as if Audrey were the judge instead of him, she lectured Sally with an inventory of reasons, beginning with, "You have two biological parents you live with, together, in the same house you were brought home to from the hospital when you were less than two days old. You've gone to the same school, K through twelve, and kept all of your best friends. Ours is a real nuclear family and, unlike most of the rest of America, you live within several miles of all your relatives, all but Uncle Neil, who more than makes up for it by staying in touch. Unlike the rest of the world, you haven't suffered any economic shifts or unwelcome surprises. Neither of your parents has been downsized, so you haven't had to get a part-time job to help out. Come to think of it, you've never had to volunteer anything to anyone, never had to give up or do without, and never, while I'm at it, shown any gratitude either." Now she zeroed in on Sally. "One car gets wrecked and you just ask how soon we can get another one. So you won't have to be inconvenienced by having to adjust, by having to, yes, *change*. Grow up. Grow up!" Audrey gripped the edge of the dining room table to make herself stay there, to force herself to keep going, ranting like one of those preachers who heaps accusations onto the heads of the congregation in order to save them. "You enjoy such privilege! You don't suffer enough!"

"God, Mom."

"No, I haven't finished." Since she'd already disregarded Gregory's lessons about how to argue a point without risking losing the sympathy of the judge and the jury, she had nothing to lose. "My point is, how dare you complain? No, don't answer, because it isn't a question, it's a fact, which is itself a terrible shame. I'll tell you why. Same old story, you'd say, about others less fortunate, so here's my example. The patient I saw today—you didn't want to hear about her—is another girl not much older than you, but she has three kids. Don't you understand? Nobody recruited her to go to college or wear their brand of athletic shoe. Nobody at school took her at all seriously, ever. Can she possibly make it through high school one day? Maybe. But today Tasha Howard was in serious trouble, and right now she's having to recover from losing too much blood. Through no fault of her own. No, worse, because she'd been given inadequate care."

Now Val too said, "God, Mom," but she meant, "How awful." She could identify with that, all right.

"Yes. Now listen to me. I know I've had the same advantages as you, so I'm not blaming you for not recognizing how much better off you are than I was. My mother still lives in the house I grew up in, and like you I went to good schools with excellent teachers. I was fortunate enough to have a mother who could help me, so I was able to work and know you girls were taken care of if you were out of school for some reason, or sick. Today was a good example, so this really isn't one of those speeches about how much more you've been given than I was at your age." Their faces blurred as she tried to focus on what else it was she wanted to say.

She remembered. "My colleague Louise was sure you'd be supportive. She reminded me that if I were either of you girls—that is, if Gram were me and she'd decided to go back to Mather, to finish—I'd have been in favor."

Audrey looked past Sally to Val, who covered the left side of her face with that hand, making herself blind in both eyes. Sally was tearing an oval slice of bread into such little particles her placemat looked dusted with flour. Gregory avoided her gaze, disassociating himself from her absurd comparison.

Celia said, "I guess you'll have to tell your friend Louise she could be wrong about that." Celia could maybe imagine herself as a farm woman like her own mother, but never, like Audrey, employed in a man's world. Two years at Flora Stone Mather College for Women was good enough for her. Needless to say, it was impossible to imagine starting over at her age, or any age. Why on earth would she?

Sally's disdain was just as apparent. Restored after her mother's criticisms, she responded as in a game, retaliating. "What is this, a midlife crisis?" Now that women had men's stresses and were dying of heart attacks, they also had midlife crises. A classmate's mother had taken off like a runaway kid with a guy practically young enough to be her own son. It was a huge scandal, the same as if she were a man in a previous generation. Sally sneered contemptuously, "Like Annie's mom?" Sally and Celia would agree that they wouldn't call this progress.

Sally didn't see, or wouldn't say, that she'd profited from having a more level playing field. She'd heard all about the old days from her coaches, but as a ranked athlete, she took it all pretty much for granted. If this relative freedom was made possible by attending an all-girls school, it was definitely worth it, if you asked her. Without ever having experienced discrimination, Sally knew enough not to be a fan of it.

Celia took advantage of the reference to the scandal to say, "If you ask me, the problem is feminism." Before her daughter could contradict her, she said, "You don't have to tell me how I always say that. I know. But it's all too true. Look at Neil."

Now Audrey disputed Celia. "Neil has nothing to do with this."

"That's what you think." Celia sat up straighter in her chair. "Who do you think provided homosexuals the excuse?"

Like the well-trained student she was, Sally knew how to repeat back the key concept. "Feminism?"

"Yes, precisely. Once women began to force the issue, men decided to get back. They withdrew." She'd never say Neil got his inspiration from Audrey's having been a tomboy, but the two weren't altogether unconnected, given that these two children of hers had clearly seemed to feel free to be different. "The feminists' marches and all that proved it was possible to get away with being defiant."

Val said, "I don't think Uncle Neil is defiant. He seems quite contented to me." But now she had to be careful to avoid any impression that she'd seen Neil lately. The accident was plenty for them to deal with right now, and she wouldn't want to make herself the focus of their worry by letting them know she'd run away to New York but been talked back to college by Neil. This was weird, though, watching her mom being treated like the bad girl. Val said, "Plus, Gram, my mom isn't the defiant type. Believe me, I ought to know."

"An act of revenge, pure and simple. Maybe not Neil, but the others," Celia argued, disregarding Val. "Which is why your friend the doctor is incorrect. Women shouldn't encourage this. Nobody should."

Audrey compressed her voice so that it wouldn't sound loud. "No, Mom, that's wrong. The two are completely unrelated, except for having to do with freedom. You have no idea what you're talking about."

"Freedom? Who do you think you are?" Celia said.

Now Val felt this was all her fault. She should have stayed at home and gone to Cleveland State in the first place. Never mind that nobody graduating from Hathaway Brown goes to Cleveland State, even if, like herself, barely satisfying the academic requirements for a diploma. Still, shouldn't she have stayed here in Cleveland, to keep things more the way they'd always been? Why couldn't she be a more typical first child, more like Sally? But then, would Sally blame herself like this, for everything? No way.

"There are many important points being made here," Gregory said, "but too many for one conversation, I'm afraid, which is why voices have been raised and why there's disagreement. And while I'll certainly be the first to admit to my own inability to respond in a creative way, I'm obviously not alone." By mediating, he'd achieved the desired calming effect, but now came the hard part of proposing a concrete solution. He took a deeper breath, and in a deeper voice he admitted, "I sometimes criticize myself, justly, for being so contented with a world that is unthreatened by great change. People had ambitions for me, and it's probably safe to say I let them down, quite possibly including all of you at this table. Nevertheless, my boundaries were enforced by me and me only, so that, if my world is smaller than it could be, I have only myself to blame. This isn't true for you, as the four of you know better than I, or any man." He decided to exclude Neil from this part of the argument.

"Or Neil," said Val.

"Correct," Gregory said, but it was Celia he was regarding with tender appreciation. There was the same age difference between the two of them as with himself and Audrey, and, even with his advantage, he knew how hard it was to constantly adjust. Perhaps this was why he'd kept his own world so small. Now he used his old trick of pretending to make fun of himself by sounding perfunctory, like the script of a courtroom drama. "So let's table the discussion. Any opposed?"

It was possible to take the silence to mean all were agreed.

Audrey had suffered the dumb jokes about nurses knowing more about sex than regular people, but when she and Gregory met, this was the case. True to his generation, he'd had relationships that had been "steady" enough to lead to the occasional overnight date, but sex was fraught with responsible action, whereas Audrey's generation's handbook included entire chapters on fun.

In the kitchen, Gregory loaded the dishwasher and Audrey threw her energy into scrubbing the roasting pan that could have been left soaking overnight. Val had retreated to bed with a painkiller, and Sally had driven Celia to her house on Lytle Road, not far beyond Sally's lacrosse field at Hathaway Brown. There was a home game the next morning, so Sally could bring

Celia's car back on her way to the warm-up. In any case, Celia's Saturday morning chores always kept her around the house.

Audrey said, "You did a good job getting my mother off my back. Thanks." She ran more hot water and squirted more Dawn into the pan. The bubbles rose like a crown.

"Sure," he answered, pouring Cascade into the compartment, pulling up the door of the dishwasher, sliding the horizontal lock, and pressing the Normal button.

"It's always a shock to see the things she believes." Audrey shivered, drying her hands on the dishtowel. "Her ideas remind me of the one time I did a night scuba dive, when all the nocturnal sea creatures come out from under their rocks. In the dark you can forget about pretty rainbow-colored parrotfish, because what you see are these albino slug-looking things."

Gregory leaned against the wall. "Did I know that?"

She turned and pressed the small of her back into the blunt countertop. "Scuba? A so-called resort course, spring break. During, I think, graduate school. Maybe it was college."

"With the tank and all that?" How could he not have known this about her? "That's a frontier."

"Yeah, well, that night dive finished me off."

"But still." Gregory dug his hands into his pants pockets as if he could seem nonchalant. "I don't think there's an equivalent thing you don't know about me."

"It wasn't a big deal." But at the time it was. At the time it was the best thing she'd ever done. "Maybe, except for that night dive, I'd have kept it up. Then, for sure, you'd have known." They could have been one of those couples where one introduces the other to that bright undersea world. As it was, he'd gotten her interested in tennis instead.

"When you did it normally, though, you weren't frightened?" It was hard for Gregory to imagine giving up conventional breathing.

"Oh, no, it was just amazing. Probably, for you, like flying." For her, it was better than airplanes. It was birds.

"Flying was the one thing that could make me feel like a daredevil," he said, "even though I never took the controls. I just liked looking down from there."

Audrey watched the smile arrive on Gregory's face from deep inside. "It's the same thing," she said softly. "I just liked looking around too." The difference was pronounced, however, since she'd quit altogether and he hadn't.

"I can imagine it would be." Then he asked her, "Should I try it?" And then he announced, "I'll try it!"

Now she did leave the pan to soak and pushed off from the sink as away from a dock. To think that they might have been enjoying that all this time. Surely she could have recovered the experience of fearlessness, like weightlessness, the first time back, deep into those blues and silvers. "How discouraging that I quit."

But Gregory was unaware of the depth of Audrey's regret, thinking instead of his own brighter prospects for adventure. "It's like I've been saying. Don't keep secrets from me." He was joking, as she surely ought to be able to tell from his expression.

But no. Her eyes were closed, so she remained silent, swallowing her urge to say something like "Shut up." The feeling she had was that he'd prevented her from doing it, which wasn't true.

He saw her bite her lip, and he tried to say in time that he wasn't serious, but didn't quite make it. He was astounded to see that she was crying.

"Oh, no," Sally protested as she barged through the door leading from the garage. "Again?" She tossed the car keys onto the counter. "Why can't you two act your age, for a change?"

And for the second time in less than a minute, Audrey felt like telling somebody to shut up. Instead, Gregory gave Sally a short lecture on never presuming to know the content of interrupted conversations, after which Sally left the kitchen, insulted.

When Audrey switched off the kitchen light, the front hall

drew them toward it, and so on from there up the stairs and down the hall to the comparative safety of their bedroom, where neither one made a move to turn out the lights. Audrey filled the bathtub, inspired as if by the detergent's thousands of bubbles combined with the dense scuba memory of warm water deep enough to get lost in. "No baths," she'd told Tasha Howard, going over the printed instructions before liberating her to a less traumatic weekend than she would have had if she'd hemorrhaged. If Audrey hadn't known it was impossible to have a baby and then have another one three weeks later, she might have thought that first purple clot was the head of a full-term baby pressing itself into the world. It angered her that this situation could have been prevented by a better delivery. It angered her that she felt she couldn't ever again tell her family about a medical emergency. To Gregory she said, more obliquely, "Sally doesn't know we're not the same age."

She went under, sliding forward and bending her knees in order to be submerged, her face floating like a water lily anchored on the stalk of her neck. She was pleasantly deaf, except for the returning sound of her own circulation. Now, when she closed her eyes, she could manage to resist gravity in addition to every other aspect of reality.

And when she emerged, simply by standing there she filled their bedroom with the calming fragrances of the bath oil, her shampoo, and, even though they were supposedly fragrance-free, her face creams and body lotions. Gregory finally quieted, perhaps inspired by her tranquilized example. It took him practically no time, compared to her, but the stream of the hottest water he could tolerate heated him up nicely. The impression he gave when he appeared from behind the closed door was of a charcoal briquet, red as well as gray, and shimmering.

Softened, they each moved toward the center of the bed, each reaching out tentatively with a relatively cool foot. She turned onto her side. His familiar profile had its usual ins and outs.

Placing a hand on his shoulder, she said, "I don't like to think about your father, and the reason I don't is that there's never a valid comparison. Surely not with me, because nothing I could ever do, short of that, would ever be equal to what he did to you. I would never do that." Now Audrey touched his face. "And you know that. I know you know I never would."

He didn't have to say he knew she knew he knew, so he didn't.

"All the way to Cincinnati I tried to imagine what it would be like to have that awful, fatal secret he kept from your mother, that he was thinking of killing himself. I drove very, very carefully as a result, afraid of being capable of the same thing nonetheless. But as you've known ever since that night, he's different to such an extent he's his own category. It insults me to be compared."

He placed his own hand on hers, to hold it in place. "You're right, there's no comparison. You're right, too, that nothing you could ever do, short of that, could be as traumatic." But he reconsidered, saying, "No, that's not true. You could leave me." His insecurity flicked like an insect across the space between their faces.

In the silence, Audrey heard the sound of the heating system, the hot air rising from the basement. "Not die, you mean. You mean, *leave* you?"

"Why do you think I reacted the way I did the other night?"

Audrey considered her reply. She could promise not to leave him, but she just had. "I told you I'd never do that to you. That's what it means to say your father and I aren't alike."

"I know. But what should I do if I still worry?" His discomfort ranged so freely he'd been upset by the image of her with a tank on her back, as if that danger were present. Such was her power. Or, such was his father's power.

She was made glad by their ability to speak of such feelings, but it was this that next caused her to feel the regret of not having had Gregory to talk to while deliberating how to live her own life. She'd needed his reassurance that, yes, it was a ridiculous ambition but, yes, also realistic and, yes, he'd support her in it. Or, no, it *was* a ridiculous, unrealistic ambition. She'd needed him, like a father, to advise her. "Your father's secret meant that if it were to come true, he'd be dead. If mine came true I'd be alive. And so would you."

Like the furnace in response to the thermostat, they could toss back the covers and generate their own form of heat, as then they did. It looked like sex.

And now it was an advantage that Gregory had come of age in the generation that contented itself with being good. Audrey was in no danger of being overwhelmed by a lust encrusted with the aspects of a performance. This was about continuing the conversation in not quite so many words. Better too few than too many.

"Comfort food," they called this function of lovemaking, not because it was bland but because, like meatloaf and mashed potatoes, macaroni and cheese, their associations enlarged the experience. He could know that she would rake her fingers through his hair like a fork, pulling it straight back to expose the subtly off-center V-shaped point his mother gave him, along with her grief, as a widow's peak. Audrey could know he would cater to her and sense whether she was feeling patient or impatient. He was more flexible in bed than on his feet, and she was less rushed here than where physical need was multiplied by more than two. As with those foods, there weren't many surprises, and no exotic ingredients.

"What's the matter?" she asked as she retrieved the sheet and the lighter-weight wool blanket they had changed to for spring.

"I meant to call Karen Wallace to confirm nine o'clock. Tomorrow's my day with her boys. Haircuts." He checked the time. "How did it get so late?" he asked, but then remembered, and said so.

"Waiting around for me to come home for dinner, you mean," she said. "Overcooked lima beans. My fault too." But she laughed. "That's nice."

"What's nice?" He could feel himself wanting to avoid the responsibility of Joel and Danny.

"You. For making a plan with them. How old are they?"

"Too young, of course. Joe Ricci asked me the other day how they were doing, and I was embarrassed not to be able to tell him."

"Who?"

"Joe? He's been shining my shoes as long as I've been there."

"I didn't know his name."

"He's dying too," Gregory told her, that bluntly. "Pancreatic cancer is a bad kind, I hear."

"If there's a good kind I haven't run into it." But this seemed ungenerous. She said she was sorry.

"Joe and Frank are brothers. That's where I'm going with the boys, to Frank. To the lakeside courthouse." Gregory tucked the blanket under his chin like a bib. No, like a barber's smock. A couple of tears ran down his face.

Audrey missed this because she was staring at the ceiling, at a faint crooked stain she couldn't analyze without her glasses. "Is that a water mark?" she asked him, pointing to the place. She hadn't meant to say that out loud, only to remind herself to check it in the morning.

"What?"

"Never mind. Sorry." How many times had one or the other of them said this lately? It seemed like too many.

So whatever it was, was gone.

The trouble with having had only one marriage was that it wasn't possible to know whether or not, all across the country, other couples went off to sleep, having made love, feeling misunderstood. Worse would be to not have had sex and feel this alone, except that situation had the advantage of logic. Only those multimarried few knew the answer to her question, but they were their own control group.

This itself was odd: how few examples there were in Audrey's world of couples, like Louise Schneider and her narcissistic former husband, whose marriages had been given up on altogether. Everywhere else but here the statistics went in that direction, further isolating those few—like Sally's friend's runaway mother with her much younger lover—who were out ahead of the tide, and got stranded.

"Goodnight, then," he said, as if having expected her to give him these thoughts—not that he'd have liked to hear them—in exchange for the penny he'd neglected to offer.

"Goodnight," she answered him. Wasn't it for such a moment that she had enforced the purchase of this king-size mattress? So that, unlike her mother, there could be a little privacy? All she wanted at this point, like her mother, was to get a good night's sleep, which was also the ultimate in privacy.

He stayed awake, not on purpose but by default, listening to such even breathing Audrey could be doing yoga. He envied this about his wife, how she skimmed the surface of sleep but managed, in fewer hours, to wake up refreshed. He, by contrast, tortured himself with his own inadequacies, each one then substantiated first thing in the morning when the task of waking Sally proved he wasn't up to the day's challenges, at least not spiritually.

And what if he envied Audrey for more than her claim on such restorative sleep? For instance, when her brother Neil changed everything by coming out, her older brother, Johnny, was obviously resentful for being left behind to run the family pharmacy alone. Gregory had to admit to himself that it wasn't as if Audrey had decided to reinvent herself, and besides, she could change her mind again anytime she wanted. One minute she could tell people she wanted to be a doctor, and the next decide after all to stay a nurse. For Neil, once out, there was no going altogether back, so his was a more permanent decision, which required a greater courage on his part and, for everyone else, a far larger adjustment.

On the other hand, in Audrey's case, unlike Neil's claim on an identity, Audrey faced the possibility of failure.

When he was a boy, Gregory had two families. There was his own miniature mother and a younger troublemaker brother, Rich, who was in flight to such a literal extent that later on he would enlist in the air force, instead of waiting around to be drafted by the army and get sent no farther than New Jersey. Back then, though, his mother had a customer named Mrs. Osborne, who kept a seamstress in business by ever so slightly changing sizes from season to season, and who had one child, a son, Charles. Gregory and Charles were the buddies he and Rich had never quite managed to be, and as a bonus Charles had his own playroom and a section of the garage for his fleet of bikes. His bedroom had twin beds and a pair of teddy bears in baseball caps leaning against the pillows. Mrs. Osborne gave Gregory his own monogrammed pajamas, which he wore when he spent the night there, most Fridays and Saturdays. On those next mornings he'd sit at Judge Osborne's elbow and watch him read the paper, and the sun would warm his own back while the judge recited to him whenever there was a story worth repeating. To this day, whenever Gregory ate a soft-boiled egg he would tear up a piece of well-done toast he would use for dipping. This was the way the judge ate his soft-boiled egg every morning.

At the Osbornes' round breakfast table the orange juice was always freshly squeezed, even though the frozen concentrate was considered more modern back then because it was a decided improvement over canned juice. And since they used cloth napkins for all their meals, Gregory too had a silver napkin ring, his engraved with a G because, conveniently, Mrs. Osborne's maiden name was Gleason.

In that house, nobody ever said anything in a raised voice,

though at the time Gregory hadn't understood the direct correlation between levels of agitation and amounts of money. Because the Osbornes could afford more help than they needed, they could also afford absolute rules about well-mannered behavior; in contrast, most days he and Rich threw sucker punches and epithets at each other, causing their poor mother to yell at them for not being nicer. Because she would then collapse into a heap, in tears, it was no wonder that Gregory preferred the tranquillity of privilege. Whether or not he deserved it, he always felt so much more appreciated at the big house at the end of the long driveway.

Now he was ashamed of himself for not having immediately rescued Rob's boys. He didn't know Karen Wallace well, but those few times they'd met he hadn't found her very approachable. Before Rob's death Karen already seemed brittle, so, beyond the fact that she taught math at University School, how could she cope adequately? Whatever failings his own pathetically hardworking mother may have had, Sarah Brennan's nature was as sweet as the spiced peaches she put up in quart jars and gave to her customers for the holidays. Karen's needy boys would also probably feel their mother was always too busy, which was all the more reason for him to help out. With Val off at college and Sally tied up with her crowded athletic schedule, he had more free weekends than not. Only now did it occur to him that if he took up a new challenge, not unlike Audrey with medical school, his helping out with Rob's two fatherless boys could be good timing.

Their bedroom had windows on both sides of the house, so as he lay there the urban glow from the city down the hill made its silent way through the linen Roman shades. Out front, there was no traffic on Overlook Road, nor from within the house was there the caustic secondhand sound of television or the music Val listened to when she wasn't making her own. As in most conventional center-staircase Colonials, the mostly empty living room was directly beneath their so-called master suite with its pair of walk-in closets and double bathroom sinks. There was no comparison between the Osbornes' stone mansion and this more ordinary clapboard, but the day he bought it was as important a transition as he'd ever made. At last he was the provider of ample material goods, with a dining room sideboard drawer filled with monogrammed silverware. Their everyday china included, at his request—since Audrey chose the dogwood pattern—egg cups. Not even the threat of cholesterol caused him to give up this custom he'd inherited, along with everything else, from Judge Osborne.

Now his own breathing slowed. A spring rain was audible on the roof, so he quieted his thoughts in order to listen while it refreshed his world. Audrey was like a mute, her entire experience interior, beyond his skill to penetrate. He wouldn't try, either, but he was incapable of seeing himself as withholding when she seemed to have secured that behavior for herself. So preoccupied was she, he doubted that she remembered he would be given an award the following night. With everything else going on, now including Val's accident, she would have little interest in his civic-mindedness. Not that he did either, really, as he might have admitted if he were able to be a bit more honest.

The rain increased, which was its job in these first few days of April when there was a whole winter to wash into the lake, the dirt sinking into the silt to turn the water grayer than the sky. Sally's games were never rained out, no matter how muddy the field, so he could always bring the boys there and let them run off their nightmares in broad daylight.

Picturing himself with them at the edge of the lacrosse field caused Gregory to wonder whether it would become his place to advise Karen Wallace on the education of Joel and Danny, the way Judge Osborne had stepped in with him. His own younger brother had ejected himself from the family when he joined the air force, but Gregory's choices were significantly influenced by fully funded tuitions arranged for with personal letters to the dean of admission, first at the college, then Yale's law school.

The only thing his mother provided with any confidence were the fine wool suits she'd made, which passed for J. Press.

If only Charles had lived. He'd have been the one to go off to New Haven for those same seven years, leaving Gregory behind at Ohio State. Charles would have been the fulfillment of his father's dreams, whereas he himself—not unlike his own brother, Rich—had bailed out prematurely from a career trajectory enabled by his having made the *Law Journal,* and thus the selection process that could have taken him, if he'd just been willing, to the top of Manhattan's highest skyscraper. So yes, he was capable of feeling guilty.

So were Judge and Mrs. Osborne, who regretted that they couldn't have him around after Charles drowned, for fear of becoming too distressed by their loss. That summer day before Charles died was the last time Gregory was invited to the big house until after the fifth anniversary, when they asked him for Saturday lunch and the three of them worked diligently not to be overwhelmed by their feelings. It wasn't possible for Mrs. Osborne ever again to see Gregory without measuring him against the void.

The rain was accompanied by distant rumbling thunder and flashes of lightning, true to Dick Goddard's six o'clock forecast. Gregory knew the trees would wick the water from the earth, turning it into leaves that would swarm the branches like those small chartreuse moths with wings that looked two-toned as they flipped inside out. Had the Osbornes known how they'd hurt him when they abandoned him for those five years, instead of allowing him to join them in their mourning? It was almost as if—and of course this was how Gregory experienced it as an adolescent—they blamed him for not being free that day to have gone to the beach with Charles, to have saved him.

The first time he mentioned Charles to Audrey, he was unable to finish the first sentence. It was on the third day after he and she had been introduced, and although he'd made a fine impression that night and the following day when he took her for a spin by chartering a plane for an hour, the next evening, in a restaurant, he'd broken down like a toy. "When I was a kid I had a buddy named Charles," he'd begun his sentence when she said something about how he looked like Charles Lindbergh. And so Audrey had held his hand until he found a way to speak about it, which was when he knew that if she didn't agree to marry him immediately, he'd keep asking until she did.

Now he felt a longing for her, as if she were other than right there beside him, serenading him with that calm breath that made her seem to have an endless supply. In the back of his throat and in the pit of his stomach he felt a throb, a hunger. He'd love to have this night over again, so this time he could tell Audrey that whatever she wanted, he too wanted her to get. But look: he was back to feeling regret again. At least he could recognize it and, from time to time, admit it.

What he meant was that he wished to go back to that moment at the dinner table when, by his passivity, he'd betrayed Audrey. If, when Sally challenged, "Don't tell me she didn't tell *you* either!" he'd said, "She did," it wouldn't have been any exaggeration. And if he'd dared to say, "She has my full support," wouldn't he feel better right now? In his profession he was always distinguishing between the said and the unsaid, the done and the undone, like a priest or rabbi whose job it was to demonstrate the Golden Rule for a forgetful congregation.

The temperature dropped. The rain slowed and then turned to snow. He slept. Whatever it was that wakened Audrey was articulated now in the stronger urge to pee, so she got up and guided herself unsteadily, like a patient after an operation, to the bathroom. Only the bottom half of the window was curtained because, beyond their back yard, the land dropped off and provided them with both privacy and their view of the lake. The sky was a murky, milky white.

But it snowed! On the corner of the roof over the kitchen addition, the outdoor light had been left on, which illuminated large, saturated flakes that, unlike snow, were without definite shape. Whether or not they would bind together, join forces for the morning, was of no particular consequence. It was still too early for pea shoots to have emerged in the community gardens, though only that morning as she drove to the clinic she'd seen the land being worked by those optimists who were always the first to sharpen their spades, walking backward in straight lines, placing their points against the earth, stepping down firmly. This was the predawn morning of April 4, the anniversary of Martin Luther King's assassination, marked by many community gardeners, in spite of the threat of a frost, by planting. As one of the original organizers, it had been Audrey's idea to persuade the National Guard to truck three thousand square yards of topsoil and ten tons of horse manure in from outlying farms, the same National Guard in need of a more favorable image after the Kent State massacre. The effort generated the desired publicity as well as satisfying the goal of enriching soil that had been abandoned for generations. Nothing was more gratifying than to stand in the center of that crowd of children and elders, cheering young men in uniform as they dumped dirt into mountains of possibility. No wonder March had seemed to her a good month for getting married.

"March?" Celia had complained. "March!" Her point had been that this was Cleveland, not La Jolla or Honolulu, where stephanotis grew like ragweed. For a second she'd thought Audrey must be pregnant. "Are you?"

"Mom, I'm a nurse, I know about reproduction" was all Audrey had answered. "And besides, it's never been my ambition to be a June bride."

"Speak for yourself," her mother had responded.

"I am."

It snowed that day too, which had presented logistical problems but also created a reassuring hush. The sun was bright enough to toss sparkles all around like sequins, so that even Celia had to admit it was a nice effect. Everybody made it to the courthouse on time, and Judge Osborne's courtroom impressed grandly with its tall leaded windows and the medieval gallery Celia said looked Shakespearean. It had been newly carpeted in a deep garnet, and through the faceted glass the sky's dense blue poured itself into the lake. Audrey had refused to wear the white of her profession but agreed to a dress the color of the ivory tulips she'd selected, and which, in their single tall crystal vase, had the effect of presiding over their vows. After the ceremony there was a noisy party in the high-ceilinged great hall, decorated with more varieties of marble than you could imagine there were to be quarried. The food was fine too, and afterward she and Gregory were transported the short distance over to the Ritz, where more champagne awaited. The first of their airplanes to Paris took off without delay the following morning, so by the end of the first day of their marriage they were suspended in the sky over the Atlantic in first-class seats.

These twenty years accrued, not unlike the value of the stocks she and Gregory held jointly, but the steadiness of their relationship wasn't permitted to be repetitious because their children enforced their own progress on them. Whenever nothing changed, they did—for better or worse, sickness or health, like marriage—and the anniversaries were like other perennials, in that some years were stronger and showier than others. This year was blighted, by Rob's death.

Audrey pressed the tip of her nose against the cold pane, and the sensation distracted her from another look at the snow streaming toward the floodlight, and extinction. Now she pressed her forehead against the glass, then turned her head from side to side for the same all-over experience. And, as if this could slow her pulse, she touched to the cold glass the insides of both wrists. To slow her pulse?

She was furious about Tasha Howard and having to explain to that vulnerable young woman the absurd and heartbreaking fact that, unless the placenta is fully removed after childbirth, it continues to provide as if the baby hasn't been born. The mystery was that Tasha's body kept its secret from her until the very last minute it could, which was when, as Audrey held her hand while Louise evacuated her, she'd asked Audrey, "But why?"

And the same went for Val's concealing the cause of her accident, as if only an autopsy could provide clues to the extent of her insecurities. But this was Audrey's point: these two young women could both have died, for no reason. Overnight, that ancient Latin imperative, Seize the day, was as modern as it was mandatory. Tasha Howard was all the proof Val ought to need.

The frigid ceramic tiles numbed the soles of her bare feet, so Audrey stepped back from the window onto the cheap fluffy oval acrylic rug that had no intrinsic capacity to warm them. Like a child, she almost believed the bathroom floor was a pond with snapping turtles or a river with eels, so she stood there a long time, overwhelmed. She couldn't see into her own bedroom, but from there it didn't look safe to her. Why hadn't she chosen a patterned rug she could move to like another, bigger island, instead of a neutral carpet that made their bed appear to float in that bottomless sea? What she could see was that she and Gregory were drifting in opposing currents, after twenty years of seeming to be about the same age.

Perhaps it was always an illusion that they were of the same generation, but in any case, age wasn't the problem for them that it was for those couples who had children from former marriages, those irrefutable proofs of living history. Because when they met he didn't have the adolescent children to which he was chronologically entitled, it was easy for them to ignore the ramifications of his being old enough to be in eighth grade when she was a newborn. Or, when she herself was a young teen, that Gregory was a recruit in a crisp khaki uniform.

The advantage they had was that she could be his morale-boosting younger woman without his having to abandon a longtime wife his own age. And because there weren't these living markers of a past life, they *seemed* like contemporaries, except every now and then she'd discover something incredible such as that he'd been old enough to vote for Ike. Needless to say, they were from discrepant sexual eras, but Gregory's deficits turned into advantages when he put himself in her hands.

Now she felt unable to make it back to bed. There was a short answer to the question of whether or not she would recommend the experience to her daughters.

Everyone always said they were so compatible, it would have been a shame if, given that neither of them had since been drawn *to* anyone else, either one had settled *for* someone else. Because they each considered the other to have been worth the wait, it was always fortunate they'd each proved capable of waiting. He'd made a whole career of it, he often joked, but of course he was quite serious, given the notoriously slow wheels of justice. Now she could say she'd waited her whole career too, so they were still compatible. Except for this: he was no longer young enough to start over, nor was she old enough not to.

4

CLEVELAND AWOKE to that Canadian snow Dick Goddard promised three days ago in his April Fools' extended forecast. The bright sun meant the snow would be gone by game time, but for now the back yard twinkled like sand, as if Sally's sport should be beach volleyball instead of lacrosse. The morning's *Plain Dealer* ran a front-page box with the yearly reminder to turn the clocks ahead before going to bed that night, so already Gregory felt helpless against the loss of time. Although he knew he was a poor substitute, he wanted to give more hours, not fewer, to Rob Wallace's boys. But what if they asked him to explain daylight saving time? Gregory didn't understand even that small mystery.

The road was the shiny, dense black of licorice, and every tree was a sparkler. The incongruent sun was enormous, splashing energy like paint. Joel and Danny were jumping around their yard in soaking-wet clothes, keeping an eye out for his silver Honda. When he pulled into their driveway, they shouted "Judge! Judge!" like a pair of older girls sighting a movie star. The commotion drew their wan mother from the dining room table where she had been paying the bills, which had been Rob's task the first Saturday morning of each month. On this one-month anniversary of his death, through the storm door Karen looked even thinner than at the funeral. When she saw how wet the boys' best clothes were, she pretended to be crying because she was that glad to see Gregory. The boys had been on their own only a few minutes. There was too much for her to do, all at once, all alone.

He understood. It was easy to imagine exactly what his mother would have needed, and easier to know how to please two boys whose funeral suits weren't what they'd wanted to have worn in the first place. It was quite all right to wear regular clothes to the courthouse's barber shop, as he demonstrated by taking off his own necktie. Joel and Danny disappeared to imitate him.

Since Karen's University School teaching salary was augmented by tuition adjustments for both boys, there was no issue of financial insecurity comparable to that of his unschooled mother, whose sewing skills provided what little pocket money there was, while the rest of the country was profiting from the postwar boom. Gregory was aware that his father's shadow was draped like a veil over everything lately, but he attributed this to the fact that his father had died fifty years ago. In a mere half century, then—not that Gregory would ever tell him—thirteen year-old Joel Wallace would feel the same renewed grief.

Trying to rise out of her desperation, Karen asked about everyone. But he also wouldn't want to mention either his daughter's bad news or his wife's so-called good news, so he said, in shorthand, everybody was fine. He asked her how she was and she didn't answer—there were no words—except to thank him for knowing how terrible it would have been for her to have to take the boys for these first haircuts without Rob. A shudder passed through her like wind across the lake.

"Ready!" the boys announced, now looking more like boys. They handled their own negotiation over which one would start out in front, and Gregory drove all the way in on Euclid, past Public Square and the Justice Center to the old stone courthouse. Frank the barber had told Gregory he would consider it a personal honor to cut their hair. "Such a good man, Judge Wallace was, such a pity."

"Sorry about Joe," Gregory told Frank, whose eyes met his in the mirror. Like a matador Frank waved the plastic smock before fastening it around Danny's neck. Of this impending tragedy, however, Frank couldn't yet speak.

This had never been a ritual outing for Gregory, neither as a son nor as a father, and he loved it. There were two barber chairs, three other chairs for waiting, and plenty of magazines about cars and golf. A solo act, Frank kept the pace quick and steady but never rushed. The advantage he had, in offering only medium or short, was that he wasn't a stylist. The unpredictable climate—"Hey, what's with the snow, huh?"—required a hair dryer, but not for cosmetic reasons. This was still a guy's world. You had to go somewhere else if you desired color.

Now that his extra hair was gone, Danny looked so much like his father that, again, Gregory found Frank's eyes in the mirror and held them in recognition of this. No doubt because Rob had been Gregory's protégé, he'd always seemed younger than a man of forty, but now Gregory felt certain he knew just what Rob had looked like when he was eight. Joel looked more like his mother, but the way Danny tipped his head, tucking in his chin as Frank brushed and powdered the back of his neck, was enough to prove the genius of genetics. For a moment Gregory understood why his wife might want to study science.

It wasn't necessary for Frank to call out "Next!" because everyone kept track of the order and knew to move to the shampoo chair when the customer ahead was switched over, as Joel now was. Gregory wasn't quite due for a cut, but in order to be on their schedule now that the three of them would come downtown every three weeks for regular haircuts, he put himself into the current rotation, for a quick trim. He'd never been one of those men who felt incomplete to have had only daughters, but he had to admit this was a greater feeling than he could have imagined. Here were the three of them in one of the last few places in the city where women were allowed but wouldn't come, where the magazine articles wouldn't be called "How to Please a Man" because, here in this unchanged environment, men already were.

"Take it easy, boys, and thanks, Judge," Frank said, pocketing two twenties and a ten. "You too, Mr. Ricci," each boy said, "and thanks, Judge." Gregory told all of them the truth: "My pleasure."

After burgers and fries he bought them baseball hats at a new store called Lids, and in the car they found radio stations Gregory didn't know he had. It was still only one o'clock. He was tired but not exhausted.

"Let's check out Sally's lacrosse game," Gregory suggested, although he knew that at their all-boys school they might have an attitude about the game's being played so nonviolently there was no need for vinyl-dipped foam shoulder pads or cage-like helmets. Maybe they'd feel boys' lacrosse was superior, no matter that Sally was nationally ranked. But they said, "Cool."

Gregory knew a lot about lacrosse equipment, and he'd listened to only a fraction of what Sally had said about it. Her stick was a Brine Tsunami, the same yellow, conveniently, as the color Hathaway Brown called gold. Sally fine-tuned the pocket as if her stick were a stringed instrument, and when the weather forced her to cover her carefully callused hands, her gloves had vented leather palms. She couldn't wait to play in Virginia, where this was a three-season outdoor sport. Gregory told Joel and Danny all this because, in their middle school experience of three separate seasons, they played soccer, basketball, and baseball. Talk about equipment!

On the sidelines, Audrey was standing next to her brother Johnny, whose block of a body, especially in the winter clothes it wasn't quite time to put away, made his younger sister look almost inconsequential. He wore the brown and gold school scarf, and boots worthy of Wisconsin. When Gregory reached them, he heard Johnny asking Audrey what her feminist friends thought of her quitting a woman's profession to join a man's one. Wasn't that disloyal of her?

The greetings enforced—like a penalty—a two-minute delay, and then when the boys ran off with a chocolate Labrador puppy another kid was racing like a greyhound, Audrey could answer the question. Where should she start? "First of all, I'd prefer to have told you myself, without Mom's spin. What she doesn't know and you do, or should, is that these days there are many male nurses and many female doctors. The two professions are more like the difference between being an actor and a director. Both essential, but it's the director who makes the decisions and therefore gets either the credit or the blame. That's what I want. My 'feminist friends' don't have a problem with that." Audrey shook the cold from her hands and admitted to herself that she should probably have stayed home with Val, who needed a mother more than a nurse *or* a doctor.

Gregory's leather shoes were the wrong choice for these sidelines, since the cold snap stiffened the ground while the steadily melting snow turned the top two inches of earth to the consistency of cake frosting. As if he were one of those friends, he said, "That's right," prompted by the awful plausibility of Audrey as his widow with the need to provide. As Karen does now, with Rob gone. As his mother did, but couldn't.

Audrey said, "See?"

Sally's coach carried a Warrior ball bag like a big canvas purse, and she could be heard insisting to the referee—deferentially, as required—on using orange lacrosse balls because in patchy snow they were more visible than yellow. Hathaway Brown also won the coin toss. The game was under way.

Sally played attack, riding the field like a champion working up to the Triple Crown. For shoes she wore exclusively Adidas, this particular model's carbon outsole for traction and because its compression-molded midsole included a heel insert. She was officially sponsored by Adidas, so she knew all there was to know, which was much more than most people wished to. Johnny had one of those piercing whistles he let loose before every "Go-go-go, Sa-lee, Sa-lee," so it was neither necessary nor possible to talk once the clock started. Johnny was Sally's godfather and her first fan, and in return she always dedicated her first goal to him.

None of his own three kids had their act together so far, and none was athletic despite Johnny's former fame as a quarterback at Ohio State. His wife could still do the cheers and, at the end of long parties, could be easily persuaded to revive things by leaping up into an X, jabbing the space around her with her four little hands and feet. "Give me an O!" Jan would shout, her O's and X's hugs and kisses for the whole room. So far, their kids disappointed big-time, but as Celia argued on their behalf, Johnny and his wife set a pretty high standard.

At halftime, though, he had to get back to the pharmacy, so after the coach's pep talk he got Sally to promise to phone him with the rest of the play-by-play, and he trotted to his parked car as if, because the score was so lopsided, he'd been taken out of the game in order to let his younger teammates get some playing time.

Audrey turned to Gregory and said, "Thanks for sticking up for me." She tucked her arm through his.

Gregory pressed his arm against his side, squeezing hers. "You're welcome. But I'm freezing, aren't you? When we get to drive to Charlottesville every weekend, it'll be warmer." He was joking, of course, but he also realized that once Audrey went back to school, she wouldn't be free, ever, to drive to Virginia.

The second half started, and with the exception of an unfair call after an unavoidable collision, the rest was predictably one-sided. The other team's players were good sports even though Hathaway Brown took advantage of every opportunity. Soon, everybody just wanted it over. Finally, it was.

But Joel and Danny were both soaking wet, again, this time from playing with the chocolate Lab puppy they called Hershey.

When they asked Gregory if he'd help them persuade their mother to get them a dog, he stalled, so it was Audrey who quickly came up with the answer that the chocolate Lab was a Hathaway *Brown* dog—get it?—and whereas their school colors were probably something more like green or blue, why not get a blue or green parakeet instead? Birds don't need shots. Their mom wouldn't have to walk it.

Gregory saw the flaw in Audrey's argument, and not just because this was the skill he used at work. If she'd gone with him to the Wallace house, she'd have seen, from the sports equipment and all-season jackets crowding the front vestibule, that the University School colors were maroon and black.

Danny and Joel sang their new refrain in two parts, like an Elizabethan round. "A *black* Lab, then. The leash wouldn't have to be maroon, but could be."

Val had wakened with a headache, so, saving her prescribed Tylenol with codeine in case of worse pain later, she'd taken two aspirin from the cupboard above the sink in her parents' bathroom. When she bled from the suture sites she was helpless, because Johnny wasn't at the pharmacy and she was too embarrassed to admit to just anybody that she had taken aspirin this soon after getting stitches. Sure, she knew her dad took a daily aspirin for his heart, to guard against blood clots, so it was obvious that she just didn't think. Not even Gram was home to help. And when Audrey finally arrived, Val asked her, "Am I okay, Mom?" The uncertainty was an admission to her mother that she'd rather not be left all alone ever again.

The bleeding had been stopped, but as Audrey changed the bandage she could see there had been subcutaneous bleeding too: blue-black bruising. "I'm so sorry for going to the game, but you were sound asleep." She corrected herself. "That's no excuse, is it?"

In their freezer they kept a variety of ice packs for Sally's injuries, and Val held one against her own swelling. "When you're a doctor you'll wear a beeper at least," Val said. "But by then, since I'll be pushing thirty, maybe I'll have stopped making all of these stupid mistakes."

Across Val's bare legs Audrey spread the cashmere blanket that was the same pale green as the living room carpet. The three-cushion couch faced the fireplace, but the day's big sunlight poured into the room as if it couldn't be contained by the entire outdoors. Val's dirty hair was tinted plum-colored at the moment and matched her face, but it was hard to tell which looked more unnatural. Her ear had been studded with silver stars in a pattern that could be a constellation — Val's "sign" — for all Audrey knew. She really knew so little.

"Are you worried about me, Mom?"

Audrey pulled up a chair and sat as close to Val as she could get. Yes, she worried about Val, a lot. As an infant Val was precociously alert, and once she could crawl it was necessary to lock the screen doors to keep her from escaping. She was soon able to vault the railing of her crib, and all their clumsy childproofing attempts failed against her skills as a born magician who made all her tricks look easy. Val tried all foods — as well as all nonfoods — and was called "the ultimate consumer" by her pediatrician, especially when, before she talked, she could sing commercials.

She'd adored school, but only until the end of second grade, when, as her third-grade teacher put it in a parent conference, behavior began to matter more than it had up to that point. According to the tests, Val had none of the problem "learning styles," but she also had no patience at all, as every test administrator pointed out. With her peers, as with her teachers, she was alternately most and least popular, depending on how frustrated she was with both them and herself. And her senior year of high school was a complete disaster, as if Val had aimed to surpass her school's record for college rejection. Her Oberlin interview, for instance, was doomed by her insistence on driving herself the thirty-five miles to the campus, but without written directions.

Oberlin had been her first—and most unrealistic—choice, but since she rejected the very concept of safety, applying to a "safety school" was out of the question for her.

Audrey answered, "Your impulsiveness has always been an asset too, but yes, I do. I worry."

"Me too." To support the ice pack, Val used two small pillows needlepointed by Gregory's mother. "I'm not sure I'll make it," she said, without specifying the goal she'd set herself.

Audrey took Val's hand, including her seven silver rings and cannibalized fingernails, and earnestly yet firmly, making contact with Val's good eye, she said, "Nothing matters more to me, Valley, than that you make it safely into your adulthood."

But Val had become aware of the other voices in the house, including her father's. "Please don't tell Dad I said that. Promise?" She withdrew her hand. "I wasn't serious. I'll be just fine."

Audrey said, very quietly, "I believe you were serious. I know I am when I say nothing matters more to me than you." It wasn't a question of her having a favorite child; it was the opposite of deliberate selection. Val's needs had the irresistibility of natural forces, like an undertow, as well as supernatural forces, like miracles.

Neither of them spoke for a full minute while the word "serious" echoed in the air between them. Forget about Val's "silly mistakes" and/or her "impulsiveness." What about the progression from good judgment to bad, then to worse? This *was* serious.

Val closed her good eye, but there was one more thing she wanted to say. "I wouldn't want to be your age before I figure myself out. But, at the same time, you're a good role model for a late starter like me. I mean, how can I be blamed for not getting my act together when you yourself didn't?" She opened that eye and regarded Audrey, like a fish, without moving her head. "So, I mean, thanks." Unlike a fish, her eye blinked shut.

Gregory could be heard laughing at something, which turned out to be the extra-long Hathaway Brown sweatpants Sally provided for both boys so their wet clothes could be washed and dried before Gregory returned Joel and Danny home to Karen. The aroma of hot chocolate also drifted from the kitchen into the living room.

From the hall, Sally called, "Mom?" as she came into the room. "Oh, sorry," but she continued, "you said it's okay if I take your car, right?" Sally stood at Val's feet and surveyed the damage while she rotated her head on her long neck and shook the tension from her exercised arms. "How come she's worse?"

Audrey said, "She only looks worse, but in fact she's better." This wasn't the first time she felt Sally didn't need to know the details. The risk was that she was permitting Sally to remain aloof from all human error—it went without saying that she'd had no personal experience—but at an either-or time like this, Audrey preferred to spare Val. No doubt her encounter with Johnny was a factor, given his all-too-familiar oversimplification and lack of curiosity. As for Celia, in her telling Johnny about Audrey, she'd seemed to have no impulse to protect Audrey from his demonstrated need for continuity, whatever the price.

Sally wasn't known for her empathy, but she managed to refrain from detailing her own plans for the evening: her best friends were getting their college letters this week, and needed her. She was beginning to realize that last year at this time the same was true of Val, whose letters were identical. The difference was made more obvious by the fact that, since December, Sally had been wearing a blue and orange Virginia sweatshirt.

Val pointed to her own face with both hands as she said, "Drive safely."

It was an award ceremony that had been on their calendar for three months, but in the chaos of this week the event had evidently slipped Audrey's mind. It was just as well that he was one step ahead.

That afternoon Gregory had decided to revise the speech he'd planned to give at the annual civic-award fundraiser at the

Renaissance Hotel, preferring to pay active tribute to Rob Wallace instead of the usual homily about the crucial importance of public service. And so, when he dropped off the boys he'd asked Karen to be the one to go with him. At first she'd said no, but when Joel came up with a favorite babysitter on the first try, the boys pleaded with her to say yes. Gregory was further gratified when neither one chose this moment to ask for a Labrador puppy, especially when he'd provided a transition by remembering to mention to Karen that the event was black tie.

Then, once Gregory got back home he told Audrey that because of Val, and his decision to dedicate the speech to Rob, he'd invited Karen to take her place tonight. Audrey felt only guilty for having forgotten that he'd been named the recipient of Cleveland's Good Citizen Award. There was no question about her needing to stay with Val, so it made sense to her that he'd anticipated this, no matter that, if she were Karen, the last place she'd want to be was in an enormous crowd of strangers brought to tears by the truth that Rob Wallace can't be replaced.

He looked splendid, his old tuxedo so well tailored the final fitting looked to have been that afternoon. Val and Audrey were waiting in the kitchen for their brownies to finish baking, and Val surprised them all by asking her father to invite *her* the next time, taking for granted that there would be a next award. Gregory said, "Sure, and maybe in the meantime you'll invite me when they choose *you.*" So she said "Sure!" and made him laugh when she sang her Buddy Holly imitation: "That'll be the day-ay-ay," although she left off the last line, "when I die."

Audrey had changed into her bathrobe, so she looked like an invalid too. Karen, on the other hand, looked like a thirty-six-year-old movie star who looked ten years younger. Her one good dress hung on her frame so loosely she was like a girl playing dress-up. It was as if her skin were vacuum-sealed, making her eyes larger than in real life. Her rings were so loose the modest diamond couldn't keep its head up. What a mistake.

He disagreed, and he told her how breathtakingly much she

looked like his mother with her hair up, held in place not by those old-style invisible hairpins but by what looked like sterling silver chopsticks. She could be his daughter, of course, but the longing he felt was the other kind of incest. He wanted her to place those pale lips on his own, just for the same fraction of a second as were her kisses for Joel and Danny—quick, distracted, ambivalent about leaving them for any reason—as she told them goodnight.

"Have fun, Mom," said Joel.

"We'll be fine. Here's our watchdog," Danny told her. They were in luck because the babysitter, a University School senior, was wearing a T-shirt with a Black Dog logo on it.

With their haircuts making them look younger than they had that morning, they looked too young to be left with someone who was just barely a legal adult. It reassured Karen to know that she would only be downtown and could always take a cab home. She promised them, "I'll kiss you goodnight in your sleep, so don't wait up."

"And you know you can count on me, Mrs. Wallace," said the young man. Already he'd microwaved a pouch of popcorn and talked the boys into drinking Sprite rather than Coke, telling them matter-of-factly about the effect on the brain of caffeine. "We'll be practicing equations. Right, guys?"

Karen had the genuine authority of those effective teachers who, in daily practice, are equally capable of giving and receiving respect. The boys smiled at the thought of another kid teasing their mom.

Gregory was thinking about the few times his mother, like Karen, had felt compelled to go out. One time he remembered was when Judge Osborne came by one evening to drive her to the big stone house to take in all Mrs. Osborne's dresses after Charles died. Much later he'd learned that Mrs. Osborne found it impossible to make the arrangement herself, in case, when she called, Gregory answered the phone.

Karen covered her thin shoulders with a shapeless wool coat, her regret just as plain. Now, by her worried expression, Gregory thought she was giving him permission to become her own Judge Osborne, the man who would provide for her sons as he would have for his own.

But in the car, naturally, they talked about such things as haircuts and baseball hats and, yes, Labrador retrievers. She was making such an effort it took the energy of a second language, and at the end of each paragraph she would sigh with fatigue and regret at the prospect of having to think of yet something more to say to him. What a mistake. She had felt obliged to go out and had made herself believe Rob would have wanted her to.

The hotel was on Public Square, across from where the extravagantly designed wrought-iron arc light at the Society for Savings Bank marked the fact that Cleveland was the first city to have outdoor illumination. Gregory was interrupted in his attempt to tell her this by the synchronized valet parkers who opened the two car doors as they chimed simultaneously, "Welcome to the Renaissance Hotel!"

In this past month Karen never went anywhere without a supply of Kleenex, which was why she'd had to carry the fringed evening bag that made her feel as if she were pretending to be someone else. She was accustomed to carrying a canvas book bag, not a purse embroidered with tiny round mirrors that were supposed to be the eyes of birds. In real life Karen wore trousers, not a long skirt with matching shoes whose toes were as bad for her feet as the heels were. She wore turtlenecks, not a scoop of a neckline that revealed the concentric circles of bone connecting clavicle and sternum. She had nothing to say to any of these hundreds of people, unless they wanted refreshed, along with their drinks, their memory of advanced-placement calculus. Suddenly she saw how it was possible to function in the protected world of the University School, where what she knew still mattered more than what she felt.

Like a couple, Gregory and Karen walked up the staircase from ground level to the mezzanine, where the white marble fountain played below a cascading artificial bouquet of wisteria and peonies. Entering the pastel apricot Ambassador Room with its deep blue velvet drapes and gold-on-navy patterned carpet, Karen heard a voice exclaim, "Mrs. Wallace!" A beautifully assembled middle-aged woman reached out her hand, which was why Karen did the same. But it wasn't for a handshake, it was to bestow on Karen's arm a touch of consolation. "Zachary Wheeler's mother," she said, Zach being the president of the sophomore class in addition to the clumsiest math student she'd ever taught. "Zach told me about your husband," she then added. Her discomfort was evident, but this was because she was afraid of expressing her surprise, given how recently he'd died, that Karen would be out at an event like this. "Zach's home working on his geometry." But then her also exaggerated laugh disclosed that she wasn't serious. "I'm afraid he gets it from me," she apologized, as if carelessness were a genetic trait.

Karen hadn't foreseen that this gathering would be packed with private school kids' parents, who, after all, funded the city's charities in addition to running all the businesses and every profession except teaching, politics, and the arts. Behind her, two fathers were comparing college acceptances. "I got Princeton. What'd you get?" "*I* got Harvard."

Cocktails ended and, as if this were a school assembly, everyone jostled their way toward their assigned seats, comparing the numbers on their place cards. A woman who was also way too thin, although deliberately, delivered Karen to the head table. "You'll be Mrs. Brennan, all right?" she asked, then said, "Sorry, what *is* your name?" Karen would have answered, "Karen," but too quickly the excessively thin woman vanished altogether.

Gregory apologized too, for having been whisked off to get pictures taken for the next morning's *Plain Dealer.* "Mayor White's here," he said, "but has two other functions to get to, so we did a 'preenactment.'" Since, therefore, anything was possible, with a powerful sense of entitlement he sat next to Karen instead of the woman who'd earned her place at his left by organizing the event. Either that woman would be spontaneous enough to mix up the entire table in order to claim her rightful place beside him, or she wouldn't. This wasn't Gregory's problem.

The salads were in place, mounds of leaves that looked as if they'd been stripped from flowers rather than lettuces. A round of goat cheese had been rolled in crushed pistachios to improve the chalky texture for those who were accustomed to cheddar balls with walnuts. There was already too much to eat, but the waiters had no personal stake in whether or not the plates they took away were empty or full. Because saltwater fish would have to be flown in, the main course was halibut in a lemon beurre blanc, along with indigenous fiddleheads. This came and went as efficiently as if the schedule were fixed by an airline. Wine and more wine appeared, and while individual tarts floated to the table in a kiwi sauce that looked like grass—so the tartlets appeared to be mini-gardens—the women at the table agreed the food was a lot of fun. "Good evening," the master of ceremonies said five or six times. Like a train gradually arriving, the room slowly quieted. "Good evening," he said again, but now with proven results.

At last, the stated purpose of the evening was reached and Judge Gregory Brennan was introduced, at length, and called from his place at the table near the podium. The ovation was also sustained, and standing.

"Thank you, thank you," he said the same five or six times, "and good evening, thank you." Election after election he'd won their votes, so they were his constituents. Who was he to ask them to keep silent their approval of him?

Karen was so miserable she didn't think it could get worse, and then it did. "Let me tell you who Judge Wallace was" was Gregory's opening line, "since he deserves this award you've given me. I'll tell you why." And then he did, by describing the drop-in children's center according to his own original, limited vision: as a way to keep the dignity of the court when, for lack of an alternative, the parents of juvenile offenders brought even younger kids to the courtroom with them. "I saw the children's center merely as a convenience, that is, until Rob Wallace taught me the better reason for it." Karen vividly remembered the passion Rob brought to this discussion at their dinner table, when he explained to Joel and Danny why it was so important.

"He said, 'I don't want juveniles to suffer the shame of looking bad in front of their younger brothers and sisters, and I don't want those littler kids thinking it's routine to appear before a judge. I want those parents or grandparents to know I'm talking to *them,* that I'm intervening, putting on some pressure, as then *they* must. I don't want them focusing on their younger kids who haven't been arrested yet, because I want them to believe, as I do, that these juveniles aren't ruined until their parents and grandparents believe they are.'"

Approval circulated the room like a current, and when Gregory felt everyone there knew the extent of Judge Wallace's worth, he said, "But, he believed, not *then* either. He'd say, 'They're not ruined until the system thinks they are, by losing faith in them. The system should never think that, and, as long as I'm there, it won't.'" Now a hush fell over the room.

Karen felt invaded by the implicit assumption that this roomful of people could claim to have known Rob. It felt to her as though all that was left of him was being divided among them, as though these memories of him were no more valuable than his suits or ties. She'd never been overly possessive of him, but now she was. Now that Rob was dead, she felt he ought to belong exclusively to her and their sons, not to these strangers who cared nothing for those poor kids in his courtroom, for whom he'd felt responsiblity. Karen put her elbows on the table and placed her arms together, supporting her face in her two hands like a globe on a stand. All the earth's water poured from her.

* * *

"Have you ever been to Paris?" he asked Karen, who said, "Never." Of course he didn't say that if Rob hadn't died, he'd have been again recently. Karen couldn't think of anything more to add.

He was driving in the right lane, behind a city bus that stopped every two blocks, diesel exhaust pluming from the tailpipe with each repeated acceleration.

Karen said, "This is making me dizzy. The fumes."

"Sorry," he said.

In their silence he realized he'd thought of Paris for an additional reason. There, ten years into their marriage, he and Audrey had experienced the pleasures of trading secrets, and he was aware of how much he didn't know about Karen. In Paris he and Audrey discovered the sixth-century church Saint Gervais–Saint Protais, which had Doric, Ionic, and Corinthian columns *and* a flamboyant Gothic interior. Audrey said they should refer to it as a "sixth-sensory" church because the normal five senses weren't sufficient to appreciate it.

In Paris they'd talked forever, and they'd each been surprised to learn things about the other that even in ten years they hadn't learned. Audrey told him about running away from home, on the second day of fourth grade, because her mother had made her wear ugly shoes. Gregory told her that one time he stole a copy of *Esquire* from a kid's dad's basement workshop, from a cupboard where there was a flask too, which the two boys drank from in burning sips.

Another summer he and Charles Osborne pretended to be lifeguards by wearing whistles on a pair of red and white lanyards Charles had made in arts-and-crafts class at his day camp. For Gregory the lanyard was merely ironic, since to this day he hated swimming in muddy-bottomed lakes. But for Charles it was tragic, because he was the more accomplished swimmer but nevertheless drowned the next summer, while his mother sat with the *Reader's Digest* under a beach parasol. The detail Audrey hadn't known until that night ten years ago, crossing the Pont Neuf, was that Sarah Brennan had kept her son home that day. Gregory hadn't been able to go in the water on account of his having had fourteen warts on his hands, burned off and swabbed brown with iodine, which then leaked through the bandages like bad blood. Charles had been envious because Gregory exaggerated how horrible it was, telling Charles it hurt like pure hell, every single application worse than the last one. And then right there on the Pont Neuf Gregory had burst into tears and told Audrey his whole life would be different if he'd not had warts on his hands. He'd have saved Charles. And later on, Charles would have been the one to get into Yale with his father's help.

Karen told him, "I shouldn't have come." But she meant he shouldn't have asked her either.

"I hope you don't feel like I forced you," he said. He would hate to impose his will on anyone, the way Jack did that long-ago morning when he prevented Celia from getting twin beds. In Paris, Audrey had told him her lasting wish was that she'd barged into the kitchen and shouted at her father, "How dare you treat your wife like this?" Audrey was still ashamed that, not only had she not dared do that, she'd also never told her mother she knew anything about it, like a coward pretending it never happened. There on the Pont de Solférino, Audrey promised herself—out loud, so he could hear her and hold her to it—to bring it up with her mother. Whether she ever had, he didn't know.

"Well, yes, I do feel you forced me," answered Karen, adding insincerely, "but thank you for what you said about Rob." Her house was between downtown and his house, so she didn't have much farther to go. This was as painful as when she'd run out of energy with ten minutes left of a class. She wished there were a way, as in class, to get Gregory started on his homework.

He was wondering if it had to do with Karen or with what she represented. Was he drawn to her counterintuitively—a moth to a porch light—or, less fatally, because he wanted her to know that he suffered too? All he knew was that, all night, he was incapable of taking his eyes off her. He hadn't appreciated how fine a beauty was Karen's, especially when her enormous eyes filled like pools and spilled over. He'd seen them at the end of his speech and been able to see them again in the darkness of his car, with the glare from the bus, until she'd asked him to pass it.

When he pulled to the curb, he opened his own door before Karen could have a chance to say he shouldn't walk her to the front door. He'd learned that morning that normally she would use the kitchen door, although tonight it seemed too familiar a move to have pulled into her driveway. The snow had melted on the flagstone walk, but it was still narrow enough to require them to walk in single file.

They stood enclosed between the outer and inner doors to her house, in the messy space for winter boots and coats neither in use nor yet put away for spring. She was merely trying to reach the end of this evening while he chattered on about the difficulty of loss. He described his own brave mother's attempts to balance his and his brother's losses with gains, and told Karen that this was what he thought was the real reason—not Judge Osborne—for his wanting to become a judge.

She'd heard the name, but she asked, "Who?"

"Legendary," Gregory replied, unsettled by this evidence that Rob would have been too young to have known him. "Anyway, I only meant to say that the heart of the profession is balancing loss with gain. I always give the same lecture to law students about wisdom as the balancer, justice itself the balanced. Justice, in the end, is wisdom in equipoise," he told Karen. Unlike himself, who was clearly way off balance.

And way off base. But she only said, "Some loss is bigger than that."

"Oh, I know that," he lamented, and placed both his arms around her while she stood there, like a tree. The tree his father hit? Now Val? He pressed his own grief upon her, most unfairly.

In one category he put his father's death, Val's accident, and Audrey's application to medical school. He didn't mention Rob, the true cause of his vulnerability.

She was like a wooden clothespin with her arms pinned to her torso, so she only had words. Just one would have been sufficient, but she resisted having to say "no." Instead she tried the perfunctory phrase she now disliked more than any other: "I'm very sorry for your loss." She knew he meant well, but she had no energy left. She'd spent it.

He dropped his arms from around her and stepped back as far as he was able in this small enclosure, which made him the one to say it. "No, no! It's *yours* I'm sorry for." What could he have said to make her feel he'd been so presumptuous? "Please don't ever think I'd compare myself to you."

"Goodnight, Gregory."

This worked immediately.

At home he was the last one in. Only the dim light above the kitchen sink had been left on, but the refrigerator light radically altered that effect. A Rolling Rock was the answer, he hoped. The question? So far the precise question eluded him.

In his chair in the den off the kitchen, in privacy, he allowed himself to feel embarrassed. He'd mentioned his ancient losses and then he'd added, "now too the loss of Audrey," as if Karen would have any reason to be sympathetic. As far as he knew, Karen and Audrey had met only at large, impersonal gatherings or those awkward dinner parties that included wives who had little in common. Karen looked to be of that generation of women who automatically sided against men, so it was stupid of him to think she would feel sorry for him—as if his wife had died!—when her own loss was so grievous. Reflexively, he blamed Audrey for everything. He knew better, but still he went along with it, blaming her for his having made a total fool of himself.

On the other hand, the icy green bottle rewarded him for his excellent work this evening—after his tribute, the room shook with its approval—and he granted himself the pleasure of the effect of the beer, as if somehow it was Audrey's fault that he'd become so thirsty, as if she'd withheld clear liquids in addition to sustenance.

He undid his tie and, like a woman, kicked off his patent leather shoes. Unbuttoning the collar of his starched shirt, he admitted to himself that he hadn't been *able* to think about Rob in that moment, for two valid reasons: Karen's anger at him—anger at Rob for putting her in this situation—and his own longing for consolation from her, for contact with her, which was making him feel very guilty.

In order to escape this frame of mind, he thought of turning on the late news, but he didn't want to be told something else was even more immediate than his own painful experience. Nothing was more real than the fragility of Karen Wallace, stiff in his arms. He saw all the beer was gone too.

So he turned off the light and found the banister and followed it upstairs, where both his daughters slept behind closed doors. At the end of the hall his own bedroom door was open, and he could hear his wife sleeping, exuding sodden breath. The way he smelled of beer, she smelled of semiconsciousness, even going so far as to ask him "How did it go?" without waiting for a reply before slipping back into her dream, for which that line would have equal meaning. She snored. He would say she snorted.

In the bathroom Gregory was unwilling to look at himself in the mirror because he felt so transparent: he was resentful of Audrey, so like a child he'd found ten ways to punish her, including finding her ugly compared with Karen. In fact, in their entire marriage he'd never once found himself seriously attracted to another woman, and yet tonight he would have to admit that this had been the case, unless he'd manufactured it. With his arms around that slender body, he'd felt his stomach tighten when she thanked him for what he had said about

Rob and he thanked her for that and more, whatever the hell he might possibly have meant by that. Which was when she'd said, "Goodnight, Gregory."

His white pajamas were on the hook on the door, where he now hung his tuxedo. His teeth needed brushing, but that was all he accomplished, except to empty his bladder. The beer would doubtless get him up at least once more during the night. After all, he was an old man.

A pathetic old man, Karen would be thinking, an old flirt of an old man. So poor Audrey all these years! So that's the kind of man he is, she would no doubt be thinking, if, that is, it was him she was thinking about. The chances of that were zero.

Nevertheless, Gregory allowed himself to imagine being in Paris with Karen, in adjoining rooms connected by a wrought-iron balcony where they could take their *petit déjeuner* in their satin hotel bathrobes. Karen would play the Audrey Hepburn role, making him Cary Grant. So he'd tell her the one Cary Grant joke he knew, where in a telegram to the studio a fan asks HOW OLD CARY GRANT? to which the star replies OLD CARY GRANT FINE. HOW YOU? Karen would relent just long enough to smile when he said that, which would justify the airfare.

"Oh, please!" his daughters would shriek if they knew he was capable of a fantasy about a woman whose age, 36, was the reverse of his 63. "That's *backwards,* Dad!" He would try to defend himself by saying, "At least she's twice as old as you are." But like their mother, they'd both snort derisively.

When his mother was Karen's age, there was no one the least bit interested in her, which was why, when Judge Osborne picked her up to bring her to Mrs. Osborne (who would refuse to leave the house for a full year after Charles died), Gregory would pretend for a minute that neither Charles nor his bereaved mother had ever existed. In that precious moment there was only the judge and his own mother—also him, their only child—for the rest of their lives. Which was pretty blatant.

Now that he was able to picture Judge Osborne and his mother on that balcony in Paris, it was possible to imagine her marrying someone else, a different man altogether, so that instead of being sent to Yale in his homemade J. Press look-alike suit, he'd have bought himself a real suit and not hurt his mother's feelings, because she'd be far too busy to keep sewing for a living. In fact, she'd have her own seamstress. Or, wait, who said he went to Yale? Say she'd married a guy who'd gone to UCLA or Texas or Michigan, giving Gregory all kinds of other options, making *him* the different person altogether.

He saw that the main reason he'd have become a different person was because he wouldn't have had to go back home. Someone would have loved his mother, rescuing her from her own life by sharing it, caring for her. Then, of course, he wouldn't have felt so obliged to try his best to save his mother. From her impoverished life and then, ultimately, her cancer.

Good. Taking it to this extreme freed Gregory again, because there was no way he'd trade Audrey and his daughters for seven years in Los Angeles or Austin or Ann Arbor. No way to save her—or Joe Ricci—from cancer, or Rob—or Jack Morrow—from heart attacks, or Charles from Lake Erie. If there was a way to save himself, from himself, wasn't this the time to seize it? For a cheap fantasy on a wrought-iron balcony in Paris, hadn't he just bargained away everything that mattered to him?

He knew himself better than that, so he could admit to himself that it was out of character to project such pathetic fantasies about his mother onto Karen Wallace's slim frame, as if they were Mary Pickfords and their Douglas Fairbankses could be as handsome as, and much nicer than, the real one. As if their Romeos were none other than him! Good! This was so ridiculous, not even he was capable of so self-servingly twisted a fantasy. Now he could be grateful that, as far as he knew, he had never talked in his sleep. Sally and Val would destroy him with their mockery.

Quickly, he made his way to his side of the bed, which—better than the Paris Ritz—she'd folded back to welcome him home. The Egyptian cotton sheets were smooth but cool, and he coiled his body to concentrate whatever warmth there was. Audrey yawned in her sleep, stretching toward him without intending to convey anything at all, but making him react. How? With more longing, for *her* now.

When they were in Paris celebrating their tenth anniversary, he was fifty-three and she wasn't quite forty, and they'd acted like perpetually young lovers. Because it was March, not April, it was possible to be wholly spontaneous, so a day trip to one of the great cathedrals could easily include a good restaurant and a cozy late afternoon first-class train compartment back to one of the glass-domed train stations. Other days, when the light was as gray as Cleveland's, they would go to a museum, and feast, and then see a black-and-white film, and pull up the collars of their raincoats as they hurried back to the hotel to make love in the afternoon. For that birthday ten years ago, back home, Gregory had given her a bidet.

Having generated a bit of his own heat, he could stretch out his legs and, in the comfort of this bed, enjoy the memory of the various reactions. The box was tied with a red bow, so their daughters guessed it had to be a television, like they'd seen as prizes on game shows. Celia and Jack were there for that family celebration, but because they thought it was a toilet, at first they weren't all that amused. A minute later, their reaction was different—an X-rated birthday present wasn't their idea of fun, in front of the girls—so Johnny and Jan pretended they were shocked too, while Audrey laughed, tilting her head back like a trumpeter. It was a week before the plumber could get there for such a nonemergency, and during the installation he'd had to call the shop to be guided through the procedure.

In Paris, she'd made him feel he held her attention totally, filling her with himself to the brim and beyond. And he'd seemed to make her feel the same way, so it wasn't a leap to envision himself—them!—visiting each wonder of the world, one after the other, and all as soon as possible. In the airplane on their way home from that second trip to Paris, they'd made extravagant plans for themselves, none of which materialized, as it turned out.

Instead, Jack died the next year, so Celia needed them more than ever. Then, before they knew it, they had an unreliable teenager whom they caught in one small lie after another, until they admitted to each other it wasn't worth the risk for them to leave town (and Val to her temptations) until things changed. At about that time, Audrey switched jobs to be more available on a more regular schedule, which made her less available to take off when the spirit moved.

Still, at some point they'd begun to plan for their return to Paris, glad that after ten years they still had a marriage to celebrate. He took the refresher course in French conversation, and they'd booked a pair of what were now called business-class seats. The moon was a slender crescent, and on the Quai des Célestins, like the last time, they'd wish on it like a star. But then Rob died.

Marjorie McCarthy had come into his courtroom to hand a note to the clerk, who then brought it to him. In Marjorie's schoolgirl handwriting the message said—although the news was already obsolete—that Judge Wallace had just suffered a heart attack and been taken from the building by ambulance. Gregory had heard the sirens.

It was Marjorie who called Audrey and then, immediately, the travel agent. It was Marjorie, too, who, at his request, called Karen Wallace to convey Judge Brennan's most profound shock and sympathy. Rob's own secretary was inexperienced, so in Marjorie's next call to her she'd outlined the protocol. Gregory wasn't sure whose idea it was for him to read from Saint Paul, but he'd done it with resonance. What he did remember was going in procession to Lakeview Cemetery and standing under a green-and-white-striped awning—the outrage of it, in March, in wet snow—and the feeling that his heart would break, although he knew he wasn't alone in that. It was shocking to him, even as one who himself came from a pitiably small family, to see that as Karen's funeral limousine was driven away from the gravesite, there wasn't anyone in the car but her and her little boys.

Now Audrey had her back to him, so he shuffled across the mattress to slide himself against her, aligning his body with hers. The loneliness he felt was deceptive, because it could be misunderstood as sexual yearning. Indirectly, it was. It was expressed with the same urgency.

They're side by side in an airplane, encapsulated but with the whole earth below and the wide-open sky holding them with invisible support. He, not Marjorie, has called their travel agent to purchase a pair of airplane tickets around the world. He wants the kind that are good for a full calendar year, where you can head off in one direction or the other and keep going with or without reservations. As a surprise he'll present these tickets to Audrey—a bidet in every hotel room in the world—on her fiftieth birthday. That's how much of a fool he is.

For the second night now, while one struggled to sleep, the other was struggling awake. This time it was Audrey, who woke up so thoroughly she believed it was morning. Technically, it was. The blurred green digits were triplets difficult to tell apart, so without her glasses Audrey didn't know if it was 3:33 or 5:55. The night before, she and Val had sat in the living room listening to quiet music while feeding a slow fire in the fireplace, two acts of recuperation at the end of this awful week. Whether it was night or morning, she felt rested.

Audrey reached with bare feet to locate her slippers, and as she went from the bedroom to the hall, illuminated by a gold stripe of light from under a door, she heard Val's voice followed by a pause that opened into Val's harmonious laugh. Echoing, it reinforced the extent to which Audrey had missed Val and their talks, which were always found in unplanned pockets of time like coins discovered in jackets. Val was more willing than Sally to confide in her mother, but since Val had the less reliable schedule, it could often seem that Sally was the more available one. However, with Sally the conversation was all about her—"all-Sally-all-the-time coverage," Val mocked like a radio host—and always, not unlike Sally herself, the conversation was muscular and on the thin side. Sally had opinions, but Val had convictions. One of these days, or so Audrey hoped, Val's belief system might expand to include faith in herself.

Audrey tapped on the door before opening it. Val was sitting on a throne of pillows like a princess with the power to summon up anybody at whatever time she wanted. "Hold on a sec," she said when she saw her mother in the doorway, "it's Neil." She'd stopped calling him Uncle Neil ages ago, but because her mother only nodded, Val specified, "Your brother Neil," and handed her the receiver as she explained, "who is in Hawaii, so he's just on his way out to dinner," as to Neil she said, "whereas your sister here is in suspended animation."

"Neil?" Audrey said.

"Remember me?" His laugh was as soft as humming.

"I wanted to tell him about my accident before he heard it from Johnny or Gram, so I left him a message in New York, which he picked up in Hawaii. I said to call back no matter how late it was, but also said it wasn't an emergency." Among Val's old talents, when she was supposed to be doing her homework, was the ability to capture the phone at the beginning of the first ring, as, evidently, she still could. "He's there for school vacation week."

So all Audrey had to ask him was "How are you?"

"Happy," he said. "We're in a small Japanese inn that has a moon-viewing room and a cube-shaped tub, plus salad and rice for breakfast. So I'll have the best show-and-tell in the whole class, I bet." He was making fun of himself, but in fact he'd won his school's Best Teacher Award three years in a row.

Val stood up and offered her place to her mother, who permitted herself to sink into it. "I can hear orchids in your voice."

"That's the pineapple daiquiri. I'm the tourist bureau's new poster boy."

Now Audrey laughed. "Phil too?"

"Today he found the shop where Robin Williams gets his antique aloha shirts. Now he looks like Robin Williams, but with less body hair."

"Tell him hello."

"The same to your own 'traveling companion,'" Neil said, a reference to Celia's first oblique references to Phil, "though I hear you haven't done much lately. Or not 'March in Paris' at least." He hesitated before saying, "And I guess you won't be taking much time off in the future either, so Val tells me." After another pause he said, "Shame on you, dear, for not sharing that news."

Val had closed the door behind her, so Audrey had the total privacy of a confessional adolescent. "I couldn't manage to find a way to tell Gregory, so I couldn't tell anybody else."

And now Neil's voice grew sincere. "Val says not everybody's real thrilled about it. You know how well I understand." From his own experience his advice to her was "Don't blame yourself."

Audrey made herself comfortable, coiling her legs and covering them with her nightgown. The telephone connection was so unencumbered by static that Neil seemed to be here in town, not that he and Phil ever set foot in Cleveland's weather between Thanksgiving and May Day. Or he could be leaning against that other wall here in Val's room, and they could be confiding their secrets as if still kids in her old bedroom with the ugly wallpaper she'd chosen and immediately outgrown.

"Promise not to tell?" she began. This was how they'd always start their secret complaints about Johnny or their parents. "I'm very disappointed by Gregory's reaction to this. And I feel blamed."

Neil said their magic word, "Promise," and then, just like old times, listened to her tell him how unfairly she'd been treated. By her husband. By their mother.

It was always Celia who was hardest on her, pressuring her toward opportunities she hadn't herself had, while at the same time needing the validation of a daughter whose choices mirrored Celia's own. Audrey tried not to blame Celia for not seeing the contradiction, but this didn't mean she would agree to pass the fallacy on, unexamined, to her own two daughters.

Neil said, "Don't expect *her* to give you what you deserve to get from Gregory."

She was silent.

"Where's he in this?"

"Wounded," she said.

"Well then."

She asked, "Well what?"

"Try not to forget the basic fact of your getting into medical school. These days they're not exactly in business to make mistakes, given the success rate of malpractice litigation." His "try not to forget" was a good imitation of her voice. "Sound familiar?"

In his earliest phone calls to Audrey from New York, when he'd felt intimidated by his own decision to move there, she'd reassured him: "Try not to forget that now you belong to a community." Neil had answered, "An endangered species," so she'd said, "Not anymore. Protected."

When Audrey emerged from Val's room she went downstairs and found Val in Gregory's chair, the small room tinted the green of an old movie Val had found on one of the more obscure channels.

"You two were talking all this time? A whole town's been wiped out. A whole war's been lost here. Or won." Val pressed the Mute button on the remote and motioned her mother into the other chair. "I'm sorry I didn't let you tell Neil yourself. It's just that he's the only one in the family who can be counted on to be interested in letting people be who they are." Val knew this wasn't really true, but it felt true. "I knew how proud he'd be of you."

"I know, he told me," Audrey said. "And he's your biggest fan too. You know that, don't you?"

"But you didn't mention the drinking part, did you? I decided not to tell him that part. It's bad enough as it is." And there was still another issue. Val hoped Neil hadn't brought it up.

Audrey reached out to touch Val's hand, which was resting on the arm of her chair. "No, I didn't mention it." She believed that the drinking was an isolated experience, not a category. The larger problem was more worrisome to her. The medical equivalent was a systemic disorder, far harder to treat than a specific disease.

"Thanks, Mom."

"It wasn't a deliberate decision."

"That's what I mean." Val let her hand be held. "Nothing in you needed to punish me," she said, accurately.

"It's because I love you."

"That's what I mean. I know you do." It was so simply said it didn't sound profound. "You just proved it."

Onscreen, flags flew, flickering the image, giving Val and her mother a pulsing, mosaic look. Planes flew too, but in the parallel lines of stunts in an air show, in formation. Because this was an old-fashioned movie, the signature "The End" appeared in script, after which the credits rolled, showing that it takes almost as many people to make a movie as it would a real war.

When Val pressed the Power button, the unflattering glow of the television was replaced by a more humane secondhand light from the kitchen. This transition became the opportunity to keep going or call it good enough, which in most ways it was.

The initiative was Audrey's. "Do you want to talk about what you call 'the drinking part'?"

Val said, "I'd mostly quit."

"Mostly?"

"It was about my running away from everything, Mom. I got

Academic Warning, so I was failing at a place I had never wanted to be in the first place. My adviser told me I could do better work if I'd just try, so I did try. I tried real hard. Except the other night when I felt those old insecurities, like, you know, that I would always only—ever—be a total failure."

"Not true."

"No, don't, since it's *been* true for me, and you know it." Val seemed prepared to continue, then looked like somebody who'd changed her mind.

Audrey couldn't exactly pretend to Val that failure and success were of equal consequence. Instead she said, lamely, "Everything always works out for the best," as if she had any reason to believe this either.

"Good one, Mom," Val told her with a small laugh.

Audrey accepted the deserved criticism with her own thin laugh. "It sounds like we're very grateful to your adviser, then."

"Very." Again, she could say more, but she didn't.

"And to you, too," Audrey said just as earnestly.

Now Val leaned forward as she deflected, "Let me ask you. What's Dad's problem lately?" Sally had described for Val how the funeral had changed him into the kind of man who suddenly weeps in front of his kids. "Is it because of that guy Rob?"

"He was devastated by that loss, no question." Then Audrey answered the question. "I miscalculated, for sure, in not recognizing the effect of Rob's death in relation to my own plans, but with Dad it's not just recent. He's unsettled by change because, like a lot of people back then, his mother felt his father's suicide was too shameful to be discussed. So, when periodically he asks, 'What don't I know?' he's serious."

"So is that a reason," Val asked, "or an excuse?"

Audrey considered her answer but chose, "Reason."

"That's what he'd say, of course," said Val, "not that it can't be both at once." With an it-takes-one-to-know-one sigh, she added, "But at least it didn't stop you from applying, did it?"

"I felt I had no choice but to," Audrey overstated, "so I

couldn't let it stop me, could I?" In reality, the deadline forced her to act, after her many self-imposed delays.

Val whispered, "I can understand all but one thing. Where did you get the confidence?"

Audrey sat forward with her elbows on her knees, her forearms extended into the space between her slippered feet, her hands clasped. "That's what I mean. I didn't have confidence then, and I still don't. I had no choice but to *try.*"

Val decided that's what she would say if she ever succeeded at anything. "Aren't you still worried, though?"

"Sure," Audrey answered too quickly, "since I might not be able to do it."

Because this was Val's own concrete fear, she shifted categories again. "But, I meant, should I be worrying about you and Dad?" So remote was the likelihood, Val had always discounted the option. "I mean, what don't I know?" she asked, and understood why her father's question was so useful. "That is, should I be worrying about divorce?"

The very word startled Audrey, who rushed to answer, "No!"

"Good!" Val was just as glad to avoid it.

Audrey knew it wasn't that easy, though, because Gregory was afraid that she would need him less, or not at all, at the point when he'd need her more. "It's difficult, but don't worry about divorce."

"Thanks. One less thing." And when Val laughed—she had Neil's harmonic laugh—she showed Audrey how wide she could open her mouth now, though it still hurt when she did. "Ouch!" She held her jaw with both hands.

"There's plenty else to worry about," said Audrey. Even if she made her way through medical school, who was to say she wouldn't make some horrible, fatal mistake, proving that she wasn't ever qualified to be a doctor. It wasn't about quantity but quality. Gregory had abandoned her to the painful solitary experience of believing she possessed neither. She and Val, in this, were sisters.

Val trusted her, as Audrey could see in her wide-open display of fear counterbalanced by faith. "But, on the other hand, you should see Neil in his classroom," Val said, easing into her own "sharing," "because he lets his kids laugh out loud, allows them to laugh at him—never, ever at each other—and gets them to laugh at themselves. Even *I* learned." Val corrected herself. "I got him to teach me. I got him to teach me a lot, primarily about myself."

Audrey didn't pick up Val's hint, but her reply wasn't wholly irrelevant. "Tonight, Neil reminded me that he was also the first in our family to understand that a secret kept is always for some valid reason."

"Like that your parents would definitely say no if you asked their permission to take off to New York for a week when you've just been put on Warning? To take a bus from Cincinnati to New York City and show up at Neil's like a runaway kid?" Val braced herself.

"You ran away? You *ran away!*" Audrey jumped from her chair and made herself sit right back down. "Look how you're absolutely right. I'd have said no. Dad too."

"I know," said Val.

But this was also Audrey's point about Val's reflexive undermining of her situation. Even with boys, every time there was an interest, Val found a way to subvert it. "Still," Audrey said, "running isn't a solution."

"The first thing, when Neil saw what I'd done, was to tell me about you. He said you ran away from home when you were ten or eleven. You'd understand, he said."

"I was nine, and only got as far as downtown, leaving a trail of clues as distinct as footprints. It was my father who found me in the shoe store, trying to give back the oxfords I'd worn for the first day of school. That was the second day." But her own had been the stunt of a willful child whose mother refused to let her wear saddle shoes because they had less arch support, whereas Val's was the conscious act of a legal adult. "Then what?"

"Then he made me call you immediately to tell you where I was. But I didn't do it."

Audrey's pulse raced. "Did he *think* you did, though? Did you tell him you did?" Nobody had the right to interfere in any parent-child relationship, and who ought to know this better than a teacher?

"Of course! He made me call home every other day, which is what I told him I did. He made me call my adviser too, which I did. Had to, because Neil was offering to tell him I'd be working in his classroom, on a project he and I designed together. The project was getting his kids to write a bunch of songs that they made into an opera, which became the subject of the research paper I just turned in. Which is what got me so worried this week, because for the absolute first time in my academic life, I cared."

Val shrugged her shoulders as she said, "I needed the freedom. I needed to get the hell out of Ohio for a minute, that's all." But she recalled all too well her terror when she arrived at the Port Authority Bus Terminal and was pressed up against the tile wall of the bathroom by a woman who demanded a cigarette or a dollar and, when Val gave her the dollar, demanded another. "So you can relax, Mom," Val said ineffectively.

"No, I can't." Audrey pushed her feet against the floor like a swimmer at the bottom of the deep end, out of breath, pressing herself toward the surface of the water.

And so did Val. Together they got up from their chairs to close the space with such a tight embrace, their two heartbeats bumped into each other like hands clapping.

PART TWO

5

GOOD FRIDAY and Passover overlapped this year, so on Overlook Road two houses stood empty, because Sheila and Herb Golden and Lou and Betty Brown always stayed away in their winter homes in Florida and Arizona until just after their respective holidays. These parallel schedules were determined by this night's first full moon after the spring equinox, a triangular convergence with paganism that seemed suited to these multicultural times. In a lighted dining room tonight, one family would eat ritual foods symbolic of ancient suffering, while in the front yard of the house next door, in the worship of commerce, dozens of gaudy plastic gumdrop-like eggs would be hung on ribbons from the branches of a gray birch. Now that the forsythia was in full flower, those bushes looked less like balls of string. The daffodils were open too, but, for fully secular reasons, it was the sun, not the moon, by which they were oriented.

From where he stood, Gregory saw that a crew was at work in the Goldens' yard, getting it ready for their return by raking up winter debris. At the Browns', the driveway was taken up by a large UPS truck, delivering to a housekeeper the boxes the Browns had sent slightly ahead of their own departure. The neighborhood was coming back to life and would turn fully green, given the right temperature.

Perhaps he was taking a cue from the season, permitting himself to feel rejuvenated. Having complained to Audrey that her plan ruined his of riding off into the sunset, he had to admit that he was looking pretty fickle. Only a week ago, as he prepared to spend last Saturday morning with Joel and Danny, he'd felt like celebrating his old age by getting still older. During his career he'd never taken it for granted that he'd live to get the chance to redeem his pension, and suddenly, presented with Audrey's alternative, he'd imagined himself keeping up with his Yale classmates (many of whom had new wives younger than Karen) by taking in the world from the smartly varnished teak deck of the *Sea Cloud*.

Now he brought the newspapers into the kitchen and scanned the *Plain Dealer* with two unrelated hopes: an idea for today's outing with the boys, and to make sure his week's most dispiriting legal case hadn't made its way into the paper. It was bad enough, without added publicity, to have had to dismiss a case because of an abuse of the spousal-privilege provision. What the court didn't need was a write-up that could only make the system look, in a word, stupid.

The prosecutor's case was based on the driver's willingness to describe for the jury the argument she and her boyfriend were having when he lunged at her and grabbed the wheel as she was accelerating from a full stop for a red light. An eyewitness saw the car veer into oncoming traffic and heard him shout at her in some unidentified language other than English, but in order to prosecute him, there needed to be evidence linking causes and effects. The woman had apparently told her lawyer that she and the boyfriend were no longer seeing each other, despite the fact that they'd been together for several years and may have had at least one child. Now married, however—quickly, last week, without notice—she no longer could be forced to testify against him, so she refused. Gregory had no choice but to dismiss the case.

To the jury he had offered his own set of assurances that,

though obviously imperfect, a system erring on the side of privacy was preferable to the potential abuses of a system without confidentiality privileges. Spousal privilege was in his view as sacred as the other exclusions—the trust maintained by doctor or clergy or journalist or attorney—but there were no excuses for any false manipulation of the system. Judge Brennan had sharply warned the newlyweds, as well as their lawyers, who both insisted they'd never advised their clients to marry as a way to get around the law, that if there was any evidence that this marriage was a fraud, the charges could, and surely would, be instantly refiled. "Need I remind you," he'd sternly rebuked them, "that, no matter what may have been the cause of this accident, the victim is no less dead."

The outcome had greatly displeased Marjorie McCarthy, who had never married but who'd never have married a violent man, not to mention having an out-of-wedlock child. Nevertheless, to protect the dignity of the court, Gregory knew that Marjorie would also be checking the newspaper to make sure there had been no mention of that trial. She was no fool, so she didn't want him to look foolish either.

Next he studied the *Plain Dealer*'s suggestions of ways to spend his second Saturday in a row with Joel and Danny Wallace. His hope was to persuade their mother to come along, to escape the ridiculous ritual preparations—eggs dyed in jellybean colors, arranged in cellophane-grass nests—of their first family holiday without Rob. Gregory remembered nine years back, to the Easter after Audrey's father's death, when Celia was unable to permit anyone else to occupy Jack's chair. It would have been better if they'd all pretended that day was no different from any other day. If, say, they'd looked in the newspaper to find a better idea.

In today's there was a feature about the Museum of Natural History's elaborate new "PLANET e" world, which begins, like the actual world, with a Big Bang. The problem was, it prided itself on being "interactive," and although this was of value for restless boys, a young widow might feel she'd already had to confront the earth's fiery core. More fun would be a touring world-class magician who was capable of fooling anybody with unimaginable tricks. Or—but no—the Rock and Roll Hall of Fame would be too chaotic on the Saturday morning of a big weekend. When Gregory scanned the theater listings he realized his ideal in the revival of *Peter Pan* at the Playhouse Square Center. He dialed the automated ticketing system and ordered four for the matinee because, on the best night of his life, Judge and Mrs. Osborne had taken him and Charles all the way to Broadway to see Mary Martin crow better than a cock while flying without wings.

He thought Karen would be able to understand his wish to relive the memory of his place in the Osborne family before their own tragedy. Already, he felt this close to Karen. Realistically, though, he admitted to himself that she would need convincing to come along, since the whole point was his being a surrogate father to her sons. He'd called her only once this week, to reiterate the sincerity of his standing offer for Saturday mornings, but all week Karen had crossed his thoughts like swallows—elegantly, voraciously—sweeping the sky free of insects. No, the grace was entirely hers, the hunger his.

He took a bowl from the cupboard and was about to reach for the Cheerios he ate for his heart when he had a better idea. Instead of merely fixing himself an ordinary breakfast, why not arrive in Karen's kitchen with a box of giant fresh-baked frosted cinnamon buns? Celia's cinnamon rolls were considered to be the best—hers weren't frosted but were so soft and sticky the grandchildren had to be persuaded to share with the adults—but commercial buns were probably irresistible too. His stomach rumbled with the thought. The more difficult question was what kind of hunger this tugging in his stomach was all about.

Like all desires, this one was involuntary, so, as if it were an erotic dream, he knew better than to disavow it altogether. Fully awake, he was dreaming himself onto the wide screen of a cinema complex—himself playing Judge Osborne, as himself—in what looked to him to be such a blatant fantasy, it seemed as harmless as conjuring up conversations between his sad mother and the man of her dreams. What harm could there be in reinventing Judge Osborne as the person he could well have been: a man in an unhappy marriage to a woman who buried herself alive with the body of her son; a man who would have been much happier with Gregory's sweet mother, whose life he could have saved in the process; a man who might have been a real hero. What was the imagination for, if not to set the world right at last, reversing every wrong? Well? This wasn't completely unlike his day job.

Gregory recognized that he was also permitting himself to blur the distinction between his mother and Karen, but only in the good cause of the welfare of her sons, who each deserved the benefit of every doubt. Nevertheless, he had to admit that he'd dressed more carefully this morning than last Saturday, when all he remembered about his clothes was that, in an effort to look casual, he had taken off his necktie. Today he wore a brown and gray tweed cashmere sport jacket over a russet-colored cashmere turtleneck sweater, gray flannel slacks, and precisely matched socks tucked into new penny loafers that, like him, aspired to look classic yet modern. With his polished exterior, no one could get the impression that, inside, he was too nervous.

In the real world it was nice and sunny and the sky was the color called French blue, notwithstanding the fact that on maps the dotted-line border with Canada, Cleveland's weather source, was no more than a few miles offshore. Gregory prepared for the worst by tossing into the trunk a coat and boots worthy of space walks. He would take the long way, to see whether the cherry trees at Severance Hall were in bloom, and swing by the Rockefeller City Greenhouse to glimpse spring being forced under glass roofs in displays brimming with trumpety white lilies. The genius of the great-grandfather, the original John D., who'd lived in the neighborhood and worked downtown in his brown iron building at the other end of Euclid, was in providing what he termed a "standard" fuel that, for the first time, could be relied on never to catch fire by accident. Say what you will about the man, in Gregory's opinion he could do no wrong, having started out in business motivated by the desire to make people feel more secure.

What a great place! The Cultural Gardens equally celebrated Booker T. and George Washington. On a nearby corner lived the city's Mayor White, a black man, as, obversely, the Supreme Court's Justice Black had been white. Gregory loved this town for having been a port city for slaves escaping from Kentucky and a destination for "Western Reserve of Connecticut" settlers on land costing forty cents an acre. It was a land of opportunity, historically, which had also made a recent, amazing comeback. As opposed to New York, where work consisted of pushing buttons, here people manufactured goods, to be carried off on mile-long freight trains. No wonder he felt he'd been turned under, like the rich earth beneath his feet. Now he had a mission as well: making sure Rob's boys wouldn't want to move away from their mother.

He himself had been caught between his mother's needs and Judge Osborne's displaced ambitions for his Charles, who would have better satisfied his father's wishes than Gregory could ever prove capable. Through college and law school he'd kept up by overcompensating, but once in the Wall Street big leagues he'd admitted, first to himself and then, one difficult afternoon, to Judge Osborne, that his being good enough at his work to be considered to have some promise wasn't the same as loving it. He'd only wanted to come home and become a small-time lawyer, and maybe consider standing for election to the Court of Common Pleas. Ironically—if that could be called the right word for a far greater failure of promise than his own—Rob Wallace had seemed destined for the higher courts, perhaps ultimately a federal judgeship or a seat on the Ohio Supreme Court. Not that Rob's failure was ever for a minute voluntary.

Gregory was never envious of Rob's clear talent, because one of Rob's skills was his absolute tolerance for everyone. Therefore, he was capable of celebrating each person independently, which was why Gregory always felt Rob's support without any hint of thinking less well of him for having, in some eyes, squandered the opportunities he'd had. There was no telling what Rob could have made of these chances he had passed up. Now, too, there was no way of knowing.

Joel answered the doorbell and Danny came running from his cartoons. The cinnamon buns happened to be their favorite treat, and although they'd only vaguely heard of *Peter Pan* (the movie, not the play), what could possibly be wrong with an adventure story about a boy who lived in a world without any girls? Before Gregory got his chance to invite their mother along, they decided there should be no women either.

Later, though, he got his chance to sit with Karen on the same couch. She'd spent the day covering the surface of the dining room table with laundry folded into fewer piles than before, but which still included Rob's pajama tops because she wore them, and assumed she always would, as nightgowns. She'd made herself open Rob's bureau drawers in order to wash his favorite sweaters, to pack them away with mothballs for when the boys were old enough. The sweater of his she wore now was the same color as Rob's amber eyes, and although she'd rolled up the sleeves it was still so big on her she looked again like a girl playing dress-up, this time in her dad's clothes. She'd washed her hair. It was still wet. To Gregory it seemed she'd washed ashore, shipwrecked. He wanted to be the one to save her. Or, better yet, to be marooned on a tropical island, only the two of them. He knew how unhelpful it was of him to want her to join him in scenes from old movies set in another hemisphere, but he figured that as long as she couldn't read his mind, there was cause for neither harm nor alarm.

"Herbal tea okay?"

He said, "Good," though he'd rather have had a beer. He followed her to the kitchen like the puppy the boys wanted, glad for the excuse, back in the living room, to move from the chair onto the couch.

She retreated into the far corner of it, doubling up her legs like wire fencing. "Thanks for taking the boys." Because of school, the only chance she ever got to be alone was in the middle of the night, when it wasn't possible, without the neighbors calling the police, to stand under the shower and scream like the victim of the most obscene crime. That's how she'd spent this past hour, which was why she could barely keep her eyes open.

"Danny was disappointed that it was Cathy Rigby when it could have been a guy. I never looked at it that way before, but of course he's correct. Why was it, I wonder, that Mary Martin was cast as Peter in the first place?" He set his mug on the table, on an upside-down magazine in place of a coaster.

Karen regarded Gregory across the steaming top of her own mug. Because, as a math teacher, she was above all else pragmatic, she said, "That was before my time, but I assume it would be because no one was a bigger star."

"You must be right," he decided with a smile, "and so it would have to be a woman for all time."

"Not necessarily," she said.

"You're right, of course. Again." They weren't arguing about this, he hoped. "We're not disagreeing, are we?"

"Well, yes, we are." She shrugged, since it didn't matter to her one way or the other.

"I get contradicted all the time, as a man in a family with three women. You must know the feeling." Oh, no. By mistake he'd alluded to Rob's death.

But Karen said, "I'm used to it, from teaching in an all-boys school." Did he think he'd get her to complain about being a woman? In the context of loss, gender was meaningless. Or, at the moment, as his discomfort in her presence seemed to prove, merely annoying.

Gregory couldn't think of a reply, so he said, "I'm very, very sorry."

And they sat in silence until Karen quietly said, "I'm so sad today I don't know what to do about it," and pulled her rope of a body into an even tighter knot. It defeated her. She'd have to get through the rest of the school year before people would stop making impossible requests of her, such as SAT scores that would get average boys into the colleges their irrational parents had chosen for them. She had no time for her own boys' applications to the summer programs she couldn't afford for them anyway, not that she could afford to let them out of her sight even overnight. "I can't manage, some days."

He felt a kind of joy in her willingness to confide in him, no matter that she seemed to be refusing to make eye contact. Gently, he said, "I very much want to help you. May I? Will you let me?"

But she told him he already was helping her out a lot, with the boys. Warily, she left it at that, because there were others, including two of her teaching colleagues, who apparently felt that without Rob around to appreciate her, they should. What they didn't know was that she and Rob had their code words. They'd never break that code.

"No," he said, "I mean help you, now, in addition to them." He couldn't quite reach her hand with his own, so he had to settle for bridging the space to some extent, by placing his hand, palm up, like a shallow bowl, on the blue cushion between them. His true age would be revealed by the veined back of that hand, but even this more protected underside looked mottled. Could she read his palm? Where was the lifeline? What if he didn't have one?

She let the long sleeves fall over her wrists, so her hands disappeared altogether. If he was coming on to her, like those others, she could only laugh at the preposterous thought, first, and then tell him he really ought to be ashamed of himself, a married man who was—she'd done the math—practically twice her age.

"Financially," he improvised, as if in the meantime he'd found the moneyline.

"What?" Her voice rang with the authority of a teacher catching a student in an obvious lie.

"Help out a bit," Gregory said lamely, pretending he'd meant that in the first place. He was sure there wasn't this confusion when Judge Osborne approached his mother with his similar offer of help. That is, unless that too was laced with an older man's desire for a woman who had the power to make him feel more— well, yes, this was the real issue—manly. He felt exposed: the poor sap on *Candid Camera* or, worse, the criminal caught in the act by an FBI sting.

Coolly she said, "If you're talking about money, we're fine." But the distress Karen felt was acute. Gregory too? Why was it that in these five weeks, so many men felt entitled—uninvited, unwelcomed—to act like her personally designated rescuers? Or, rather, to try to *pretend* to rescue her when what they really wanted was to possess her.

"You misunderstood me," he tried to convince her. But it was, clearly, only his vanity.

So Karen decided to let him believe her when she responded, "Oh? Okay." At least he wasn't as clumsy as most of the others, one of whom actually told her—talk about blaming the victim— she was so vulnerable, she was profoundly, irresistibly sexy. Sexier than ever, he'd insisted, as if complimenting her for succeeding in her grief where all the other ordinary widows failed.

"That is, please believe that I don't mean to make it your fault, misunderstanding me. It's completely my fault, and I apologize." Now he felt the nausea of fearing for his life, as if falling into an abandoned well with slimy mossy walls. He could barely see the sky, and she was definitely not peering down at him with concern. It was all he could do to keep from calling for help.

"Don't worry about it," she said, to reward him, like a teacher, for his honest effort.

"But I will worry, I know," he said with a winning smile,

"since I already do!" He uncrossed his legs and stood up, feeling them give a bit and wondering if he might actually fall flat on his face. "I'd better get going." He hated herbal tea, which now he knew for sure as well. Just as falsely as everything else he'd just said, he told Karen, "Thanks for the tea."

When she said "You're welcome," she was no more sincere.

Val had taken the bus home for the holiday weekend and, met at the terminal by Audrey, had suggested stopping off at Tower City to check the shops. Across a café table, she'd told her mother she'd recently met "somebody." He was in a band too, she'd said, and for the moment that was all she would be willing to divulge. But her eyes were sparklers, and her speech was interrupted by the sighs of the sleep-deprived. Later, in the kitchen while faux-marbleizing a dozen eggs, they'd listened to music that combined comprehensible lyrics with reckless instrumentation, a demo tape of the very band in question. Its name was Road Show. His was Rex. Val wasn't sure of his last name.

Sally had gone for a long run and was back now, running in place in the middle of the kitchen so that, before making it into her hot shower, she wouldn't seize up like a car engine. Neither of the other two cared to imagine what it would be like to have a body like hers, requiring constant maintenance.

Gregory returned to this mix and was greeted as if he were a *BBC News Hour* broadcast: no detail too remote for them. Like a reporter, too, he protected sources by telling only a portion of the story, but with the effect that he felt smart and funny as he described his trip to Never-Never Land. His daughters were the right age to have had the benefit of the Disney animated version and had already been exposed to evil Captain Hook. But even their childhood experience was by now relatively ancient history. He felt as if, like Peter, he had just barely escaped near-certain death.

Val took over, saying, "Now that you're all here, I've got news for you. Ready?" She stood up, striding to silence the music, turning in place theatrically, so that the far greater effect than of her bruised face was of her purposefulness.

Sally's face clouded, however, as she scrutinized Val. All last year, whenever the family was gathered at this kitchen table, Val had been high. Night after night she'd sat here as if in an observation booth, a nonparticipant no matter how hard the others would each be trying to engage her. When asked about her day at school, one night she'd announced that she'd changed her name from Valerie to Valedictorian, which made her, and only her, laugh. "Who could blame me for being a misfit," she'd challenged bitterly, "when I come from a family with no sense of humor." This would be when Sally would ask to be excused from the table.

Val said, "I know you're used to me as a failure. And, frankly, so was I. But, as I just said, I've got news." The whites of her eyes were so clear, nobody could doubt her.

And anyway, Sally was finally inclined to give her sister the benefit of the doubt. This had been an awful week for a couple of her best friends whose first-choice colleges sent rejection letters. Sally was hoping Val could advise her about consoling them, since Val had had the same experience. Sally was so solemnly respectful, for once, she wasn't exercising a single one of her more than six hundred muscles.

This didn't escape Val's notice. "Well, I hate to say it because everybody told me this too, but the fact is, everything, even failure, is an opportunity." Returning to her place at the table, Val winked at Audrey to show that her right eye had sufficiently healed, then continued, telling Sally, "You can quote me." To her father she said, "I know I haven't exactly been a model of perfect behavior, especially not last week, but listen up. You're about to hear me say the word 'success' now, for the first time ever." Val paused. She would have imitated a drum roll, but her healing jaw wasn't flexible enough for that. "Imagine a trumpet fanfare," she invited, "hear-ye-hear-ye–type thing."

Now Audrey was worried Val might be high, but Val distracted her with words Audrey couldn't believe she'd heard. "You what?"

"I got an A on my research paper about opera," Val said again. Actually, it would have been fun to be just a little high right now, to watch each of them react.

Sally first, by leaping into the air with enough noise for a whole team. "You *see?* You *see!* It's never over until it's over, *is* it?" She lifted Val's chair off the floor, with Val in it. This was what Sally meant the other night by a normal family!

Gregory's response overcame the fact that once again he hadn't been clued in. This time at least he could be wholly enthusiastic, and was.

Audrey felt a disappointment she couldn't quite articulate, which had to do with Val's not having confided her ambitions. If she had, wouldn't they have given her their unconditional support? Couldn't Val have used it? Audrey's immediate reaction was muted by this realization that Val had deprived herself of their support the same way she herself had. But while this worried her enough to make her feel sad, Audrey refused to cause Val to feel, rather than celebrated for having told them, punished for not having told them sooner. Audrey threw her arms around Val as she said, "Congratulations!"

And now came the fun part, when Val got to tell them what it felt like to stay up all night because she couldn't quit learning about the amazing relationship between story and song. She never knew, just for one little example, that the impulse to subvert was both ancient and honorable. It was her idea to call her paper "People's Opera" and combine the research with the tapes she'd made of Neil's kids turning their personal stories into songs, but her professor really got into it too, Val said, and wanted her to consider being a music major. "As if," Val said, "it would be a toss-up between music and, say, astrophysics!" The bruise had evolved from purple to blue-black to a yellowish gray, so half of Val's face, like a hit song, looked gold-plated.

In the court system Gregory witnessed rehabilitation in cases where he wouldn't have predicted it, and vice versa. Though he hated to admit it, until now he hadn't ever been completely surprised by Val. "I've been wanting to surprise you one day," she said, to which he responded, no matter that it wasn't wholly true, "I knew you would."

"The anxiety got to me last week," Val said. "I got back in touch with last year and doubted myself. It was such a bad feeling because this time, unlike last year, I felt I deserved to do well. But I didn't believe I could." And then she said, "Last week I couldn't bear to tell my adviser about the accident, in case he told my professor, who'd know how irresponsible I am. So it meant everything to me to be able to hang out here, waiting it out. I never had that experience of home as a sanctuary, which is why I wanted to be here to tell the three of you, in person, all together, that at last I finally got some good news." Not even Neil knew yet, which was saying something.

Sally demonstrated a genuine deference to the complexity of her sister's life compared to her own. Her own triumphs had been earned too, but hers weren't complicated by self-doubt. Because hers was such an easier way to live, she hadn't understood why it wasn't the same for everyone. Who would choose problems when there were so many solutions out there? As a result, she'd thought of Val as deliberately lazy. As a hardworking athlete, that was the one thing Sally hated. Now she bestowed her highest praise. "I admire you for turning a loss into a win."

Then Sally asked Val if she'd mind talking to a few of her friends who'd benefit from learning to deal with their disappointment. Val knew from this experience that failures overturned by successes are like the soil of spoiled land, needing more nourishment than would seem necessary to someone who doesn't know the first thing about gardening. From her mother, in the plot they'd worked together on the land rescued by the

Community Gardens Initiative, Val had learned that the mere act of turning over the earth was just the beginning, and that in itself was straining. "Sure," she said, "invite them over. Group therapy."

Val didn't believe these three couldn't entirely identify, since they'd never been genuinely surprised by their successes. Sally expected to remain undefeated her whole life, the way time after time her father ran unopposed. Not even her mother—and, really, who else's mother would have dared to want to be a doctor when in the same amount of time she could become a full-time grandmother instead?—not even Audrey seemed to be aware of the odds against Val's becoming a serious student.

Val grinned at the thought of herself as some sort of demonstration plot in the community garden. She laughed. What wouldn't grow now?

Their invitation to dinner was to the apartment of a much younger colleague of Audrey's, a resident married to another resident who'd recently given birth. Because Gregory admitted that he'd have preferred to skip it, Audrey was flattering him by saying, "You're good to be so attentive, and I'm sure Karen is extremely grateful." She was drying her hair, so her voice was raised to outdo the volume of the small appliance. "And thank you for being willing to come tonight," she half shouted at him, making him feel guilty.

Gregory didn't attempt to reply, but he noticed she wore a dress he hadn't seen before, which appeared to be a size smaller than anything she'd worn in the past several years. It had seams his dressmaker mother had called darts, where the fabric could be eased to follow the female form, fitting the rib cage while flaring to showcase the line of the breast. This had been Gregory's first anatomy lesson, the afternoon his mother caught him in the small bedroom that doubled as her sewing room, examining the padded standing dress form with his hands. With her arms raised, Audrey seemed to be offering the top half of her body to him. The fabric was slinky too, and the color of a very fine chocolate.

"No?" She incorrectly interpreted his look. Having quieted the hair dryer so abruptly, she left a larger void than the shrill noise had contained. Though the purpose of the shopping errand had been merely to find something for Val to wear to church the next morning with her grandmother, Val had talked her into the dress.

"Not at all. Yes." It was sophisticated enough for Paris.

She stepped toward him. "Good. Then could you cut off the tag? I needed you to help decide." She turned her back to him and over her shoulder handed him the little pair of scissors from the medicine chest. Tipping her head forward, she exposed the clasp of her beads, which, like everything else, started out small and got bigger.

He pressed his mouth against the place just above the clasp, at the base of her skull. Her shampoo was new too, he thought, but here he could be wrong. He was.

She leaned against him nevertheless, so that, if he wished to, he could touch her. He did. "Val told me she has a boyfriend." Audrey hoped Val's Rex was worthy of her, wondered what kind of parent would name a child Rex, hoped it was some kind of stage name, wondered if they'd had sex.

"Will she introduce this one to us? Celia could take him to the club and we could interview him." He kissed her neck again. And yet, still, Gregory permitted himself a fragment of an interruption, which was like a single note of a song on the radio of a passing car, an image as unrepresentational as an out-of-focus photograph. It wasn't a deliberate thought—Karen on her couch, in profile, her face in her hands, the back of her longer, thinner neck exposed like a wild bird's—but it came and went away like a trained pickpocket who will be long gone before you notice you're missing anything.

"Don't stop," she said.

Without that flash across the screen of his own mind, he could have imagined pulling the zipper the length of her spine, or, more aggressively, using those scissors of hers to cut all their clothes away. But he couldn't. He'd ruined it. Or Karen had, for him. So he just clipped the tag.

"Good thinking," Audrey said good-naturedly, "since we'll probably be late as it is. You know how it is with psychiatrists, the only doctors for whom the trains always run on time, no matter what."

"No matter what chaos," he said, feeling exposed, "at the station."

"They're both still in training, though, so we don't have to worry as much." Audrey turned in place, to face him. "And anyway, we're not worrying about Val for once, so we can be completely honest when we admire their new baby and agree how rewarding it is to have a child." She touched the meticulous knot of his necktie with her left hand as, intending to kiss her manicured fingers, instead he kissed her wedding ring. She was about to say she couldn't imagine being a new parent and a resident married to another resident, but she didn't want to bring into this moment the inhuman demands imposed by medical training, when in fact she almost wished she'd never had the idea. "I love you," she told him in a tone that said she meant every word.

Then, in the car, because either Danny or Joel had moved Gregory's passenger seat to the laid-back angle of a patio chair, he adjusted it for Audrey while hovering over her. It occurred to him to ask if they couldn't stay home tonight, but he knew she'd have to say no, as he'd have if they'd been invited by a younger associate of his.

"What is it?" she asked.

But if he were to tell the whole truth, he'd have to admit now to the sudden adjacent memory of what must have been his and Audrey's first meal at Rob and Karen's dining room table. Karen was pregnant, but all Gregory noticed about her was that she didn't trouble to disguise her rudely obvious yawns, for which

Rob had apologized the next morning. Identifying with Karen, Gregory answered Audrey, if only somewhat accurately, "I was only wondering how soon we can leave the party." And, since they were still in their own driveway, she laughed.

As they headed down the hill from their house and passed the university, Gregory discovered himself admitting that the commute to medical school would undeniably be convenient. As he found himself with this thought, he naturally wondered what it might mean—his belated acceptance and/or support of Audrey? his own change of mind about the future he anticipated?—but decided not to ask Audrey what she thought, since they were already at the curb in front of the apartment building. On the sidewalk, he asked, "Is it just us?"

"That this feels like so long ago in our own lives?" Their first apartment was a house, though, since when they were newly married they were, as their respective peers considered them, established.

"That too, but I meant will we be the only guests?" Their first table could seat six at most, but now their dining room had fourteen chairs lining the walls like a fleet of museum guards.

She said, "I believe so. Anyway, their baby's only a few months old, so it can be an early night for sure." If that was what he meant.

"And which one of them, again, is it you work with?"

"Him. Jeffrey. And her name is Virginia." They were buzzed in immediately, as if their approach had been observed, including Gregory going back to the car for the good bottle of wine he'd forgotten in the back seat and which he carried by its neck like a tennis racket. Audrey carried, like the baby it was intended for, a box the size of the tiny moccasins Val had helped her to select at Tower City.

Everything in the apartment looked brand-new, including their round-faced daughter, who showed her gums to Gregory and reached for his pretty necktie, which, at Jeffrey's recommendation, he slipped into the pocket of the jacket he also willingly gave up at the door. Their hosts were close enough to their college years to dress down whenever it wasn't required to dress up.

"Thank you!" the new parents enthused, as together they opened their baby's present.

"Tiger Lily," Gregory guessed.

But Audrey corrected him: "Sacagawea." The tag proved it, providing a mini-history of the heroic Shoshone interpreter-guide. "Hardly show biz," Audrey added, but in a matter-of-fact way.

"Whatever," Gregory said self-mockingly, imitating kids. He ignored his impulse to explain why Tiger Lily had occurred to him rather than the real-life Sacagawea. And it was good he did, because evidently he had insulted nobody. As opposed to Karen, whom he could imagine being offended by his reliance on the lowest common denominator, it was clear that these people were willing to credit him for his good intentions. Even while he wondered whether Karen also disapproved of his selection of *Peter Pan*, these other three had moved on to another subject altogether.

Gregory felt himself relent into enjoying the promise of an evening out without having to worry about the impression he might make. He relaxed into the intimacy of this little apartment where the dining room table was mostly used as a desk. Besides, their baby was so constantly in someone's arms—his own at the moment—she had no need for moccasins, since her feet would never touch the ground.

The table was set, but for five. Louise Schneider was the answer to the question who else, and the answer to Gregory's other question was apparently not: Audrey's surprise seemed authentic. Then, when Louise leaned close enough to greet Gregory with a polite kiss, the baby, who was still in his arms, grasped her pearl necklace, providing them the chance to turn the other cheek.

Workplace gossip dominated, but, Gregory noticed, unlike

among his own colleagues, it took the form more of problem-solving than one-upping. Nobody said, "Listen to this, here's a good one," daring everybody to have a better one.

At a certain point when the talk grew more serious, Virginia "presented" a case. She was troubled by what she felt to be her inadequate response the day before to the teenager whose parents dragged her in, at nine months pregnant, complaining that whenever they asked to know what she was going to do about the baby, she'd only close her eyes and mouth and cover her ears with her hands. "Get her to say something," they demanded, but all Virginia got her to say was "When I know myself, you'll find out."

The table's centerpiece was the Catalan paella pan whose combined ingredients were arranged as if by Picasso in a display of saturated and impassioned color. Everyone took the equivalent of second or third helpings, and kept adding one last mussel or morsel of sausage available only either back in Barcelona or here at the West Side Market. "Not in any cookbook," said the grandson of the one who'd almost starved without the recipe when he first came to America. "Family secret."

"Every family has its secrets," Gregory said, intending to cue Virginia to continue. Because he feared being asked to expose his own secret, with his free hand he helped himself to yet more of the saffron rice.

Virginia persisted, "All I could think to say to her was let's talk about that, which was when she told me there was nothing to say. So I broke a rule." Virginia opened her eyes wide to receive whatever wisdom or blame might come her way. "I did all the talking."

"Good!" said Louise. "And?"

"She agreed at the end of the hour to make another appointment for the day after tomorrow." Here was the catch. "But by now she's already a few days overdue, so what if the baby is born this weekend?"

No one was sure which of the many possible good questions

she might be asking. In the meantime, Virginia burst into tears, unable to imagine *not* being capable, for whatever reason, including denial, of having a full-term baby with no forethought.

Finally Jeffrey knew what to say, which was that although it was clear the young woman didn't want to talk about it, she could well have *thought* about it. More directly helpful was the way he put his hand on her hand.

And Audrey said, "When I think about our Helena at Metro, who sometimes prepares all day long for an appointment she then misses, how can we really know what's going on, or how to help? Isn't it true that all we can do is be there in case something happens or someone says something?" She asked Virginia what she'd said.

"All the wrong things." Virginia pulled a Kleenex from the pocket of her hyacinth-blue velvet shirt and, like somebody with a bad cold, blew her nose. "But can you imagine? She'd refused to attend childbirth preparation classes! Jeffrey and I learned so much at ours, and look how much we already knew about what could happen. It makes me feel so *sad* for her."

"For the baby too," said Jeffrey, "and the father."

"And the girl's parents," Gregory added as his own point of identification.

Virginia said, "I gave her my pager number," addressing Louise as the one with seniority, "and I know that wasn't right."

"Not wrong, naïve," Louise replied. "But once I'd have done the same thing. It's that awful fear of not being indispensable." She'd been a physician as many years as Virginia had been alive, so no wonder she knew better. "It's that terrible sense that the worst could happen."

"Yes!"

"When, in fact, so could the best?" This was Audrey's contribution.

"You see how good you are at this?" This time Louise turned toward Gregory to say, "She's a natural. The way you are with this baby."

He said, "So you can perhaps ignore all the terrible things you've heard about me?" He didn't know where this came from, but before he could take it back, she'd answered it.

"Yes, because it's also my fault, since I gave Audrey the idea in the first place—not of not telling you, so don't worry—of going ahead and applying and, later on, waiting and seeing. I told her to think it over, but I also said she was under no obligation to discuss it, not with me or you or anyone else." Louise shrugged her shoulders as she said, "So sue me."

"Don't assume," he said, "I haven't thought about it." When he laughed, the baby loved it.

Louise saw the bewilderment in their hosts' eyes, so she explained, "She's beginning medical school," and both Jeffrey and Virginia said, "Wonderful!" Jeffrey added, "I wondered before chilling the champagne if anyone drinks champagne anymore." Anyone a little older, was what he meant.

For Audrey this second wind was primarily a renewal of the spirit, but luckily the flesh wasn't entirely weak. Last week's all-nighter may have been unusual in the recent years of her regular schedule at Metro, but she'd found it wasn't so terrible to be alert enough to be of some genuine use. And as a daily last resort, a tube of Erase would come in handy, according to another "nontraditional" medical school student whose once larger brown eyes had receded (not unlike the hairlines of her male counterparts) due to her concentric circles emblematic of chronic fatigue. "I'll think of my eyes as closer to the brain now," she'd reported resourcefully.

"Are you up for celebrating this, Your Honor?" Louise asked Gregory mischievously, while giving him a chance to redeem himself in her eyes.

He was already feeling that he'd had more than enough to drink. And in fact his thoughts had moved to Audrey's pregnancies, because both times she'd had the news confirmed in appointments she'd scheduled so she could come to the courthouse during the noon recess to tell him right away and in person. Both times she'd been waiting for him in his chambers, and both times they'd wept like babies, like Virginia, about the fearsome privilege of having a child. If Audrey had thought herself entitled to have kept that news from him because she thought it was exclusively hers, then he could have been justified in reacting so selfishly. He ignored Louise a moment longer in order to appreciate Audrey, who was more beautiful in brown, he decided now, than any other color. Finally he answered the question with a firm "Yes."

"Then the law *is* perfect justice," Louise complimented him. Her next, more technical question was why the system punishes doctors as if their mistakes were committed with deliberation.

The plates were cleared and, as promised, champagne rushed up the sides of flutes that had been a wedding present. Gregory was aware of having had more to drink than any of the others, but everything lately seemed to require huge effort. He improvised a suitably pompous reply, seeking to prove to her that the law is the poor creation, so the province, of mere mortals, whereas science, being infallible, is blah blah blah something or other, and so on. All he meant was how rare it seemed to be in his own profession to hear any authentic talk about human service, unlike these people who, all jokes and complaints aside, honestly hoped to help out and, he saw, weren't too cynical to admit it. He told them this. Was he drunk? Perhaps a little.

At the same time Gregory bounced the baby on his knee while remembering how impossible it was to string two thoughts together when a darling child wants 100 percent of your attention.

Audrey drove home, and as they went from the garage into the kitchen Gregory took two Rolling Rocks from the refrigerator. "No thanks," she said, but he'd already opened both bottles.

In the next room Val sat in her father's favorite chair to preside over a few of Sally's friends, who sat silent as acolytes. Gregory leaned against the wall, listening in. The ceiling light emphasized the folds in his face, but like a boy he opened his mouth and poured the beer into it. With the charmed baby he'd been like a grandfather, but now it was as if he felt a need to show off for the girls. These conflicting presentations could have converged to steady him, but they didn't. He rolled up his sleeves, then he undid a shirt button, as if anyone, including his wife, cared to see his chest. He was just trying to catch up with them, so he wouldn't feel so extraneous. "Isn't it a wonderful thing to start over?" he asked. He was regarding Val with a tender pride, so she felt obliged to say something. "Sure, Dad."

Audrey supposed that, technically, it was still possible for her to want to start over in the sense of having another child. And, in terms of age anyway, hadn't Gregory been close to her age when they had their children? But his example didn't help, because of his simple advantage as a man. For her as a woman it was impossible to imagine giving birth at the age of a half century, no matter that a lot of old men—young old men, his age—seemed to think nothing about it. Only last week a retired man from Seattle came in with his child and a third wife young enough to be his granddaughter, who was in town for some sort of job interview. On their way out of their hotel the little boy stumbled and landed on his chin, which was sliced open like a fruit. And because he'd had his thumb in his mouth, his very sharp baby teeth ruined the thumb too, possibly for all time. They'd come to Metro so as not to frighten the boy with an emergency room, where Audrey then directed them because, as anyone could see, the boy required the expert services of a plastic surgeon.

Gregory drained the first bottle and, since he'd already opened it, picked up the second. Audrey moved closer to the hallway door but didn't go upstairs, in case he might get the wrong idea that she was going on ahead to prepare to have sex with him. In this roomful of women, he seemed to think himself the centerpiece rather than the odd man out.

Sometimes, when he'd had this much to drink, he'd be so

greedy with need he was like one of those keyboard synthesizers with an array of canned rhythms—cha-cha, bossa nova, jazz, rock—playing itself. This was an unkind characterization of him, Audrey knew, but it wasn't as if she'd invented the concept of female orgasm, even if she *had* introduced it to him. In the beginning, it was almost as if he'd feel obliged to make her precisely that responsive to him, as if he refused to be satisfied without her achieving orgasm too. Those times, it wasn't that she wouldn't, but couldn't (and didn't mind that she couldn't), which he'd seem incapable of understanding until, finally, she'd say that she didn't want him to keep trying; she wanted him to stop, in fact. The reversal was that on those occasions when Gregory didn't seem all that old, she didn't seem all that young.

In the first month after Rob's death, she'd made herself available to Gregory without any regard to reciprocity, but his grief, since it was larger than Rob, seemed to drain him of all desire. If they were to manage to come together, it had a for-old-time's-sake feeling, which admittedly wasn't nothing. Weren't they lucky to have old times? This was what Audrey often told herself in this last month, although she would have preferred to tell him about the struggle of carrying the burden of a concern she couldn't share with him because—as if her demand were greater than he could possibly meet—sleep would overtake him. His spirit would sputter like a candle, and their bedroom would fall into such a darkness that her own breath would quicken, as with fright.

She felt scared now, too, by the mixture of Gregory's alcohol and their anger at causing in each other such real disappointment. In Family Practice she saw examples of the abuse of women who were able to ask for a little professional help only if they believed that, this time for sure, they'd die. Audrey knew she had no right to compare her privileged situation to theirs, but in these past ten days since telling him about medical school, his anger was being expressed in all these unfamiliar ways.

And now? He looked as if he were trying to attract lightning by being the tallest one in the room. "Sit back down," she wanted to say, for his own sake as well as everyone else's.

He appeared to be attempting to show Sally's friends how perfect a Peter Pan he'd be. At least he wasn't standing on his chair, jumping off like an even bigger fool. What Audrey didn't know was that he was really playing Karen, passing off her lines as his own. "It's probably because at the time no one was a bigger star than Mary Martin, which is why she got the part. And from then on, only women got it, no matter that Peter is the original Lost Boy." Maybe that part wasn't what Karen would have said. He didn't know.

"Interesting, Dad," Sally said.

"No, seriously," he argued, "isn't it wrong?"

"Isn't what?" asked Audrey, who could see that the others were embarrassed enough to want to go home. "That the part wasn't given to a guy?"

"Yeah, Dad," Val said. "Who cares?"

The others said they guessed they better get going. "Goodnight, Judge and Mrs. Brennan," they said as they filed past, using their private school manners but, in a lapse, not making eye contact.

Sally followed them out the door but, as if she were the parent, she said, "I'll be right back." She meant, "I'll be right back to deal with you."

Gregory sat. As if he might faint, he leaned out over his knees. "Val, dear, I'm very sorry if I intruded."

"You didn't, Dad."

"But I must have. Look at your mother's face."

It was true that Audrey looked suspicious of him, also concerned. This was no longer an issue of sex. But she didn't recognize it for what it was.

"Don't worry, Dad," said Val, "really. It's no big deal. It's just that nobody our age cares about Peter Pan. I think it's nice you do." She smiled at him in order to camouflage her own urge to laugh. "Seriously." Filling the void, she continued, "But the real test would be Joel and Danny, I guess." She was grinning like a real fool.

"Please don't mock me." He couldn't feel more miserable. Why didn't they stick him on an ice floe and watch him drift away? Why condescend to him? He might be old, but he wasn't senile.

Sally pushed through the door from the garage and said, "What are you, drunk?"

So Audrey said, "Don't be disrespectful."

Val said, "I'm sure Mom didn't let him drive, Sally. You can leave him alone."

But Sally asked him, "Could you *be* any more humiliating?"

Gregory raised his head and looked at each of them, but none was looking back at him. He was unable to hold their gazes, never mind their regard. It was as if he couldn't keep up with them and saw that he was running in place while they all disappeared down the superhighway. They didn't seem to know they had outdistanced him. They didn't know how lost he felt. They didn't see he was missing.

He could be dead. It will be like this when he dies, won't it? They'll go on with their lives without consulting him, without informing him, celebrating all their victories.

"Leave him alone, Sally," Val said. "Leave the poor guy alone."

Audrey asked, "Do you feel all right?"

"No, how could I?" he said, because Val will graduate from college having made her own way, on her own terms, as an honors music major, let's say, and who knows, probably become a career musician, maybe even a famous one. And Sally will graduate from U.Va. as an All-American Atlantic Coast Conference champion athlete. Audrey will become a doctor in spite of the fact that the world needs more nurses, not more doctors, and at this same kitchen table, one day, she'll tell her next husband that the same way her overly conservative father did, her first husband held her back.

"Here, Dad, here's some water." Sally wondered if she ought to pour it over his head.

"Here, Dad." Val offered him a damp dishtowel to press against his forehead. She'd never seen him this bad.

Gregory looked at the three of them and transformed their bewilderment and worry into opposite expressions of enormous optimism: eyes bright with belief in themselves, smiles wide with pride, laughter exploding from their lungs as the simple reflexive byproduct of their ample life's breath. For them it won't be anything like the way it was for him when his father died, because these three won't be worse off.

Not only that. Karen Wallace will remarry too, because, unlike his widowed mother, she won't have lost her trust in men. In him, yes, obviously, but there's a man out there somewhere who will be perfect for Karen. She'll know her sons need a father, and, unlike his mother, she'll be able to obtain one for them. It won't be him.

When Gregory acknowledged this, his hands trembled with the recognition that he must have imagined marrying Karen Wallace and being a father to her sons. He must have imagined himself reincarnated as one of those grandfathers with new babies, impregnating Karen with his chromosomes in order to have a baby to redeem his own misfortunes. It was possible that, while bouncing Virginia and Jeffrey's baby on his knees all evening, holding her, kissing her, tickling her, and getting her to laugh, he'd been thinking of Karen and wishing that she could be the mother—since he could pretend to be the father—of that daughter. It was as if all night he'd been forcibly overachieving, trying to prove himself, but not, as it appeared, to those at that actual table. Instead, he'd been proving himself to a phantom Karen Wallace! He felt deranged. He felt he must have been transparent to those two psychiatrists, who were no doubt discussing him right then, recommending treatment. He felt utterly powerless against these horrible feelings. That afternoon, if Karen had let him — what *wouldn't* he have tried if she'd let him? — he could have told her he loved her!

"What's the matter with Dad?"

"Is he sick?"

"Gregory?" It was as if he had dematerialized. All color was gone from his face. "Are you all right?" Audrey got behind him and slid her arms under his as Sally pulled out the chair so Audrey and Val could guide him onto the floor.

"What's the matter with him, Mom?" Sally had seen the effects of dehydration and heat exhaustion, but she'd never seen a heart attack or a stroke. What if he wasn't drunk in the first place but having some kind of nervous breakdown?

"Is he sick?" Val had seen plenty of binge drinking. "Daddy? Do something, Mom." Was he even breathing?

Audrey checked his pupils and his pulse. He had one.

"*Daddy!*"

Gregory managed to push Audrey's hand away, protesting that he needed neither a doctor nor a nurse. In an earlier age it would have been sufficient to say he'd had a fright.

They all helped him upstairs and Audrey took over, assuring Val and Sally that he'd be better in the morning. He managed to undress himself, and Audrey buttoned his pajama top while taking his temperature. It was normal.

When Audrey was out of his sight, brushing her teeth, Gregory concluded that everything he *thought* he felt about Karen he *really* felt about Audrey instead. She was the only one he'd ever wanted, really, and Karen was merely an expression of that overpowering feeling. He was normal! It was *normal* for a basically contented person like him to want nothing to change! He was drawing back from a precipice he'd been foolishly considering jumping off of. Like some guy on a ledge he'd been rescued, by her. By his wife! By Audrey! He may be drunk, but he wasn't incapable of recognizing he'd been saved from himself.

She, meanwhile, was hoping he'd fallen over the edge, but only into a dead-to-the-world sleep from which he wouldn't awaken until it was time to go to church, then on to her mother's house, where, it was a safe bet, Celia wouldn't bring up medical school, or anything controversial. That was all Audrey asked: just to get through the next however many hours while she figured out whether his behavior was caused by arrogance or insecurity. If those were the right choices.

He'd have thought it impossible. Alcohol and sex, in his limited experience, never made for a very effective combination, so he was surprised to be able to translate the depth of his feeling into an erection. But look! In the immediate blackout of her switching off the bedside light, he showed it to Audrey by pressing it against her, by rolling onto her like a poorly designed sport utility vehicle.

Audrey held her breath, suspending every form of animation. She knew how to do this because, as a girl, she'd skated. It was her escape from the boundaries of anatomy and the laws of physics. If only it could still be that.

She'd loved the ponds and the rivers the years there was dense ice, smoother than Steuben glass, etched by her spinning stops. In deep winter Audrey would fly along the ice as gracefully as a water strider on a summer lake, its water-repellent legs tiptoeing in box steps across a surface consisting of a single molecule of water. It was the feeling Audrey would have when the ice was invisible because it was the same black color as everything beneath.

Indoors, in rinks, instructed by skaters who worked the opaque white surface of that fixed amount of ice as if it extended well beyond the safety boards, her best move was that zigzag direction shift, when her body would keep going forward just as fast or faster, but with her skates facing backward. To achieve this, she would lift into the air for the pivot, weightless, then press back down, easing like an engine into higher gear. Her feet would reach out behind like arms, with her body seeming to twist in place, as if it were possible to rotate around her spine like that. She had practiced this again and again, though not so the spectator ever saw, or knew.

But could she do it on land, on demand?

6

WHEN THE PHONE RANG, it seemed to Gregory that only minutes had elapsed after falling asleep. "Judge?" It was a boy's voice, but he didn't know whether it would be Joel or Danny.

"Hi." He barely knew if it was night or morning. His memory didn't extend beyond imagining how he might feel if everything were different. If he could have had less to drink.

"Guess!" In the background there was soprano giggling.

"Joel?" In truth, he didn't know their voices as well as their faces.

"I mean guess *what*."

"Oh. What?"

There was a pause. "'Chocolate' rabbits. Get it?"

"Bunnies!" Danny corrected Joel. "See?" Clearly, Danny should have been the one who got to make the call.

"A pair." Joel knew he should be happier, since this was intended to be a compromise.

"A pair of brown bunnies, tell him, two boys," Danny coached Joel, who knew the difference between a puppy and a member of the rodent family, whereas Danny was excited enough about having a pet to be happy. Joel said, "You didn't know?"

Gregory considered. Did he? "I still don't," he answered.

"Mom gave us two brown rabbits in a cage."

"They're *cute!*" shouted Danny, who didn't want to hurt his mom's feelings the way Joel had when he let her see how disappointed he was.

"We thought it might be your idea," Joel said, "so we called to thank you."

"*You* thought," Danny blamed Joel.

"I thought." Joel sighed. This was one of those times when his dad would know what to do, not to mention that if he were alive, he'd have said, "No, don't get them stupid rabbits, just go ahead and get them a dog."

Danny had seized the phone. "*I* wanted to tell you to come over."

"Now?" Gregory had no idea how he was going to get out of bed.

"He can't," said Joel from the background.

"Maybe he can." So Danny asked, "Can you?"

But Joel took back the phone and told Gregory firmly, "We're going to our cousins' as soon as Mom gets out of the shower."

"Maybe later, tell him." Now Danny was angry. "*Tell* him!" Then he said, "You asshole. You ruin everything." He could be heard sobbing.

So Joel simply hung up the phone.

From her side of the bed Audrey asked, "Who *was* that?" She'd heard Gregory say almost nothing.

He saw where to begin, since of course Audrey had been at the lacrosse game too. She'd suggested parakeets, so maybe the rabbits had somehow been her idea. Gregory asked.

"No way," she said.

"That's what Karen got the boys. A pair of them, as you suggested." He was lying flat on his back like a sunbather, except that his body was so tense there was no resemblance to a day at the beach.

"Hold it." Audrey propped herself up so she could look down on him as she said, "Don't ever get rabbits, I'd have advised, because the only way you can tell which sex they are is by internal exam."

"That can't be true."

"But it is," she said. "So whatever they tell you in the pet store is only true if they've really bothered to look."

He didn't believe her, or, rather, he didn't want Karen not to have known this.

"People make the mistake of thinking a rabbit is like a cat." Audrey rolled onto her back. "Still, I can't believe Karen would do that. All she had to do was ask the science teacher at school." She laughed sympathetically, but to him it didn't sound that way.

He got out of bed in order to get away from her, but his legs worked poorly and his head was heavy enough to pitch him forward like someone about to vomit before reaching the toilet. She seemed to be heckling him. "Don't you remember when Marcia Morgan got the call from the vet, that instead of neutering their nasty rabbit, they'd done a hysterectomy?" Audrey said with a sharper laugh, "Which is a lot more expensive, the vet explained, because it's considered major surgery." Because he'd made it all the way across the room to the bathroom, she called out to him, like an outraged consumer advocate, "Hundreds of dollars, Marcia said."

Her laughter was so shrill he thought it sounded mean, so he poked his head back into the bedroom and shouted, "If you're so goddamn smart—"

She gave him a fraction of a second to find a way to say he didn't mean it the way it sounded. When he didn't, she asked, "What's the matter with you?" even though he'd closed the door and she could hear the shower running. So much for the promise of the resurrection.

In the kitchen, in her nightgown, she scrambled the eggs with the intensity of aerobics class, which Val observed by commenting, "Go, girl!" Val wore the new long skirt they'd selected together, and with outrageously big black shoes, she looked as forceful as she felt. Finally, she could be part of a family holiday without being the source of worry, the subject of furtive conversation. "You go, girl!" she said one more time, and poured herself a glass of pulpy orange juice. "Happy Easter!"

"You too," Audrey answered. She wasn't out of breath, but the effort provided her with an excuse for not sounding all that happy.

"Why isn't it Merry Easter and Happy Christmas? Why not Merry New Year or Merry Birthday? I guess Merry Passover doesn't sound quite right, but why not Merry Hanukkah?" Val gulped her juice and asked, "Who gets to make those kinds of decisions, huh? Who decides?" To show she didn't expect an answer, she said, "Sorry. Want some?" as she brought three more juice glasses from the cupboard.

"Thanks. But I'm not quite ready for all this happiment," said Audrey.

"Awesome," Val said. "You do catch on quick. So, hey, listen to this one. A name for a law firm specializing in malpractice—Sticks and Stones—you get it?"

Gregory stepped through the doorway, taking advantage of the joke. "Good one."

"Hi, Dad. I made it up myself." Val scrutinized him for signs of the night before but, especially for an older guy, he looked to have made a pretty decent recovery. "You look fancy." His Como silk tie joined the dense brown of his eyes with the navy of his blazer. His ivory shirt made his teeth, by contrast, brighter.

"You too," he said. "Nice skirt."

"My personal shopper," Val said, giving Audrey all the credit. And because her mother was cooking Canadian bacon while prying English muffins apart in the correct way, Val added, "And a world-class cook too. Allow me," she offered, tying an apron around her new skirt.

"It's all yours." Without having made eye contact with Gregory, Audrey left the kitchen, claiming she was going to get dressed.

So he followed her into the hall. "I'm sorry."

"What's the matter with you?" She turned to confront him, gripping the banister. "That's a serious question. You're so unpredictable, you seem unstable."

"I know, and I'm sorry." He offered no explanation.

"What's the matter with you?" she asked again. If he still blamed her for having thrown him off balance with her news, she would know it was something else.

"I guess I'm still a little off balance," he said, unable to come up with a better excuse.

So Audrey took the stairs two at a time, and at the top, Sally had to jump out of her way, which she was good at doing. And when Sally came down those stairs, swinging past her father at the bottom, it seemed choreographed.

He should follow, he knew, but without a plan he was afraid of making it worse. Was there a choice? So he climbed the stairs after her. Since he'd already made the bed, already having stalled that much in order to postpone having her confront him, he sat on a corner of the mattress as if in a saddle, resting his nervous hands on the Charisma bedspread between his legs. His ankles and knees were at right angles, his elbows too. He could have been a stick figure drawn by a child.

Audrey wasn't glad to find him there when she came from the same shower into which he'd vanished with the words "If you're so goddamn smart—"

But now Gregory was mute.

In the shower she'd determined it had to be Karen. But in what way? As a gift to him, she'd managed to respond to his clumsy sexual initiative, which was the reason she now felt so manipulated by Gregory. Audrey wasn't wearing her glasses or her contact lenses, so he was, in fact, just as blurry as he seemed. To compensate, she looked at him so hard it had the effect of staring him down. Then she marched over to the bureau and snatched her glasses as if otherwise he might steal them too, in addition to every reason to trust him. She wore a towel around her head like a helmet, and the thick terry-cloth bathrobe was like armor. Her voice sounded calm, but it was made that way by disappointment. "Since you're making me ask the question, here it is. What's going on between you and Karen Wallace?"

"It's about Rob." This had the advantage of being mostly true, but that didn't make it a good answer. He had to let his gaze escape to the tips of his leather shoes, rather than to acknowledge by his expression that she'd posed a valid question. He'd never before been accused of anything of which he was guilty. Amateurishly, he added, "It's none of your business."

Audrey told him, "Since it's about me—though not primarily, I see—I'd say it is my business." She widened her stance as she said, "Don't insult me, furthermore, by pretending this is about Rob, when you're only using his two poor little boys to get whatever it is you want from his wife. Widow, rather."

Gregory rejected Audrey's accusation by pointing a finger at her. If it could be true that he was using Joel and Danny for his own purposes, he'd have abused everyone's trust, including his own in himself. If that was true, he'd be like a sailor lost at sea for being too stupid to bother to have learned celestial navigation.

He withdrew his hand from the air and secured it, in a fist, inside the pocket of his blazer. This part *was* none of her business, in the sense that it was private. A thought struck him: what if it could be true that there was another reason, in addition to Mrs. Osborne's grief, for why Judge Osborne had abandoned him for five years after Charles's death? What if his mother had rejected Judge Osborne's advances? It had been so easy for Gregory to imagine the judge's attraction to another woman—to ease his own sorrow—but what if his widowed mother had refused Judge Osborne? The thought stung Gregory, since it would explain everything.

"Mom? Dad?" There was a knock, but the door remained shut. "Dad? Mom?"

Audrey regarded her husband with a feeling that frightened her, less because of what she'd seen in him than what she'd confronted in herself. If at any point in these past twelve days he had asked her not to go to medical school, for whatever valid reason, she would have felt obliged to honor him, never guessing he had the capacity to take advantage of her for his own purposes. He'd had this power over her by virtue of her genuine regard for him, which wasn't reciprocated.

She quickly took the four or five steps to the door, where she stood like a war monument. It was Sally, who fixed her eyes on the rug under her mother's bare feet and recited, "Val asked me to tell you everything is ready, so she would appreciate it—these are her words, not mine—if you'd come to the peace table."

According to Celia, her first-born child, Johnny, couldn't do a single thing wrong, especially on a holiday, when her husband's extravagant charms were most missed. Still, it was as if poor Johnny were Jack's willing understudy and knew every cue, every line, but wasn't as good an actor.

Already, Audrey felt tired. Her sister-in-law had woven individual wicker baskets for everyone in the family. Presumably, next Jan would tackle Russian nesting dolls, combining advanced woodworking techniques with her talent for folksy portraiture. "I can make anything," was her motto, "as long as there's an instructional manual." To outfit her basement workshop, she had purchased tools from Home Depot, a surgical supply house, and a store called Krafty Krafters.

"I got your news too late," Jan admitted with a nervous pout, because in Audrey's basket sat a little chick wearing a nurse's cap. "You're too hard to keep up with," Jan complained instead of offering congratulations, as if Audrey ought to answer, "Sorry!"

Gregory filled the ice bucket and sliced lemons into wedges

and limes into rounds, dividing what had been Jack's tasks with Johnny, who was lighting the back-yard gas grill for the butterflied lamb. Because Jack's chief religious belief had been "Live and let live," when he'd learned one year from the *Plain Dealer* that the origin of the traditional Easter ham was as a proof of not being Jewish, he wouldn't let Celia serve ham on Easter anymore. In terms of activities, however, there were no substitutions to the fixed menu. As if her young adult grandchildren were still kids, Celia hid colored eggs for them to find along the scavenger-hunt route, and the table decorations were always made by an old-world confectioner, Mr. Leopold, who this year devised white-chocolate straw bonnets adorned with bright ribbon-candy bows polkadotted with miniature jellybeans. And since Celia's favorite colors were these same pastels in every variation from room to room, there could be no more apt setting for this designer holiday. "No earth tones need apply," Val told Audrey, since the skirt she'd picked for herself was a copper-beech-colored crushed velvet, a departure from basic black on Gram's account. Her cousin Jill wore Pappagallo shoes of robin's-egg blue, for example, and Jan was costumed age-inappropriately in buttercup. "Wardrobing is a genetic trait, so you couldn't help yourself, is all." Audrey was exhausted. "Blame it on my three shades of gray."

"Line up!" Celia organized them so Johnny could blow his father's whistle for the start of the hunt. "Don't come back until you've found them all." Sally posed like a racer at the edge of a pool, poised to push off into a head-start dive of an advantage. "No fair! No fair!" complained Johnny's two lumpen sons, Jackie and Steve. Johnny blew the silver whistle like a tuba.

Gregory made Jan a screwdriver, and the same for Celia minus the orange juice. "Martinis are back," proclaimed Johnny, who'd never stopped drinking them. "No can do," Gregory declined, settling for Sprite. Audrey was content with plain club soda. "You're no fun," Johnny said, the way he always did when they refused to drink too much. An instant later he raised his glass and said, "Here's to you, big guy," to which Celia added, as if her husband were here in the room, "Happy Easter, Jack, dear."

Gregory was standing between Celia and Audrey, as if they were lined up in chronological order to demonstrate the same fourteen-year age difference between Celia and himself as between him and Audrey. He felt isolated in a sort of Neither-Nor Land, a Peter Pan forced to keep his feet on the ground. Of the two women, of course he felt closer in age to Audrey, but this was no longer as simple as when they'd been synchronized like a pair of watches set, admittedly, to his time.

Johnny asked, "Who was it who said 'Psychology is destiny'?"

To which Audrey responded, "Bi."

"Who?" Celia asked.

"*Bi*, not *psych*ology."

"I'm not following you," Jan told Audrey.

"Biology," she said a bit too sharply.

"Oh."

"Never mind who," Celia said, leaving the circle to settle into the skirted chair with the little matching upholstered footstool.

"Sor-ry," Johnny dredged up like an artifact from the ancient civilization of his childhood, proving to his know-it-all sister that in fact *history* is destiny. "Sorry I asked."

It was up to Audrey to recover the mood, so she said, "No, you're right, I think. It should have been psychology in the first place." Weren't they all living proof of that?

Gregory moved to the couch, by the bowl of smoked almonds. "I agree with you both." His behavior confirmed all three hypotheses.

"So that's settled," Johnny pronounced, unable to resist adding, "but then, if I may ask, Audrey, why go back to school to study *bi*ology?" He gave himself a dividend, as he called it, but nobody else was ready. "Just kidding," he said. "But hey, what great news about Val, huh? That I *do* call good news. It gives me hope, frankly, which I could use, frankly."

"As who couldn't?" said Celia. She hadn't been able to bring herself to tell anybody about Jackie.

Audrey backed up to the fireplace, to allow that heat to remind her to cool it.

"He's referring to Jackie," Jan explained, "who—"

"No, I'm not," Johnny said.

"Not now, please," said Celia. "And anyway, since life is full of surprises, he'll be fine too." Not that anyone in the family had ever been kicked out of school for cheating. She never thought she'd hear herself say she was glad Jack wasn't around for this one. Cheating was the one mistake, he always told his own kids, that he couldn't abide.

"I'm referring to the fact that I don't have a goddamn kid who's good at business, so no goddamn kid who'll help me out with the pharmacy one day. I'll never retire, because I don't have a goddamn kid to inherit the goddamn thing. That's what *I'm* referring to. Sorry, Mom, but now and then I've got to tell it like it is." The expression on his face changed from sour to sweet, as Johnny turned to Gregory to ask, "Speaking of retirement, what's new with you?"

Gregory inhaled so sharply it was good there wasn't an almond in his mouth, or he'd have choked. "Well," he began, but even so, he'd breathed in a fragment. He couldn't continue.

Never in her life had Audrey performed the Heimlich maneuver on an actual choking victim, but by training she was ready at any moment to clear an airway. Once again, it wasn't necessary.

"You see?" Celia scolded Johnny. "I'm not the only one who's uncomfortable with all that swearing."

Gregory laughed, so they all did. Then Celia said, "Anyway, let's change the subject. Tell us about your brother, Rich. What's he up to these days? His news is always more interesting than yours." This was no exaggeration, usually, so Gregory already knew it couldn't be an insult to compare poorly to his vagabond brother.

He gulped his Sprite, knowing that if he gave them a second or two, someone would interrupt and he wouldn't have to admit having no answer to either question. His brother was always away, if never more than a cell-phone call away. "He's probably in Shanghai or someplace."

"How nice," said Celia, "since Neil is on his way home from Hawaii. But, of course, direct to New York."

Johnny confided, for Gregory's benefit, "I haven't talked to my brother lately either."

"But that's just because of Jackie," Jan added too quickly for Johnny to stop her, "so you wouldn't have to tell Neil what Jackie did."

So Audrey asked, "What did he do? What's the problem?" as if this were an examining room and they were complaining of aches and pains.

The kids could be heard arriving at the other end of the house, so there might be time for only a word or two. Johnny said, "Expelled." His wife was more explicit. As Sally could be heard denying indignantly, "I did not!"—unsaid was that she never had and never would cheat—Jan added, "Plagiarizing." And just as Sally burst into the living room with more eggs than all the others put together, Jan compounded the crime. "Lying when confronted," she said.

Celia's boy-girl-boy-girl preferred order would work out perfectly if Neil and Phil could have been there, or, even better, if Jack were alive and Neil still single, so to speak. Before anyone knew for sure about Neil. Not that Phil wasn't great.

Jill talked and talked while Audrey pretended to be alert to more than the key words ("sorority," at the moment) when in fact all she could think about was whether Karen Wallace might have any possible attraction to Gregory other than as a substitute father to her boys. Gregory sat diagonally across the table from her and was being monopolized by her mother, whose fine looks were never better displayed than when she presided over a meal. Audrey noticed the backs of their hands and their necks, where their ages couldn't be concealed or camouflaged. She examined her own hands. They looked batiked.

Jill was saying, "I'm in a women's studies course, so we look into the pressures on women to conform, or not."

"Are there pressures to nonconform?"

Jill's bow-shaped lipsticked mouth turned up at the corners as she said, "That's what I'm asking."

"Ask me," said Val, who had Jackie on her other side and would rather be studied than hear from him why he felt she'd deserted him, by not yet having been kicked out of her freshman year.

Jill slid her fork under a mouthful of potato, careful not to combine food groups. Her brother Steve argued with Sally about the relevance for the regular season of spring-training batting averages, so Jan took a second helping of lamb and served Johnny too, who, like her, hadn't been included in the conversations on either side of him. Only then did Jan remember the sweet, grass-colored mint jelly that had been put on the table but not circulated to her. Nothing was right. All she could hope was that everything would eventually improve.

Audrey felt sorry for Johnny, who was leaning back in his chair. She could see he'd bitten his nails down to where they looked torn, and that the end of his belt didn't quite extend to the belt loop because the buckle was on the last notch. What if he were to say he'd decided to sell out to Rite-Aid? What if he'd announced *that* while the kids were on their scavenger hunt? Instead, he could only imagine himself dropping dead while waiting on a customer. Naturally, he hadn't said this in so many words—or Celia would have become distressed, since her Jack collapsed at the pharmacy and died in a hospital corridor before Audrey could respond to the page—but he saw his days extending all the way to the horizon, not a single day different from the one before. And if there had been no Johnny, would that be her?

Audrey took a sip of her wine, the inexpensive "special occasion" Beaujolais Celia always served, but before setting the glass down again, she tapped it with her salad fork. At least the crystal was first rate. "I want to say a word," Audrey began, "or two." At about this point in the meal it would often be Gregory who said something, so Audrey was claiming her own authority in addition to the point she wanted to make. "Thank you, Johnny, for being the one—there only had to *be* one, but there *had* to be one—who took over from Dad. No one had to ask you to, and nobody did. You just did it." For what was a strict improvisation, she seemed fully rehearsed.

Johnny sat forward in his chair on all four legs.

"And for these nine years you've kept us independent." When she said "us," Johnny's eyes grew shiny with his surprise, and she wished she'd said it before.

"Hear, hear," said Gregory.

But Audrey ignored him. "When it would have been easier to go out of business, you stayed. We'd have understood—we still would, just so you know—but you didn't sell out when you could have. You refused to sell out. I'm proud of you."

"Me too." This time it was Jackie, who left unsaid, in order not to shift the focus from pride to shame, that he could see what a mess he'd made of his life so far. He'd have to improve if he wanted to get into any college of pharmacy.

Johnny put his elbows on the table, but neither to provoke his mother to correct his bad table manners nor to prevent his wife from giving direction. Johnny placed his elbows on the table in order to bury his face in those hands with the fingernails he'd made ragged with his teeth and his desperation.

After dessert, Celia was carried off by her grandchildren into the living room, where they would sit by an invigorated fire. Some years they didn't need a fire at Easter, but this year, when spring had come early in terms of the earth, the air seemed too far behind. Gram was always happy to talk about the weather—midwestern chitchat—on the way to new jokes. No matter what the weather was, there were always new jokes she could tell them the antique versions of. The children would protest each time, "The very same punch line? No way!"

Gregory removed his jacket and tie and rolled his sleeves to above his elbows, scraping the plates Audrey washed and Johnny dried and Jan put away. The kitchen table had replaced the booth of their childhood, the newer cushioned chairs more comfortable in recognition of the fact that the human back could take a lot less abuse. Audrey wondered how many cumulative hours they'd each spent sitting around talking. It would take a calculator.

"I've got to admire you," Johnny told Gregory, "on the way you're handling Audrey."

"Oh my God," said Audrey, "*handling?*"

"Coping, he means," said Jan, who knew about coping.

"I can't take any credit," Gregory said immediately, "because I'm not handling it too well. Just ask Audrey."

"Right. Why not 'just ask' me?" challenged Audrey. But she threw back her head so her burst of laughter could rise to the ceiling like a balloon. "On second thought, don't ask." They weren't ready to be discussed like any old troubled marriage, because they didn't yet know for sure how bad off they were.

"Happy to oblige," Johnny said. At home he'd refuse all serious conversation unless the music was turned down first. With "Jumpin' Jack Flash" in control, why bother?

But like a quiz show contestant, Jan wanted the definition of a general category, so she asked Audrey, "It's your midlife crisis, right?"

"Maybe. It began as my midlife solution."

Jan nodded appreciatively. "Did you just make that up?" The Stones made her shout too, but to be heard.

Audrey reached behind her to quiet the music to a dull roar, as Celia would say. She answered, "I'm not kidding."

"Say more," said Jan.

In these twelve days, this was as close as anyone had come to asking Audrey why she would want to begin medical school. She had no idea if her original reason had any validity, but she didn't want to miss this chance to hear herself say, "I decided to think of fifty as a glass half full. Soon I'll no longer have other people's schedules to work around, so I saw I'd be free to resume surgical nursing, which I left for the reliable hours at Metro. But if I could go back to that, I saw I could go sideways too. Or go forward. If I were freer to decide, there'd be more options for me to consider than I was seeing, or than I'd really ever seen. How free was I? I wanted to imagine myself as a fifty-year-old, free."

If she'd made them uncomfortable, one of them could make a slighting reference to the controversial sculpture near city hall, the giant red metal rubber stamp spelling FREE, but no one did. So Audrey continued, "And it really proved to be a good exercise, because there was almost no idea I came up with that didn't seem believable. So what if I'd be fifty-four, finishing school, and fifty-seven before I'd have finished with my residency. The only way that made no sense would be if I didn't like school. But I love it! I always did." This realization had been a discovery, a recovery. "You remember, Johnny, how I insisted to Dad that I wanted a real college education, not just the hospital-sponsored nursing program that hadn't yet been phased out altogether. I told him I wanted to study Latin so I could read Julius Caesar, not just the names of body parts. Maybe I wanted to go to college so I could go on to medical school one day." Audrey's voice was without regret or blame. College in the sixties had been its own radical act, and anyway, she'd found nursing. To be a surgical nurse was to go to school with each first cut.

"So you want to be a surgeon?" Johnny hoped to God his own kids got their act together a lot sooner than this, but he urged himself to remember the goal was that they'd all get where they're going eventually.

"Well, no, never. I'll never become a surgeon now, but that

would also have been true if I'd had the idea of medical school ten years ago. Surgeons get good at what they do by doing it over and over and over. Becoming a surgeon, having been a surgical nurse, would be like watching bicycle racing, not having ridden as a kid, and thinking there didn't seem to be much to it. So, no, not a surgeon. But your average doctor? That could be me."

Johnny asked the obvious question: "But, if I might ask, why would you rather be an average doctor than a first-rate nurse?"

"You already asked me that." This time it sounded less insulting than at the game, but Audrey reminded him, "At Sally's game, you called me a traitor to other women." As if Johnny could speak for women!

Gregory remembered him saying "disloyal," but didn't feel confident enough to say so.

It took all Johnny had for him to draw a deep enough breath to tell her firmly, "No, that was a different question and, as you pointed out at the time, informed by my ignorance, and Mom's, about the way the two professions work. My question this time isn't about men and women or even about doctors and nurses. I'm asking why be a beginner when you're already an expert? No, here's my real question: how the hell do you have the *energy?*" Johnny himself was so depressed, he could barely get out of bed in the morning.

"The energy?" Audrey felt all hers drain away. Didn't she tell patients at the clinic that it was natural at midlife to experience fatigue, to need more rest, to have more trouble retaining information? She resented Gregory for his unavailability, since she ought to have been able to ask if he honestly thought she could do it. Normally, objectively, he'd say yes or no. She'd be able to believe him.

Gregory could have told Johnny he knew this feeling too, but, again, he lacked the confidence to join in. Or, wait, since Johnny was capable of making the effort to refine meaning, so should he, since this wasn't only about confidence. It was that he didn't feel entitled to join in, which was because he *wasn't* entitled. He'd been no support whatsoever.

"You're right to ask," Audrey answered Johnny. "What if I don't?"

On the ride home, Sally took them all by surprise by offering to drive Val back to Cincinnati. Hathaway Brown seniors got an extra day off, so, as long as Audrey or Gregory could take a cab to work in the morning, she'd stay over with Val. Sally had never seen the place, but now that she was willing to take Val more seriously, she was kind of curious. And if she caught a glimpse of Rex—despite the name—all the better.

Back at the house, Audrey stretched out on the couch beneath the Sunday papers and the pale green cashmere blanket, as she felt her body completely relax. She and Gregory needed this opportunity to end the day better than it had begun, as he seemed to agree when he used the Classified section to start a fire and offered to make a pot of tea. Neither of them recognized, although they rarely drank tea, that this could be a clue.

For Audrey there was no mystery. She'd been studying Gregory all day, and she'd concluded that they were even. Whatever displaced attraction he felt for Karen was his way of retaliating against her. By not having consulted him she'd hurt him, and she understood how he felt, because when Val admitted that she'd run away to Neil, it hurt. Here was the benefit of an analytical mind: it was possible to see the things that needed fixing.

She watched the fire. Banners of flame spiraled up between the logs contained within the walls of the brick fireplace, behind the fitted screen. It was like observing a wild animal in a cage, a restricted version of all it would be capable of doing on the outside. This difference between captive and free struck Audrey as another object lesson: not to let those things go unfixed.

When Sally and Val were little, Jack and Celia often took them on an outing after the family buffet at the club. Sometimes

Audrey and Gregory would take a long drive on these Sunday afternoons, but more often they'd take advantage of the opportunity to go home and make love. This would be when they could catch up with each other. It would be when she'd be most aware of her capacity to enjoy sex, when the house was empty of their daughters and filled with the fading afternoon light. And if they were to slide into a nap and the last of the daylight slipped west from eastern to central time, they would savor the moment of waking up and not knowing where they were, until one of them clicked on the bedside lamp and they were restored to their cozy king-size bed on Overlook Road. It had been years since this routine, but Audrey was aware of the idea taking form within her. It could grow, not unlike hunger.

In that bedroom, twice, they'd acknowledged being ready to have a child. She'd been the first to endorse him when, near the end of each judicial term, he'd talked about standing for election again. He'd seconded her moves into and out of surgical nursing and always taken as seriously as she did the courses she took in order to keep current. At a certain predictable point their daughters broke with the routine of having their Sunday afternoons taken up, which meant that Audrey and Gregory lost the regularity of those opportunities. Now look: a Sunday afternoon, an empty house.

Everything felt elongated, pulled like Sally's curly hair into a pair of braids, extended like Val's fingers by her drumsticks. Audrey enjoyed the sensation so much, she yawned. She yawned, you could say, utterly. This meant that although she had the idea of going into the kitchen to suggest to Gregory that they forget about the tea, she didn't quite have the energy for that. Anyway, any second now he would be on his way back to the living room. The air seeped from her like a slow leak from a tire; she could travel, but not too far or too quickly. The fire shimmied in place, going nowhere, while mesmerizing her. Her steady breath kept the slow pace, stretching like muscles across longer intervals. Her mind held the image of the two of them in the room right above her, in the bed right above this couch, the two of them having ascended along with the smoke from the fireplace.

In the kitchen, while waiting for the water to boil, Gregory checked the phone messages. All day, off and on, he'd been thinking about those bunnies, a distraction he'd justified because the basket Jan made for him contained a miniature rabbit wearing a long black robe. All day, too, he'd felt guilty for blaming Audrey for knowing more about rabbits than Karen did, no matter that he was really angry at his wife for upsetting their balanced life. Gregory plainly knew it wasn't her fault that he couldn't stop seeing Karen's face flash on the screen of his consciousness periodically, not unlike subliminal advertising. No, he wasn't blaming Karen either. It wasn't Karen's fault that she couldn't be lovelier. He knew better—he knew he knew better—than to be so foolish. Karen would disapprove as thoroughly as Audrey—or he—did.

The nearly boiling water danced in the kettle as he listened to Danny's voice, whose innocent message was that they were back home now, so could Judge please come over and help them choose good names for the bunnies? Joel wasn't cooperating—he said they should be called Rover and Spot—so if Judge was free now, they could sure use his help. Danny had twice said the word "help," but it wasn't as if he were drowning, like Charles Osborne, calling "Help!" And anyway, he'd also said "Judge" twice, which Gregory could have taken as a sign to use doubly good judgment.

After Audrey's accusation he felt compelled to prove that he wasn't guilty of using those boys—he loved them!—and yet, by the relief he felt in hearing Danny's voice, it seemed this was the excuse he needed, which was the proof that he was looking for an excuse, which meant he *was* using them.

Instead of filling the teapot with water sufficient for two, he put a tea bag into a mug and watched the water darken. He didn't erase the message, so Audrey could hear it herself. Who could criticize him for not resisting the appeal of a boy with an unchanged voice? He carried the mug to her, hoping she might have closed her eyes so he could say, later, that he hadn't wanted to disturb her. Yes, her chin rested on her shoulder, and she'd tucked the blanket under her neck like a terry-cloth bib, as if he might be prepared to feed her.

His note to Audrey was a lie, because he wrote, "I've been summoned," when everyone knows a summons isn't the equivalent of an urgent request. Further proof that Gregory was fooling himself was that he left his damp toothbrush for her to find, not that she would. In his courtroom he'd seen this kind of secondary evidence, but only in divorce cases when a vindictive spouse's lawyer had read too many boilerplate mysteries. No wonder Gregory couldn't relate to that.

It was still light out, although the sun had settled behind low clouds. During this bright day the buckeye leaves seemed to have been magnified by the deepening green of cumulative photosynthesis. The early tulips had arrived, messengers signaling that the earth was unfolding into a new season that can't be restrained any more than, after every night, morning. The power wasn't lost on Gregory, who had decided not to call to say he was coming over, in case Karen answered the phone and said not to.

The bunnies' ears were like peace signs, four brown fingers in pairs of V's. Their eyes were too big, but at least they were brown too, rather than the pink of a show-business rabbit, so they looked real. Danny picked up the smaller of the two, but not by the neck, as Joel insisted was how it was done in nature. "Yeah, but," Danny protested with a wail, "that's by their enemies just before they kill them."

Joel countered, "Oh, grow up."

The wire cage was in a corner of the kitchen, so Gregory didn't know where else in the house Karen might be. Maybe she was dozing on the living room couch and, like Audrey, wouldn't wake up when he approached.

"She's not here," said Joel, who saw him wondering this.

"She'll be back soon," Danny added, as if his mother had told him to relay this to Gregory.

"I don't think so." Joel held out a carrot to see whether his rabbit would interact, but then was too impatient to wait around.

"You're mean! You don't deserve a pet!" shouted Danny.

"Just because I'm willing to let Mom think I don't mind, don't expect me to spare *your* feelings. You gave up on our campaign for a dog, so don't complain." Joel crossed his arms, burying both hands, unwilling to join up with anybody ever again.

"I did *not*. You *liar!*"

"Look how happy you were to get these things—"

"So?" Tears were streaming down Danny's shocking-pink face.

Joel stomped out of the house, leaving the kitchen door open and taking off down the driveway.

"Wait! You're not allowed to leave me alone!" Now Danny was in a panic.

Joel called back over his shoulder, "You're not alone." He knew at this moment he would never choose to be a father. It was too great a chance to take, given the real possibility of dying.

Gregory was barely able to retrieve himself from memories of his fights with Rich. It was no wonder that to this day they spoke so rarely, when they'd hurled such anger at each other and never recuperated by any admission that it was way too hard to act as if they were all right. Was this the first time he'd been forced to see what it was like for Rich to have been the younger brother? He'd never thought anything could equal the hurt of having been the older one.

"I hate Joel," Danny moaned in an echoing voice, like a wind driven by a more substantial weather system. "You see how mean he is to me?"

Gregory absorbed the impact of Danny's small body, enfolding him, wishing to keep him safer than he could. "You're both entitled to feel how you feel," he said, "because this is such a horribly painful time." He'd have preferred to negotiate a reconciliation by chasing after Joel and bringing him back here. Then he could have told them how well he understood, from being exactly like them. Audrey was wrong. She knew nothing about real loss.

But Danny disagreed. "No, he isn't. Only I am." He choked on his misery, pumping himself into Gregory like a fist. "He's thirteen, but I'm only eight."

"It's true. And it's a big difference. You're right."

"I just wanted something that could *love* me." Danny reached into the cage, but both rabbits jumped as far away as they could get. There were no words to cover his disappointment.

Gregory took the couple of steps to the kitchen door and pushed it shut. "Maybe they'll relax if we sit here on the floor next to the cage," he said. "Think so?"

"Maybe." Danny said the word in two syllables hyphenated by a shudder. In case, he hooked the fingers of one hand through the side of the cage and said, "Here, Pete, here, Pete."

Gregory tipped his face to rest his cheek on the top of Danny's head, to surround the boy with his pure commitment, without the complication of his own miserable history. It was better that Danny not know anything beyond his power. He was his own best example that it was never possible to understand permanently.

The telephone rang and startled all of them all over again. Danny jumped up from his protected place within the circle of Gregory's arm, to catch the phone before the third ring could trigger the answering machine. Gregory heard Danny say, timidly, "Hello?" and, more comfortably, "Oh, hi." He replied to a series of questions with answers like "Uh-huh" and "Pretty good," "Yeah" and "Nope," and then "Light brown" and "Maybe Pete" and "I'm not sure because he hasn't picked his yet, but maybe Repeat." Danny was leaning against the kitchen counter, but now he crossed back toward the cage as he said, "Yes," and "Okay, sure," and then, handing the portable phone to Gregory, "It's for you."

Gregory told Audrey the truth, that he couldn't leave until Joel reappeared and/or Karen returned, but he understood why Audrey told him she didn't believe him. All he could say, especially in front of Danny, was that he'd be home pretty soon, and all he hoped now was that Joel would show up first so the boys could resolve things while he slipped out the kitchen door like an appliance repairman leaving Karen's kitchen in working order.

But Karen arrived before Joel did, and with a cold glance she made almost unanimous—all except for Danny—Gregory's wish not to have come in the first place. She crossed the space of her kitchen, regaining her territory, and turned her back to Gregory as she phoned Joel's best friend's house and, barely inquiring if Joel was there, told the other kid to tell Joel to get the hell home.

"You can leave now," she said, not that he hadn't gotten the message. This was between her and her son, so Gregory was like an administrator brought in on a classroom problem best solved by teacher and student. Her authority was intact, even if earlier she'd been done in by her computer printer's refusal to provide the handouts she needed for her Monday morning first-period AP calculus class.

"I didn't mean to interfere," Gregory said, while Danny offered in his defense, and to further isolate Joel, "Judge got here in the middle of me and Joel's fight."

Karen's point was that Joel wasn't allowed to leave the house, not for any reason. How was she supposed to depend on Joel if he left whenever he felt like it? This much she said aloud, but the real issue was, wasn't this what Rob did to her?

In response to her impenetrable silence, Gregory picked up his blazer.

"If you hadn't come here in the first place, Joel would have known better." So this was Gregory's fault, not Joel's. "You're the grown-up." And what she meant by "in the first place" was "ever."

"I'm very sorry for interfering, but this was Danny's invitation, not my initiative."

Karen arched her back and wheeled on him like a flamenco dancer. "Don't you *dare* use my children against me!" The anger she felt right now felt good to her because it was so uncomplicated.

"He's not! He's telling you the truth!" Danny was crying now, again.

"No, your mother's right," Gregory managed to say as Danny ran from the room, with his mother following close behind him.

It was only a minute or two before a figure appeared from out of sight, shortcutting across the corner lot by jumping over a low hedge, running along the heaving cement sidewalk, now turning into the two-car driveway, taking the curve on an angle like a motorcyclist.

Gregory wanted to escape Karen's anger, but he also wanted to make things right by offering an official reason for having come. Like a gift in the mail, he got the great idea of naming the children's center the Judge Robert Wallace Center. It would be easy to sell his colleagues on the idea, and as a result of the Good Citizen Award there was already public support for it. He pulled on his jacket to prove that he was on his way out the door, and he listened for their voices to see if he could tell Karen. He heard nothing, however, except the shuffling of the rabbits.

Joel burst through the door and called out, "I'm home," as he ran through the kitchen to find his mother, leaving Gregory to stare out at all the other places he should be instead of here.

As he drove home, he rehearsed his idea of naming the children's center for Rob, but he was also forced to recognize that his behavior was as defiant as those delinquent boys who stood before him in his courtroom. He saw that this deliberate experience of risk was out of character for him, but this gave it a strange allure. He'd never been able to identify with them so fully as now, when he felt more alive than he had in too many years. Watching Joel jump over the hedge, he'd been able to see the same impulse in himself, the rush of fear and fearlessness.

The skunk cabbages were a brighter green than he'd ever seen them, and the soil that rooted them was black with nutrients, the birch bark pure white on those slender trunks that clumped like a group of women in conversation, sending little leaves at each other like tidbits. He felt like a stranger to himself, and this was a new feeling. It wasn't just Audrey who had the chance to start over. He was surrounded by the defining proof, in nature.

From the doorway into the living room he could see she'd kept the fire going, along with her burning feelings. Employing a trick of the trade by offering the available truth rather than the whole truth, he said, "You fell asleep. I didn't want to wake you up. I had to drop by to tell Karen about my idea of naming the children's center in memory of Rob. But then Karen wasn't there."

Audrey examined him as if he were a patient of hers, for evidence suggesting foul play. "But I thought you went there at Danny's request."

"That too."

"That *too?* You had *that* reason this morning, presumably, with Danny's other call."

"That's right." It was all too easy to see why people got caught in their lies.

Audrey glared at him. "So you spent the day searching for an additional reason?" She made it sound like a question, but it was an accusation. "Coming up with a cause Karen couldn't refute?"

"No, not at all. I just came up with it."

She rose from the couch and put her hands on her hips. "I make a better lawyer than you right now." All she meant by this was that she had the ability to see through him.

"So no need for you to go to law school, you mean?" He pressed his head against the door frame for something more than support. Of all the things he could have said, why that? Why not, simply, agree with his wife?

Now she sat again and gestured to a comfortable chair, and as she watched him move toward it, she observed his bad posture. Maybe it was the thickness of the rug, but he seemed to shamble across the room. When he sat in the chair he put a hand on each knee, like an elderly patient on the edge of an examining table for the last dignified moment before the doctor said to lie down and roll over.

He said nothing, not wanting to risk choosing the wrong thing again.

"Now you're going to listen to me," Audrey said, "until I've said everything I haven't told you." She had to place a pillow against the small of her back, since the couch had been bought for his legs, not hers, and was too deep. Another distraction was her long gray silk scarf. She removed it from around her neck and dropped it on the floor, where her gray suede shoes lay facing each other like yin and yang. "Without interruption from you."

Her voice vibrated in her throat, and not only because speeches always made her nervous. Her hands were cool, as if her heart were reluctant to pump sufficient blood. Her mouth was dry too, but if she got desperate, there was always the mug of tea she'd let become stone cold. "If I were you, and you were me, and you were my age and had decided—say, when Val was five and Sally was four, when *you* were forty-nine—that you wanted to do something different—if you were me, and I were you—how do you think I would have reacted to you?" This much she'd practiced, verbatim.

"If, say," she continued, "you thought you wanted to go back to school to become, let's say, a professional pilot, wouldn't it be impossible for all these days to elapse without our really discussing it? Don't you think I'd have taken you seriously enough to ask you to tell me more about what was prompting such a radical change? Don't you think I'd have taken you *seriously*? Don't you think I'd have tried to figure out how to help make it *work?*"

Because she'd had most of an hour to formulate her argument, she took her time. "I think I'd have answered you something like this: 'So we can sell our house, no problem. The kids are in school, and I can work two shifts if necessary. My mother can help out, and would be happy to. That's all possible.' I'd have said this immediately." She let a pause linger before adding, "Because that's what I'd have wanted to hear myself be able to tell you if, instead, let's say, in an upset, you'd lost the first election of your career and had to find something else to do with yourself."

"Thank you," he said. He'd only shifted in his chair to take a breath, and barely that.

"No. What I mean is that I'd have *wanted* to help you. I'd have asked you to tell me what you were feeling, and we'd have talked. We'd have talked it over, wouldn't we have? Because we were partners." Her parents' poor example was useful to her, if only as a negative role model. "Because I was your wife, I would want to help you." She didn't say it would be her *job* as his wife, because for the moment she wanted to keep separate the anger she felt for what, only the night before, she'd required herself to give him, when she should have refused.

So far, her voice had been balanced so perfectly that, if they'd been speaking in a foreign language, without subtitles, no one could have guessed what she was about to say. Her gestures spoke too, though, as she said, "But then, of course, if I were you, the husband, it wouldn't have occurred to me to feel guilty for having wanted something more, so it wouldn't have occurred to me to wait until my children finished high school. It wouldn't have been a problem. Or not *my* problem, anyway." She shook her hands as if flicking water from them.

Audrey drew in a shallow breath so as not to waste any time. "If, as the husband, I'd come home one night and said I was going to run for the state legislature, or mayor, or Congress, would my wife ask, before anything else, why I didn't tell her sooner? Or let's say she did, let's say she blurted it out. Would that justify it? Or make it the last word? Wouldn't she have wanted to come up with something else too, a better reaction?" This proved to be too many words, so she took a deeper breath.

All he said was "I wanted you to have told me. I wanted to be given the chance to help you. I *wanted* that!"

"But you didn't say so, did you? And you never made it past your first reaction, did you? So instead of discussing it with me, the way we've always made decisions, including those of far less consequence, you withdrew from me, leaving me to prove to myself that it was a bad idea." Because she was feeling so insulted—so hurt—it seemed too mild to say merely, "I resent that." She said it twice.

"I don't think it's a bad idea," he said.

"That's irrelevant now, because you've found a way to make everything more impossible by creating a new problem. Or I *think* it's new, anyway. I mean this infatuation. Karen Wallace." Here Audrey checked his reaction, but either he accepted the criticism as warranted, including her disdain, or he hid behind a facsimile. So she pressed it. "Karen Wallace, out of the blue. If I remember right, you never much liked her. Until Rob died."

Gregory closed his eyes, but only because he wasn't able to close his ears.

Now Audrey raised her voice, stressing the consonants. "It infuriates me that, that first night, you accused me of having surprised you. And I let you." She moved to the fireplace and, in separate graceful motions, shifted the logs so skillfully with the poker that wings of fire came from underneath to wrap them in a light that flared gold. By this time in the year, after a long season of fires, the ashes were too deep, no matter that they were supposed to be some sort of advantage. Audrey stirred the ashes with the poker, gently, like soup.

The heat penetrated her clothes. "You equate *surprise* with *se-*

cret, but they're not the same thing, are they? It was never a secret from anybody that whenever I had a chance I took a course, sometimes to update my license but more often because I liked watching the ways doctors convey information. Case studies were as interesting to me as your own were to you, and you knew this, because sometimes I'd toss out a problem from the Neurology Case Scenarios seminar. I'd lecture the girls that the lessons were more important than the information. Then I'd describe the case of the severely alcoholic man whose tremors were in fact Parkinson's related, or the one with throbbing headaches upon waking who turned out not to have a brain tumor but caffeine withdrawal, since on a normal day he'd drink ten liters of Classic Coke. You remember, I'm sure, because it was never any secret that I loved school."

"I remember," Gregory said.

Now a bit too warm, Audrey left the fire and returned to the couch. She reached for the long gray scarf she'd dropped to the carpet, and she folded it and refolded it. "If I'd been able to tell you, perhaps you'd have supported me. When I studied so hard for the MCAT, you did, no matter that it wasn't clear to you that if I did well enough, I'd maybe have the option of being a full-time student. Back in the fall I wasn't sure if I was doing it for myself or Louise, or I might have had the opportunity to float the idea by you. I regret that. But it's too late now, isn't it?" A pair of headlights rounded a corner, swept the room, and disappeared. And while as an image this was always a possibility, she didn't know, with regard to Karen, whether it was or not. She had no idea, was the point, because although Karen was the occasion of her experiencing for herself the difference between a surprise and a secret, she didn't know which of those Karen was, and didn't want to have to ask. She made herself do it. Otherwise her argument was invalid. "I have a right to know how you feel about Karen Wallace and what your relationship is."

It served him right, he could admit, but that didn't make it any less new as an experience. Unlike practically every other man he knew, he'd never been enough attracted to other women as to have to reel in his curiosity. He'd never been distracted like this before, wondering how he might look to a person he hardly knew, who had plenty of troubles of her own and who showed no willingness to reciprocate. During his dinner speech at the Renaissance Hotel he had imagined Karen admiring him, and the effect was to strengthen his legs, his voice, his spine. He'd remembered to smile and to leave room for their applause at the end of key sentences. Karen's vulnerability had the effect of a seesaw, lifting him up.

All week he'd been subject to wild mood shifts. In a single second he'd pout and grin, flicking between opposing emotional states as if he were switching channels. At the moment he looked real and fake, fake and real, without her knowing which was which. This was how she saw that, the night before, in the dark, she'd given him the benefit of the doubt, and shouldn't have.

So she augmented her own strength in a similar way, by wrapping Louise Schneider around her own slumped shoulders. Louise would whisper in her ear to remind her that if he was going to leave her for Karen Wallace, or any other woman, wasn't that all the more reason to reinvent herself by plunging into the harsh demands, but greater rewards, of vocation? And look how close you came (Louise would tell her again and again) to deciding, because of *him*, to postpone your application for yet another year. Think how stupid you'd feel, Louise would say. Think how angry.

Gregory was sure there was an explanation, so he took another minute to locate it, as if while raking leaves his wedding ring had slipped off his finger. He would find it even if he had to dismantle the whole pile.

She could wait too, the whole night if necessary. Her limitless disappointment would keep her awake regardless. He had many choices of things to say, of course, but even if he recanted, it would feel forced, like the confession of a prisoner of war. "I'm asking you again," she said. "What is your feeling for Karen Wallace? What's your relationship?"

"I wish I knew," he responded, knotting his fingers together so his life wouldn't slip through them.

7

GREGORY'S BREATHING was like speech, and because in coming to bed he hadn't turned his back, it was as if all night he were whispering to her in an unbroken code. Not even he knew what he meant by the breath that fluttered from him until interrupted by a sputtering choke, a gasp abruptly resulting in a measureless silence and the resumed, quickened pulse of his moist exhaling. With this much activity going on behind her back, how on earth could she sleep?

The time passed unnervingly, rearranging particles of digital light, like finger paints, in one approximate shape after another. She had no way to know what time it was without giving in to the decisive act of locating her glasses and settling them in place. And why? To know exactly how many more minutes had been lost.

It was hopeless. Too many times she came too close, feeling the sweet elasticity of near sleep and believing in its power to overcome her, only to discover herself, a second later, in the hardening midst of cognition. It was perverse to pretend to the imaginary sensation of scuba, being suspended between dimensions with an oxygen tank strapped to her back like a knapsack, gliding from coral to muted coral, fish to Technicolor fish. She knew she couldn't be dreaming, because she'd devolved into a woman who felt certain she would never sleep through the night again, who couldn't be redeemed by mere thin pale moonlight. The famous question What do women want? had a profoundly simple answer in her case. These three or four hours back again, for a start.

The sense of futility made Audrey feel as if all light had been extinguished at once, total shocking blindness giving over to an incremental night vision that, by comparison, seemed like sight. And now she could see enough to get up and get dressed. At the hospital the distinction between night and day was primarily a matter of documentation. The staff functioned around the clock without undue reference to it.

From the parking lot she entered University Hospital by the automatic doors of the emergency room she then bypassed as she walked toward the lobby. The glossy corridor was lined with grainy photo enlargements of past medical discoveries as fundamental as the wheel. In that more dressed-up era it was impossible not to tell which was the doctor, which the nurse, and their patients all looked a lot more, well, *patient* than today's, who enter the health care system as wary consumers ready to become activists or, when called upon, litigants. Back then, so it appeared, everyone had blank looks, including medical personnel in caps and pin curls or cravats and starched collars, posing stiffly, holding enormous syringes.

An intern came down the hall wearing his surgical blue face mask pushed up onto his forehead like a triangular rhino horn, as if, in his pale green paper booties and puffy cap, he could otherwise be mistaken for the kitchen staff. Another intern's white jacket had pockets so packed with equipment they could have been a pair of saddlebags: pocket formulary of the most common drugs, penlight, tuning fork, stethoscope, pager, date book, notepad, logbook, "cheat" book called *Critical Care Secrets,* and the so-called "peripheral brain" quick look-up guide. For any nurse this would be the middle of the eleven-to-seven shift, but these two interns had signed on for the duration. Audrey said,

"How's it going?" The reply was "Fairly quiet." Which she already knew or they wouldn't be on their way to the cafeteria. Compared to them, she was rested. But this didn't mean she couldn't use the caffeine.

At a table, someone had left behind a straw wrapper torn into so many pieces it was as if the assignment were to isolate every bone there is between the skull and the pelvis. Audrey sat there just to be around other people. Violating patient confidentiality was no risk at this hour, when nobody from the outside was there to listen in on irreverent conversations about how people behaved in emergencies. Staff confidentiality was violated too, but with them no names were used. None were needed.

At the table behind Audrey sat two more training physicians, one of whom let himself be overheard because, cutely, he used the Greek "*priapos*," giving it the force of a proper noun by making it sound exactly like "Prick!" They were discussing a surgeon Audrey remembered from her days in the OR, whose teams never functioned smoothly because of their absentee rate. The other guy couldn't agree more, even if he resorted to the more puerile Latinate insult "Anus!" Too bad they were too tired to laugh.

They were so young. Not only their language, but the food before them: pancakes and sausage and pepperoni pizza and fried-chicken-mashed-potato-gravy and huevos rancheros *and* a towering brownie deluxe. Free food could get them to any optional lecture or demonstration, because their metabolisms were like furnaces hooked up to vast open spaces like airplane hangars, and they could eat like that—like Sally—at any time of the day or night. Sipping her black coffee, she worried that she would never keep up with them, with their ferocious energy and quick, elastic brains. Despite her years of experience, compared to them she felt like an old-style car whose windows had to be cranked open, a vehicle without even power steering.

And yet, if she were to join this conversation, she could add the one about the time she witnessed this same surgeon demand of a student, "Why did that patient die?" when the patient *just* did and was lying there between them like a major failure made worse if the student couldn't come up with a valid enough reason for it. "Surgical shock?" he guessed, which was equal to saying the heart stopped.

Her own did too, for that moment, because the student was expelled from that surgical rotation right then, when all the surgeon said was "I have a machine to tell me that." These days that surgeon was clearly still resorting to humiliation as his prime teaching tool, but now Audrey identified in a new way. Another time, for his own amusement, he'd made another student recite suture types—ethmoidofrontal, ethmoidolacrimal, ethmoidosphenoid, bifrontal, biparietal—but only Audrey had seemed to notice how the student's breathing became superficial, how she trembled under the burden of such arbitrary control. In the hierarchy, the only ones who have the power to look down on surgeons are the internists, and when they can't solve a problem with intelligence, the joke goes, they call a surgeon. How, with ever-diminishing brain cells, would she stand a chance of amassing such intelligence?

Fortunately, in the relatively user-friendly culture of Case Western Reserve, that surgeon was both a cliché and an exception. Nevertheless, the task was made more and more difficult, in her required continuing-education courses and in daily learning the new technology, by the obvious fact that it got harder every year to process information, then to focus the memory on the task of retrieving it. Unlike younger students, Audrey could be confident of having to "double book" her brain in order to absorb terminology the other students took in reflexively. She could be sure of having to carry in her own overstuffed jacket pocket a tube of Erase, to conceal those deepening circles under her ever-diminishing eyes.

Well? At least the coffee had substantially improved in the years since she'd left the hospital for a clinic setting. Now it had body and flavor, so she could experience the caffeine in relation to the cup of coffee. Now it was like medication, in that if you stopped taking it, there would be known consequences. Before, like the cause of an unexpected death on the operating table, this was much less well understood.

A notable advance was the "Code White" call that alerted nurses to convene in silent protest against any doctor taking unfair advantage of a nurse. Others would arrive on noiseless feet to witness, by intimidation, the intimidation. It wasn't a foolproof system, because some doctors went off like firecrackers and the incident was over too quickly to summon any but those nurses who were already on the corridor. But in most cases it worked. Audrey knew that it would naturally be to her advantage as a doctor to know that Code White wasn't about manners but rights.

But as with that notorious surgeon, such abuse of power was the exception in this institution that prided itself on being the origin of the idea of replacing with a pregnant woman the cadaver customarily assigned for continuing study by every incoming student. The difference was obvious—one had two futures, the other none—but such common sense was radical in itself. Another revolutionary change, originating here, was to understand the human body as a set of interlocking systems rather than subsets of separate subspecialties. Audrey was lucky that Case Western Reserve was her hometown medical school, rather than one of those traditional hierarchies where the concept of "cutthroat" wasn't only a metaphor.

In this cafeteria a gentle improvement was that on each table was a small vase containing a floral mix assembled from abandoned bouquets that, like the released patients who left them behind, were still intact for the most part. Volunteers performed the task of rescuing the buds that were about to open and giving them another chance to improve the quality of life. In the little vase before her was the proof that, in a hospital, there were more than medical specialties. Some of these flowers came from the Southern Hemisphere in waxy tissue paper layered like skin, while others were cultivated under glass and transported across state lines in long-stemmed buckets. These were nosegays, little opportunities to delight the senses with whimsical mixtures of color and shape, whereas in a previous era there would be just salt and pepper shakers or paper packets of sugar and sugar substitute to placate the taste buds. Leaving the last lukewarm sip of coffee in the bottom of her thick-lipped ceramic mug, Audrey took advantage of the welcome opportunity to enjoy a perfect rose.

The lobby of the hospital was decorated like an airline terminal, except that instead of numbered gates, corridors had been named for major donors. Because this was a teaching hospital, for each task there were always observers, who were then interrogated. In these predawn hours, third-year interns did the actual walking and talking, but the attending physician was always reachable by phone. It seemed that the progression from the rumpled white jacket to the pressed knee-length coat—as from understudy to star—was the gradual ability to empty those overstuffed pockets of information you'd absorbed and equipment others carried for you. For almost an entire minute, Audrey was the only person in this lobby, but she squandered the opportunity by feeling unequal. In one of the chairs she sat, and before she had a chance to decide where to go from there, panic rushed like the contents of her unsettled stomach up her throat and into her mouth. If she'd opened it, she'd have screamed. Instead, she wept like someone whose lover was in Intensive Care with no chance to make it through to the next morning.

They had always used their wedding anniversaries to congratulate themselves for choosing each other. Over a fine meal they'd tally up their compatibilities, never keeping in mind that the majority of marriages underwent such daily challenges as poverty or disease or the occasional natural disaster. How spoiled they were by the luxuries of such reliable ease as to be newcomers to the popular worlds of sudden change. Whose marriage couldn't last under the circumstances they'd enjoyed?

Neither had it occurred to them to plan for the future by speculating about how they might cope in an imagined crisis situation. That too was taken for granted, so it was a total surprise to her to see that, with this first instance of a problem, instead of leaning toward each other, they were inclined to fall away. Their reflexes were tuned so as to cause them to jump back, to run. Not only Gregory, she admitted to herself, but her too. Look at how she'd fled her own bed for this solitary wandering.

Normally, he would be the one she'd confide in, so these second thoughts would have mirrored walls to bounce off and fall at her feet for her to kick away or put back in play. She would be able to tell him she was fearful of not having the strength to endure the ordeal, and he, also older, would review the pluses and minuses. But now? If she confided to him that she was fooling herself in thinking she was equal to those half her age, he'd agree, pretending to sympathy while conjuring up his own escape into a future as youthful as Karen, as gratifying as her boys. He'd stare down at her as from his bench at those whose lives were ruined, who'd fooled themselves terminally. The bitterness she felt toward him took on the taste of the coffee she was afraid she might vomit into her lap. She took an enormous breath and let it go, folding her arms around herself while she repeated the ancient technique of a deliberate focused breathing, which made things both better and worse.

In this same hospital, her daughters had been born with such relative ease that Gregory could have had no idea how much more likely it would have been for something to have gone wrong. He'd been her labor coach, but she hadn't really needed the support of someone to talk her across that bridge, because Val and Sally met her halfway, and they each carried the other. Gregory never knew, to this day, how complex a transition that was, or that she'd accomplished it without him.

Now Audrey was sobbing like the bereft, bending over her knees, convulsing in spasms that exaggerated her condition by making it harder to breathe. If she was so self-sufficient, why was Gregory capable of wounding her with his blatant, pathetic lies? He was punishing her for this same self-sufficiency he never fully knew she had, and this was, in his own terminology, an injustice.

In their twenty years of marriage no third person had intruded, nagging at their fidelity to each other. During the cyclical downturns typical of long-term commitment, they'd managed to pass through without being lured by the Sirens of the quick fix. Why only now? It had to be because for the first time she showed a willingness to imagine life without him.

This wasn't true. In fact, it was the opposite. Audrey heard her own gasps—not the kind that come with realization, but her attempts to catch a breath—and understood that the reason the births of their daughters had come to mind was that this was a similar moment. That is, she had proven herself capable of an act of strength, but now she required all the help she could get. To be a single parent would be difficult in a similar way as getting through medical school alone. It could be done, but couldn't be recommended.

"Ma'am, are you all right?" It was a security guard, offering her a paper cone of water. "Here, drink this, okay?" He handed her a stack of paper towels too. "Can I call somebody?" The concern in his eyes conveyed his debate with himself about her condition.

"Yes. Thank you. No." At least she could get the words out, shorthand answers to his larger questions.

"I was afraid you were needing real help." He didn't specify seizure or stroke, but communicated the fear, even here, where there was real help to be had, of finding himself in such a situation.

Audrey poured some of the cool water onto the towels and pressed them against her face. "I was, and thanks so much." She tried to smile. Then she tipped the cup to drink the water, deciding not to caution him that, on the other hand, it wouldn't have been such a good idea to offer her even this tiny amount of water, in case, instead of the simple, generous common care he had provided, she'd needed emergency surgery.

With no particular destination in mind, she kept walking the beige industrial-strength linoleum hallways, making a right angle turn every now and then, stopping once to repair her face with the cosmetics nobody bothered with at this time of night, no matter how much the effect might improve an insomniac patient's spirits.

Covering the entire ground floor in this fashion, after a while the wide tan elevator doors became more obvious to her. Suddenly she knew where to go to place herself on the frontier—the Neonatal ICU—where, by definition, nothing you can see existed in your experience the day before.

The last time she'd visited this unit there were two differences: it was smaller because there were fewer babies, and the babies were each a lot bigger. In their transparent beds—plastic boxes on wheels—these wore miniature blindfolds because the lights had to be bright enough for the nurses to miss nothing at all. It jolted her to see how the scale was reduced to the extreme, where IV needles were like pins and a "spot" Band-Aid could almost wrap around a premature wrist. Whose adult hands could be sufficiently agile to tend to the enormous needs of these minuscule infants? Her own?

Almost none of these babies could be fed by mouth, but for weeks or months their valiant mothers would pump their milk, ready for the day when they might finally nurse their babies. Gladly would they have given their milk to anyone else's baby, but they couldn't do that either. These parents sat vigil, semidormant, like bees in an interdependent hive. As in a monastery, the faith was kept alive by the fervent hour-by-hour practice of it.

Here was the new, too, the ultimate in the contemporary: births as multiple as berries. At the moment, infertility was overcompensated for by an unnatural yield, whose survivors would move through the population like the previous generation of girl babies adopted from China, these now elementary school–aged daughters whose glad, earnest parents journeyed to them by way of the same ladders of infertility tests undertaken by their younger counterparts. To accommodate these sudden numbers of babies, manufacturers already produce carriages wider across than sidewalks, and soon, for a few years, some company will make bunk beds for three or more. The phenomenon will have to bubble through the school system and out into the future like a digested meal, and it will, so then one day again, when the medical protocol results in single births, twins will resume their ancient role as the fascinating exception to the loneliness everyone feels.

But if the miracle of modern medicine is also predictable, why was it so hard for Audrey to see what part to play in it? Even with the advantage of suspending her own disbelief in order to accept that Louise could be right, that she too might learn enough to be the decision-maker in a unit like this, one question still remained. Presuming she could know, when a life depends on it, how will she *know* she knows?

"Can I help you?" asked a young nurse the third time she brushed past Audrey, who was about to advise her to stop rushing around like that so as not to agitate the babies along with everybody else. "Do you have a minute?" asked Audrey in return, but of course the answer was "Not right now."

Audrey busied herself, waiting. As in a department store, she could have responded, "No, thank you, I'm just looking." That would have been the truth in addition to an answer that didn't make her sound like some pharmaceutical salesman with an attaché case full of free samples. Also, now she had to come up with a way to use her minute.

But since she already had a way, once the nurse came back to the desk and actually sat down, Audrey could introduce herself with the question "Do you mind if I ask why you decided to become a nurse instead of a doctor?"

The nurse scrutinized Audrey's credentials by reading the plastic tag she wore clipped to her breast pocket. Satisfied, she answered with a self-confident efficiency, "I wanted to have everything." She didn't look as voracious as she sounded.

"Oh?" Now Audrey seemed the novice. Never had she heard that particular answer to the question this young woman automatically turned right side out, like a sock before tossing it into the washing machine.

"You know what I mean even better than I do. Compare yourself to a doctor your age, I mean. You see? Which of you has free time?" She blinked her eyes and popped a peppermint into her mouth. "Want one?"

"Free time?" Audrey didn't know if they were talking about time for marriage and a family or, say, mountain biking.

"For, like, a life," the nurse said, twisting the cellophane wrapper and tying it into a knot before discarding it. "My college roommate went to med school—and we had the same board scores, incidentally—as I almost did too. She does a twelve-hour shift, which works out because she has a baby who stays up late and naps all day. But she admits that she hardly ever sees her nursery schooler, who has to keep regular hours and is almost always asleep by the time she gets home. Her husband helps a lot, but because he's a doctor too, they're like relay racers, always alternating." She shifted the mint from one cheek to the other as she pointed to an efficient stack of Nursing Assessment/Plan of Care forms. In a decisive voice that rang with the power she'd given herself, having chosen one way over another, she completed her uncomplicated answer: "I would rather be a nurse and marry a nurse."

Now Audrey unwrapped the red and white pinwheel peppermint she'd tucked away to save for later on.

"Now that more men are becoming nurses, and for the same reason I did, this is finally becoming possible." Then a buzzer sounded and she jumped up to dispense something more concrete than casual advice. Audrey watched her, admiring her example of confident self-knowledge, knowing self-confidence. With this affinity for the perfect balance, she could have been an engineer.

Before the current seven-day work week, when Morrow's Pharmacy could still afford to close its doors for thirty-six hours, on a rare occasion the phone would ring at home and Jack would willingly oblige by driving over to the shop. Back in those days nobody ever called at night, as if the ability to wait until morning were a skill that hadn't been passed on to the present generation of consumers. According to Johnny, the whole business had shifted from treatment to maintenance, so now the economic strategy was to get the population onto as many drugs as possible. Gone were the days of nonprescription remedies. Now the advertising prompted, "Ask your doctor," whose options were governed by the partnership between the pharmaceutical companies and the insurers. In this business these days it was harder to make a living, Johnny said, than to make a killing.

Yet from this desk Audrey observed that, as this young nurse moved about the Neonatal ICU, her efficiency gave courage to those women and men whose babies were tethered to the finest machinery of extreme means. The strength of her focus was like a transfer of power, a succession from the technology, through her, to these babies, who seemed to return limitless courage. Audrey watched her place her hand against the bowed head of a brand-new father. This must be what she meant by wanting to have, like, a life.

From a window at the end of a corridor, the sky vibrated with its pearly light and was like ice melting before her eyes, giving up its opacity for transparency. Audrey knew ice the way a sailor knows the wind, not to tempt it with oversimplification. Erie was the shallowest of the Great Lakes, and for that reason it was also the most unpredictable. A barge could make its impossibly crooked way up the Cuyahoga River relatively uneventfully, after a rugged lake crossing more like the open ocean. In spring or fall only daredevils would windsurf, and the winter equivalent of ice-boating was subject to such brutal conditions that not even teenage boys thought the thrill was worth that trouble. In her own safer world, smoother ice formed on back-yard ponds or in rinks where skaters had protection from the dominant species called hockey players. Still, it was easy to catch an edge, or to land wrong when a turn had been executed perfectly. If she were to try a double axle today, there would be no way she'd land it.

She drove from the University Hospital to the Community Gardens Initiative, where, having given back the plot she and Val had worked together for all those years, there too she could only be at best an interested bystander. These managed plots were already being worked by those whose regular jobs would keep them busy the rest of the day, until the evening offered up another hour. This was no time for the heavy lifting of garden maintenance, but fine for the tidy task of sprinkling lettuce seed in shallow furrows created by drawing a finger down a row as down a lover's arm. Mainly, this was just an excuse for those gardeners to start the day with pleasing spring calisthenics. She remembered the good feeling of arriving at work with dirty fingernails. Better were the days when she and Val pulled carrots. Best were ears of corn rushed home like organs harvested for transplant.

It was never about hunger, though, so now Audrey took that insufficiency upon herself, in spite of the fact that, back then, when the land was divided into garden plots, political activism was its own form of nourishment. These days someone in the world died of hunger every four seconds, while right here on a typical late summer day, a zucchini large enough to feed a family might be tossed onto the compost heap simply for being one zucchini too many. She herself had been that guilty.

With Val the intent had been to provide object lessons, one after the other, like seeds: if Val planted she'd reap, just as if she studied she'd get a passing grade. Audrey had tried to be available in case, while thinning beets, Val decided to explain why she was failing first-year French for the second time. Preferring Italian was all Val could offer as an excuse, by which she meant the boy two plots over, whose grandfather sang like a gondolier. Now Audrey wished that at the time she'd found Val's answer, if not charming, then sufficient.

But Val had such a disdain for structure as to seem in willful opposition to her mother, who couldn't make it through the day without checklists. "You should move to New York for the city planning," teased Val, "since you obviously love your gridlock." Val had a point. Oversimplification shouldn't be confused with a genuine solution, like the summer school course taught by a clever teacher who played Edith Piaf and Jacques Brel ballads for the drill-like repetition. "*Voilà!*" sang Val.

Audrey got back into her car, heading downtown and across the suspension bridge to the West Side. She had her desk at the clinic, and since she could see she had a need to organize herself by categories, she went there now, to draw two lines on a sheet of paper, one vertical and one horizontal, dividing it like a gardener into quadrants. There were four possible combinations following from whether or not she decided to change her life and/or if Gregory changed his:

she: *yes* / he: *no*	she: *no* / he: *yes*
she: *yes* / he: *yes*	she: *no* / he: *no*

Like a schoolkid, she set to work filling in the blank spaces with implications—losses and gains for each—and was well into it before she could see that, with this scheme, she had distributed the weight equally. She'd deflected her attention to him even now, as if it were her permanent job to make herself compatible with him, as if she weren't free to choose for herself, as he did. Here was her proof that their marriage was too old-fashioned to make the necessary transformation.

Therefore, on the next page, pressing the point of her pen like the tip of a knife slicing a melon, she drew one line down the middle to signify that *her* choices were her own Yes or No, no matter what he chose. Audrey thought about that "free time" motivating the young nurse in the Neonatal ICU, and she wondered how she might have counseled her if she'd been her college adviser, or her mother. Would she concentrate on the "time" or on the "free"? And in her own case, which was which? That is, she could begin medical school, have no time for anything, and still be free. But wasn't she already free? Wasn't this what it meant to leave her house in the middle of the night and have someplace else to go?

Her third attempt was somewhat more anecdotal: the case-scenario method, which was more suited to these deliberations because ambiguous questions were permitted to prompt equally vague findings. She could present a case as if it weren't her own and study it. Take, say, Gregory's anniversary gift to her.

With its crisp army corners—the way he'd learned to make a bed—the slim rectangular box had been wrapped by the jeweler whose logo was made superfluous by trademark gold-foil paper and indigo satin ribbon. At their table for two, with their champagne to toast these twenty years, he'd handed it to her like a conductor's baton or, if she preferred, a magic wand. She'd slipped the box from its wrapping paper almost too easily, as if to be able to return it untouched by human hands. It could have been a pen or a bracelet or a watch, which it was. A watch such as Mrs. Osborne might have worn to Severance Hall for the orchestra's opening nights. The face was encircled with twelve diamonds, so no numbers would be necessary.

"It's an antique refitted with a quartz movement," he explained because she was already pulling out the crown to wind it.

"Thank you," she said quickly, inadequately.

"You don't need to wind it, that means."

She had just removed her own watch for the only time in however many years it had been since she'd bought it for herself, for the stopwatch function and the fact that if she ever took up scuba diving again, it claimed to be that waterproof. "It's the wrong time," she said, "so I thought I'd change it." She held it out to him in the palm of her hand, so he could see.

He'd forgotten that he'd picked it out long enough ago that he'd be presenting it in Paris, so it was set six hours ahead of eastern standard time. He couldn't believe his disappointment in all that had happened to him in the meantime, including, now, her reaction.

She said she was sorry, that it wasn't a complaint. "It's beautiful," she said, but unconvincingly. It may be suitable for the Ritz, but there was no way she could exclaim, "It's me!" In place of that she repeated, "It's beautiful."

The waiter might have had his own opinion, but, this being the Ritz, his smooth face was without an expression of any kind. This wasn't the first time jewelry had been unwrapped in public view, but usually it would be an engagement ring and everyone would forgive a moment of enthusiasm.

"I'll return it," Gregory said as he took the watch from Audrey, slipping it into his pocket like a tip for the maître d' on their way out.

In this veteran waiter's memory, he couldn't think of a time when such a gift as this was refused. He approached their table with a water pitcher with a rolled white napkin tied around its silver neck. Refilling their cobalt goblets with ice water, he hoped to restore them to their senses in addition to their good behavior. Of course he'd heard all the stories of those royal entourages who roasted goats on spits in the hallways—so anything was possible for the right price—but so far none had as yet found an excuse to visit Cleveland.

"I'll simply return it," he felt compelled to say a second time.

So, she decided, she'd let him.

As it turned out, by the time the waiter paraded to their table with a complimentary Grand Marnier soufflé, they had partially recovered. Since her gift to him was back in the room, a cashmere bathrobe lined in silk—not him, either—they were even, sort of, in spite of the fact that her real present to him was the nonrefundable deposit on the reservation she'd canceled at the last minute, at what would have been their once-in-a-lifetime three-star restaurant. She hadn't bothered to tell him that part, although now she just might.

She was back at that page with the line drawn down the middle, with them on either side of the divide. She began to feel her own heat circulating in her body as she wondered if this was the moment when she might be forced to decide whether or not her husband was in love with someone else.

Audrey and Gregory had met for the first time in the routine way, by being "fixed up" by Gregory's upstairs neighbor, who didn't know how much older he was than her "old friend" Audrey. Bonnie moved out of the building practically immediately, so they'd nearly missed each other altogether.

The way Audrey remembered it, over a dinner of lasagna Bonnie asked Gregory what his father did, and he answered that his father had been dead for thirty years. Since this was longer than Bonnie had been alive, she'd asked how that was possible, never imagining—and what a fuss she made, backing herself into and out of that corner—that Gregory was already over forty, when, famously, her generation's cutoff point was thirty!

On the ride home, which he had politely offered in such a way as to provide Audrey the excuse to say no, she redid the math and told him, "If your father died at thirty-nine, you've already surpassed him." This was when he'd said she was the first person he'd ever met who instantly understood everything about him.

Since Karen was the math teacher, no doubt she had reached the same conclusion and he'd said the same thing, or so Audrey was capable of imagining. Up to this point she would have said Karen needed Gregory the way a sailor needs the Coast Guard, just to be there, in case. It wasn't Karen's fault if he thought of himself as heroic, as long as all she wanted him to do, like the Coast Guard, was to provide some support for her boys.

But yesterday afternoon in their living room, when she'd confronted him and he'd only told her he wished he knew what his relationship to Karen was, she'd been more specific, asking him directly, "Are you leaving me for Karen Wallace?" Even as she said it, it seemed more possible than she'd have thought.

He'd said, "But that's ridiculous. What would she want with me?" He'd seen this was a good question, but not the best there could be.

So had she.

"What would I want with *her?* When I have you, I mean."

Audrey was conscious of the lurch in her stomach. She pictured it like a smooth stone she'd tripped over, and flipped over, revealing its moist, dark connection to the earth. If they separated, they'd become one of those marriages that, like former colonies, couldn't survive the transition to their liberation. They'd have survived the transition into captivity, but not independence. Their marriage would fracture. They'd be a statistic.

Audrey had to admit that she'd taken his support for granted, but she also saw the meaning of taking support for granted: a fundamental reliance, as on a support beam in construction. Demoralized, how could she be capable of the demands of medical school? Why would she subject herself to such an ordeal? The terms of her own ambition presumed the sound support of their marriage. Was that presumptuous?

It wasn't yet the hour when regular life would resume, but it was almost time. Soon, if she were home, she would be waking up and beginning this day which, without having been extended by her by several hours, had already promised to be too long. Was she trying to prove that she had sufficient energy for medical school? If she were at home and this were a normal morning, she'd wake up, as she practically always did, a fraction of a second before the alarm and give herself another minute or two to get her stamina, and hopes, up. Audrey was about to realize, at several minutes before six on this Monday morning, that her own alarm was about to waken Gregory, who didn't know she was missing.

Like a child, he'd moved to her half of the bed, taking over her warmth without fully waking. The buzzing alarm clock fooled him into thinking it was his own, so he got up and took his shower, dressing for the day before he noticed the time. Standing at the door to Sally's empty bedroom, he forgot that she wasn't supposed to be there. It seemed as if the house had been evacuated.

Rushing to the kitchen, Gregory found Audrey's note explaining nothing more than that she'd left the house earlier than usual. She hadn't put the coffee on either, the way she always did. While it brewed for him alone, he let his focus widen to include the world of their back yard. The grass sparkled, each pointed blade silver like the tines of many hundreds of forks. The flower bed against the low stone wall provided protection for the bleeding hearts with little pink puffy flowers and doily-like foliage. The triangular buckeye now had the shape of an A-frame. Way off, the lake took its color from the gray sky, making it possible to seem to see all the minerals.

In that same distance a small plane made its descent to Burke Lakefront Airport. From that window it looked like a seagull, but Gregory recognized it as a Cessna. As a small boy he'd loved the idea of flying, and the impulse had persisted until, in New York when he made the first extra money of his life, he'd taken a series of flying lessons in order, like a bird, to examine the surface of that world, as if to confirm how hard it would have been to build a nest there. He hadn't continued with the lessons for one reason only: as much as he loved being in the cockpit, he was more interested in looking all around him than in attending to the controls. He poured himself a glass of orange juice and peeled back the skin of a banana, and by the time he looked back up, the plane had apparently made its safe landing.

The airport was where he'd taken Audrey the morning after their first meeting. He knew her address because he'd driven her home, so he'd sent her a bouquet of pure white triangular Casa Blanca lilies, with a small card that said only "RSVP."

She'd replied immediately, telling him that the lilies' perfume couldn't be contained within the walls of her small apartment, which was his cue to ask her out. Later, she told him she'd already decided what to answer. It was a matter of realizing she'd come to that conclusion unconsciously, instinctively, trustworthily. Audrey had told him she could hear herself saying yes because she had already imagined it—so it existed within her—which was how she knew what she wanted to answer. She was far too careful a person, she told him, to leave such a thing to impulse.

And from the airport they took off in a chartered plane no bigger than a limousine, which was when she'd realized that she ought to get ready to answer him when he asked whether she'd be free the next day too, and the next, which was when she could see she'd already decided yes, and felt free to tell him. Then, when she asked why he'd left New York, he knew to tell her she must be the reason.

That is, after Yale and Yale Law and his two years in the army in New Jersey, he'd been recruited by one of the top Wall Street law firms. But then he'd left almost as quickly as he'd come, returning home to Ohio, where he became president of the state bar association and positioned himself to run for the judgeship he'd held on to ever since that first election. Having satisfied Judge Osborne's sublimated goals for his own son, he was ready to find a wife and enter into the private life he had postponed since the age of thirteen. Even his mother was ready for him to find the right woman.

He studied the string of bead-like bubbles on the surface of his coffee. In Audrey's note to him, she said he'd have to take a cab to work because, since it was still dark when she'd left the house and since Sally took her car to drive Val back to Cincinnati, she'd taken his. "Also," she wrote, sounding more like a mother than a wife, "don't forget to shut off your alarm."

Marjorie McCarthy was already at her desk when he arrived, despite the fact that he'd been the one with the head start. After sympathizing with him over his having had to wait for the taxi, and without seeming to contradict him by wondering why he wouldn't use the Rapid Transit, she got down to business by asking him, without ceremony, "How stupid do they think we are?" With a fingernail lacquered fresh each Saturday morning, she pointed out the story's headline: "Sneak Bride Kills Case." Never herself married, it infuriated her to watch Judge Brennan's valuable time wasted on domestic disputes. "A vehicular homicide and guess what? She marries the guy and doesn't have to testify." Her fingernail was an arrow, and the target the *Plain Dealer* for having published the story. "It shouldn't be allowed," Marjorie said, resuming her typing as if drying the polish on her nails, touching the keys with the plump undersides of extended fingers. "Do you want to write a letter to the paper?" she asked, and then, when he didn't reply, she said, "I hope you had a pleasant holiday at least." She was prepared to share every detail of her own nice Easter, not that he'd ask.

With so many other choices of things to say, it seemed meager of him to reply, "Fine, Marge, and yours?" as he slipped into his chambers to read the article to see how bad it was.

Saving him the trouble, she said, "You're mentioned, but favorably. You're quoted as saying you'll refile the charges if there's evidence that the marriage is a fraud." She added, although with no evidence at all, that it probably *was* a fraud. "Still, I know how you hate publicity. Should I complain for you?" Marjorie had made friends with the mayor's secretary, she'd called there so often.

"But you're absolutely correct," he said in a voice that carried back out to her. "We should do something about this."

Quoting him, Marjorie recited from memory, "There should be a fraud exception which wouldn't recognize spousal privilege in hasty marriages with criminal charges pending."

Gregory returned to the antechamber, where Marjorie McCarthy's desk had sat for too many years for her to keep track. He was about to say she should be the one to go to law school—as he did whenever she prompted him like that—but how could he use that any longer as a throwaway line?

"You're supposed to tell me I should go to law school," she said without raising her head from the notes she was typing up, "so I can answer that I'm too old now not to retire and take one of those round-the-world cruises."

Gregory stood there in awkward silence. All he wanted to say was "I mean it, Marge." With her instincts, she should—should have—and he should have encouraged her. Look how flimsy an excuse retirement was made to sound, too. Now he wondered if he'd really wanted to retire or if he'd just needed to be an obstacle, an impediment, to Audrey. Was he that much of a bully? As a judge of character he was supposed to be an expert.

Marjorie stopped typing. She'd be sitting at that desk until the last day of his career, whether he retired or keeled over. Unless she did it first.

He said, "The judiciary ought to force the legislature to change the law on this. Spousal privilege should never be able to be abused. By anyone. So you're absolutely correct."

"No privilege ought to be," she asserted firmly. God knows she'd had too few of them in her own life.

Gregory hung his suit jacket on the back of his door, behind the robe he wasn't quite ready to put on. Was Marjorie's job satisfaction the result of her knowing that she was smarter than anyone knew? And did that make her content or merely self-confident? For someone surrounded by women, he still had so much to learn.

For example, Marjorie wanted him to tell her to schedule certain phone calls for his morning recess, to take action on this outrage against the judicial system by getting it onto the agenda of his colleagues. She allowed him a minute to give the direction, then suggested, "Why not put it on the agenda of your Third Friday Lunch? I'd be glad to take care of that for you if it's a good idea." She knew it was.

"Marge, you're brilliant," he said, no exaggeration.

"Oh, and Judge, one more thing, and I'm sorry for getting sidetracked. There was a call on the machine as I came in today, from Judge Wallace's widow, who wants you to call back."

Marjorie brought the message slip to him. She'd provided "Day" and "Evening" options in her legible large print, but she added neither anecdote nor attitude, leaving him to wonder plainly why Karen would be calling him. He'd been planning to phone her today with the news of naming the children's center for Rob, until Audrey apprehended him like a thief with marked money.

In a manufactured voice he asked, "Did Mrs. Wallace say when I might reach her?"

"The machine picked it up as I was coming through the door," Marjorie said, adding defensively, "I just missed it, which is the reason I disapprove of voice mail. With the old system, a person would call right back and I'd learn everything necessary to know."

Gregory knew he wouldn't be able to listen to Karen's recorded voice because, unless there was a real message, Marjorie's method was to listen twice to verify she had the numbers right and then to erase it. She didn't approve of electronic clutter any more than the regular old-fashioned kind.

He closed the door to his office, knowing he would be too distracted during the first court session if he didn't try to reach Karen, while also knowing that, with his luck in the last twenty-four hours, he wouldn't be successful. And his luck held.

The University School receptionist was kind enough to look up Karen's teaching schedule, and told him to call back at 11:20, first lunch, when Karen had a free period. She'd also be happy to put a note on the bulletin board in the faculty room in the meantime, if he wished to leave his name and number. This wasn't an emergency, was it? From his title, she couldn't help but wonder if there might be some trouble.

"No," he answered, providing more information than was strictly necessary, "I'm just a family friend." But there would be trouble if Karen were to call him at home, so he needed to convey this to the receptionist without making her suspicious of him. He specified times when Karen would be likely to reach him during the rest of the day, and reassured himself with the knowledge that she was very familiar with the intricacies of a judge's schedule. To be safe, he lied. He was busy that evening, he said to say.

When he opened the door he walked over to the water cooler and drank deeply before telling Marjorie, calmly, that he was expecting to hear from Karen Wallace again. Since this was the truth, there was no reason for him to feel awkward, but he felt as guilty as if he were prepared to send Marjorie to Dillard's lingerie department to buy a present for "Audrey" in the wrong size. He caught himself wondering what Karen's size was, and guessed petite. Unless her long legs made her a tall. Clearly he knew nothing about women's clothing.

But this fantasy was enough to return him to that feeling on Karen's couch, when, if he'd really been out of his mind, he'd have said he loved her. He guessed he did now, because the heat he felt in his face was sure to prompt Marjorie to ask if something was wrong. "Yes and no," he'd have to answer.

He was always uncomfortable with those conversion-experience divorce cases where one or the other of a longtime married couple discovered the true meaning of life in someone else—in someone else's *bed*—and wanted to divide the property. He was known around the building as the judge with the least personal experience of marital counseling, but who always required more of it than the other judges, who knew that sometimes it works and other times it doesn't. He tried never to be smug about it, but behind his back they called him Judge Clean. If they only knew.

And if it came to that? Marjorie aside, Gregory didn't think he could face the rest of them either.

The sun was still surprisingly high in the sky as he drove from the Justice Center to Karen's house in the flamboyant red Camaro he'd rented as yet one more extravagance. She hadn't called, but he'd left a second message that he'd stop by. He'd left a bit early so they'd have extra time.

The front yard was a mess. If there were tulip bulbs at the edges of the grass, they'd never make it through the darkly sodden leaves, which looked like random patches of asphalt. The neighbors' squares of lawn had been carefully aerated and fertilized, but this orphaned turf proved how little time it takes, even up north, for nature to ruin itself. Two new bicycles locked to the fence appeared abandoned, as if they were prematurely old, and the blue plastic recycling crate looked hit by the garbage truck. Gregory hated to be so hopelessly retrograde as to say to himself that this place could sure use a man.

By now he had learned the family never used the front door, so he came around to the kitchen purposefully, like somebody sent to read the utility meters, lined like pickets along the garage wall. Since the back door was wide open, he could look in and see Karen at the counter, throwing out most of the day's mail, and Danny, who was crouched in the other corner by the wire cage, regarding the bunnies with what looked like reverence. The rabbits looked smaller, as if in their total fear of humans they'd retracted.

When Gregory knocked on the storm door, she looked up and displayed a belittling irritation, as if he were proving to be altogether too much trouble. Danny hugged him, but Karen said, "I left you a message at home, when I got yours that you'd be leaving work early. Joel has a dentist appointment. Orthodontist." She clamped her mouth shut as if to protest the expense, of time as well as money, no matter that the dentist's prediction could have been made simply by looking at Karen's own jaw. Danny had Rob's mouth, which was perfectly aligned.

"And we're starting grief counseling," Danny told him with an expression that conveyed he had no more idea what that entailed than if they would be beginning lessons in Arabic.

"We're leaving now." She meant he shouldn't bother to take off his coat.

"Joel's just brushing his teeth while I feed Pete and Repeat," said Danny.

"Fine," Gregory said, although if he'd been more honest he'd have said, "You called me at home? Did Audrey answer the phone? Did you indicate that I'd said I was on my way here?" Pulling into this driveway, he'd had the unwelcome feeling of wondering what Audrey would think if she should happen to drive by Karen's house right then and catch him in the act. He'd always felt both sympathetic and unsympathetic toward those men or women having affairs, hiding their cars, never knowing in any public space if someone who recognized them or who knew their spouses could read between the lines of their fraudulently bland looks.

When would he stop learning such awful things about himself? And, in the meantime, what was there to say right now? If Karen knew that within the past several minutes he'd fantasized about their having an affair, she'd kick him out of her house for good. The only initiative she'd taken was to call the office, which she was pretending she'd forgotten.

Joel came down the narrow, uncarpeted back stairs, jumping over the bottom few steps to land in the kitchen like a stunt man. When he smiled, Gregory could see for the first time what a bad overbite he had. "Hey!" Joel exclaimed, pleased to have a bigger audience than he'd known.

"Hi," Gregory said.

"So you can come to the game? Awesome!"

"No, he can't," said Karen.

Gregory asserted himself. "Why not?"

"Because your message this morning said you're busy tonight. That's why I'd called: Joel's championship basketball game. Joel was supposed to ask you on Saturday, but he forgot to." She didn't refer to the second opportunity, Gregory's stopping by yesterday, but her impatience with him was adequately expressed in her lack of investment in his being at the game.

"No problem," Joel said, practicing good sportsmanship.

"But I wish I could have," Gregory quickly responded. What he meant was that he wished he still could.

"It's no big deal."

"I have to be home tonight, though." Gregory felt like an adolescent who was being grounded for staying out too late.

"Maybe next time," Joel said, even though this was the one and only championship game.

"Next *year*," Danny corrected while trying to make it sound sooner than in reality it could be, especially after this year.

Joel pulled on his baseball cap as if to say baseball season was already under way, to underscore the unlimited potential he had as an athlete.

"Ready?" Karen grabbed her key ring from the counter. It sounded like too much small change.

Because Gregory's rented red Camaro blocked Karen's minivan, Gregory had to back out first, which wasn't all bad, since he was in a bigger hurry. He was realizing two related things at once: his still not having had the chance to tell Karen about the Wallace Center meant that he'd have another excuse to see her; and, if he rushed home, there was a chance of getting there first —that is, before Audrey—and erasing Karen's message in time.

Back on Overlook Road, Gregory had no opinion about anybody's yard. He was feeling the recklessness of a young man at risk, a physiological state that managed to merge euphoria and panic. And the garage was empty. Audrey wasn't there.

Karen's phone message said, "Gregory. I won't be home when you get here, but you can call me late tonight." Like an anonymous note, he erased it so quickly he could barely remember if it said anything. He hated this feeling of knowing Audrey had every right to be suspicious of him. It was the first time he'd ever had it.

He took off his coat and draped it on a chair. Since he was unused to being the first one home, he was uncertain what to do. It was too early for the news, too soon to make himself a drink. Because he saw he'd left the coffee machine on all day, he poured the bitter remains into the sink, destroying more evidence. He'd left an empty house and was returning to it still empty, so he was forced to encounter another new experience: what if Audrey and Sally had abandoned *him?* He wondered if, in that case, he would make it to Joel's basketball game after all. Now he was ashamed of himself. No wonder men always seem to remarry immediately; they're incapable of managing life on their own. Not to mention unable to see themselves, as Marjorie McCarthy would say, as anything but the victim.

Audrey's car pulled into the driveway, but inside was Sally, back from Cincinnati. "Hey Dad, new car?"

He said, "Have I ever owned a car that wasn't silver?" But he saw she couldn't care less.

"Have I known you your entire life?" she responded. "In fact, I've known you only a fraction of it."

"Where's Mom?" he deflected from the issue of his age.

"Aren't you the one who's always forcing pleasantries on the rest of us? Like a simple hello? I drive four hours and arrive home and all you ask is where Mom is. As it happens, I talked to her and she's at some reception. But what's with you, anyway, Dad? What's the deal here? This is getting tiresome." Without letting him speak, she said, "I'm going over to school now to put up posters for the 10k, so I'm not around for dinner. Mom knows all this."

"What reception?" he asked, but Sally ignored him.

The Hathaway Brown Carnival was in six days, when with

the 10k Race for Charity the school proved its dedication by raising thousands of dollars for social service agencies. The school motto exhorted the girls to gain "preparation for life"—that is, the mind and the heart—by means of an "abiding passion for learning" as well as a "constant devotion to good character and service to society." So important was the race, Sally had been working to sign on more sponsors than anybody else, aiming to break the school record by running it like a sprinter, earning double the donations if she got in under some impossible time. She'd been training too, not that he'd seemed to notice. In any other two-week period, the anticipation of the race would have dominated everything else. But then, there wouldn't have been so much else.

He poured his ounce-and-a-half and sat to click on the news, where he knew Dick Goddard would be, making an appearance at the top of the show and coming back with the fuller picture at the bottom of the half hour. To Gregory it seemed ages since he'd had the luxury of worrying about the weather. Daylight was rapidly fading, so the smoky flickering glint from the television was the defining light. He'd become one of those geezers who nodded off in his chair while his ice cubes melted. Not even Celia was too lazy not to go around the house and make it appear lived in. But he couldn't relieve the gloom, he just couldn't. With his legs stretched out in front of him, he could see his polished black shoes all too well. He thought about Joe Ricci's pancreatic cancer for the first time in a week, a significant portion of all the time Joe had left to him.

The day's stories boomed out at him, but he couldn't concentrate on anything but the fact that a minute ago he'd felt like a teenager and now he felt like the opposite. The scotch hurt the back of his throat, probably because he'd held this sip in his mouth too long, making this sad admission to himself. What if he choked on it and died? Who would know that at the last moment he had recanted?

In this posture he was discovered by Audrey, who corrected the mood immediately by going around the house and turning on all the lights.

"I was getting worried," he said quite truthfully. He didn't feel he had the right to ask her where she'd been, but he meant it when he told her instead, "I'm glad you're home."

"I left word with Marjorie that I was going to be late. She said you'd left early." If Audrey had been told anything more than that, she didn't say.

And for once he didn't evade. "I stopped to tell Karen I wanted to propose naming the center after Rob, but they were just leaving the house for appointments. So I didn't get a chance to."

"She has too much else to deal with, you know."

"Without me too, you mean? I know. It's already the second time I've tried, and failed, to tell her about it." He smiled, but mainly so Audrey wouldn't think he was complaining. There was a silence now, which grew.

Audrey released a long-held breath, exchanging it for a new one. She didn't look at him when she said, "She called me today at the clinic."

"Karen?" His expression was what Audrey was avoiding seeing.

"To say she'd made an appointment with someone I'd recommended to her."

He knew this wasn't a reference to the orthodontist. "The grief counselor?" This proved Karen had also called Audrey before today, asking for help and, clearly, getting it. As opposed to his own interference.

Now Audrey sat down in the other chair. "Karen told me she's been worried that I might be bothered by your involvement with her boys. But I said I wasn't. I told her it was a good thing for them." Audrey tipped her face to him when she said, "And I told her it was helping you, too." This was the conclusion she'd reached in the middle of her own day, when she told Louise she was afraid of his leaving her, to which Louise responded, like an instructor, "No, fear isn't something you can experience in anticipation. It's dependent on real circumstances." Then Louise persuaded her to go to the reception at the medical school, to prove exactly this point.

"It's not helping anybody," he said.

"I told Karen it was helping everybody but her." Audrey didn't tell him that then Karen had said, "And you."

"And you," said Gregory.

"Yes, but this isn't about me." Audrey had been right to argue that applying to medical school wasn't about him—"It isn't *about* you!"—and she was right again. "It's about *you*. Finding your grief for your father, for example."

When he now said, "I love you," he expressed the feeling he'd had for Audrey at first sight—better than love at first sight—of complete human safety.

"You were wanting to rescue her, be her hero, save her from her loss. Bring him back." The words settled into the space separating them, and the middle distance evaporated. By her natural compassion she saw how good she was at this.

Gregory nodded his acceptance of this news that, after all, his power was always only ordinary, no matter how he wished to have saved his father from the death that drained his mother of the rest of her life.

But then Sally barged in, complaining that the entire school was locked! Onto the kitchen table she flung a stack of "Rock the Block! Run for Charity!" posters and said, "By the way, Mom, Val said to tell you she's coming home next weekend. Suddenly it's like she loves home. Have you noticed?" Sally was speaking exclusively to Audrey. "And, Val said to tell you, Neil and Phil too. We talked to them last night. She had to tell them about Rex, I guess." Only now did Sally allow herself to smile. "Neil asked what breed Rex is."

Audrey said, "Well, first of all, hello. Welcome back." She opened her arms to Sally, who smirked at her father to make sure he noticed. "What breed *is* Rex?"

"Not pit bull, I hope," Gregory said, only a little forcibly, gratified that Sally didn't snatch back her smile.

Sally didn't, because it was more like old times to laugh at Val's expense, so it was as if everyone had fully recovered. "So we planned a carbo-stoke party here, for Saturday, which I hope is okay. Neil and Phil have one every year, before the New York Marathon."

Gregory noted that Sally wasn't necessarily asking permission, but to show he was a good sport, he said, "Fine." Audrey was rummaging in the kitchen cabinets as if already checking the spaghetti supply, but she offered, "Tuna, is all."

He opened the two cans and squeezed out the liquid. Nothing would taste as good as this sandwich, and he said so. Sally draped cheese slices over her two halves and put them under the broiler until they blistered. Audrey made herself a salad. They sat down to eat, equal but separate.

When they finally got back to the subject of Rex, Sally said, "I'll only say two things about him. His real name is Jasper, so Rex is his road name or whatever, and he always calls Val Valerie, like Gram does. Which, by the way, I think is weird. He spikes his hair into a sort of crown—so Rex, get it?—and he plays in a band, although she may have told you that. I heard him play. He's pretty good." Sally had no need to say what she really thought. Anyway, with boyfriends Val always moved along.

"What's the second thing?" asked Audrey.

"Well, he's *way* old."

PART THREE

8

GRAY LIGHT gave form without shadow. Through the kitchen window Audrey could see that the back yard had advanced into on-time spring, the buckeye flowering less tentatively, having by now leached the poisons from its young shoots. It occurred to her that in this same period Val might have escaped her toxic adolescence by the same means, whereas Sally's own first-stage rocket would be shed in the sky, and she'd be long gone before it would be found. Audrey noticed next that her face wasn't reflected in the glass. The advance of an hour, brought on by daylight saving time, made the window only transparent. The lake in the distance was the same color as the kitchen sink, she saw, the rugged gray of stainless steel.

On this deadline day the dark-roasted coffee infiltrated her, but instead of agitation Audrey felt calm. Sally had tried to be encouraging by telling her, "Mom, Val and I agree that you've got to try med school, because if it's too hard, you can always quit." But then she'd added, in deference to her coaches, "Don't quote me."

Audrey sipped her coffee slowly, fixing her eye on that farthest-away solid-looking water in order to understand what she knew she had to have understood all along: all her work in reaching this decision had occurred long ago, ending with the day she'd mailed her application. Today was only the day for saying whether she'd go through with it, because in applying she'd had to decide for herself what she would do if they said yes. Once she knew *her* answer was yes, she'd sent in her application. These two weeks had existed purely for insurance purposes, as a way out if all else failed.

This wasn't a revelation, but it was news: Audrey knew herself better than she knew she did. This was why it wasn't necessary to blame herself for not seeming to have properly investigated the pros and cons during the allotted time for her deliberation, nor to resent—nor to have resented—those whose own needs had intervened and required her immediate focus and care. That is, she was capable of being just as careful with herself as with everybody else.

So she took an extra minute to discover what made this a familiar feeling, and therefore why she trusted it. There were no distractions here in her kitchen, but still she didn't want to risk losing the thought by pouring herself orange juice or cold cereal, toasting a sesame bagel, freeing triangles of grapefruit with a curved knife and, next thing she knew, emptying the dishwasher and thinking about what to make for dinner. Instead, she fixed her gaze on the buckeye. Now the white pyramidal blooms looked like candles. An accurate count wouldn't be necessary, but it was Audrey's impression that there were more flowers on it this year than last.

At the clinic, Helena was already there but arranged in a different chair, in the corner. She told Audrey, "Morning, Doctor," from behind the wraparound opaque sunglasses worn after cataract procedures, while spread across her lap was the day's newspaper, as usual. "Good morning, Helena," answered Audrey, once again not bothering to tell her she wasn't even close to being a doctor. She had seen Helena the day before and could only wonder where she'd found those glasses. Helena said, "Let me ask you this one, Doctor. Are you late or am I early?" Audrey said she was a little late. Helena said, "Just checking."

Louise was delayed too, but by hospital rounds. Because it was essential to know what was going on upstairs in relation to what came in off the street, she systematically rotated through the specialties. Today it was Pediatric Orthopedics, so by the time her day began, she could already have the belief that there were practical solutions for practically every problem. This was heartening work, perfect for those in the profession who, in another life, might be plumbers or carpenters: problem solvers, fixer-uppers. Like evangelical healers they had the power to command "Get up and walk!" And get results.

Helena greeted Louise with, "Morning, Doctor," but had to repeat her earlier question in order to orient herself. So Louise said, "You're on time, I'm the one who's late," but, unlike Audrey, she thought to ask why Helena had moved out of her regular chair. Helena replied almost too softly to be heard, "I'm trying to see if I can manage in a chair without arms." Her own fleshy arms had disappeared under the newspaper, which Louise understood had been spread across her lap for that purpose. Louise said, "Since not enough light gets through those dark glasses, please don't try to read your paper," to which Helena replied with a smile, "Doctor's orders."

Audrey was sitting with a Nursing Assessment/Plan of Care form. Already this morning she'd had a yes response to one of the safety questions, so, as required, she'd had Social Services on the line to determine the need for further action. The aunt of a patient had brought her in to Metro with a plausible enough explanation for the girl's sprained wrist, so Audrey hadn't expected the clinic's scripted disclaimer to yield anything. Alone with the girl in the examining room, she'd said, as usual, "Because so many people deal with fear and abuse in their relationships, we've begun to ask some routine questions of all our patients." She made it sound like some kind of survey when she asked, "Are you in any relationship in which another person tries to control you?" and "Has anyone physically harmed you in any way in the last twelve months?" When Audrey asked the third question, "Do you ever feel unsafe at home?," the girl responded, "Once in a while, sometimes."

Because she was so thin, she looked younger than a seventh-grader but, not unlike Val at that age, her narrowed eyes were outlined in black and shadowed in a reddish color designed to camouflage the fact that the whites of her eyes weren't all that clear. Audrey asked the first two questions again, rephrasing them, and now she got different answers. She explained to the girl, now calling her by her name, Dolores, that Social Services would follow up with her. Audrey brought Louise in, who examined both wrists and suspected an earlier fracture that hadn't mended properly. Just as Louise was about to order x-rays, the receptionist delivered a message from the girl's aunt that she'd had to leave for work. Now Dolores could talk all she wanted, and did, beginning with the fact that her aunt had been out of a job for four or five months.

Audrey's stomach rumbled audibly, like a large vehicle on a bad road, inspiring little confidence. Handing the patient the separate signed forms for Radiology and Social Services, Audrey told the girl that she'd done the right thing by coming in, but it was a sickening feeling nevertheless. No matter how inappropriate it was to compare this girl to Val, it was scary to imagine what these next years would hold for her. If Val's accident had been only a little worse, she might never have known she'd earned the first A of her life. Dolores seemed not to have had any such chance so far, and who knew if she would? The colorless hair on her head was so stressed, it looked as if it could easily snap, like toothpicks.

Audrey gave her two notes for school, one merely to explain her absence and the other to recommend intervention. She also gave her lunch money and directions to the cafeteria, in the event all this took the rest of the morning. In response to Audrey's question, Dolores said she didn't know who her legal guardian was, maybe her grandmother, but no matter what, she couldn't leave her little sisters in case something happened to them. Something? When Dolores exhaled, the breath that had caught in her slender throat carried the bitter smell of cigarettes.

"Don't ever give me your money, Doctor," said Helena, "because I always lose all my money." She'd moved out of the experimental armless chair to gain the familiar support of her particular place. Now she wore the wide wraparound glasses like a velvet headband, and it was possible to see behind her chafed skin that in another life she would be pretty. "I always lose all my money," she repeated, fussing with the buttons on her pink cardigan sweater, "like you."

Audrey thought of the Cincinnati nurse who'd taken charge of Val and made her call home. That shift had ended by the time Audrey got to the hospital, and then she'd neglected to find out the nurse's name in order to thank her for taking that initiative. As if care were a chain letter, all Audrey could do was pass it on and hope no one would break it. But now, as she leaned against the door of her office, she couldn't say for sure if, according to the Hippocratic oath, in intervening in the life of this girl, she'd done no harm.

One night this week during dinner, she and Gregory tried to get Sally to say something more about Cincinnati. "It's not too bad a school, you know," Audrey began, hope vibrating in her voice.

Sally flooded her mouth with milk and was silent.

Gregory said it was his kind of place, or would have to have been without the intervention of Judge Osborne's tuition for him at Yale. "Co-op education was invented there, so for almost a hundred years now, kids could earn their way through college." He was boasting on behalf of his brother, who was one of those kids who took time off for Korea but made it back and finally finished up. "It always bothered me," Gregory was able to admit for the first time, "the way Hathaway Brown made Val feel like such a failure for going there. So what if Cincinnati accepts almost everybody but can't enroll more than half of those? So what if they don't bother with essay questions on their application? So what if the electronic organ was invented there? What snobs private school people can be, when in fact the University of Cincinnati has one of the best state-run conservatories in the nation." He preferred "nation" instead of "country" in such an argument, as if the Founding Fathers were somehow involved.

"And, it turns out, Val's lucky to be there," Audrey said, "since they take music so seriously. It's a good opportunity, in the end, isn't it?" She'd be very happy to be convinced.

"I mean, so were antihistamines invented there," Gregory added. "Also the U.S. Weather Bureau. See?"

"Yeah," said Sally in a lifeless voice as she started to clear the plates. She wasn't going to be the one to tell them that while it was true about Val's A on that one paper, they might want to ask Val how the rest of her courses were going. If, for instance, she ever went to class. If, here in mid-April, she'd even bought the books. Now she wished she'd let Val take the bus back to school. She hadn't wanted to know this much.

Audrey asked, "Is there a problem?" Sally was rinsing the dishes, speeding things along.

"No problem." Sally wasn't going to be the one to tell them Val's roommate was furious because Rex had basically moved in there. When Sally drove her back to school on Easter night—and it wasn't as if she had nothing better to do!—Val and Rex had dragged her to some foul place where everyone was stoned. Not Val, but only because Sally watched her like a cop. And then, and *then,* sharing Val's room forced her to listen to the two of them all night. They sounded to her like toilet plungers.

Audrey hadn't pressed Sally to say more, because she didn't assume Sally's mood was caused by Val. The forecast for the weekend wasn't great, for example, and although the 10k was a rain-or-shine event, revenues, if not spirits, were sure to be dampened.

"Plus," Gregory had gone right on, "the athletes are good

enough for a number of them to turn pro." He wasn't giving up, neither on Val nor on his argument.

Sally didn't answer at first. "Yeah, but," she said, unable to resist, "guess how many of their star athletes graduate? Zero."

"That can't be true," Audrey protested, wanting it not to be.

But Sally only said, "Ask Val. Because she's the one who told me."

From the windows of the old courthouse dining room the sky and the lake traded blues, the one intensifying the other by an energetic mirroring that looked magnetic. The windows were sealed shut for reasons of security, but the restoration project's budget evidently extended to simple window washing, another old-world skill. This room had elaborately carved ceiling rosettes and was painted in dense, grandmotherly tones. This was the meeting of a group that called itself Third Friday Lunch, as if to prove, since they were all members of the Ohio bar, how plainly pragmatic they were. Too suspicious of Harvard to count themselves Pragmatist disciples of Charles S. Peirce and William James, they were nevertheless steady measurers of practical consequences. "No Poets Need Apply" was their joke on themselves, but Gregory nevertheless refused to sit with his back to those windows. And just then, to please him, a little jet took off from the Lakefront Airport, on the southwest runway, aiming for him.

Next to Gregory at their long narrow table sat a litigating attorney who couldn't help himself. The week of April 15 was a natural time for complaining about tax legislation, but it wouldn't be considered appropriate to get personal. "I'm dead," said Hank Ferguson when asked how he was.

Already it was easy to feel sympathy for Hank. His former law firm had gone under in the eighties economy, and although he'd been taken instantly by another firm, at the point in his career when he might have been allowed to ease up, Hank was instead accountable, along with the youngest of the associates, for more and more billable hours. Plus, he'd had a public and punishing divorce, having had the bad luck to leave his longtime wife just before the stock market crash in 1987, which swamped him and his partners. It could get worse?

"Shoot me, I always said I'd say," he said, breaking the flaky crust of his hard roll and slathering it with butter, as if he hadn't heard—or else, as if he had—about the link between diet and heart attacks. "It serves me right."

Cream of spinach soup would also be Hank's last choice, if asked, but there it was, thickened after the fact by the addition of cornstarch. Unintegrated, the shiny white flecks looked toxic against the dark overcooked spinach. Because Hank had asked Gregory if he agreed, about the soup at least, in case he didn't want to get into the other stuff, Gregory responded, "How come?"

"How come it serves me right? Thank you," Hank replied with a quiet laugh, "since I do hate to break the rules against discussing our personal lives." He slid the soup out of his way. "But since you ask, as you know I have a young family, which means I have two families. Five tuitions altogether. After taxes, I'm too broke to be merely depressed. I'm finished. Last night my wife told me she wants to become a social worker. Not like we used to think of them, volunteering here and there to help out, but a licensed therapist."

"Sounds like you could use one," Gregory said, like Val when Audrey had made her announcement.

"Thank you, I could. Good line. I'll have to remember that one," Hank said, "for when they lock me up for child support failure, as well as every other kind."

Gregory didn't want to tell Hank he understood all too well, because he didn't want to shift the emphasis onto himself. He hated it when complaints were traded back and forth like insults ("You think *you're* stressed!"), one-upping each other like gameshow contestants.

"My wife tells me it's not her fault she was that young. She says, 'Since you were so vain you married somebody so much younger than you—who hasn't had a complete life, unlike yourself—how can you be surprised?' Who could argue with that? I can't, is the truth. I know that. But does she have to call it *vain?*" Hank took a gulp of water and, with his thick teeth, reduced an ice cube to chips.

"How old is she?" Gregory couldn't picture her.

"Forty-something, as it's called now."

"Forty what? My wife's forty-nine."

Hank reconsidered Gregory. "You too? I didn't know that, or I forgot. My kids this time around are ten and eight. How about you?"

"Mine are older. Everybody's older, including me." He had no need to point out that he'd never been required to pay alimony or court-mandated child support. Gregory guessed Hank would call it a narrow escape, if he were to know about Karen. By comparison to Hank's, his own life appeared simple. Everything was voluntary, with the one exception of Audrey's decision.

"At least your wife won't want to switch careers on you," Hank said. "Mine used to work for *Cleveland* magazine. What was so wrong with that, I ask. Plus, it's income." Hank's voice was a little too loud and prompted an audible silence that, as if these men were musicians, fell back into a synchronous action.

Gregory would rather talk about anything else but money, so the subject hadn't been raised in spite of the fact that Audrey's tuition costs, unlike the girls' college funds, weren't planned for. He'd mentioned his retirement without reference to the discrepancy between salary and pension, but that wasn't the same as neglecting to mention more than a hundred thousand dollars in unanticipated costs. In order to get Hank's reaction, he decided to try out the idea. "Well, my wife is beginning medical school, so—"

So Hank roared like somebody who'd been told the best joke

in the whole world. He had no reason to believe Gregory could be serious, but he felt better anyway.

"I'm serious," said Gregory, happy to admit that they had this in common. He was even more glad—though it made him feel appropriately guilty to admit this to himself—that he didn't have a second wife and a second family. What if, like Hank's new wife, Karen decided to quit being a math teacher and, because she was good with numbers, enter business school? That would make six tuitions. The same as Hank.

The soup was cleared and a plate loaded with "oriental chicken" was put at each man's place. It was the kind of dish none of them would have picked from a menu, but there wasn't infinite time during this weekday lunch recess. Now the meeting was called to order, to get to the topics of common interest. Thanks to Marjorie, Gregory had placed two issues on the agenda. The first was the spousal privilege, and in presenting it he footnoted her properly.

"Bad luck," lamented a colleague on Gregory's behalf. "As they say in Boston, nobody wants to be in the paper unless it's for a birth announcement or a death notice."

"Too true," another said, "and I agree with your clerk."

"My secretary," said Gregory. "Marjorie McCarthy."

After a silence, somebody joked "Whatever" in a poor imitation of the tone favored by the current generation, from which most of the court house secretaries came. Hank Ferguson's second set of children qualified him to instruct them in the vernacular, but Hank had sufficient troubles without passing himself off as an expert opinion in ruined language.

"Marjorie McCarthy has been in this business longer than some of us at this table, and when she says the time is right, I tend to believe her." While working to persuade either his own peers or juries of a defendant's peers, Gregory liked to rest his reading glasses on the ridge of his forehead. They looked like headlights—fog lights—and gave the impression of doubling his resources. He said, "We should propose a bill, I think," claiming the idea as his own since, after all, his was the court the defendant had manipulated, with the perfectly legal assistance of his girlfriend—former girlfriend—and their pair of lawyers. Gregory felt a responsibility to the woman bringing the charges in the name of her truly innocent-victim husband, who'd had the misfortune to stop for that red light. "A spousal-privilege bill that gives us real power if it's abused."

"Power to restrict it, you mean, don't you?"

Gregory said, like a bridegroom, "I do," and they all laughed, agreeing to come back next Third Friday with concrete suggestions for an immediate plan of action.

And since this was how they always did their business, they went on to the next item. Again Gregory leaned forward to present what he expected to be an easy sell, because Rob Wallace had been about to be elected to this lunch group when, that very same week, he died.

"Shouldn't his widow be consulted?" someone asked, not at all in disagreement, only, as he put it, to touch all the bases.

"If you like, I would be glad to," Gregory said. On a strict need-to-know basis, this was all they needed to know.

Of course someone else raised the issue of precedence, since no decision could be reached otherwise. But it was pointed out that in the naming of most programs, and the same was true of buildings, especially government buildings, the only major restriction had to do with the person in question no longer being alive. Alive, there was always a risk the person might bring discredit upon an institution by some unforeseeable lapse.

One of the men said, "But since he's dead, no problem."

Gregory asked Marjorie to make a reservation and leave word for Audrey that he hoped she'd let him take her out to dinner. His week had been filled with small annoying cases, which kept little firms in business but gave the impression that the law was for sale to the highest bidder. It didn't help to have started the week by looking like a fool in every conceivable way, but he'd still managed to remain aware that this was Audrey's day. He was glad not to have made any plans of his own for the weekend. He wasn't a candidate for the 10k race, no matter that he could use the charity.

On their way out for the evening, Sally came into the kitchen with her enthusiasm revived by the group labor of assembling a plywood booth for the bake sale, with a brown-and-gold-striped awning in case it dared to rain. She felt released from the self-imposed pressures of record-setting by remembering that Carnival was a joint venture, so the point of the Race for Charity wasn't to win it, but to run it.

In this spirit Sally agreed to take Audrey's car to pick Val up at the bus stop. She posed like a cartoon of a teacher with her checklist, asking briskly, "Any other questions?" Her hair was pulled back severely and held at the base of her neck by a barrette from which it exploded, propelled as if by aerosol. "And we'll stand by, waiting for the family's marathoners, who are driving here as we speak." She cut an orange into quarters and slipped one into her mouth like a mouth guard, sucking the flesh efficiently. Rinsing her hands, she shook them to dry as if they were feathers and she a duck. She had a few more calls to make, so she vanished from view, like a duck, to pop up again in a new, nearby place.

Gregory said, "Today at lunch I told a guy you were starting med school." He left out the part about not being taken seriously.

"And you survived the thought?" Audrey returned his smile.

Now he was the one who laughed as he said, "Survived? You know me, I'm never comfortable as the survivor."

"It's learnable. Everything is." Or so she hoped.

Optimistically, then, in Gregory's silver sedan they headed away from the house and across the city, then across the river, to the place he'd chosen because they had never been there. He'd asked Hank Ferguson for the recommendation, figuring the clientele would be younger at Lola Bistro than in the Ritz dining room. When he told Audrey this, her laughter filled the car.

Lola's was jammed, and it turned out that the crowd at the bar was young enough to drink bottled beer and largely base their opinions of each other—not unlike the chef—on the presentation. The majority looked to have come from work by way of some gym, where, if their skin wasn't naturally brown, they could manufacture color by improving blood flow. The walls were dark, so the pressed-metal ceiling captured all the light while ricocheting the harsh sound of happy voices at the start of a weekend. Audrey and Gregory were given an out-of-the-way table, as if they were out-of-towners who, when they made their reservation, didn't know West Cleveland had become this hot.

As opposed to the waiter at the Ritz, this one expected originality, so when Gregory said, "Whatever Lola wants—" his waiter's forced smile conveyed his boredom with such an obvious reference. "Lola gets," Gregory said, indicating his wife. Audrey ordered twin flutes of champagne.

The champagne came with exquisite bubbles rising from the stem in straight lines, like the seed-pearl baby-girl necklaces Celia gave her three granddaughters when each was born. Gregory raised his glass and held it in the air, waiting for hers. "Here's to Doctor Brennan," he said in such an authentic way as to make it impossible to tell no such person existed.

There were specials to hear recited, but since they weren't ready to begin contemplating the menu, they listened as if to a foreign language neither of them spoke—mango vinegar, fig yogurt—knowing they could always ask to have the entire thing repeated. With practice the waiter was only going to get more fluent.

"Can you say how you decided?" She still hadn't told him *what* she'd decided, but by his smile he hoped to convey his full, albeit belated, support.

"Well, earlier this week I made lists. If this, then that; if that, then this. Which was a pointless exercise. Which surprised me." She rested her fingers on the edge of the table like a pianist preparing to play an arpeggio. "I tried it twice, once with you and once without you."

His face registered shock, as if she'd intended to imply that Plan A and Plan B were equal. "Without?"

"Without *considering* you."

"Don't mind me," he managed to joke, "if I feel sorry for myself for a second." He counted it. "There!"

Audrey let herself be charmed, marginally.

Gregory pushed his glasses onto his forehead to indicate his lack of interest in the menu and the full attention he wanted to give her. "Say more."

"I made a grid with four sets of alternatives, including yours, and next I drew a line down a page, two columns, Yes and No, but both of them mine. Since I'm always helped by list-making, I was surprised to find this exercise didn't help at all. Not that I knew it at the time." The waiter seemed to know not to interrupt to ask if they were ready to decide. He hovered and pivoted. The busboy brought a breadbasket, but it wasn't his job to speak to customers. "At that time, last Monday morning, you were being the inconsiderate one. I imagined you thinking about leaving me and starting over with Karen. No, don't," she stopped him from speaking, "it was *my* imagination. Don't correct it."

So he didn't, realizing in time that, the way two wrongs don't make a right, her oversimplification would be made worse by his own oversimplification.

"I had to figure out, for example, if I'd qualify for loans or be considered too much of a risk for paying them back. I probably would be, by the way, but that was useful, because it helped me to see, in that case, that I'd find some other means. But," she said firmly, "this isn't my point at all. Why was there no *process* for me? Where was my *choice?*" She didn't have to mention her organizational skills—she was already famous for them—so instead she reminded him, "When I got my Med/Surg credentials it was only a matter of budgeting time. This is different. This isn't about weighing pluses and minuses to decide Will she? or Won't she?"

"It isn't? But you'd still have to decide if you will or won't." When exactly *was* the deadline, if not today?

"Yes." Audrey paused for emphasis. "But I'd already decided."

And why wouldn't the waiter assume they were ready to order? His "Have you decided?" seemed redundant, given the number of times he'd heard them say it.

"Yes," Audrey said, selecting what she remembered of the specials he'd recited. Gregory ordered the same thing and at random chose a red wine to go along. It was as if they were in the exact-change lane.

"Here's the enlightening part," she said, sounding trivial in order to avoid sounding melodramatic. Because of the noise in the room, she was forced to speak louder than she'd have wished, but she had to say this because it had taken her such a long time to get here. "The fundamental stance, for a woman, is to know in advance the answer to the question 'If he should want me, do I want him?' It's a wholly practical consideration having to do with the need to say no in time."

He was listening intently, in spite of the fact that he hated generalizations like this. "Only for a woman?" he asked, proving he didn't get it yet.

"If the only power a woman has is to say no and mean it, and be taken seriously, she has to know in sufficient time." She knew she sounded like a sex-ed counselor.

"Wait. You're talking about sex here, or rape, or what?" He placed both his hands on the table to show he had nothing to hide.

"Yes, rape, but not per se. As regards decision-making."

This was the kind of talk he couldn't stand, because it sounded exactly like law school. Gregory frowned.

"Don't frown," she said.

The waiter wanted to be watched while he expertly demonstrated the wine opener, but Audrey ignored him as well. "It's ingrained behavior," she told Gregory, "a legacy."

"It's fine," Gregory said about the sip he'd been given to taste, and the waiter withdrew without bothering to tell them their smoked trout would be out in a moment. From his point of view, this was obviously a business dinner. The woman was the boss. The older guy was trying hard to impress her. He hoped the next table would be more interested.

"What I'm saying," Audrey went on, "is that it's the lesson of inferiority to try and anticipate situations. I'm not saying it's how I'd choose to be, but only how I am—how women are—for good reason. When it isn't a clear case of mutual consent, to be taken seriously a woman simply can't decide at the last minute. So unless somehow she loses her power to choose to have sex or not, she'll have thought about it, and she'll have decided. Unconsciously, if not consciously." She was drinking ice water. "Self-protection."

"Let me see if I've got this right," Gregory said as the waiter set down their wide plates drizzled with a wasabi cream sauce so pale it was barely chartreuse. But he sounded like the loser the waiter had figured him for when he asked, "Is this key lime sauce?"

During the main course, which was a quail with tiny tangy berries, the subject was changed back to the familiar territory of Val and Sally. Gregory asked if she'd discussed her theory with them, and if so, whether they agreed.

"You make it sound as if I've invented some new product that needs to be tested before *Consumer Reports* gives it their seal of approval. It isn't a *theory*. It's a scientific observation." There was practically nothing on these little bones, and Audrey felt guilty for having robbed a nest.

He was watching Audrey and saw she had the same problem: either the silverware was too big or there wasn't enough food.

She said, "What's the central question here?"

"How is everything?" asked the waiter, not waiting for an answer because by now he knew better than to expect one. Now she was quizzing the poor guy.

"What do women want?" At this point he'd do anything to please her, including quoting Freud.

"Correct." She sat up a little straighter, to be the same height as Gregory, who somewhat slumped. "It's implicit that whether you or anybody else ever asks, I'll know the answer to that question because I'll have thought about it." She waited for him to raise his head and turn his face toward hers, and when he did, she saw how difficult this was for him, no matter that, in principle, he loved these discussions about what motivates people. "For you, wanting and getting are connected as cause and effect, aren't they?"

Gregory was unsure of the meaning of her question, but his answer was very clear. "Well, sure. Shouldn't they be? Isn't this what we're trying to teach our daughters? 'Whatever Sally wants, she gets'? Like Gwen Verdon in *Damn Yankees*. Nineteen fifty-five." After a pause, he added, "And now Val too."

But she wasn't willing to let it get away from her. "Whether or not I *get* what I want isn't wholly within my control. So it's more like the Rolling Stones." Was this a complaint? Not really. Or not merely.

"Or not *always* get what you want," said Gregory, pleased with himself for having caught Audrey's reference.

She tried again. "My having thought about it means I wouldn't have been capable of applying to medical school unless, if I were to get in, I was able in my own mind to say yes. So these subsequent two weeks were not about decision-making." She could see he was still puzzled. "It's like the time between the day you and I met and when you asked me to marry you, when I knew I'd answer yes. Or like the interval between engagement and marriage. It's for the lesser intelligence of cold feet."

Gregory raised his glass and, without being so mundane as to say, "I'll drink to that," he held that thought suspended between them until she'd picked up her glass and could join him in being glad, at least, for that.

"Me too," she said.

Her smile was what the waiter had been waiting *for*, so now he described the desserts. To celebrate, Audrey ordered one made with five kinds of chocolate. "Now it's your turn," she said, pulling her chair in closer in order to feel the back against her own. Nobody could be expected to finish five kinds of chocolate.

In his lap Gregory was rolling up his napkin as if it were a red bandanna he was about to tie around his neck and run away from home. "Not here," he said.

And before Audrey had time to feel deflected, a woman approached their table and proved his point by coming too close and having to rock back on her heels in partial correction. She said, "Sorry to interrupt, but I really have to tell you I think about you every day." It wasn't clear which of them she was addressing, until she said, "You gave me my verdict. Thank you."

He wanted to say, "No, the jury delivers the verdict, I'm the one to impose the sentence," but she was smiling so enthusiastically, whether drunk or not, he couldn't bring himself to be didactic.

"So thanks again." She was nodding her curly head to include Audrey in her thanks, as if Audrey had been the one to prescribe antidepressants.

What could he say but "You're welcome." To Audrey he suggested, "Let's go somewhere else."

The waiter set the bill between them, closer to Audrey. "Whenever you're ready," he said, backing away to convey the impression that he hadn't overheard a single word all evening long.

And as they walked to the front of the restaurant and saw the Friday night crowd in full exuberance, they discovered as well that by a different standard—more people were arriving than leaving—it was still early. By comparison, outside, the street called Literary Road was quiet.

This was the neighborhood of the West Side Market, where she and Sally had stopped for delicacies the day she got her ticket to medical school. They were also in the vicinity of the Metro-Health Medical Center, where ambulances brought victims of trauma from all over the city, all night, because no one could be refused care.

"Now it's your turn," Audrey reminded him, fastening her seat belt for the journey.

"You're right, it is." They reached the lighted river, where his willingness to talk was apparent because, although he was still considering what to say, his mouth was open, like a door.

When Gregory first came back to Cleveland from New York, he was aware, by his own defensiveness, that most people assumed he'd failed. Everyone was too nice at first, making him feel more acceptable than he'd been made to feel the years he lived here. "Oh, thank goodness you're not better than us after all," they practically said, which always made him find a way of saying something bad about New York. After a while, he began to say what he liked about Cleveland, but still there remained a discomfort. That is, until he met Audrey.

Back then his car was a silver Beetle, which his neighbor Bonnie said he'd probably bought because he was old enough to know the music of the Silver Beetles, one of the Liverpool band's ancient names. Bonnie unfairly accused him of passing himself off as younger than he was, but when Audrey said that his being over forty meant he'd outlived his father, he'd become aware of feeling, for the first time in his life, free.

He asked, "Care for an airplane ride?"

Audrey knew he couldn't be serious, so she said, "Sure, anytime."

He was serious. The day after that night they met, he'd hired a pilot like a limo driver, to create the impression of spreading the whole world at Audrey's feet. If the crooked Cuyahoga could find its way to the port of Cleveland, then so could they, and with greater ease than the barges winding downriver like food through the city's intestinal tract. At the river's mouth, in daylight, the color of the water changed to green, but tonight it was like patent leather, appearing—impossibly—waterproof.

The willow trees alone would have been worth the trip, fountains of budding branches like beaded curtains across doorways, shimmying with the activity of a breeze. The streetlights backlit them as if to demonstrate that Cleveland's city planners, and planters, had been to Washington, D.C., to study spring evenings. Gregory allowed himself to be influenced by these willows. No tree was more exposed, year-round, in leaf or not, in its states of heartbreaking grace.

He stopped at the farthest end of the parking lot, where they idled while he told her he felt stripped of the protection of his own worthless pretensions. He felt found out, like a liar caught in a senseless deception. "Look how much I took for granted," he said, turning off the headlights to make the outside world invisible, restricting their frame of reference to his own behavior.

Audrey pressed the door-lock button for added emphasis and so they couldn't be dragged out of the car and killed before he could finish his sentence.

"I would have said we were partners in the new style, the typical working couple with kids, equal partners. I'd have called myself contemporary, believe it or not." He waited for her to laugh, in case she couldn't help laughing at that, but she didn't react. "I guess this is too obvious to bother saying."

"I'm not going to interrupt you this time, or anymore. Just talk." Her reassuring voice was appropriate to a darkened room.

He turned off the engine. "It was my first reaction to blame you for daring to imagine changing your life. I must have felt you weren't free unless I gave you my permission. But I *don't* blame you," he told her, "and I'm very sorry if it looked like that to you." He kept his face in profile, so she'd know he wasn't finished. "It wasn't about blame," he saw, but a deadlier sin: envy. He asked, "Do you think it could be that I was envious of you?" Even as he admitted the word into the public record, he knew it was so. Another way he knew was that he felt ashamed.

"Yes," she answered immediately, preventing him from striking it.

"It would explain my behavior," he found himself capable of saying, "if I were jealous of you for having the chance to start over."

"Say more."

"I don't know more. It's not something I'd be proud of." Then he could admit to Audrey, "It would mean I was envious of you for being young enough to begin again. Envious of your ability to believe your life will be sufficiently long. An admission that you possess something I don't have." He could feel his heart being squeezed. "I would hate myself, and so would you, if, for those reasons, I refused it for you."

"It would prove that you were human."

In the old days he'd have pushed in the lighter now, to buy time. When the glowing orange coil made contact, searing his cigarette, he'd draw the smoke in and deliberate what to say. Back then, he always had a cigarette burning in the wide glass ashtray on his leather-topped desk, the victim of his own secondhand smoke long before the threat had been realized. Back then, he was a rising star bound to disappoint everyone by leaving the city for Cleveland. Nobody could quite believe it, but nobody said so. "If I'd stayed in New York," he told her now, "I'd never have met you." This was an exaggeration too, since for all he knew, without him in her life, she'd have gone to medical school on time. "Unless you had ended up my mother's oncologist. We could have met that way, out in the corridor. If I'd given you a few more years on your own."

"What I mean is that it would prove you were human. To want your life to be longer than it will be."

The night was cool enough to require the heater, so he started the engine again. "As you can see, I refuse to imagine my life without you." With the absurd exception of that night after his speech at the Renaissance Hotel, he hadn't imagined it. But that night was a delusion. "And I couldn't dare imagine yours without me," he admitted. "Here's what I want to say to you as clearly as I can: my decision to retire was an improvisation."

"*What?*" She knew it!

"I didn't intend it. When it became a way to obstruct you, I didn't intend that either." He wasn't in profile to her, nor was he able to face her directly, even in the dark. "After Rob died I wasn't thinking of quitting, but the opposite. Of continuing his work." If his voice was too flat to seem sincere, Gregory honestly didn't mean it to sound that way. The problem was larger than that. "I was feeling obliged to continue his work."

"That's what I thought," she said. "By which I'm not saying 'I told you so,' only that you'd seemed to feel there was too *much* work he'd left undone, not too little. That's not quite what I mean either."

"I know," he said, so she could know they were on the same side. "But I felt so inadequate compared to Rob. I believed then, right after his death, that I'd come back from New York because I wasn't up to it. As opposed to the way, with his gift, he'd have been." He let go of most of what remained of his breath. "Do you think that's why I canceled the Paris trip?" He turned toward her. "I'm sorry we didn't go, so all this wouldn't have been left unsaid."

"Me too." Another car joined theirs, at the other extreme end of the parking lot. Lovers, she hoped, although, no matter how much the Cleveland shoreline had been improved, Lake Erie was no Seine, whose willows were ancient, monumental. In this part of Cleveland, after dark, it was still true that nobody dared to stroll.

"Plus, we could have used the romance."

She laughed softly but was waiting to see if he would bring it up now.

And he did. "And so, as for Karen, well, that was to punish you for changing the rules, I guess." He shifted in his seat. It sounded right to him: if not valid, at least correct.

"Yes, it did. Punish me." She could hear her own hurt.

"I owe you an apology for these two weeks."

This was more than she was looking for. She took it.

But Gregory wasn't finished. "What you were saying back at the restaurant bothered me."

"Why? Because it was true?"

"That too, but I mean because of what it showed me about myself. You talked about 'women' and 'men' and I couldn't abstract myself. I know I've never raped you, or anybody, and never would. But when you said you'd had to have your answer ready ahead of time, I recognized that what you meant was your belief that I would have tried to talk you out of it." He pivoted his whole body, like a weathervane.

"Yes, I was most afraid of that. Or that if you didn't succeed, you might have tried to coerce me." She knew that what she was about to say was true. "Because then, I saw, I'd have had to divorce you."

The door to the terminal was unlocked, so they entered looking like customers and were greeted by a man dressed as a pilot.

"May I help you?"

Gregory admitted he had no idea whether it might be feasible to go flying. "Tonight," he clarified, "right now." He was careful not to sound as if he might hijack the plane if the pilot said no. "If possible."

The pilot worked for a charter airline, but was already booked for the evening. Something was going on next door at the Rock and Roll Hall of Fame, and at midnight he had to fly his passengers back to Pittsburgh.

Without hesitating, Gregory asked, "What's your position on double-booking for a half hour? I hear all the airlines do it." He slipped his hand into his pants pocket as if to bring forth a wad of hundred-dollar bills.

Following the pilot through the glass door, they walked over to the little white plane that was parked like a taxi they could catch for the short ride home. He unlocked the door and, with a welcome irony, said, "Welcome aboard," after which, in toneless compliance with federal aviation regulations, he gave them their orders like a policeman reading them their rights. With both engines going, conversation would be impossible, even though the pilot put on his earphones and, unlike the waiter at Lola's, couldn't have heard a word they said.

Which of them would have been the one to ask, "Is this crazy?" and which one of them would have answered, "Yes!" And what would be the meaning of "crazy"? As it was, Gregory sat behind the empty copilot's seat—this *was* crazy—and Audrey behind the pilot, on either side of such a narrow aisle that they'd had to shape their bodies into question marks in order to board. Because the aisle was so narrow it was natural to hold hands.

If their yard were bigger, Gregory might have given himself a tractor mower to ride around like this, high up, gently bouncing, rolling toward the runway, in partial suspension with the motion of the twin propellers. Gregory was already feeling weightless, his useless legs folded as neat as a paper clip. They could be breaking not just the rules but some law he ought to know about, but—too late! they were already airborne!—there was no stopping them. He loved this feeling of pulling against gravity.

Beneath them, Cleveland was instantly transformed into constellations, so that they could be flying upside down and gazing at the sky. And look how much was new! Every time either of them came or went from Hopkins Airport the landscape was improved upon. But they'd never flown like a flag over the glass point of the pyramid temple to rock and roll, or hovered like the blimp over the new football stadium, built on the site of the old one as if to preserve sacred bones. From the air, Jacobs Field was as pretty as an amusement park, polished in anticipation of another winning season. Cleveland wasn't all new by any means, but now it was famous for being new, not merely for having been so dirty the river once caught fire.

The New York jokes about Cleveland got so tiresome he'd been happy to trade them for New Yorkers' jokes on themselves, which, like the bagels, were fresh every morning. When he'd returned home from New York, this city was at its most laughable, but now the jokes had been discarded like pieces of string too short to save no matter how frugal he might be. He'd run away, but he'd run back.

He'd once been chosen by one of the senior partners to work on a big case that required him to fly to Brussels every other week. There his French improved so quickly he was tempted by that perpetually receding horizon's chance to see how far he could get from the memory of his father. The senior partner had trouble understanding why Gregory would return to Cleveland when he had the opportunity to go so far in the other direction, but Gregory had understood the need to stop avoiding the realization that his father killed himself, yes, but not solely on purpose. Gregory had needed to come home to learn that the acts of a sick man aren't wholly voluntary.

The buzz of the airplane's twin propellers was stereophonic reinforcement of his knowledge, gained over time and realized in the intervals between episodes of self-doubt, that he was contented in this life, which fitted him like his tailored suits. He wouldn't have chosen it for himself, but that didn't make him incapable of embracing it when presented with a good alternative. Or of choosing it once again, right this minute.

Not long ago, Gregory's brother told him he was thinking of

moving back now that most of Cleveland had been renovated into a kind of trophy house. Rich had lived everywhere, which could be proved by the debris he'd left behind, but he hadn't been back for any amount of time since their mother's funeral, after which he'd boarded his plane holding her Singer sewing machine like a briefcase, leaving everything else for Gregory and Goodwill. Gregory knew Rich would live in the restored Warehouse District, as if he were starting over again. He always did, like someone just out of rehab.

So, like a localized headache Gregory felt the pressure of his own near miss: succumbing to the myth of the surface overhaul without first updating the infrastructure. He hadn't returned to Cleveland from his big chance to amount to something because this city was fulfilling its promise, but because it was where he was from. Where he *is* from.

He rested his forehead against the small window as the pilot banked to bring the plane back from its turn over the lake to cruise the suburbs to the east. Gregory almost felt he could be falling from the sky, so immediate was his grief about all that he'd almost lost. If he could have been heard over the noise of the airplane, he would have told this to Audrey because, twice, she would have been his lost opportunity.

Now he saw himself from outside himself, and it embarrassed him to admit that he'd tried to appropriate her opportunity. He'd never claimed credit for an achievement of hers, but it was as if he couldn't let her feel entitled to a future without, like an agent, taking a percentage. Unlike an agent, he wouldn't have enabled anything. Quite the opposite.

And in the meantime he'd let himself become distracted at work and, uncharacteristically, overlooked the obvious clue that the "missing" witness could have been absent as a way to evade testimony. If his secretary had been in the courtroom observing the case, she'd have prompted him, and if she'd been presiding, no lawyer would have dared try it in the first place. As it was, thanks to Marjorie, that particular lawyer will be very sorry he ever came to her outraged attention. Gregory felt a little laugh rise in his throat. He squeezed Audrey's hand so he could assure himself she was there.

Below her feet was Case Western Reserve Medical School, along the rim of University Circle. Audrey noted that this was what she'd searched out first, before the geological formation of Cleveland Heights, where she could spot their house on Overlook Road from high above it, and, below the ridge, the white lights of Morrow's Pharmacy that made it look like an ocean liner. Shaker Heights offered up Hathaway Brown and its dark playing fields and the school buildings where Val always learned by doing. Academically a late bloomer, she was precocious in the kinds of skills that could get her in trouble. The settings for Audrey's own exclusively good-girl life, from her very first hour to this one, were traceable from this porthole window barely bigger than her own face. How could it look so expansive, so beautiful?

"Look." Audrey tried to speak over the steady drone. "Look at the plan." She meant the way their landscape had been organized by the artful tycoon Patrick Calhoun. This overview gave her an appreciation of what he'd been able to see at ground level, the vision in the meaning of envisioning. The only other time she'd flown this low above Cleveland she hadn't noticed this, because it was daylight and because she'd fallen in love with Gregory. "The lights have shapes! Look how we're surrounded by stars!"

He wasn't able to hear her exact words, but with her other hand, the one he didn't hold, she was pointing both down and up. It had come to her too that looking at the ground was like looking up at the sky, as if they were in some kind of cosmic net hammock and could see everything forward and backward and inside out and upside down. Now Audrey experienced the world as a sphere, as advertised, although this was the first time she was seeing it from its center. Their little plane blinked like more stars, but it traveled across the sky, more like the moon. Now, were they as three-dimensional as could be?

His flying was like her skating, or like scuba, for its offer of a version of an out-of-body experience that didn't require dying. This they had in common, although for each it was more a hobby than a passion, which might be why they were so suited to each other. The day after they met, when he took her flying like this, it could have been as true that he'd go on for his pilot's license, just as—if, say, she'd persisted in her interests—their life would have included her worlds within worlds. As it was, they were who they were. Audrey liked surfaces and depths. Gregory preferred someone else at the controls.

Who could blame him? What she saw she liked about this experience of wraparound stars was that it was somebody else's job to know which way was up, or, failing that, to know how to find out in a second or less. It was this, after all, that made *her* free, just as underwater there was a certified instructor monitoring the oxygen supply. While skating as a girl, she'd always kept herself safe from thin ice, because she knew the difference between limitations and limits.

As they came in for their landing, the plane bounced on incompatible air currents, lifting them out of their descent, tipping them side to side, causing her to wonder, while landing on one wheel, if instead of the other wheel touching down, the wing tip were to graze the runway, rolling them into a giant fireball. Before she had time to picture it, they'd landed.

Gregory was the last one out and liked the way the pilot had the authority to take his wife's hand as her feet touched the ground. Now, although up in the air he'd recommitted himself to his practice of the law, a sudden thought intruded. Eventually he would be forced to retire from the bench, required to cultivate other interests. He knew better than to pretend to qualify as a pilot, but he could allow himself to imagine his wife the doctor assigned to a helicopter, evacuating lives from deadly situations. So maybe he'd be allowed to go along for the ride.

In the car, however, she had no interest in pursuing such fantastic images of herself rescuing people from worst-case scenarios. The idea irritated her. She said so. Then she admitted that the idea frightened her and made her sad.

"Don't be sorry," he coaxed as he touched Audrey's face, "since I'm the one who should be."

"I didn't say 'sorry.' *Sorrow.*" Which intensified it.

"Well, me too, in that case," he said. They weren't too far from the courthouse, but he turned left on Carnegie and also avoided the Renaissance Hotel. All he really wanted was for them to get into their own bed. Beyond that, he saw, who knew?

"Now I'm sorry too, though," she said with a forced laugh.

"No, don't. As I already said." At least his laugh was genuine. "But how about postponing sorrow until tomorrow. If only for the rhyme." Even he could admit he was sickeningly charming.

They were on their way up the hill to Overlook Road. "Don't you think they meant to call it Over*view* Road?" she asked. The Browns and the Goldens had arrived back in these days after their Easter and Passover observances, and their house lights made a difference to Audrey, especially now that the moon had moved into its weak phase. She was already looking forward to the next full moon, leaving this cycle behind, like one of those disappointing months when a woman hopes to be pregnant, and believes she is, only to be proven wrong.

Audrey's car was in the garage, so it was possible to think that both of their daughters were safe, sitting at the kitchen table waiting, not for their parents to fall from the sky, but for Neil and Phil to come in off the interstate.

And so they were, drawing up their lists like professional shoppers. Val said, "Look, I won Most Improved!" She rotated her head like a clay sculpture on a wheel. The discoloration was gone. Her elastic flesh had used its memory to regain itself. She presented herself for their hugs and kisses. Not even Sally failed to be genuinely impressed, after four days, by such definite progress.

"They called to say they're only as far as Pittsburgh," Sally announced, "so Neil told us to go to sleep, although we won't. You can," she said, making it clear she hoped they would.

"Rex also called," Val said, "and is also coming." She wasn't asking permission.

"Tonight?" Audrey didn't want to have to wait up for anyone. There was also the issue of where, with Neil and Phil in the guest bed, to put him. Unlike Celia, she didn't have a policy about sharing bedrooms, but this didn't mean she wouldn't prefer to consider the question, in relation to her own daughters, in the context of a somewhat familiar face.

"No, tomorrow."

Val clearly hadn't told Sally that Rex was coming. Sally's only comment was "He's no runner," to which Val responded, "Neither is Dad. So?" They were looking in opposite directions, Sally at her mother and Val at her father.

"Speaking of me," Gregory said, "I'm planning to help out in the morning, so save some of the work for me."

"Don't worry," said Sally, "we have big plans for you." This was a reference to the fact that the past two Saturdays he'd disappeared before Sally had a chance to ask to use his car.

Now Gregory and Audrey took themselves upstairs, released to their own company by these two who never bothered to ask them what kind of evening they'd had. Gregory was relegated to amusing himself by wishing he'd mentioned, ever so casually, they'd gone flying.

The discrepancy for Audrey was that this was the day she'd expected to feel free of the burden of her choice, but, as she'd articulated it to Gregory tonight, her mind was made up the day she'd had to hand deliver her application in order not to have missed the deadline. That was only one day in a series of days when Gregory seemed to rely on Dick Goddard's weather forecast as the worst news he was capable of encountering, as Sally seemed to notice by sparing him her most controversial plays, not to mention the earned penalties. Val had taken advantage of being out of mind by staying out of sight too. Only Celia barged in with her varieties of soup and recycled advice about how to cope with all unexpected loss.

By a comparable logic of opposites, Audrey decided that the momentary sorrow she'd felt tonight once they were back down on the ground could instead have been an index of a great joy. The sadness was an expression of the surprise she felt in discovering how *happy* she felt, a recognition of how rarely, lately, her heart had been lifted up in an unanticipated experience of beauty. This sorrow was an instruction never to let her life pass before her eyes. She wasn't dying.

She busied herself with the task of brushing her teeth with a brand of toothpaste that took credit each time she had reason to smile. Her face became shiny with the traction of terry cloth, and gleamed when she stroked it with another product that claimed to be a collagen replacement, a medical oxymoron.

She was glad to have something to tell him that she didn't need to articulate in order for him to know it.

9

ON THESE SPRING MORNINGS, the birds called like crazy in eager imitation of each other. Celia knew them by name, by breed, because those that stayed through the winter fed at her banquet table and rewarded her by letting her watch them mate. Once the storm windows were raised and the screens lowered, she'd offer her advice about nest building by setting out whatever materials she thought would make the nest more comfortable. Martha Stewart was a client of the advertising agency Neil's partner, Phil, worked for, and although Phil would never say anything bad about Martha Stewart, Celia was the only other person he could imagine who might think she knew better than birds.

Celia wasn't in the habit of laughing at herself, but in a sunny corner of her kitchen, in her element, she wouldn't refuse Phil's genuine compliment of being compared to Martha Stewart. "Why thank you, Phil, dear," Celia said, passing to him the Fiestaware plate of warm cinnamon rolls she'd made for him with sufficient brown sugar and pecans for pralines. She could do the other kind too — white frosting and walnuts, for Gregory — but she knew Neil had more sophisticated tastes.

The trouble with having such a handy daughter-in-law as Jan was that her own, more modest achievements went somewhat underappreciated. In her small sharp voice she told Phil, "Martha would have glazed the plate too, in what she would claim to be her own potting shed. But then Jan can do all that. Plus, she'd have shingled the little roof from cedar trees she'd raised from seedlings in the corner of the back yard, right where the potting shed is now." Celia patted Phil's hand with her faithfully manicured fingers while she pretended to be distressed to offer any negative feedback about his agency's most successful client. The secret she let Phil in on was offered in the spirit, not of criticism, but of a telemarketer. "This is because Jan's a more thorough recycler than Martha."

It was still too early for Phil to be authentically awake, but when he nevertheless joined in, by laughing—at the thought of Martha Stewart taking advice from his own, so to speak, mother-in-law—he found it was technically possible to laugh first thing in the morning.

Phil and Neil had driven from New York straight across the treadmill of Pennsylvania, arriving on Overlook Road, exhausted but wide awake, a little after midnight, way past Neil's bedtime. They'd been persuaded to come for the 10k race—no distance at all, Sally had said, for a pair of marathoners—since, as Val argued, after their vacation trip to Hawaii, they could think of Cleveland as close by. The fold-out couch in the room over the garage was where they always stayed when they visited, even though, as Celia told them year after year, she had plenty of guest rooms. "We just need one," Neil would tell her when she'd say they should have stayed with her because, now that the house was empty, all she had was guest rooms.

"But we need only one." When Neil said this once again, Phil stroked Neil's face with his eyes, following the paired curves of his dark eyebrows to under his visible cheekbones to where other, vertical lines ran along either side of his mouth, down to his squarish chin. Phil observed that Neil's thin nose came from his mother, but not those round brown eyes that, opened wide, made Neil look like a good-quality stuffed animal. Phil once proposed the theory that in a previous life he'd belonged to F.A.O. Schwarz himself, as if, like Hugh Hefner, all moguls have their own personal bunnies. When Neil smiled, his bright button eyes were as alive as any real animal's, and when those lines around his mouth grooved into crescents, and his powerful teeth proved the utter worth at whatever cost of a decent orthodontist, then with his own eyes Phil was saying I love you.

And though Celia smiled, recognizing devotion when she saw it, a sadness crossed her face. She saw the generic resemblances between the two, who had the same short haircut, the same collarless shirt, the same completely even Hawaiian tan. She said, "I wish two things. I wish you two had been home for Easter, and I wish it had gone better." This was an example of the way she still actively missed Jack, wanting him back when she felt the kind of grief you feel when you're startled by feeling happy. But rather than only enjoying her ability to be glad that her son was so clearly adored, she went on to complain, "Audrey and Johnny are both impossible now, and so's Jackie, the cheat, but at least Jackie has the fairly good excuse of being a kid." Celia hated to hear herself sounding like such a grouch, like those she volunteered for once a week, some of whom had much more legitimate complaints, such as having been evicted from their homes by their own children and placed in foster care, like orphans or wards of the state. But there it was.

Neil's expression changed again as he asked his mother, "Would you like to hear my just-for-what-it's-worth opinion?" From Audrey he'd heard that Johnny was having a hard time, but in their long phone call Audrey hadn't complained to him about Celia. Neil would have thought Celia might be happy to have someone—her own pharmacist son the next best thing to a doctor—to tell her complaints to, someone, that is, who couldn't so easily rush along to another patient. But then again, he'd also have imagined his mother capable of being glad for his own clear contentment.

Neil rested his hand on his mother's knee, their short fingers the same, except that in his case they'd become a professional asset. In his fourth-grade classroom the scissors were three-quarter size, like the chairs and tables, and he could string beads or shoot marbles, depending. Agile hands were useful for a pharmacist too, of course, but not mandatory. And for a nurse? The less invasive, the better. All the more for a physician.

Celia smiled again, but artificially now that she'd wished nothing would ever, ever change. "And to think we called Jack the conservative one," she said with the cute little shrug of her still strong shoulders, signifying that she needed neither Neil's intervention at the moment nor his opinion, thank you very much.

She wouldn't come to the party because it sounded too noisy for hearing aids. Voice upon voice created the unnatural shriek of metal against metal. "Deafening," Celia called the experience, "never mind that I already am." All you had to do was to be old enough to remember the sound of trolleys, she assured them.

It was never necessary to prompt Celia to relive the old days, and Neil gladly listened to her most of the time, knowing there would always be some detail he hadn't heard. But it made him uncomfortable when she snagged him for her semiannual inventory of the ways every one of them disappointed her. Celia seemed to feel none of them could possibly live up to the legacy of rugged values on which the honorable state of Ohio prided itself. "Our refugees didn't just step off the boat in whatever port they could afford the boat passage to. First they had to get a horse, build the railway, or escape from slavery however they could." She always missed the direct connection to Neil, who had turned the earth under his feet, planting his path like a garden all the way from here to New York City.

"I disagree," he said when Celia mentioned Johnny now. "Johnny's basically content with his life. I know. I worked with him all day."

"It's pretty late for Johnny to change his name, though, if that's his point."

"His name?"

"The 'Junior' thing. Nobody does it anymore, or haven't you noticed? Anyway, he did it himself, naming Jackie. That's his real regret, don't you think?" Celia never lost an opportunity to show her disapproval.

Like a good teacher, Neil said she had a good point. Obviously, she didn't want to hear that his name was the least of Jackie's unconfronted troubles.

"Then there's Audrey," Celia intoned, "who can't see that her husband's dying on the vine."

"What?"

"Gregory is an advertisement for premature old age." She looked to Phil, as the expert advertiser, but he'd given in to the full-time job of eating another cinnamon roll. "And there she goes, planning to spend all their retirement money on tuition. Don't tell them I said so, but his future could look more limited than it used to. He's getting bad publicity about cases he's presiding over, so I wouldn't be at all surprised if in the next election Gregory gets challenged."

"What do you mean?" Neil asked.

"You know how much he hates publicity. I haven't seen him for a week now, since Easter, but he seemed in bad shape and was very quiet, even for him. I'm afraid he's losing it. You know how men do, or seem to, sooner than women." The only saving grace in Jack's premature death at seventy was that it would have been a crime if he'd gotten smelly and ornery, like so many. "I'm afraid he's running on empty lately, if that's the current expression. If you know what I mean."

When Neil and Phil arrived at the house last night, Gregory hadn't been awakened by the commotion, but Audrey, the lighter sleeper, had come down to greet them. Neil could have told Celia that under Audrey's bathrobe her nightgown was on inside out and backward, the label showing like a rabies tag, but he knew Celia would be disgusted by this sort of telling detail. "I saw Gregory this morning, and he seems great."

"Well," she said, "you wouldn't say that if you'd seen him recently."

Because Neil was unable to laugh at this proof that Celia's problem—not listening—was greater than that of not hearing, Phil could tell that Neil was in his censoring mode. So Phil tried to compensate by coming up with a new topic. "How about Val!" he suggested, but saw Neil slump under the weight of that prospect.

"Well," Celia jumped in, "there's a sad story for you. I ought to know, since lately I've spent a lot of time by her bedside, so to speak. She spends all her time on the phone."

"Mom, everybody spends all their time on the phone. Stop this, will you?" Neil saw her face crunch shut with hurt, but he'd had it. Often, after visits like this, he and Phil would amuse themselves by inventing the things she'd tell the others about them the minute they left town. But Val wasn't fair game. With his fourth-graders she'd relaxed, because she'd seemed capable of remembering having had whatever it takes to be popular. As she'd confirmed to him on the subway that afternoon after school, she'd lost that sense of herself, like a satin hair ribbon that slips off your ponytail without your knowing it. She'd lost that sense of feeling good about herself—of being one of the popular kids—around fourth or fifth grade. It had been missing ever since.

"So!" Phil gathered the plates and told Celia once again that these were the only cinnamon rolls capable of making Martha Stewart roll over in her grave.

"She died?" For a second, Celia doubted her ability to know everything. Also, not that anybody ever seemed to notice, she made exceptions for the dead in speaking ill of people.

"Well, no, but when she does, I'm sure she will leave detailed instructions." Actually, this was a whole new area for Martha to explore, a huge consumer group of those who don't ever want to die but, if they have to, will want it to be done right.

* * *

Back at the house it was already lunch time. "This is going to be big," Sally said, piling smoked turkey on a roll, "for something with no planning." With planning, she'd have hired a tent with see-through flaps. There'd be one at school for the race, with tables for registration, quartered oranges, and miniature paper cups of donated spring water. Oh, well. "Next year we'll have a tent."

"Oh, right," Val said. "Which means our star attack here goes to her coach and asks if she can miss a game in the middle of the season because there's a 10k Race for Charity back home. She explains that she'd had the tent reserved for a whole year, so—"

"You're flattering me," interrupted Sally. "Athletes don't just jump to the head of the class like math geniuses. But you're right. It's unrealistic."

Their parents didn't fail to note that Val wasn't in the habit of flattering Sally, nor had Sally ever in their memory told Val she was right about anything. But their parents didn't speak, because they were the audience.

In her chair at the kitchen table, Sally stretched as if demonstrating exercises for party planners. Her big blond hair had been let go altogether, so it got huge as she tipped her upper body from side to side. She wore navy and orange nylon practice shorts and looked like L.A.'s idea of what a prep school girl would wear around the house on a Saturday.

Val wore her trademark black and was dressed like a city kid in shoes high enough off the ground to qualify as both fashionable and precarious. Now that her fingernails hadn't been stripped to the quick, she could afford to wear fewer than her seven silver rings, useful for distracting from the mutilation. She was applying a quick-drying onyx nail polish that could have been the Kiwi paste Joe Ricci used on her father's wingtips. For almost the first time in her life, Val was taking care not to color outside the lines.

Audrey leaned against Gregory, who draped his arms around

her neck as if this were a way to carry him. He rested his chin on her head, a perfect fit because Audrey was precisely a head shorter. She could feel his chest rise and fall with even breaths, so it was easy to synchronize her own with his. Gregory had spent most of the morning at the Sam's Club warehouse, because he'd been put in charge of buying in bulk.

Sally glanced over her shoulder as she said, "Danny Wallace called, by the way, Dad, to find out if there was a game you were planning to bring them to. I told him there wasn't, on account of the 10k, but I guess they were expecting you to call. I said Joel could start the race with me, since he's cross-country."

It was clear that Sally was as innocent of the complexities as Danny, and Gregory wasn't about to fill her in. When he answered blandly, "That's nice of you. Thank you. I'll call," Audrey felt his throat move and heard his voice as if it were coming out of her own head. "I'll call him back in just a minute."

"Their mother's who, again?" asked Val.

"It's their father," Sally informed her. "Or it *was*." She could have said a lot about Karen Wallace, such as that she was best known at University School, and therefore also at Hathaway Brown, for giving bad grades to seniors who needed good grades for college applications whether they deserved them or not. "Who died."

Now Val remembered Rob with her own moment of silence.

"Anyhow," Sally reiterated, "that's that. Everything's set." She looked back at her list: everything was checked off. "Oh. I invited them to come tonight, but I told Danny there would be no kids his age."

"Come *here?*" Gregory said, forgetting he'd already brought them here himself. He could feel the tension beginning to accumulate along his jaw.

So could Audrey, but she also noticed that he made no move toward the telephone. She asked Sally, "Who of your own age is coming?" These days, kids wearing pagers and cell phones made it a little too easy to spread the word of a party, but there would be enough adults to discourage more than those who were invited.

With a small smile Sally only said, "The usual." In order to better withhold her surprise for Val, she pulled her legs up to her chin and rested a cheek on her knees, hugging herself for lack of a better thing to do with her arms, closing her eyes so as to relax even those small muscles.

"And," Audrey asked Val, "your friend Rex?"

"Any minute," Val said, blowing on the dabs of polish that made her fingers look as if they'd been caught in a car door.

Neil and Phil arrived back at the house with shopping bags filled with fruit from the West Side Market. Phil displayed a melon he said would be three times that size at a tropical roadside stand, but Val identified with it just as it was, because, she said, the mottled skin resembled the bruise on her face in its last fading stage. Gregory disagreed. That is, maybe it did, but he didn't want to have to remember Val's face split open to reveal—yes, like a melon—bright juicy pulp.

Neil said, "Only human bruising is that complicated. Right, Audrey? Since fruit doesn't have seven layers of skin."

Val nudged Neil with an elbow. "I don't anymore, either," she said, and shook her hands as if to scatter her sequin-like fingernails. "But let's get to work around here, folks, or we'll never be ready on time." She assigned to Neil and Phil the task of figuring out how to prevent cooked spaghetti from becoming one with itself, asking, "So do you make a sauce or what?" Sally replied that she'd already taken care of that.

Gregory used the kitchen phone and, Audrey noticed, had to look up the number.

Danny answered, taking advantage of caller ID to go right into his prepared remarks. "Joel's babysitting me, but only because our mom had to go to some kind of a math convention. All three of us figured you'd call, since you promised to do something fun with us every Saturday." Danny's adaptive personality enabled him to say, "Which could have included chores like shopping for the party, we think, but we don't mind so much now that Sally invited us."

Gregory felt almost too stunned to speak, but he managed to come up with the only permissible things to say. "You're right, I promised. I'm sorry." Impermissible was the other truth he'd been living with for these few minutes, which was that he'd forgotten all about the boys.

"We're pretending, in front of our mom anyways, that it was your idea to invite us to the party tonight." Danny's protective tone conveyed that he felt almost as sorry for Gregory as they'd been feeling for themselves. "Because we wouldn't want our mom this mad at *us*."

Audrey was hoping for an early impression of Rex, who had called Val to say he'd been delayed by car trouble. Tolerantly, Audrey told Val she thought the problem might have been preventable with regular checkups, but that it was typical of kids to think they could run their cars without changing the oil now and then. Val said, "He isn't a kid."

Then all at once, at five minutes before the hour, there was the transition between the end of the preparation and the start of the reverse flow, as if everything from then on would run backward until the end of the party, which then would become the beginning again, this time of the cleanup. These few moments permitted the absolute poise of the unblinking eyes of storms. Audrey and Neil stood together in a corner of the dining room where it wasn't possible to see the front door. Neil asked his twenty questions.

"For me," she responded, "medicine is like working a jigsaw puzzle, in that I've always been looking for parts of the sky that have straight edges. It's about putting a frame around empty space, defining the size of problems, but always, too, it's about starting with the sky, making sure there is one. In the clinic I've studied Louise Schneider and learned she has the opposite orientation: the reason she's great for that job is that what she loves best is diagnosing. She has a problem-solving mind, so she's looking to rule out possibilities in order to locate the right answer."

Neil was nodding. Finding the means to ends was what he was best at, but it wasn't a set of skills he'd always had.

"As a nurse it's very different, because there are mainly two ways of behaving, which is that either you're following directions by doing what you're told to do by someone else, or you're doing the obvious. It's been good for me at Metro because Louise encourages me every day to look at what's between the entry level and the outermost reach, and to begin to feel entitled to form my own opinions." She leaned her weight into her elbow, which was resting on the mahogany sideboard that had come to Gregory as a bequest from Mrs. Osborne. This was a good place to have found, in the midst but apart, and she felt protected from any immediate need to play hostess. This event belonged to Sally and Val, both of whom had told her she could relax because they'd thought of everything.

"Tell me," Neil said. "I want to know what specifically allowed you to let go of yourself in order to think differently."

"It just happened." Audrey was wearing her favorite denim jacket, which had a deep pocket convenient for holding a bottle of beer. She took a cool sip. "It happened, and then it accumulated."

"But I actually meant to ask you about changing your identity. Wasn't it hard for you?" As he looked into his sister's dark eyes, he saw himself every morning in the old days, staring into the bathroom mirror, daring himself to risk the truth. "Or wasn't it?" Maybe there was nothing harder than what he'd done.

She tipped her head into the palm of her hand propped by her elbow. "And it still is, right?" So they talked about her recognition that, for her, the main factor wasn't their father's disapproval, but Celia's. "And she won't be outlived," Audrey said matter-of-factly, without any disrespect.

With a sad smile Neil said, "You're right, I was waiting for him to die. My unhappy life was like my being married to an abusive spouse I couldn't leave. As soon as he died, I could convince myself to admit how I hated my life. And then once I didn't have to defend it, I could change it. I could leave. You didn't wait."

"Oh yes I did! Waited and waited, all these years!" Because now she laughed, she conveyed no bitterness. "Celia's influence was that I never dared to risk the possibility that if I altered the balance, Val and Sally would suffer the consequences. I suppose I was afraid of what it might take to shift the weight. But what's more important is the thing you're talking about, claiming your own life because you recognize it's finite, so, if you don't, you could use it up and never have the feeling of being free. This took me just as long as you. Maybe longer."

"But in your case nobody had to die." Neil had the uneasy look of someone who'd worked his way all through this and still resisted the outcome. Jack was still alive in those early years before there was adequate education about the potentially fatal consequences of the AIDS virus. At that point he was still willing both of his sons into the profession only Johnny had any desire to join. By the time Neil set himself free, after Jack's death, the world of gay men had become considerably safer, which was why, while blaming Jack, Neil also credited him for having guaranteed the opportunity to come out.

"No," she said, "but *I* could have died before recognizing this." She closely watched her older brother realize that this hadn't been what he had meant but was exactly what he meant. Celia was a separate issue and beside the point, in a way. That is, at this stage in her life Audrey wasn't waiting for Celia, or anyone else, to die. It was a function of midlife to be able to see that the death she ought to be thinking about was her own.

From the door into the kitchen Val was watching Audrey and Neil lean toward each other with their questions and answers. That corner of the dining room, under the sideboard, was where she'd hidden herself in games of hide-and-seek, so it was where she could always be found. Was she feeling lost? Val hated to admit to herself that Rex might not take the trouble to come to the party. But where was he?

The house was filling up with sculpted young women who looked capable of running however many kilometers there were to be run. Each costumed herself identically in multipocketed khaki pants and smoothly fitted cotton T-shirts in this season's colors. They leached a serene confidence, the way garlic is exuded from Mediterranean pores, and no matter what their particular ethnic backgrounds they were Sally's look-alikes, all poster girls for privilege. Val's own, graduated classmates were away at college, and anyway, they always prided themselves on making their parents go temporarily insane by minor acts of clothing or grooming defiance. Strictly as a throwback, Val wore her String of Pearls pop-it necklace, the flaked luster notwithstanding.

In the spirit of good intentions, naively, Sally had told Val it was too bad the band couldn't get back together for this one night. Val said that would be like rounding up the Little League team when the players were senior citizens, but Sally asked what would be wrong with that? What was wrong with simply getting out there, no matter how out of practice you were? After that, it became a personal challenge to get the others to come home for this weekend, so close to final exams. But there they were.

Each looked different from the time before, as from the time before that. If one was slimmer the other was heavier, and there wasn't a true hair color among them, not that it would have been worth keeping track of that. Like Val they favored black, but, like her, there were whimsical touches—licorice bubble gum—to show the world not to worry. They lifted Val into the air and bore her off like a trophy.

Into this chaos Karen Wallace arrived. Joel looked more like the other kids, because he had the height of a seventh-grader who could stand still and grow before your eyes, but Danny was young enough to be searching the room for Gregory and/or junk food. Karen was looking first for Audrey, not Gregory, which was evident when she and Danny split, like a highway, in two directions.

Karen could already tell by the unfamiliar faces that she wouldn't be able to stay at the party as long as the boys would want to. The perfunctory question "And what do you do?" was made worse now that the honest answer was "My husband just died. That's all I do." It had always been bad enough to have to hear from strangers about their more finite fear of math.

Clear in the open gratitude of the expression on Karen's face, however, was that Audrey's willingness to meet the concrete need of a medical referral had been a far greater gift than Audrey could have been aware of. Even at her best, it wasn't Karen's style to open her arms, but to Audrey she did. What could Audrey do but to put her own arms around Karen's slight frame, more like a cape than an embrace.

And like the blink of a firefly, it n eeded to last only a fraction of a second to leave not just an impression but an afterimage. Quickly too, then, and equally authentically, Audrey had to get the hell away from Karen, so she motioned to Neil to take over. "You're both teachers!" she said as she skated across the room as gracefully as that girl who wore a small circle of a skirt and pushed off from the zigzagged toe of her figure skate. Neil and Karen ought to share their stories, the concept of "sharing" originating in the classrooms of schools not unlike their own.

Gregory watched Audrey as she came to a stop on the other

side of the room from him, by the French doors leading to the flagstone patio, where the band set up their instruments under floodlights that gave a theatrical glare. The air temperature would have been described by Dick Goddard as "April in Paris," but the weekend-replacement weatherman had used the more prosaic "unseasonably warm." What this meant to the band was that they could play their hearts out, outdoors.

In her deep-pocketed denim blazer Audrey looked hip, if that was still a word—or a value—whereas now it was Karen who seemed so depleted that her mouth had a sour look. From a distance Gregory could see the lines in her skin, proof that, like a fruit, she was aging from within, at the core of her being. Such an ungenerous characterization shocked him, making him more fickle than he'd already shown himself to be.

Eventually, however, he and Karen each found themselves brought to the same corner of the living room by Danny, who wanted them to agree on a definite plan for him. Gregory quickly supplied one: since neither of them would run the race the next day, how about the two of them watch it together from the sidelines? So Danny raced off to observe Val and the band do their sound check.

Karen told Gregory in a voice irritated by all the other noise around them, "I wouldn't have had to come here tonight if you hadn't disappointed Danny." She felt too much like a teacher when she told him, "*Never* promise a kid something you're not ready to deliver. Like a regular plan for Saturday mornings, if that's what he's led to expect. Not that you ever bothered to clear *that* with me first."

"I know. I'm very sorry. I meant to make a plan on Thursday when I stopped by, but in the rush—not that I'm blaming you for being in such a rush—I failed to." He'd also repeatedly neglected to mention the decision to name the center for Rob, which he neglected again now, but this time deliberately, in order to give it its proper due at last. "I should have called, but I got home too late last night, and this morning Sally sent me off on errands." Lame excuses, all.

Altogether furious with him, Karen said, "As far as I'm concerned, those are fairly valid reasons, but Danny needs an excuse that makes sense to *him*. So does Joel, for that matter." This was working for her, to treat Gregory like a parent on Teacher Conference Day. He would know how to receive criticism if she made it sound like expert advice. That lasted a minute, and then Karen began to feel too depressed for words.

And, for a change, he didn't fail to read the signs.

They were standing near a high-backed upholstered chair, which Karen could use as a prop, or a shield. But, to her surprise, she didn't seem to need it. She told him directly, "Now I can see that my anger at you hasn't been deserved. Until now." As if he were a student, she had the power to hold him back or, if she chose, to promote him. She didn't care what he thought of her, and neither was it important how little she thought of him at this moment. The issue was bigger than all that, Karen told him. It was the same exact size as her children.

"May I make a plan with Danny and Joel without involving you?" So far, every plan he'd made with them had tried hard to give that completely false impression, but now he honestly meant it. This was the feeling he should have been having all along.

She studied him, as if a figurine, for cracks.

So he explained, "I imposed on you the story of my father, but I didn't tell you he died when I was precisely Joel's age, when my brother was Danny's age."

He had to wait for Karen's response, because her unblinking eyes were on him like a fixed camera for closed-circuit television. If this was another come-on, she and her boys would be out of there instantly. To persuade her, he had less than five seconds, counting backward, beginning now.

"Please. They need me."

Karen could admit to herself that she had better uses for her anger. And so, for once, she took the easy way out, by answering "Yes."

Across the front hall from where they stood, Neil and Phil carried steaming chafing dishes into the dining room, barely setting them over their pans of water before kids assembled to empty them, cafeteria style. Sally had made Phil toss tasteless shredded cheese into the pasta, like stale breadcrumbs scattered in front of Central Park benches by old people who sat there all day long. But, as was true for the New York marathoners lining up to carbo-load once a year, did it matter to them any more than to the pigeons what brand they were eating? So what if the cheese had separated! No one, apart from Phil, cared to notice or seemed to mind. Long ago, Neil had promised Phil that if he could stop being a control freak for a minute, he'd get a glimpse of the rewarding life of an inner-city teacher. It was certainly worth it.

Johnny and Jan arrived fresh from exercising, shampooed, eau de cologned, dressed as for the morning. Jan brought a sheet cake with lemon-chocolate decorations, saying as she always did at Hathaway Brown functions that it was more fun to work with school colors that had true flavors.

Neil greeted them, and Phil complimented Jan on the cake, which was beyond the wildest imagining of amateurs. "It's why we're late," explained their son Jackie, who was hungry for more than the sea-salted pretzel crumbs in the big wooden bowl on the sideboard; who was starving, in fact. He disappeared into the kitchen and came back with a jumbo box of Cheez-Its he took into the living room as a conversation starter. "Want one?" he practiced on Sally, who said, "No thanks."

It wasn't that Gregory took anything for granted, and yet it was true—he realized this, with the cake—that he hadn't seen Audrey's upcoming birthday from long enough ago. His own fiftieth would have suited him better if it had been resorbed like the tail of a tadpole instead of celebrated with the surprise party he'd experienced as such a setback. Hers was coming up soon. He hadn't begun to think about it yet, or not from her point of view. Well, now he had. He decided to be of more use around the house, and went to grab a garbage bag.

The doorbell rang, and Audrey opened the door wide enough for another sheet cake to be brought through. "Hi, I'm Audrey," she said.

"Jasper."

Audrey didn't see his yellow spiked hair as a gold crown, as a means of wondering if this could be Rex. What she noticed first about him was that he looked undernourished. His white skin made his black stubble look as if it had been applied by a pointillist with an indelible pen.

"Valerie invited me."

"Well, fine. I'm her mother, Audrey." She could have said "Mrs. Brennan," but he looked a little too old, and impolite, to call her that.

"So is she still here?" He made it seem as if Val's plan was to leave first chance she got.

"Well, yes. Her band's about to play." She still hadn't taken that one step to either side, to signal that she was welcoming him in. It was possible she wasn't.

He shrugged, and brought two stained fingers to his mouth and whistled as if for a taxi. From the other side of the house—from outside on the patio, actually—Val ran, almost mowing her mother down, throwing her body against his. It was plain that they enjoyed pressing their tongues into each other's mouths while making devouring sounds.

In the more than twenty-five years since Audrey's introduction to nursing, she'd seen enough to make her sick to her stomach, and some of it had, too. But not like this. This was a man who had his tongue in her daughter's mouth while keeping his eyes open in order to wink at Audrey. It might have been harmless—"You didn't want to let me in, did you? I forgive you"—

but it felt as threatening to her as if he'd said, "Don't mess with me. You got that?" This sense was confirmed when Audrey heard Sally say, "See? I told you."

Gregory was in the kitchen tying a knot in the top of a garbage bag that weighed nothing because it contained paper plates and plastic forks. Audrey burst in and Sally followed close behind, not so much to talk about that disgusting kiss she was only glad Gram hadn't had to witness, but to repeat, "See? I told you he's old."

"So then, how old is he?"

"How old is who?" asked Gregory. Maybe he knew.

Now Sally had to stop and think how to put this without possibly hurting her father's feelings. "The same age difference, Val told me, as between you two. So, fourteen plus Val's nineteen equals what?" Once she had taken the SAT for the last time, she gave away the multiplication tables and, as it amused her to say, the multiplication chairs too.

"Who?"

"Rex!" Audrey let her weight fall against the refrigerator door, which caused the magnets to drop to the floor, along with the random photos, expired school notices, and the rest of the lacrosse schedule.

"What, he finally got here?" The ignorant expression on his face meant he was still hopeful of liking Rex. Wouldn't he be forced to, even more, by an age discrepancy? "Like the two of you, I assumed he'd be a college kid, but, well, maybe he is! Of all people, Audrey, you shouldn't think less well of him just for being older. How are you going to feel when it's you?"

"You missed his entrance," she said.

Sally was all too glad to get the feeling that they could use a moment alone, because anyway, she wanted to check out her friends' reactions. "You know where to find me," she said as she pushed through the swinging door into the dining room. First of all, wouldn't kissing like that *hurt* only a couple weeks after a car wreck? But, mainly, isn't it crazy to think that less than a week ago Val was passing herself off to these same friends as someone whose act was together?

Audrey said, "Come with me," and led Gregory into the garage, where he turned on the ceiling light she turned back off. The outdoor light gave them just enough to work with, because it pulled from the shadows his wooden tennis racket and her figure skates, and illuminated their old license plates, hung on nails.

There it was: the silver Beetle's plate from 1978. Every car he'd owned had been a silver sedan, whereas Audrey always picked a station wagon in any available primary color. There was not one vanity plate, though he wouldn't have minded an "Empire State" as a souvenir. "There's the Bug," he said, "with the sunroof that had to be cranked open."

There were rakes and shovels, a bale of Canadian peat moss ("*tourbe de sphaigne*") and a partial bucket of SnoMelt granules, the rolling garbage bins and plastic recycling crates, and the lumber left over from the no longer brand-new kitchen addition.

"What's the matter?" he asked, afraid that she'd say their entire history.

Audrey sounded as if she were talking to herself. "It isn't that he's too old, it's that she's too young! He can be thirty-three, but she can't be nineteen, that's all. By twenty-nine, I'd had a life."

"You make it sound like you didn't afterwards."

But she refused to respond.

He said, "Celia would say it's a good thing, because of the way boys are so slow to develop character. At the time I found it rather irritating, the way she insulted your brothers right to their faces, trying to flatter me for not having been rebellious. But there's something to it when you sit in a courtroom all day long." Even in this indirect light, he could see she didn't want to hear about it.

"I don't want to hear about it, and not Celia either," she said flatly, "because Val's just getting going, don't you understand that? This is her first chance to begin to believe in herself, don't you *see* that? She can't have somebody like *him*. He's altogether wrong. He pushes her around, I can already tell. He whistles and she comes *running!*"

"Come on, Audrey."

"He does! She did!" If they were still in the kitchen, her voice would have been way too loud not to be heard. "I can't stand that."

"You know better than to tell her, don't you?" he said, leaning against the garage door, which from the outside looked like it was one panel. Inside, where it hinged, the metal bars connected at joints as crucial as knees or elbows. Above his head the shoebox-sized motor was suspended from the ceiling, and the track ended in a pair of stiff silver springs. Everything was more complex than it seemed, and, perhaps, more than it needed to be. That part wasn't for him to say. Or her either.

Val kept a Ziploc bag of fake pearl necklaces in her bureau drawer, so the musicians were adorned like ladies even though they played not just like men but madmen. The lead guitarist wore her guitar below the belt and plucked the strings as if masturbating. The bassist played so straight up and down it never failed to shock whenever she dropped onto her knees for solos. Val's legs jumped all over the place while she sat like a spider on her little stool, scrambling the air with plain drumsticks that were like copper whisks whipping sound, like egg whites, into stiff peaks. Her drum kit was missing the splash cymbal, but she was managing to get good sound from the crash and ride cymbals. The foot pedal was more responsive than she remembered, and the bass drum sounded good with the floor tom. The Hathaway Brown set was accessorized beyond the highest standard, but this too was pretty fine quality for part-time amateur drumming. Like so much else, she had taken it for granted.

"Thank you," said Val, breathless with their effort. "We're a bit stiff, but its great to be back here playing together." She'd stepped out from behind her drums and held the microphone like an ice cream cone on a summer night, turning it in her hand, not feeling up to the challenge of it. "I'm a little nervous too, because String of Pearls here—note the newfound glamour as we all age so gracefully, off at college—has been trying to convince me to sing. As you may remember, I don't do that. That's Becky's job," she said, pointing to the rhythm guitar player. "Her voice has been described as 'buzzing like an electric knife sharpener' while reaching into a 'delicate falsetto warble.'" The keyboard played a fat chord, squashed.

"Sing! Sing!" shouted Danny, who had heard them upstairs, when Val showed the others some of the melody.

"Here goes. The song's called 'Flies,' and I guess it's got to be a solo, since that's how I wrote it. But instead of my weak *a cappella,* we've got a special guest artist tonight from Road Show, who's agreed to make me feel a whole lot less lonesome up here." Becky twanged her guitar most mournfully. "Girls and ladies, gentlemen and boys, please welcome Road Show's drummer, Jasper Rexford!" From out of sight Rex materialized, slipped neatly into Val's place behind her drums. Val turned around, her back to the living room, facing the yard and the lake and everything unknown, and then, like an actor, prepared, she turned the rest of the way back around. She held the microphone with one hand, using the other to snap her fingers to set the pace. The pace, you could say, was extravagantly slow.

One I, two eyes, driving blindly, crying,
flying nine times ninety,
blindly lying. Lying dying.

Val's voice was so soft it sounded more like humming. Gregory was shocked that this was a song about Val's car accident, since he'd made the assumption that "Flies" was going to be a song about airplanes. In the flash of his mind's eye he'd pictured Val going for her pilot's license, the two of them in a cockpit. This was painful to listen to, made more awful because she let her voice crackle like a big-time country singer and whine like a spoiled child.

Nine lives bye-bye, lifetime dying. Fruit flies,
no time, no ways, nowise!
No surprises: fruit flies finite.

Val was swaying. Rex was barely touching the snare but conjured a faint sound that could have been insects too small to see. Her humming buzzed, Rex tapped the crash cymbal with three or four fingernails. Since Val's eyes were closed, she couldn't know she had their attention so utterly, along with the silence of their suspended breath for her to fill with the next verse. Audrey wasn't certain what the words meant, presuming she'd heard them accurately, but she knew for sure they conveyed the next thing to absolute loss. She couldn't help noticing that Rex wasn't watching Val; he appeared to be searching for his own reasons to be engaged and, so far, seemed not to have found any. Because all song exaggerates, Audrey's worry wasn't caused by Val's grave lyrics but by Rex's look of boredom, which made her wonder whether it was the music that wasn't sophisticated enough for him, or Val herself. Audrey hated to think of her daughter as one of those who throw their body and soul at rock stars. Not that Road Show and the Rolling Stones had anything more in common than a mere few letters of the alphabet.

Firefly lightning, third eye brightening, nowise
frightening. Lifeline fireflies,
guiding my blind inquiring I.

The tuneless melody moved the lyrics from place to place, and because the room was very quiet the last note held, only dissolving, as smoke does, when the molecules drifted too far apart. "As you can see," Val said before there could be a reaction, "I'm still working on the happy ending."

Audrey knew what she meant, but the rest of them seemed to disagree and energetically signified their favor, until Val called, "One-two-three-and," to get the band to assemble for a real song. Resuming her regular role, she said, "We'll only play one more for you, for now, because we don't want you to get too tired for the Race for Charity tomorrow. Which I just decided to rename, by the way." In fact, it was hard to believe that it hadn't ever before seemed to occur to anybody at the school, including her. "To the Race for Justice."

She said nothing more in order to prompt a consideration of the distinct difference between charity and justice, no matter that uncharity and injustice are closely enough related to be similarly experienced. Rex gave her a drum roll that went on forever, until finally everyone relented sufficiently to recognize that, all these years, the 10k race had been called the wrong thing. "Yeah! *Yes!*" Val saluted Rex as his exquisite roll faded into its echo.

Sally was the first to react to Val's idea, with the piercing shriek that would have made her a good sports fan even if she weren't a skilled athlete. Because she was, she knew the value of effort better than most, so she was perhaps more open to the old concept of pulling yourself up by your bootstraps. After all, she was the descendant of Ohio Republicans, although, on the other hand, being young, she was entirely in favor of new ideas. Mostly, Val's song awed her, so as far as Sally was concerned Val could change anything she wanted. Plus, it turned out that Road Show was a band her friends had heard of before.

Who knew better than Gregory that justice can have no equal? He chimed, "Hear, hear," not that he was the expert when it came to knowing about being discriminated against. This seemed to be the right moment for him to speak, maybe even to give a speech. He had plenty to say about Val's song—or was it a ballad?—because of all she had been through. In preparation, he placed his plastic tumbler on the mantle and structured his thoughts, discovering that he might rather prefer to begin by saluting all the other members of the band, and end by circling back to Val. He missed his chance, however, because he suddenly felt intimidated by the fact that apart from the Wallace boys, Neil and Phil, Johnny and Jackie, and a few random dads he didn't know too well, and of course Rex, these were all girls

—sorry, women—and who said they had any wish whatsoever to hear from him? Besides, he'd already embarrassed himself in front of a number of them, exactly a week ago. What if he'd had too much to drink again?

Now, though, he could experience a letdown effect, so his breath slowed, his arms forfeited their tension, and he unlocked his knees. This was not the army, where he'd learned how to stand at ease just as at attention, but that difference was as great as between this letdown and the other kind of letdown he'd expected to feel because, if for no better reason, it was familiar. So where was it? Audrey was wrong, for once, at least about Val's boyfriend, who seemed pretty nice from this distance, especially for someone who, according to Joel, was already more or less established in the business. Where was his own familiar ability for feeling disregarded? Gregory looked for it everywhere but couldn't find it.

Neil knew all about the difference between justice and charity, having come from being held in respect, as the heir apparent at the pharmacy, to being eyed with suspicion. It was hard to teach children how to give each other the benefit of the doubt when their own parents weren't capable, or willing. The bias was all the more plain because Neil could watch their thought processes in action. These parents always seemed surprised when he smiled—tolerantly, wearily—while they proved to him—while claiming the opposite—that they couldn't see him as a person without first discounting him as a gay person. Did they think he wasn't able to see through them? What did they think he did all day long with their kids if not to study their unique minds in order to help them learn as best they could?

The air was sweetly cool, and it was too early in the year for insects, including Val's fireflies. The sky was the blue called marine, even though the lake was without color, a void bordered by those lights of Cleveland that, like a small child on the shore, are allowed to go to the edge and no farther. The yard was filled with the music of young women who admittedly took their styles from male rock stars, but who, in a different time and place, wouldn't be players at all. The moon had been reduced by half, but because the night was so clear it looked fuller and seemed brighter than it might have. A plane crossed the sky above them, west to east, bypassing Cleveland. If the sunset could have been tied to its wings like a parachute, anyone who'd missed it on its way through the first time could have had a second chance.

Val took the microphone again. "So, one more song." Singing all by herself, she'd fixed her gaze on the point in the far corner where the ceiling joined two walls in a Y angle, spotting herself like a dancer so she wouldn't get dizzy from the tremendous effort of performance. The others set down their beers and took their places as Rex moved into the audience. Now there was no need for her to feel shy, since she was no longer carrying inside the secret of her first song.

Audrey stood by herself, watching Val stroke the drums with her sticks in what looked like concentric circles. She'd been afraid Val would forfeit her place in String of Pearls to Rex, but he clearly wouldn't have been available. Because Val presented for viewing only one side of her face, Audrey could suspend most of her doubt about whether Val would make it. In Val's case the self-doubt had been nearly fatal, whereas in Audrey's own life, hers had resulted in a paralysis that appeared to have been temporary. In the medical world, this wasn't unheard of.

Neil stood between Phil and Karen, off to one side. He and Karen had talked, or tried to, but their classroom situations were too different. Val couldn't have felt this good about herself in Karen's classroom, because almost nobody did, which was how advanced-placement calculus worked. In his, where kids weren't competing with each other, he could get Val to get the kids to write a song they would turn into an opera, just as he could get her to turn her own opera into a song.

String of Pearls liked to play its own ironic arrangement of "You Can't Always Get What You Want," and now they played it—dedicated it—to Audrey. Becky sang it, never quite pronouncing the *t* in "can't" but at the same time making it sound more like the "cain't" of the old Broadway show tune she was way too young to have heard of, much less heard. Now Audrey let herself become distracted by the sinewy image of Mick Jagger prowling the stage, screaming out the lyrics, "I'm jist a girl who *cain't* say no. I'm in a tur-ri-ble fix!" She checked to see if Gregory could be as amused, since he was the only one in the room who, as a boy with Charles Osborne and his parents in New York, might have seen *Oklahoma!* with the original Broadway cast.

The connection didn't appear to register, though, since he was tranquil, standing by the fireplace with his two hands on Danny's shoulders, his slim fingers like the stripes on the epaulets of pilots. Joel stood next to them, close. Because the three of them could have been a portrait over the mantle of another living room, emotion caught in Audrey's chest. At first she didn't know if the feeling was small or large, but she stopped herself before she had a chance to resist. The territory had been made to expand by her own daring, and by his too. What could be bolder than to be reinvented as a parent, especially in place of your own.

Audrey withdrew her attention from Gregory and permitted herself to move to the music, rocking from one foot to the other and back. It was possible to achieve perfect balance by placing equal weight on both feet—she'd done this—but now she could tolerate risk. She could shift all her weight, dancing, because she believed that there's a middle ground, called the air, and that the air is its own dimension.

NOVELS BY

ALEXANDRA MARSHALL

THE COURT OF COMMON PLEAS

"A novel of unusual warmth and humanity." —**Anita Shreve**

The Court of Common Pleas offers insight into the complexities of modern relationships. A husband and wife, after twenty years of marriage, seek opposing futures: Judge Anthony Clifford, at retirement, wants to travel the world with his wife, Audrey; Audrey, soon to turn fifty, has been accepted to medical school and plans to embark on a career as a doctor. **ISBN 0-618-25753-5**

GUS IN BRONZE

"Above all, this poetic story is about the small, strange, and important ways people have of expressing love." —***Christian Science Monitor***

Strong, lovely, vibrant Augusta—Gus—is dying of cancer. In her last weeks she sits for a portrait in bronze—a brave final gesture for her husband and three young children. *Gus in Bronze* illuminates the sad and comic ways a remarkable woman and her family grapple with unthinkable loss. **ISBN 0-395-92490-1**

SOMETHING BORROWED

"A glorious portrait of marriage, divorce, and true love." —**Alice Hoffman**

A novel "full of wise observation, mordant wit, and a fine comic sense" (*San Francisco Chronicle*), *Something Borrowed* tells a story of unresolved relationships and unexpected second chances. Gale and Gary are a divorced couple reunited after fifteen years at their son's wedding, where, to their own astonishment, old passions are rekindled.

ISBN 0-395-92489-8